THE UNLIKEABLE DEMON HUNTER: FALL

DEBORAH WILDE

te da media
vancouver

Cover design by Damonza

Issued in print and electronic formats.

ISBN 978-1-988681-16-0 (paperback)

ISBN 978-1-988681-17-7 (EPUB)

ISBN 978-1-988681-18-4 (Kindle)

ISBN: 978-1-988681-32-0 (Large Print Edition)

1

The five leaked song titles from Rohan's upcoming album that I found on the fan boards were either A) written about me because Rohan wanted to publicly profess his forgiveness, B) not written about me because I was no longer lyric-worthy, or C) written about me but in a completely unflattering light.

"Silver Lining" was the first title I learned about. A case for either scenario "A" or "C" depending on whether I was the silver lining to the tragedies Rohan had faced in his life or I *was* the tragedy. And if it was the latter, what was this silver lining's name? Because she and I were going to have words.

Next was "Tourniquet of Phrase," which was just mean and suggested that he had to staunch the words that came out of my mouth. Another one for the "C" column.

"Rhapsody in You." As the Magic 8 Ball that I'd had for all of three days as a kid before Ari had dissected it to prove it contained neither magic nor science would have decreed in favor of the "A" column, "All signs point to yes."

Unless the "you" in the title wasn't me.

Moving on.

"Asp." Like the death snake that killed Cleopatra? Did he think I'd be the death of him? Seriously? I'd saved his sorry ass from a magicless life. In fact, I'd probably saved him from a reality in which he moved to the top of a mountain in a fit of emo pique, went off-grid, and eventually ended up with a peg leg because he sucked at gardening and couldn't produce a single fruit or vegetable. The point was, I'd fixed things. Badly, perhaps, but he also wasn't a legless mountain man, so there. And he calls me the asp?

And then there was the final leaked title. The title that no matter how I spun it, never left the worst-case column, and in fact added a subsection of "get ready to be dumped and hard." "Age of Consent." Because we all knew how he felt about consent.

I decided to take it from the top again and see if perhaps reading them for a seventh time changed anything when a strange noise caught my attention.

I slid my phone into my pocket and peered across the kitchen.

Ari Katz, my twin brother, was humming. Sure, sunshine streamed in through the open glass sliding door, the late July sky was a picture-perfect blue with fat pillowy clouds drifting lazily by, and the pop song streaming off Apple Music was pretty catchy. It would have been plausible, nay, likely even, that another blond guy would bob his head to Katy Perry and hum while doing dinner prep, but my brother? The guy who'd been tortured, liked weird art, and whose magic was the literal manifestation of darkness?

Not on your life.

I dumped more oil and balsamic dressing on the salad in the large wooden bowl that sat on the counter in front of me, pondering that Sherlock quote about eliminating the impossible blah-blah-blah to get to the truth.

And the truth's denim-clad bubble ass was currently bent over in front of the fridge.

Kane Hashimoto elbowed the fridge door shut, holding by a pair of tongs a raw slab of T-bone that glistened with marinade.

"Do you have..." he glanced around. "A plate?"

"Because your meat is dripping?" Ari asked in a mild voice.

"If it was?" Kane popped a hand on his hip, a cocky smirk on his face.

This foreplay made no sense, since no one, and I mean no one, at Demon Club was getting laid. While Kane's words sounded a sexy challenge, his arrogance was belied by a look of light panic in his eyes. It seemed unlikely to stem from needing crockery.

Ari, to his credit and my astonishment, didn't blush. He licked his lips. Slowly. Except again, less foreplay, more cheerful determination, like he was faced with a wild stallion he had to gentle and nothing was going to deter him from his path.

Kane broke out in a full-body blush: from his razor-sharp cheekbones, across his bare sculpted torso, and down into his waistband. He ducked his head; even his spiky black hair looked flustered.

My brother trained a fond expression on him and handed him a platter.

"That's it." I threw down the salad servers. "What is going on with you two? Because ever since you came back from that mission in Osoyoos, you've been all..." I circled my finger around at the two of them. "That."

Kane transferred all three raw steaks from the marinade bowl onto the platter. "You need a life, babyslay."

"We kill demons, remember? Lives are overrated. What

3

I need is cold, hard information so I can stop driving myself crazy."

Blue-gray eyes met dark brown as Ari and Kane shared a look.

"When's the last time you spoke to Rohan?" Ari said.

I thunked the salad bowl into my brother's chest, making his faded green T-shirt ripple. "Salt this. And don't deflect."

"There's nothing going on." Kane tossed the words out over his shoulder, oh-so-cavalierly, and stepped outside. He had the platter in one hand and the BBQ tongs in the other.

Ari shrugged and tossed a dash of salt onto our salad. "You heard the man."

If I had a twin sister, I'd have had the details ages ago. No matter. I'd break him.

"If you two are dating, then tell me. Don't pretend it's not happening out of some kind of misplaced pity. Don't want it. Don't need it."

Ari set the bowl on the dark granite counter next to the forks and plates I'd already gotten out, then plucked Ro's favorite purple guitar pick from between my fingers. I blinked, surprised to find that I'd fished it out of the front pocket of my shorts and had been rubbing it like a lucky rabbit's foot.

Again.

I swiped it back before my twin confiscated it in some misguided Rohan intervention.

Ari glanced outside at Kane on the flagstone patio by the stainless steel BBQ, grilling and singing away. "There's nothing going–"

An alarm blared from upstairs, startling us.

"Mischa!" I yelled, sprinting for the foyer.

The three of us ran up the curved staircase to Kane's bedroom.

4

Technically, the surveillance cameras we'd installed in Mischa Volkov's townhouse weren't legal. Neither was the B&E that had allowed us entry while he was at work. But what were pesky laws when the fate of humanity was at stake? I'd made the call and would make it again in a heartbeat.

Kane dropped into his desk chair, tapped the keyboard, and shut down the alarm on our side that had been triggered by Mischa's garage door opening. He peered at the various room views displayed on his monitor, Ari and I hovering at his shoulder. "Look at his bed. The top sheet is messed up."

Mischa wasn't Rasha like Kane, Ari, and myself, but he'd spent some time in the military, given his hospital corners and blanket that was usually so taut you could bounce a quarter off it.

"About the right size and shape for a suitcase," Ari said.

. "The tracker," I said.

"On it." Kane brought up another window, this one displaying the blinking light that represented Mischa's car's turning off his street. "Wherever are you going?"

Over the past few weeks of watching Mischa, it had become clear he was a man of habit. Or a dude trying very hard to stay under the radar. He worked a boring nine-to-five job, shopped and did meal prep for the week on Sundays, and aside from the rare drink out with co-workers, didn't socialize. Not once had he left his house on an early Saturday evening like now.

Ari and I sat down on Kane's mattress and settled in to learn his destination in tense silence. Well, tense silence and cramming as much steak into our mouths as possible to temper the excruciating wait while Mischa drove along the highway for the next forty-five minutes.

Over the past month, we'd hit more dead ends in our

investigation of what Rabbi Mandelbaum and his select group of Rasha were up to than a fairgoer in a house of mirrors. Ferdinand Alves and Tessa Müller were still dead, Sienna Powell was still missing, and we still had no definitive clue as to the rabbi's agenda.

I crossed my fingers for a much-needed break, perking up when Mischa took the turn off for the ferries at Horseshoe Bay.

"He's going to Bowen. Gotta be. What's the wait time for the ferry line up?"

Ari opened a browser on his phone. "He'll make the one at 7:10. With the crossing that gives us about a sixty-minute window."

Kane nudged Ari's knee with his. "You good to go?"

My brother wiped off his mouth and tossed his napkin on his plate. "Yup."

Kane handed me an iPad mini, which I tucked into my waistband against the small of my back under my flowy blouse.

"There shouldn't be any buffering problems," he said.

They followed me into my bedroom where I stuffed my feet into runners, tugged on a pair of fingerless gloves, and pulled on a balaclava, carefully tucking all my hair under it.

"You sure you don't want me to take you?" Ari said.

"My portal mishaps were so two weeks ago. I'm rocking Witch Magic 101. Later, gators."

"Just make sure you don't end up in the duck lake at the petting zoo again. That was a hard one to explain." Ari squeezed my shoulder. "And be careful."

"You, too." I pulled them into a hug, rubbing my cloth-covered cheeks against theirs. "If this is the start of all hell breaking loose, I want you both to know how much you mean to me. And also that you'll need to feed me second dinner later because I expect I'll be hungry."

Kane pushed me off of him. "I feel like I'm being groped by Deadpool. Go."

I closed my eyes. Witch magic was based on the idea of infusion and elimination. All I had to do now was eliminate the spaces in between my start and end points. It was still somewhat surreal that I was now my own mode of long-distance transport, but I gotta admit, witches beat Rasha hands down in the magic department.

I took a deep breath and vanished, landing in the small forest clearing out back of the single-storied, very rustic log cabin that Mischa owned on Bowen Island, and startling the crap out of the herd of deer grazing there. As I didn't end up all Han Solo embedded in the damn animals, all was well. Most of them bounded off, but one snorted, turning its disdainful gaze on me.

I flicked it the finger and strode into the press of Douglas fir.

Ari and I had spent the past couple weeks unearthing everything there was to know about Mischa, including that he owned this property. He hadn't tried to hide the fact or anything, but then again, he probably hadn't expected to be under surveillance.

I inched my way closer and closer to the house that was set well back in the woods. It had been cool under the tree canopy, but the temperature shot up pleasantly as I skirted the back lawn to the bushes under the living room window. I elbowed my way into the brush, doing my best to avoid any brambles, and cautiously raised my head to peer inside.

A man with shaggy brown hair sat sprawled on a battered sofa, texting. One of Mandelbaum's Not-So-Merry Men, this hunter had actually trained at the Vancouver chapter years ago. He tossed the phone onto the cushions, rose, and padded into the small galley kitchen.

I slid my burner phone out of my pocket and fired off a

quick text of my own. *He's here.* My phone buzzed two seconds later with a thumbs-up emoji. I stashed it in my pocket, and portalled into the cabin.

"Howdy, neighbor." I'd never spoken to this man before, so he wouldn't recognize my voice.

Ilya Volkov's double take and barked Russian profanity were priceless.

I planted my hands on my hips and cocked an eyebrow. "Come on. I nailed that landing. That was a solid ten by anyone's standards. Even the Russians. Get it. Russians? 'Cause you're... Okay, do you speak English?"

His furrowed brow got more slanty and scowly. "I don't talk to witches."

Ten points for recognizing I was a witch, and a big sigh of relief that he hadn't realized I was also a fellow demon hunter, since the exact total of all female Rasha was me. Those fingerless gloves hiding my Rasha ring had been an excellent idea.

Even if he'd seen any photos of me, say in the center of a dart board owned by Rabbi Mandelbaum, my balaclava obscured my face so my identity was hidden.

"You just did. Talk to a witch. Because you answered–" I yelped and portalled behind Ilya and out of the path of the knives that rose of their own accord from the butcher's block and flew across the cabin to impale me.

They thunked into the wall in a reasonable outline of my head and torso, quivering from the force of their embedment.

"Telekinesis! Aren't you a special boy?"

Ilya spun around and was caught up in a net of my magic electricity. He struggled, but he wasn't going anywhere.

I spared half a second to get the cabin layout and assess what else Ilya could use as a weapon. It was one big room, with the only inside door leading to a small bathroom. There was a rumpled bed in one corner, barstools shiny with age pushed haphazardly up against a high round table, and a living room area with a sofa and flat screen TV. The room smelled vaguely of cedar.

It was two steps up from "serial killer in the woods."

"I just want to have a little chat," I said. "And before you do something stupid like try and eviscerate me again, look at this." I moved in close enough for him to see the iPad screen.

His twin brother Mischa was strung up by his wrists in a dusty warehouse, his mouth duct-taped, and his head hanging forward, sporting a fat purple bruise over his left eye.

Ilya's mouth flattened out into two tight lines, but he didn't speak.

Since he was still caught fast by my magic, I pulled him toward me, as if he was in a lasso. Yeehaw!

I got all up in his face. "Answer my questions and we all walk away. Fail, or hurt me in any way so I can't give my team members the signal, and you'll be attending Mischa's funeral. Nod once if you understand."

He glowered at me. His snotty disregard for his predicament was pretty impressive, given he was levitating a couple feet off the ground.

"Think it over. I'm gonna get a drink," I said. "You want anything? No?"

Leaving him in my magic net, which honestly, was so low-grade it didn't even qualify as strong-arming, never mind torture, I strolled to the fridge and flung the door open. I staggered back, throwing an arm over my mouth and nose and slammed the door shut, breathing in the scent of the orange floral perfume clinging to my sleeve.

9

Sadly, trying to overpower the stank of the sour milk burning my nose hairs was a losing proposition.

The creepy stuffed owl mounted to the wall with the clock in its belly showed that I was twenty minutes into my allotted sixty.

My phone buzzed with a text from Ari. *Took private water taxi.*

Shit. That shaved a good fifteen minutes off my window of opportunity.

I dropped my magic and Ilya plummeted to the floor. "Talk."

One of the bar stools flew across the room and smacked me across the small of my back. I howled, crumpling face down, the iPad slipping from my grasp to bounce on the hideous area rug that boasted a pine cone motif. The person who'd looked at that rug and thought "that's exactly what I need to tie my room together" needed to be shot.

I pushed myself up onto my knees. "Your brother's gonna die."

"He'll die for the cause." Ilya raised a fist–to show his solidarity, or just toss a sofa at me, whichever. I wasn't taking chances.

I blew him into the television. He splintered the screen, the set crashing sideways onto the floor. I snatched up the iPad and marched over to him, shards of glass crunching under my shoes.

"Fucking zealots."

Give me a villain with verbal diarrhea anytime. Placing the iPad within easy reach, I splayed my hand on his chest.

Ilya stiffened and gasped, my magic wreaking havoc with his heartbeat.

"You feel that, right?" I said. "Arrhythmia. A classic. I could give you trippy visuals that would make virtual reality look like 8-bit. It's all in the synapses and magnetic pulses. But for my purposes today? Lungs." I ground my palm into his ribcage. "Ever burned your lungs? I made a troll cry last time I tried it."

The troll had been on a murderous rampage and had killed two hikers. Killing him had been a mitzvah. This? Not so much.

Ilya's skin turned bright red, his eyeballs bugging out of his head. This was fucking ruthless, but the fate of the world might literally be at stake if I didn't stop Mandelbaum and I was desperate for a break. Ilya was my last resort.

I steeled myself and did what I had to. "Think of this as your own electric chair session. Your flesh is swelling and stretching. It'll break soon, but I'm hoping you catch fire first. Apparently it comes with this cool popping sound like bacon frying, so if you're not going to talk, I might as well get in some practice time."

Ilya thrashed against my magic, his mouth slack, uttering garbled sounds.

"Did you want to reconsider? Great. What's Mandelbaum's agenda with the demons?" I dialed down the voltage coursing through his system.

He opened his mouth... and spat in my face.

My magic flared with a sharp snap before I strapped it back down under control, wiped the spit off with the hem of my shirt, and tapped a key on the iPad.

"Stage two," I snarled into the iPad's built-in mic.

After Kane, unrecognizable in his own balaclava, drove his fist into Mischa's side, Ilya closed his eyes to block out our persuasion tactics.

I turned up the volume on his brother's strangled screams, punctuated with meaty thwacks. "Don't like it? You could stop this. Just say the word."

Still nothing.

According to the Brotherhood, Ilya Volkov was dead. He hadn't allowed Mischa to believe that lie and I'd been banking on his connection with his twin to get him to crack now. Since he'd snuck away from whatever nefarious agenda he'd been working on with Mandelbaum to come see Mischa, his brother had to matter.

Personally, I would never have even let Ari suffer stage one.

I glanced at the owl clock. Ten minutes left if I was lucky.

Ilya turned as bright red as a boiled lobster and blood leaked out of his nostrils.

On screen, Mischa's tenderizing continued.

"Huh. Bones breaking really sound like the crack of a wooden baseball bat." I let up on the magic for a moment in case he wanted to share.

Ilya wiped the blood away with his sleeve.

"You better have the balls to kill me because I'll hunt you down for this," he said through wheezing breaths.

"'Balls?' Don't need them. It doesn't seem like yours are helping you terribly much at keeping it together, does it?" Fuck. He was really going to sell his brother down the river. I cranked my magic up again.

Ilya's hair was smoking—on his head, on his arms, on his face—but he didn't say a word.

Seven minutes left.

"Stage three," I said into the mic, holding the screen up once more.

Mischa's face was a bloody pulp. His head lolled at an awkward angle. Kane raised a gun and fired it into Mischa's knee.

Ilya flinched.

I mentally fist pumped. "Last chance. The cause or your brother."

The pool of sunshine in the cabin had been dwindling down through our encounter to the last dull rays of twilight. The oppressive gloom now pressing in on us went a long way to setting the appropriate ambiance for the grand finale.

Ilya turned his face away from me.

"Shitty birthday gift for the two of you," I said. "But kudos on your devotion to the cause. Kill him," I said into the mic.

Words I never thought I'd say. Especially to a twin.

Several months ago, a Rasha had taken down a ward and facilitated the kidnapping and torture of my brother at the hands of a monster. I hadn't been able to understand that kind of betrayal and yet here I was, the monster now torturing Ilya and blithely ordering Mischa's death.

I truly was a Fallen Angel, trying harder and harder to hold on to some of my light.

The image jerkily zoomed in to Kane placing the gun against the back of Mischa's neck.

"No! I'll talk." Ilya rushed his words, his eyes glued to the gun trained on his brother. By the time he neared the end of his debrief, he was practically slurring, his words were tumbling out of him so fast.

Good thing the iPad was recording all the important intel he was spilling because my entire focus was on keeping him pinned in place. Physically and emotionally, I was exhausted. My vision swam and my breathing was labored, but I didn't want to release him until I had the full picture.

A car crunched over the gravel, coming closer up the drive.

My time was up. iPad in hand, I released Ilya, but in the split second before I could portal out, he used his telekinesis to blow me through the window.

Glass exploded around me, cutting into my flesh as I sailed into the air and landed in the driveway with all my weight on my left ankle. My foot twisted, giving way beneath me with a hot burst of pain, and I slammed forward, breaking my fall with my knees and one forearm on the gravel.

Glass sparkled in my lashes like diamonds, embedded all over my skin like I was a human disco ball. I closed my eyes, using my magic to buzz the pieces out of myself, while blood streamed freely from dozens of gashes, soaking into my clothes and providing an underlying silky texture for the swath of road rash striping my body.

The balaclava was ripped from my head.

Ilya squatted in front of me, blinking in confusion. "You? But..." Headlights from the approaching car illuminated the evil glee on Ilya's face. "No matter. Now it's your turn to die."

"Ilya! Happy birthday!" A man exited the car, carrying a bright pink pastry box that looked cheerfully discordant against the tableau of broken window, bloody Ilya, and me, holding the iPad aloft in a weird Lady Liberty impersonation. The man was hale and whole, in perfect health except for the shocked expression on his face as he slammed the driver's side door. "What happened?"

"Mischa?" Ilya did his second double take of the day.

I had one way out. Mischa hadn't seen my face yet so there was only one person who could rat me out. I bracketed Ilya's face with my hand and pulled on his memories of me, eliminating them.

The one good thing about Rohan's absence was that it had left me with a whole lot of time to nail several witchy arts. This was one of them.

Ilya's face went slack, his eyes unfocused. Memory wipe accomplished.

Go, me. Gelman seriously needed to start handing out gold stars to her star pupil. Or rugelach.

Mischa's booted heels rang closer and closer. "Hey!"

Exit, stage left.

I landed on the back lawn at Demon Club, sweaty, bloody, and in copious amounts of pain, prepared to lay here under the cloudless night sky until I was either found by friends or eaten by wolves. I was tapped out and neither my magic nor my inflamed ankle were capable of getting me back into the house.

Ari discovered me about five minutes later. "Shit, Nee."

He pulled out a jagged shard that had been too deeply lodged in my collarbone to pop out with my magic.

Fire blazed down through my shoulder. I turned my head and vomited onto the grass.

He carefully scooped me up and carried me inside. "Did you get the answers?"

I nodded, waving the iPad. The screen was cracked but it still worked.

Kane bounded into the kitchen. "How did it look? Am I brilliant or what?"

"She's injured and exhausted. Wanna give her a minute?" Ari carried me into the TV room and lay me down on one of the oversized leather couches.

They got my ankle propped up with a cold pack, my back settled against a bunch of pillows, and let my accelerated Rasha healing magic do its thing.

Kane reheated some Hawaiian pizza for me, allowing me to shovel in three pieces before once more demanding I sing his praises.

"Yes, you're a genius. Really." I licked sauce off my fingers. "I'm not being snarky. Even I was uncomfortable watching it and I knew it was staged."

Kane had used hundreds of surveillance photos we'd taken

of Mischa to create a 3D rendering of his face. Knowing Mischa and Ilya's birthday might be an occasion for them to meet up, Kane had mapped Mischa's head onto the footage of a purely fictional torture session we'd filmed. My best friend Leonie had hooked us up with a couple of film student friends from university to help make it happen and man, were those dudes warped. We told them we were filming a short horror film, and they immediately had a dozen disturbing ideas to improve it.

Ari, having a similar build to Mischa, had played the body double when required, while the prop body the film boys had brought along had taken the brunt of the damage.

Kane had worked on the resulting footage around-the-clock, and that was what Ilya had watched. Kane had remained at Demon Club to stream it and stay in contact with me to switch up scenes as needed. Blessings for stage makeup, camera angles, and fake blood. Oh, and high-stress situations that smoothed over any suspension of disbelief issues.

"Play the audio file." I scrubbed at my arm with the damp cloth my brother had brought me. Sure, I'd stopped bleeding, but being coated in dried, flaking blood wasn't a step up.

Kane and Ari's expressions grew grimmer and grimmer the more they heard of Ilya's babbling.

The Brotherhood's Executive was comprised of six rabbis who oversaw the organization. As its head, Rabbi Mandelbaum wanted to usher in a new era with some very big-picture thinking: in this day of CCTV and iPhones, the rabbi didn't think that demons—or the Brotherhood—could be kept secret much longer.

Fair enough, except his plan was to strategically unleash the spawn on the world, swoop in, and play hero. He'd intended for Tessa, a witch in possession of dark magic, to cause an earthquake in a major urban center. By pinpointing the right stress trigger, she'd have set off earthquakes across the globe. Mandelbaum would then have deployed Rasha to all those cities, since demons were drawn to disasters. With those places compromised and on high alert, no one in the organization would have thought twice about the redistribution of hunters.

Then, using demons bound against their will to carry out orders, again thanks to Tessa's black magic, Mandelbaum would unleash the second wave of spawn on the public in those cities where the Rasha happened to already be conveniently stationed. The Brotherhood would present itself as the only de facto option before any other militaristic group could even think about trying to pull rank. Not that the military could kill demons, since their deaths could only be brought about by magic, but Mandelbaum didn't even want them getting a toehold on the situation. Plus, he could claim he was preventing unnecessary loss of life from the military.

In one stroke he'd reframe the ensuing terror of people finding out about demons into a huge relief that we'd had these secret heroes all along. The Brotherhood would be universally adored and Mandelbaum would be the most powerful man in the world.

Thanks to Ilya, we also finally confirmed what the deal with the modified gogota had been. An early–and abandoned–line of experimentation to try and make demons even more challenging to kill when they sent them after their enemies.

Like Rasha who strayed from the fold.

I hugged a pillow tight against my chest.

"Go team," Kane said, his body rigid.

Ari sat with his head in his hands.

"You okay, Ace?" Ari had grown up being Team Brotherhood all the way.

"I knew something like this was coming, but to hear it spelled out so matter-of-factly?" He dragged in a shaky breath.

"The trouble with this plan?" I polished off my last crust. "Tessa's dead. The use of dark magic burned her up from the inside about a month ago. Ilya said that Mandelbaum hasn't figured out how to do this without a replacement witch."

"I'd throw a parade," Kane said, "except Ilya also mentioned that the rabbi was actively looking for one."

Heaven help us if he found a woman who had that ability–either the one currently AWOL or the one trapped inside me.

2

Since I was all dented, I spent Saturday night binge watching the final season of *Orphan Black* off my laptop. *Supernatural* might not have had the same allure for me anymore now that my day job was destroying the things that went bump in the night, but clones and my Tatiana Maslany crush held up just fine.

By the last episode, I was a teary mess, rolled up in my blankets like a burrito. Battered and bruised, my body ached and worse, my heart ached. I was a puddle of emotions by the final credits, thanks to this stupid show that had given me all the feels.

I put the laptop on the pillow next to me and massaged my temples. For the past month, my head had felt trapped in a vise exerting a continuous, low-grade pressure that pinched the front of my face and made my eyeballs ache in gritty weariness. I hadn't been able to take a full breath either. I swear my lungs had seized up inhaling on a gasp that horrible night that Ro had left, and never managed to come unstuck.

But I'd have taken ten times that pain if I could have traded away mornings, because bright and early, every day,

I would hang in that moment before full wakefulness, a smile blooming across my cheeks, and roll over to face my boyfriend, only to be jolted with the brutal reminder that he wasn't here. My eyes would snap open, my brain would trip over his absence, and the totality of my loss would swamp me anew.

Being alone put me in that same swamp.

Kane and Ari were out because it was Pride weekend here in Vancouver, which was where Leo and Ms. Clara were as well. I was too battered on every level to be out partying with them. In my fragile state, the smart thing to do would have been to turn off the light and go to sleep, but I was restless. And yearny, which totally needed to be a word. Maybe I'd write the Word of the Day app people.

I fumbled in my side table for Snake Clitspin, my trusty S-shaped vibe, hit the power button, and scrolled through the settings to the particularly delicious pulse/vibe combo guaranteed to get me off in minutes. Kicking off my underwear, I brought him close to my clit Cuntessa de Spluge, Snake whispering *you know you want it.*

Heat pooled in my belly, my lady parts growing damp.

Snake brushed over my clit and my entire body jumped to attention. I slid the vibe inside me.

Calloused fingertips biting into my sides.

No. Sisters were doing it for themselves. I palmed my tit, massaging the sensitive flesh.

Rohan shooting me a lazy grin as he licked my nipple.

Focus. It was Snake and me and that's all I needed. My breathing quickened.

Hot gold eyes feasting hungrily on my naked body.

I canted my hips, emptily aware of being filled with silicone instead of Ro's hard, hot cock. The tight swell inside me receded, and the more I chased it, the more it eluded me.

That glorious fullness of him, thrusting into me, driving me deeper into the mattress.

My thighs clenched at the phantom memory.

I grit my teeth, blocked out all images of dark haired, brown-skinned men that I ached for, and gave 'er. Fifteen long minutes and four setting changes later, I came with a whimper, not a bang.

With a snarl, I tossed Snake away. He hit the wall and bounced to the carpet, buzzing merrily.

I wanted to buzz merrily because I hadn't buzzed merrily since the night my life had gone to shit, when I'd made a deal with Lilith, the most powerful witch alive, to possess my body in exchange for giving Rohan his powers back.

He'd trapped her unconscious inside me. And while my malevolent tenant was still out like a light, I'd rather have dealt with her than the constant replay of the wreckage that was my relationship.

The Vault it was. My heart was a parched desert, but my biceps were hella toned from whaling on the punching bag.

I turned Snake off, replacing him in the drawer with a stern scolding to up his game next time.

Two hundred and forty-two steps from my bedroom to the Vault. All I had to do was put one foot in front of the other and not deviate from the route. I limped out the door, careful of my not-yet-healed ankle. Leaning heavily on the bannister, I navigated the stairs to the main floor, and that's when my stupid betraying feet led me astray.

I clutched the doorframe of Rohan's bedroom. Uh-uh. I wasn't going in. Wasn't going to lay on his bed like an addict, sniffing his pillow, terrified the last of his musky iron scent had finally faded and would portend him fading. From my photos.

From my life.

I didn't need to turn on the lights to find his hoodie with the blue zipper and blue cowl neck. Snuggling into it, I crawled under his covers. I was injured and he had a better mattress with way more plush bedding so it was only natural to want to recover here. However, I stuffed my burner phone under his pillow, because phoning him was where I drew the line. I wasn't a pathetic clinger. Our time apart was a slowing down, not a break up. I knew all that, and still, in the dead of night, I'd find myself bathed in sweat and uncertainty.

Why was I the only one who ever reached out?

That wasn't fair. Ro had put himself on-call from hunting, insisting on taking all the vacation days he'd accrued but never used since he'd become Rasha. Hunters weren't great at work/life balance. (For the record, I had zero vacation days. I'd been at this gig for almost five months and I had yet to qualify for an extended coffee break.) He was focusing on his dad Dev who'd had a heart attack and was still recovering from double bypass surgery. Any leftover time was focused on his music. Which didn't mean he wasn't focusing on us.

In a quiet, secondary way.

As I pounded the pillow into flat submission, a flash of black caught my eye, wedged between the mattress and the wall. I stretched my fingertips to snag it. It was one of the velcro cuffs from the bondage system I'd bought that one time we rented a hotel room. I dropped it like a hot potato, but it was too late.

I was assaulted with images of Rohan, not sexy ones, but playful ones, like the time I'd ambushed him washing his car with an arsenal of water balloons, resulting in the water fight to end all water fights and both of us soaking wet, doubled over laughing. The marathon of Prince hits he'd played for me to tap to, while wearing eyeliner with his feet half-stuffed into a pair of my heels to give me the authentic Royal Badness experience. Every memory of him fighting alongside me, talking to me, feeding me.

And then suddenly hating me.

My brain caught up to my fingers a second after I'd hit speed dial. I tried to end the call before it could actually go through, much less ring.

"You're up late," Ro said.

We both were. Vancouver and Los Angeles were in the same time zone.

The huskiness in his voice shivered through me. Whiskey-soaked. No. Stripped down from singing.

I wished I could have seen his face but our one attempt at FaceTime after he'd left had been an unmitigated disaster. I'd spent the entire phone call deconstructing every single expression, not to mention that seeing him somewhere that wasn't with me was too hard. Too raw. The call had gotten weird and we'd defaulted to these voice-only calls that let me believe in the continued intimacy of our relationship. Since then, we'd fallen into this place where we only had about three safe topics of conversation, the first one being his music.

"Did I interrupt a recording session?" I said.

"Nah. I was just screwing around with a new melody."

Yeah? What about Josie and the other Pussycats? I tamped my paranoia down. "Nice. The writing's going well then?"

He made a frustrated sound. "It's this last song. I can't get it to fall into place."

Rohan updated me on the progress of his album, sharing the latest anecdote of his mom Maya, a famous record producer, and him butting heads over the creative direction. Rohan had told me that she'd previously refused to work with him for just this reason and the fact that she'd agreed to for his solo album had his fans going crazy with excitement.

I didn't begrudge him his happiness or quiet satisfaction, I just wished I got to be there with him, listening to him record, because there'd been a couple times that these anecdotes popped up on his fan boards, and while I'd heard them first, they weren't any more exclusive and personal for me than any other rando.

Case in point, the leaked song tracks that didn't include any mention of "Slay," the tune he'd written for my birthday when I was still his world. His home. Now, I wasn't sure that song was going to be on the album at all.

"How's Dev?" I said. Topic number two on our phone call countdown.

Rohan snorted. "Driving everyone crazy because he thinks he can go back to work full-time. Mom actually paid Liam fifty bucks to get him out of the house before she murdered him for pestering her."

"I'm glad she didn't have to incorporate prison orange into her wardrobe." I wrapped my arms around myself, pretending he was the one holding me. "But your dad's health is good?"

"Yeah. The doctors are really pleased with his recovery. What's tonight's T-shirt?" he asked.

I debated whether to press for more than the minimum of personal information about Dev, but I didn't have it in me to beg for scraps, so I let Ro steer us onto our final topic–and the end of this awful call.

After Ro had gone back to L.A., I'd slept in one of my many snarky T-shirts, like that could somehow armor me up against the night. My discerning taste in quips had always amused Ro, so I'd mentioned it, as part of my "entertaining persona," a.k.a. conversation topic number three.

"'I licked it so it's mine.'"

Right on cue, he chuckled, strained though it was. It was kind of forced, this little ritual of ours. No longer the easy banter that had always flowed between us, more a cautious, careful feeling our way through. I kept telling myself that careful was good. Careful reminded you that you had something precious to lose.

Careful was killing me because it was too close to indifference.

"Hey," I said brightly, "did I mention I flew ass-first out a plate glass window? I don't recommend it."

"Never a dull moment. How badly did the demon bite it?"

Right. I hadn't actually intended on telling him about today. He'd stepped away from all Brotherhood conspiracies and I hadn't wanted to drag him back into all that when he was still sorting out his music, his dad, and us. I didn't want to remind him that I was the one exposing corruption in his Brotherhood, that I was a witch, that I was more trouble than I was worth.

"Same as always," I hedged.

"You worried that *she's* listening?" Ro's words were measured.

"Lilith?" I did a thorough body scan, but didn't sense my occupant. Too bad I couldn't collect rent. My body was valuable real estate. "No. I don't feel her at all."

"She's incredibly powerful. You don't know what she's capable of. She could be influencing you without you knowing."

I sat up. "Is that what you think? That you're speaking to Lilith or some brainwashed version of me? Is it a phone thing or would you still be wondering if you were looking into my eyes?"

"Don't blow this up." He paused for a fraction of a

25

second too long. "I'm sure I'm talking to you. I was just checking you were okay."

Magic flared off my skin, scorching a hole in his damn hoodie.

"You want to know why I really went through the window? So you can decide if it's me or not?"

Cue his barely veiled annoyance and alpha posturing that I was about to make his head explode with something dangerous that he didn't really want to hear but that he would ultimately support because Ro always had my back.

The seconds ticked by.

"Well?" he said.

I pressed my lips together tightly for a breath to compose myself, then I launched into my Ilya encounter, the fake torture session, and everything I'd learned. I left out the part about Ilya recognizing me. What was the point? I'd dealt with it. Rohan was probably worried enough that I'd encountered Ilya at all.

It was a terrible way to dump the details on him. I'd have freaked if he dropped a story like that on me from hundreds of miles away.

"Sounds like you've got it handled," Ro said.

I shot the phone the finger.

"We need to find Sienna before Mandelbaum does," he said.

"Top of my To Do List." I switched the phone to my other ear and stretched out on my back. "We also need to make sure that he doesn't learn about Lilith."

"Do you have any less shitty news to share?"

Fuck you. I wasn't the harbinger of doom.

"Nope," I said breezily. "You should actually consider this a mitzvah, Snowflake."

"I should, huh?"

"Absolutely. If it wasn't for me, all this info might have been a surprise for you at some later date, blindsiding you."

"So I should thank you for ruining the surprise?"

"Well, yeah."

He gave an aggrieved sigh. "You understand that this is not a typical surprise."

"I'm not a typical girl. Plus, I don't like surprises."

He laughed. "It wasn't your surprise."

It was the first time I'd heard him laugh unguardedly in a month. My treacherous heart kicked up, while my brain cautioned me to get off the phone before I begged him to care about me again.

"I don't like them for anyone." I pulled the sleeves of his hoodie over my hands. "Listen, I gotta run," I lied. "Meet Leo."

"It's almost three am."

"Pride weekend. After party thing. You know how I roll."

"Right. Have fun. Be safe."

Safe like *don't run into a demon in a dark alley because I worry about you* or safe like *use a condom because I am totally banging all these other people?* Had I been friendzoned and not even issued a memo? Ro was a decent enough guy that he'd tell me if we were officially broken up, wouldn't he?

I burrowed deeper into his blankets, shivering violently. "Rohan..."

"I'll let you go. Talk soon." He disconnected.

I couldn't keep living in this limbo. I had to know where we stood but I dreaded it at the same time. We were very different people and our relationship had had its share of challenges, but I thought we'd make it. Had that deal with Lilith proven to be one thing too many for him to accept? If we were reunited, would he always look at me and see her?

Had all my previous fears about us being us until we

weren't come true and Ro had ditched the relationship persona for the singer-songwriter one?

Or had he found someone else in L.A.? Someone easier to be with?

I don't know how long I lay there, staring at nothing, feeling everything. Clinging to the thought that at least I hadn't fallen in love with him like I had with Cole. At least I hadn't been that stupid.

My own silver lining.

The lights flicked on and I was crushed by a heavy, sweaty body making kissing noises.

"Get off." I shoved Kane away. "I'm still injured, you jerk. And you're getting gold sparkle dust all over Ro's bed."

Kane rolled off me, sprawled out on the mattress, hogging all the space. He was dressed in blue skinny jeans hanging low on his hips, exposing a strip of taut abs between them and the red tank top that had ridden up.

Ari lounged in the doorway in his usual all-black attire, Mr. Dangerous with his stubble and blond hair that was slightly scruffy. He looked up from his phone long enough to raise an eyebrow at me in concern.

I shrugged. "How was the party?"

Kane shuddered. "It was all children."

"Says the ancient twenty-five-year-old." I poked him. "What's with passing for normal?"

Kane vibrated with outrage. "Breeder is not normal."

"Calm your tits. I meant normal, fashion-wise. Your choices are usually diametrically opposed to the rest of humanity. But this? It's almost like you're not trying to impress the masses for some reason." I cast a pointed look at my brother.

"I don't try, babyslay. I just do. My blessing and my curse." He rubbed his eyes. He looked haggard, shuttered, and totally unlike his glittering self.

I nudged his shoulder with mine. "How you doing there, buddy?"

His answering smile was too bright, too stretched. "Glorious as usual."

Before I could press him, Ari let out a soft, "Damn."

"What's up, Ace?"

My brother frowned at his screen. "Gary Randall was hit by a car. It's bad."

Kane dug his own phone out. "How bad?"

I groaned. "Whatever."

"You don't understand," Kane said. "Gary Randall is–"

"Left wing with record number of assists," I said. "Picked by the Ducks in the lottery round, threw around a bunch of tantrum slurs on social media about how he was going to dominate that team and they'd better keep up with him. Subsequently traded to Tampa Bay, his dream pick with an astounding contract, especially for someone straight out of Junior League. Did I miss anything other than the fact that you're one of the many fanboys who thinks this dude bro is the second coming of hockey?"

Kane propped himself up on one elbow. "You like hockey?"

"Nee hates hockey," Ari said.

"Our mom loves hockey and I was forced to watch."

"I willingly watched," Ari said.

"Because you're defective. If I never see another puck drop, I'll be a happy girl." Still, I peered over Kane's shoulder to watch the viral footage of Randall drunkenly celebrating his signing, then stepping off the curb and crashing into the front of a car so hard he cracked the windshield. There was even lift off. The footage cut off with him slamming onto the cement while people screamed.

I winced. "Yikes."

"Will he play again?" Kane was frantically scrolling through his news feed.

"Doesn't say yet," Ari said.

Kane rolled off the bed and trudged out the door. "This is a sad, sad day."

I made a shooing motion at Ari. "Go. Comfort him."

"I'm not... I wasn't the one Kane was trying to impress tonight." His hand tightened on his phone, a flash of annoyance crossing his face before he peeled himself off the doorframe and followed Kane.

That left me lying alone in my absentee maybe-boyfriend's bed, wearing his clothes like a pathetic security blanket.

Romantically, the Katz twins were nailing it.

3

You had to love a guy who had the balls, literally, to go fully regimental in a kilt while walking on his hands. Welcome to the Vancouver Pride Parade, the happiest place on earth this sunny Sunday.

My father squinted at the underwearless, upside-down, dangly man keeping pace alongside the float ahead of us for Numbers' Cabaret, a longtime popular gay club here in town. "How does he keep his balance?"

Hips shaking to the infectious disco groove pumping out of the float's speakers, I tossed more rainbow-packaged condoms from my beribboned basket at the deliriously pumped-up crowds that lined both sides of Robson Street.

"*That's* the question you want to ask?"

"Really, Dov," my mom, Shana, chided.

One of the barely-clad boys gyrating on the slow-moving Numbers platform, all buff in tight shorts and rainbow beads with dewy skin like silk, tossed my mom a whistle. She caught it one-handed like the star softball player she'd been in her youth, blowing it in time with the beat.

"Okay, my little raver," I said, clamping a hand over it. "I know you're pumped up for Pride, but let's remember that hearing is also important. You taught me that."

Mom laughed. "No. I taught you listening was important. Admit it, you're just jealous you don't have one of my magnificent homemade T-shirts."

"I'm really not."

My parents had donned matching bright pink shirts proclaiming "I love my gay son." Mom was even wearing rainbow-colored leis around her neck. This was the only time of year my mom was less than impeccably groomed, so points to her for how much she loved Ari.

I, however, was wearing the fantabulous "I'm not gay, but my boyfriend is" shirt that a drag queen had bestowed upon me years ago. Technically, I identified as heteroflexible, but that didn't make for a catchy T-shirt.

I'd already texted Ro a photo, in hopes that the phrasing on the shirt might get me some answers about our status. Also to show how busy I was having fun this weekend. No moping around for me.

My goal for Pride? Find mine because it had gotten sadly lost this past month. It was time for me to move forward with my life and today was the day I decided whether Rohan was going to be part of it.

"Ow!" The burly man who I'd just winged on the head with a condom glared at me.

I waved weakly. "Sorry, safety first!"

Mom nudged me. "Put whatever is worrying you aside and enjoy yourself."

"You're right. Today is a happy day."

It really was. My family had started marching in the parade when Ari was fourteen with the PFLAG group at the University of British Columbia where both my parents taught. It had embarrassed him almost as much as he'd loved it.

I loved it, too. Paradegoers were packed ten deep: everyone from elaborately decked out drag queens to buff women from the Dykes on Bykes contingent in sleeveless tuxedo shirts, to burly men in tank tops and flip flops, and families with toddlers holding melting ice creams as they waved at the floats. Rainbows abounded and smiles were wide. Even the harsh heat couldn't dampen spirits, and I was determined that no demon would change that on my watch. I tracked loud voices from my left, but it was just some people jostling for premium front-row space.

Behind us, the crowd broke out into hooting cries of appreciation. Mom and I turned around in unison.

"What are they doing now?" I asked, rising onto tiptoe for a glimpse of the LGBTQ firefighters in full uniform behind our group.

"Ohhhh." Mom's eyes widened and she stopped walking.

"Mom!" I tugged her forward, her head swiveling around like *The Exorcist* baby's. "Multitask. Move and describe in accurate detail."

"They got out the hose, drenching each other. Very well-built, these first responders of ours."

Dad sucked in his small gut with a wry look, and then shrugged and let it out, hoisting his "We love *all* our kids!" sign higher.

"Bitch!" Blair Lisowski, a gorgeous diva who was the only person in the world who could speak to my mother that way, bounded up to us in a cloud of vanilla perfume, and gave us both loud smacking smooches. She wrinkled her nose at my still faintly nicked-up skin. At least I wasn't limping anymore. "Did you go through a windshield?"

"Kind of?" I said.

"Happy Pride, darling," my mom said. "You look fabulous as always."

"Yeah, great look." I nodded in approval at her crocheted bikini top and the flower swizzle sticks threaded through her hair. "Very *Love Boat* Lido Deck."

"Finally. Someone who understands what I was going for." Blair, who had been Blake when I'd met her years ago at a faculty party for our mothers' history department, clapped her hands. "Brava, sister from another mister."

It wasn't really a stretch. I'd been forced to watch that show with her as teens more times than I could count when our families had our semi-regular dinner parties.

"What am I, chopped liver?" my dad huffed.

"Never. Happy Pride, Studly!" Blair threw her arms around my dad, who hugged her fondly. "What's shaking in the fascinating world of law?" she said. "Unleash any new courses on an unsuspecting student populace?"

Dad rubbed his hands together, spinning the sign he was holding. "I'm doing a second-year course on the reality of reopening cold cases with their exhausted leads and lack of probable cause versus advancements in technology and how fresh eyes, contemporary methodology, and information sharing can be valuable tools."

"Love it!" Blair declared. As a social activist, her and Dad bonded over the geekiest topics. "I'll fill you in on my chat with City Council about the zoning permits for the co-op later." She rolled her eyes. "Oy vey."

I threw a handful of condoms to a particularly boisterous group of women coming up on my left, blessing our alternate girl-child for sparing me these yawn-inducing chats with my father.

Dad cracked his shoulder to stretch out a kink. "Where's your mom?"

"Italy," Blair said. "That workshop opened up at the last second. You're my parents today."

"You got it, kid."

34

Blair tossed her gorgeous mane of pin-straight blonde hair. The motion caused her enviable boobs, that were more spot-lit than encased in her tiny bikini top, to jiggle. Female heads in a thirty-foot range swiveled in her direction.

"Where's your Alphabet person to bestow my glad tidings upon?" she said. "You're missing the second component of the LGBTQ equation, Katzes."

"The component was making friends," Ari said, catching up with us and hugging Blair. He'd lost his boring shirt but gained a plastic red fire hat, a rainbow flag cape, and a sunburn on his nose.

"Way to level up on the attire, bro," I said, adding in a lower voice, "See anything?"

Ari shook his head. He and Kane had been doing sweeps of the parade ground as they marched.

"Yowza," Blair squealed. "When did you get hot?" She ran a hand over the tattoo of a roaring lion he'd had inked on his shoulder as a late birthday present to himself. "Me like."

"'Like' from a distance, girlfriend." Kane locked into step with us, smacking Blair's arm off Ari. He wore white short shorts that showcased his approximately 600 cut leg muscles, a too-small, pink T-shirt that read "Gay as fuck," and a purple feather boa slung jauntily around his neck.

"Did you know that 'Ari' in Hebrew means lion?" Dad said.

We all stared at him in varying degrees of "all righty," before my mom said, "Yes, it does, love."

Blair threaded her arm through Ari's. "Marking your territory, much?" She cast a scathing glance at Kane's crotch. "You'll need a bigger hose. Mosey on over to the firemen and ask if you can borrow theirs."

"Five bucks on Blair," Mom murmured into my ear.

I clamped my lips together to stifle a laugh. Joking around with my mom? This truly was the best Pride ever.

I fired off a quick text to Rohan. *Mom and I are getting along. Too bad you're not here to witness this modern miracle.*

He answered right away. *I'm happy for you.*

No little dots indicating more was forthcoming. I glared at the screen.

Pride, girlfriend. Get on that. I was going to have to ask him about us straight out, but in the middle of the parade wasn't the place for it, so I simply texted him back a "Happy Pride" and resolved to call him tonight.

"You good?"

I threw an arm over Ari's shoulder and grinned at him. "Yes." I jerked my chin at Kane and Blair still fighting over him. "Not as good as you, though."

Ari shrugged. "It's always good to see Blair."

"Whatever is going on, he obviously cares."

"I'm more than some possession to be marked and forgotten." He shook his head and stepped away from me before I could force him to share that juicy anecdote.

Ari would talk when he was ready. Meantime, I was running low on condoms, so I danced up to the Go-Go boys, waving my basket. We'd lost dangly man somewhere along the line.

The lead Go-Go dancer tapped me on the shoulder with a wand before tossing scoops of condoms into my basket from a stainless steel barrel on the corner of the float.

The bass was so loud it reverberated through me. No, that was my phone with another text.

I blew a kiss to the helpful dancer, and fell back in line with my people. "Ro says 'Happy Pride.'"

"Who dat?" Blair asked, snatching away my phone and holding it out of reach. "Hello. Why do you have a photo of Rohan Mitra and what is that divine shade of lipstick?"

I plucked the phone from her fingers. Sure enough, there was Rohan with scarlet lipstick smudged on his mouth and his arm slung around his friend and former Fugue State Five bandmate Zack Bailey.

I texted him back, my fingers flying over the letters. *I was right! My T-shirt knows all. Okay. I can be supportive about this but only if I get to choose the guy and watch.*

It's from last year's Pride and you know nothing, Jon Snow. I met a fan.

Hot jealous hooks dug under my flesh. *Yeah? Do you remember her name?*

His name, Sparky. Jonathon. It WAS Pride. Wow.

I snorted. *Did you like it?*

That's for me to know and you to find out.

Typical Ro and me banter that hurt my heart because it was such a rarity these days. It would be easier if he'd just flat out act like a douchebag. At least I wouldn't be second-guessing everything between us.

"Ahem." Blair threw an arm around my shoulders, squeezing more in threat than friendship. "Answer my questions or I manslaughter you into that lamppost."

"The lipstick? Scarlet with an orangey undertone."

Blair squeezed harder.

"Ow. Fine."

I wasn't ready to let go of the reality where Rohan and I were still together, even if he had. Today was one of my favorite days of the year, and if I said I had a boyfriend and put off the pitying glances until tomorrow, what harm could it possibly do?

"Doesn't everyone have photos of their boyfriend on their phone?" I said.

Kane rolled his eyes.

Blair gaped like a fish, her mouth working but no sound coming out. It was a thing of beauty. She punched me in the shoulder. "You. Are. Shitting. Me. Assorted Katzes, tell me she lies."

I shot Ari a panicked look. He backed me up with no hesitation and since my parents had no idea that anything was wrong between Ro and I, they added their assurances as well.

Blair whipped out her phone, fingers flying as she typed, and a wicked smirk on her face. There was a whoosh noise and she held up the tweet she'd just posted.

Goodbye, little people. Partying in more interesting circles now since my darling friend is getting #RoMantic #rockstarlife #lovestory

I grabbed for the phone like I could somehow make the tweet come back. "Blair!"

"What?"

"We're not... It's... I didn't really want this public."

"Why? Are you his dirty little secret?" She wagged a finger at me. "Nobody puts Baby in a corner."

Sure, the tweet was tagged, and his fandom was going to see it, but they'd probably think it was fake or a rumor. And Rohan didn't go on social media. He paid people to do that for him, all tightly curated and very polite. Again, what harm could it do?

I forced myself to unclench.

It took the rest of the parade route to satisfy all of Blair's questions. Obviously, I left out the demon hunting part, saying we'd met through DSI.

Between the heat and the interrogation, by the time we got to the end of the parade route my shirt was wet with sweat stains, my gold lamé mini skirt was limp, and I'd have sold my twin for a cold drink.

After making me swear I'd introduce her to Ro at the

first available opportunity, Blair took off to go find friends in the crowd. My parents were headed for their annual post-Pride lunch. They offered to treat us, but we wanted to grab some food from one of the food trucks on the beach where the party was in full swing and keep patrolling, so we bid them farewell.

Trying to get anywhere in the mad crush took forever. I'd have whined about it, but the people-watching was spectacular. Especially the sight of my brother and Kane directly in front of me, their pinky fingers occasionally brushing and their heads close together as they talked animatedly about something that I couldn't hear over all the music blasting out from the beer garden.

An older man of Japanese heritage, kind of a sexier George Takei dressed in impeccable business casual, and this seventeen or eighteen-year-old stocky guy in a Crooks and Castles "Cocaine & Caviar" hoodie stepped out of one of the pricey condo towers overlooking the water.

Kane stopped dead.

The teen pushed his Beats headphones up. "You look like an asshole."

Ari put his hand on Kane's arm, but Kane shook him off, skewering the guy with his most disdainful look. I'm surprised the dude didn't burst into flame. "It's Pride and I look phenomenal. Not that I'd expect your Rohypnol-loving ass to understand either of those concepts."

"Kaname." The man didn't raise his voice but Kane flinched. "Apologize to your brother."

Whoa.

"Half," Kane corrected, lifting his chin to meet his father's eyes.

Double whoa.

His father refused to be cowed. "There is no half in our family."

Kane laughed. "Right. You, me, step-monster, and the spawn. Cozy-cozy."

I tugged on Ari's arm because this had gotten beyond uncomfortable, but my brother had planted himself at Kane's back. I tried to make myself the third in a defense triangle, because we were being jostled like mad by the crowd and our little island was in danger of being swept downstream.

Mr. Hashimoto raked Kane with a slow, disapproving gaze, but Kane didn't wilt under it. He'd obviously learned his own intimidation from a master. Ari was next up for inspection.

"Is this your boyfriend?" His father spoke the words like they left a bad taste in his mouth.

I sucked in a breath.

Ari stepped forward. "Let's go, man. He's not worth it."

Kane laughed at his dad. "Please. You know us gay men. Incapable of all those values like monogamy you prize so much. Naw, he's just someone I like to fuck."

He clasped Ari's head in his hands and kissed him, hard.

Ari stilled, sank into Kane for a brief second, and then shoved him back.

My hand flew to my mouth, my heart breaking for the tangled mess of these two.

"Don't ever use me to prove a point," Ari said.

Hurt flashed in Kane's eyes. Then he gave a cocky swagger. "You're right. That's your thing."

I stepped closer to my twin, ready to tear a strip off Kane.

Kane's father didn't betray a single emotion. He jerked his head at his younger son. "Ren."

The kid trotted after his dad like an obedient puppy, throwing one last sneer at the guys.

Ari looked up at the sky, jaw clenched, then exhaled. "Why can't you admit your dad set you off?"

Kane threw me a humorless smile. "You getting all this?"

I threw my hands up. "Don't take your anger out on me."

"I don't get mad." Kane's eyes glittered dangerously. "I'm Mr. Good Time."

He snapped his fingers at some random pretty boy who sidled up and poked Kane's "Gay as fuck" T-shirt.

"Care to give me a demonstration?" Pretty said.

"Kane," I said. "Come on."

Kane brushed past me to slide an arm around the man's waist. "You'll do. Happy Pride, kids," he said and, taking his boy toy, was swallowed up by the crowd.

4

Ari remained in quite the mood for the next couple of hours, perking up from grim to pleasantly murderous when we tracked a trail of fights that had broken out to the brahns responsible. Sure, these pug-like demons looked cute, all wrinkle-faced, even wearing rainbow doggie collars, but one brush with these fuckers and a person was lost to the darkness.

Pride, sadly, was a perfect venue for these demons to ply their trade. For all the people living loud and proud, totally confident with whomever they were and whomever they loved, there were those grappling with all kinds of identity issues. These people came down here hoping for connection and community. Many of them found it.

But sometimes these demons found them first, sucking them in with their adorable big eyes. A single pat on the demon's head was enough for a person's self-perceived failings to start playing on a loop in their brain until it twisted, hardened into a rage that needed to be unleashed.

We cornered the demons in an alley and Ari wrapped his shadow magic around them. Tight with tension, the ropy cords wound around against the demons' necks despite their thrashing. Their eyes bugged out, their tongues lolled, the doggies emitting pathetic little whimpers.

A sense of unease crept in that we'd made a terrible mistake. "Ari."

He tightened the shadow noose even more, a determined glint in his eyes.

The whimpering increased, their little tails wagging at warp speed.

I grabbed his arm. "What if they're not–"

Their glamours fell away, revealing their true forms: fat, foot-long worms, their skin weeping like half-crusty herpes sores.

Ari stomped them underfoot until they winked out, dead. I guess I must have made some kind of noise because he rounded on me, the line of his shoulders tight. "What?"

"Beer?" I said.

He relaxed slightly. "Okay."

I slung my arm over his rainbow flag cape. "You're buying. I left my wallet at home."

We'd made it back down to the beach, the party-happy beer garden a more welcome sight than Eden, when a very familiar red-head walked by, refusing to make eye contact.

"Leonie!" I cried out in evil glee, bounding over to my best friend, who sped up. Well, she tried to speed up, but I had about six inches on her and fifty percent more determination. I snagged her by the back of her short purple sundress. "Happy Pride!"

Leo thrashed in my grip while I stuck my hand out to the tomboyish woman rocking the bright blue pixie cut beside her. "I'm Nava."

She shook my hand, slightly taken aback by my enthusiasm. "Hi? I'm Madison."

"Yes, you are," I beamed.

"Please lock your sister up," Leo begged Ari.

"I tried. They didn't want her. Hey Mads, how's it going?" He hugged her.

I narrowed my eyes at Leo, who broke free to duck behind my brother.

"Look at that," she said, totally unconvincingly, peeking her head out. "They know each other."

Madison laughed. "You're so mean. Ari and I have a bunch of chem classes together. Leo freaked when she found out. Apparently, I'm not allowed to socialize with you two."

"Not because of you," Leo assured her.

"Nope. Don't lump me in with my sister," Ari said. "I don't interrogate new kids."

"I wasn't going to interrogate Madison." Three pairs of eyes swung my way in disbelief. "A gentle questioning."

"You're a few weeks too late on my intentions," Madison said. "I've got a girlfriend now. Leo and I are just friends."

Leo batted her lashes. "She got herself a real live lesbian. Much better than me, the girl who 'couldn't decide which team to play for.'"

Madison jammed her hands in her jean pockets. "Zahara has issues with bisexuality. She was burned by a past relationship," she explained to me.

"Nope," Ari muttered.

I crossed my arms.

"And now you're wondering about me," Madison said. "If I'm just one more lesbian being an asshole to a bi girl."

Leo nudged her hip. "Come on, Mads. I know it isn't like that."

"Now that we've cleared that up," I said. "What's Leo's ticklish spot?"

Leo tried to jump up and muffle my mouth but I'd anticipated the move and scurried back out of range. She'd used my ticklish spots against me on many an occasion, but I'd never been able to do the same.

"She doesn't have one." Madison was betrayed by the tiniest flicker of her eyes cutting to Leo. If I hadn't been Rasha and trained in visual cues, I'd have bought it.

"Fine. Take her side. You two wanna come to the beer garden with us?" I liked Madison's loyalty to my bestie. While Madison didn't know that Drio had dumped Leo because she was a half-goblin and he said he'd kill her if he ever saw her again, she did know that their tentative relationship had suddenly derailed. She'd helped keep Leo from falling into a funk this past month. That counted for everything in my book and I wanted to get to know her.

"I'm meeting up with Zahara," she said. "Rain check?"

"Definitely."

Leo hugged Madison, then watched as she was swallowed up by the crowd.

"You okay?" Ari said.

"Yeah. Mads and I were never meant to be long-term, and I'm happy she's found someone. Just..." Leo shrugged.

"I know." I wrapped an arm around her waist. "Let's get you a drink."

Thanks to Leo's connections with the bouncer manning the beer garden gate, the three of us got to skip the line. We snagged a sticky folding table and sent my brother off to procure booze.

"Something up with our favorite non-couple?" Leo said.

I glanced over at Ari, patiently waiting in line for drink tickets. "No clue. Why?"

She fiddled with her mass of thin silver bracelets. "I ran into Kane about half an hour ago on a log down at the beach."

"Was he sucking face?"

She shook her head. "He was on the phone and he

sounded really agitated. I'd come up behind him but didn't say hi."

"He was probably upset about his dad." I filled her in on what had happened. "Why didn't you talk to him?"

Leo bit her lip. "He was speaking to Drio."

"Oh." I squeezed her shoulder.

She waved me off, grimacing when she touched the table. She grabbed a napkin from the dispenser and scrubbed at the sticky spot. "It's all good. If Drio is gonna define me by what I am, not who I am, then fuck him. I'm glad I never have to see him again."

Leo had uttered some variation of this so many times that she sounded close to believing it. My friendship with Drio had died that day as well, and if she missed him only twice as much as I did, then she was screwed.

Ari arrived with the pitcher. I took the precariously balanced glasses away from him and he dumped the jug on the table, beer sloshing over its side.

"Remember it's hot," he said.

"Right, right, pace the drinking, whatever," I said.

"No." He filled the first glass. "We should be able to get drunk faster."

By the time we finished the pitcher, sloshy happy Leo had made an appearance. She was sitting in my lap, telling us about a recent negotiation she'd had to do as a part time Private Investigator between two basilisks.

"So then." She cocked her fingers like a gun. "I looked them straight in the eyes and said, 'Life is full of little dangers and I'm one of them.' Booyah!"

"You've got mad skills, baby," I said.

By the end of our second pitcher, sloshy happy Ari had made an appearance. He'd pulled us to our feet, the three of us dancing in a group like high school girls to "YMCA," which was pumping out over the speakers.

Tilting to make my "C," I poked Leo, pointing out the very fit shirtless man trying to grind up on my brother. Ari had ditched his cape but kept the fire hat, now sitting at a jaunty angle. "You know my favorite guy part?"

"Your near pathological fondness for the peen?"

"Shockingly, no. Eyes." I sighed. "Ro has the most beautiful eyes."

"Shut up. Today we only objectify strangers." She rooted around in her bra.

Ari covered his eyes. "Quit it. I might see nip."

"What did you store in there this time?" I said.

"Gum. And... Aha!" She triumphantly pulled out a crumpled five-dollar bill and waved it in the air. "Yoo-hoo! Mister Hot Guy."

Ari plucked the money from her hand.

"I didn't mean you," she pouted.

"You did at one time," he smirked.

Leo punched my arm. "You told him I had a crush on him?"

"I didn't!"

"Elyse Shimizu told me in grade eight."

Leo crossed her arms. "Well, it was over by grade eight and a half, smarty pants, so nah."

Maybe I couldn't have everything I wanted, but having this? Having them? It was pretty damn good. One more pitcher and sloshy happy *Nava* would make her appearance, making the what-the-fuck's-going-on call to Rohan so much easier.

I kicked off my shoes, curling my toes into the grass and feeling no pain. So when my phone rang in my front pocket and I recognized the international number, I answered with, "Go away. I'm on my break."

"There's no rest for the wicked," replied a man with a French-Canadian accent.

"Seriously, Pierre. I've already protected the good people of my city today." Pierre had been my main contact at Brotherhood intel since the assignment where I'd been lead hunter tracking down this demon called Candyman.

"Bon. You're warmed up."

I scowled at the phone, mouthing "Orwell" at Leo and Ari.

"Hang on," I told Pierre. Brushing off my brother's offer to come with me, I pushed through the crowd and out the back exit of the temporarily erected fencing onto the beach.

"Where are you?" he asked.

"Pride parade. Ouch." Half-jumping over the hot sand, I beelined for the nearest log and sat down, scrunching my feet until I hit wet, cool grains. "Okay. What demon would the Brotherhood like me to dispose of?"

"What do you know about Gary Randall?" Pierre said.

"He's a demon? Sweet! I'm on it. One less asshole hockey player in the world." I'd gone through a phase of crushing hard on those boys. It hadn't gone well.

"Tu me gosses."

I snickered. Pierre lived in Jerusalem and he and I had never met; still, I'd quickly become one of his favorite people, since not only was I a fellow Canadian, but thanks to my years of French Immersion I was well-versed in Québécois expressions. I knew exactly how the fucker was insulting me, which we both found hilarious. Between that and the way I'd handled the Candyman assignment, I'd gained his approval.

"What about Gary?" I said.

"Watch the video footage," he said. "Right before Randall trips into the path of the oncoming car, he stops to speak with some woman. You can't see her face in the video and there isn't any other CCTV footage that caught her on tape, but there's a flash for a frame and then she's gone."

"Demony. Do we know what they talked about?"

"No. The cell phone video was too blurry to lip-read and there was too much ambient noise from the street to hear the conversation."

"Sounds suspiciously tidy."

"His doctors are saying his career is over. Could be an honest case of drunk and unfortunate, but if not?" It came out as "'onest" and "hunfortunate." Pierre tended to both drop his "Hs" on words that started with that letter and add them on words that didn't need them.

I jacked up the volume on my phone because the beer garden crowd had gotten riled up at the opening strains of "Born This Way," their enthusiastic singing drifting across the beach.

"Draw out the demon," he said.

"Oh, sure, throw me to the wolves, Pierre." I watched a tiny crab scuttle across the sand. "I'm the most unappetizing target for that kind of demon. I have a few hundred devoted Instagram followers, but that hardly makes me famous."

"Remember when you were Lolita?"

"Hell, no. I'm not playing Rohan's groupie again." I was barely playing the role of his girlfriend these days.

"Camme toé."

"I'm calm. This is me being calm." My voice rose with a tinge of hysteria.

"You don't need to be Lolita. Our working theory is that this demon was attracted to Gary's cockiness. A groupie who's now the girlfriend? You've gone public with the relationship and it's the perfect opportunity."

"I haven't–"

"Your friend Blair."

I checked my Twitter notifications which had exploded with messages from people asking if Blair had been talking about me, since her next tweet was a photo of Ari and me in the parade that I hadn't seen her take.

I kicked at the sand. Fuck! Fuck! Fuck! "That was like four hours ago and I wasn't even mentioned. Jesus. Are you stalking my friends?"

"We've monitored all mentions of Rohan for years. We had to in case his fame exposed the Brotherhood. You should be pleased. You've created the perfect way to draw this demon out."

I hunched over, my shoulders curling forward and my knees clasped tightly together. Everything Pierre was saying made sense, especially in light of this mission. I could behave like a giant diva on Ro's arm and probably attract the demon's attention fairly easily. That level of obnoxious was fun for about five minutes, but living it 24/7? I'd done it in Prague and it'd been hell. The thought of doing it again made my skin crawl.

"Look, how about..." I cast about for an alternative. "Um. Okay. Rohan is writing again. He could do a bunch of interviews. Talk about his solo career. Slam the band. That's douchey."

Pierre made a dismissive noise. "Even when Rohan acted his worst at the height of his fame, this demon never came for him. Why would that work now? But with you, we have a unique opportunity. We need you."

I scrubbed a hand over my face. The Brotherhood had never claimed to need me–officially or otherwise. Part of me preened like a cat hearing them acknowledge my worth, however, Blair tweeting a vague tweet was one thing. My relationship, if there still was one, was so fragile right now that deliberately seeking out criticism *and* a demon to shred it to pieces was insanity.

But they needed me.

I swore silently. "I'll help you find the demon, but not like that."

"Forget it."

"Pierre, I still want to be on this mission."

"Don't worry about it." His voice was cool and he hung up without our usual teasing.

I flung my phone on the sand.

"Nee? What happened?" Ari and Leo had shown up, wearing twin expressions of concern.

I shook my head, unable to trust my voice. My feet worked just fine, however, so I let them carry me across the sand and into the ocean, not stopping until I was deep enough to submerge myself and lie about where the salty water on my face came from.

5

One suck-ass sleepless night and a rushed breakfast later, hundreds of magic icy needles pierced my skin and stabbed my organs. I bit down harder on the strap of leather between my teeth, sweat dripping off my temples and running down the back of my neck.

"Anything?" Dr. Gelman's face hovered above mine.

Moaning, I strained and bucked under the magic enveloping me.

She clicked her tongue and shut it down.

I spit out the strap, my breath coming in harsh pants. "I hate you."

Gelman loosened one of her shirt cuffs with a delicate flick of her wrist. Thanks to her last round of chemo, her lung cancer seemed to be in a holding pattern. It wasn't better, but it definitely wasn't worse, and seeing her not looking like a walking skeleton never failed to make me happy. She'd managed to gain some weight, and her hair, while now totally white and still short, had lost its patchiness.

"Hate me all you want. Do you feel any sign of Lilith?"

I closed my eyes, exploring every twinge and ache from

the crown of my head down to my baby toes for a more sinister explanation than what she'd subjected me to. I pressed my hand against my sternum and opened my eyes.

"I sense a box. Maybe the size of my fist, lodged here."

The box didn't hurt. It was just there, floating. I have no idea whether my clear visual of it as matte black and seamless was thanks to my magic or an overactive imagination.

She tapped my breastbone. "Here?" I nodded. "This is where I detected the wisps of dark magic," she said. "Lilith's essence is locked in that box. Now that you feel it, you can monitor it."

Not use the magic or get Lilith out, just tell whether or not everything was super about to go to Hell. My life had become one long limbo.

"Given that spells are the basic cable of magic," I said, "and that's what Ro used to knock Lilith out, you'd think getting her out of me would be simple."

"Nothing involving Lilith is simple." Gelman placed her hands on my shoulders, sending a healing warmth inside me to relieve all the pain she'd inflicted.

My magic Domme.

"What's left to try?" I shakily pushed myself up into a seated position, rubbing my arms to get the blood flowing.

The past few weeks, my Mondays had been a series of standing appointments with Gelman as she tried all kinds of things, magic-based and not, to deal with my unwanted guest. Today's attempt had involved extreme cold. It didn't suck as hard as the herbal concoction that had left me with debilitating stomach pain and grossness running out of both ends of me, but still ranked pretty high on the unpleasantness scale.

"There is one form of stimulation you could try. Pleasure yourself and–"

I clapped my hands over my ears. "La. La. La. La. La."

"Don't be childish. I assume you have a vibrator and if not, you have working hands."

"Stop talking." My cheeks were burning and I couldn't meet her eyes.

"Have you been avoiding masturbation because you're concerned about Lilith? I understand your fears, but a powerful orgasm might shake her loose. Then I could transfer her to another vessel. We could do it in a controlled situation, where you'd still have maximum privacy. Do you want help finding stimulating material?"

I twisted the fat gold band with the engraving of a hamsa around my finger. "Ohmigod! I've masturbated, okay? It didn't wake her. End of subject."

"All right." She slipped on a sweater. "That's enough for today. I'll make some tea."

I scuffed the floor with my toe. "Did you make scones again? Because I think I deserve them."

"Your mother deserves a medal for dealing with your petulance."

I took her arm, the two of us moving slowly. "Yeah, thrilled you're getting along so swimmingly. You were supposed to bond over witches. King David. A whole host of subjects that didn't involve yours truly."

"But you're the most fun to discuss." Gelman led me up the basement stairs into the kitchen of her sister Rivka's house.

Sunshine flooded the long, narrow space which flowed into an open-concept living room, the backyard beyond visible through the glass sliding door. Rivka had a fondness for white—the walls, the furniture—but kept the space from feeling cold with brightly colored cushions, a fat, fluffy throw rug, and an enormous photographic print of a spice market.

I filled the kettle with water while Gelman busied

herself laying out all the goodies, including the buttermilk blueberry scones.

My visits with her had three components: Wizard School, Torture Time, and Snacks.

Wizard School was progressing nicely, with my witch magic coming along in leaps and bounds. I could portal reliably and had mastered eliminating memories, which was how I'd been able to make Ilya forget about meeting me. I'd even learned location spells, which weren't spells at all but a type of infusion magic. And that was in addition to all the training and studying I was still doing as Rasha. In comparison, university looked like a vacation.

It wasn't all learning about infusion and elimination magic though. Gelman, a scientist and a witch, was using me as her guinea pig to investigate how magic and science intersected based on Maxwell's Laws of Electromagnetism. Yes, she'd drilled me in the stupid name. Case in point? Today's new unit, testing whether or not I could cloak myself with electromagnetic fields that would deflect light from behind me to the front of me like an invisibility cloak.

The answer was a resounding example of how to suck hard. I could call up the electromagnetic field, but then I sat there like an electric flashlight doing a snap-crackle-pop impression.

After growling at me about my tenth failure, Gelman had moved on to Torture Time. When she'd finished working out her jollies—I mean, testing her theories on how to resolve the Lilith situation, involving my pain and/or humiliation—it was time for the best part: Snacks.

We generally puttered around making our tea, and only once we were nestled in the cozy booth eating did we fill each other in on any new developments regarding Sienna, the witch community, and the Brotherhood. Though I had yet to be rewarded with rugelach.

"How hungry are you?" I asked, eyeing the multiple platters of scones, cookies that were not rugelach, and bagels that she was laying out. "I mean, I can always eat, but that's a bit much even for me."

The doorbell rang.

"Oh, look," she said. "Company." She raked a critical glance over me. "You might want to wash up."

I flicked off the switch on the kettle. "What have you done?"

"You wanted to meet other witches."

"With some warning."

"Get over it. We don't have the time. The sooner we have more brains working on finding Sienna, the better."

"I hate it when you're logical." I ran a hand over my wrinkled clothes. My hair was limp and my makeup had been sweated away. "You couldn't tell me before your little sadism session?"

"I didn't want to listen to you whine. Be nice or I'll stick you in a Faraday Cage."

The first time she'd uttered that threat, I'd stared blankly at her, so she'd launched into a long-winded explanation that made me go from clueless to glazed over.

"You could have saved me ten minutes of my life and given me the tl;dr version that it was a dealio that nullified electricity," I'd said.

She'd stared at me in confusion.

"Tl;dr. Too long. Didn't read. Like 'in summary.'"

"I know what it means. My stupefaction is your childish reduction of the cage to a 'dealio.'"

Then I'd gotten glared at for a full half hour. Ah, memories.

"You can't say that every week and expect me to be scared," I now said.

"I'm wearing you down, making you think it's an idle threat and then bam! I'll surprise you."

"Funny." I grabbed my purse off the counter, grateful I'd kept the travel cosmetics kit that my mother had given me before the Pride parade, which, come to think of it, had seemed like an odd return to our old passive-aggressive dynamic. "You told Mom, didn't you?"

"You're welcome."

The doorbell rang again and I bolted for the upstairs bathroom. By the time I'd made myself presentable, four new women were waiting for me.

As one, they turned from the dining room table to inspect me.

The black woman closest to me was maybe five years older. A total fashionista, she could have been a model in her designer mini-dress and bling. She certainly had the attitude for the catwalk.

Next to her was seated an elderly Indian woman with a sleek silver bob and a sharply tailored business suit.

The other two women were seated across the table: a fiery red-head, probably in her early thirties, dressed in the latest post-apocalyptic chic with a partially-shaved head and a very cool Monroe piercing above her lip; and a middle-aged Asian woman with her hair pulled into a ballet bun, wearing an ankle-length sundress with a delicate floral-patterned scarf knotted jauntily around her neck.

Gelman did the introductions. "Raquel, Shivani, Elena, Catalina. This is Nava."

"Hi." I shook hands with each one in turn, making sure to maintain eye contact, my grip firm. I may have been a bottom feeder in the witch hierarchy, but I wasn't going to roll over in their presence.

"Come here, cariña." The Asian woman, Catalina, kept my hand tight in hers, drawing me around the table.

"Catalina is head of the Mexico City coven and an expert in spellcasting," Gelman said.

"She's also not letting go of me," I muttered.

Catalina stood up and placed one hand on my chest and the other on the small of my back. A wave of warmth pulsed through me, coming up short like her magic had hit some kind of wall. My entire body jerked, the way my leg did when the doctor tapped my knee.

"It's as you feared, Esther," she said in her melodic Spanish accent.

"Feared?" I did a double take. "You told them about Lilith?"

Gelman didn't even look repentant. She flicked the stainless steel lighter engraved with her initials she always seemed to have on hand, even though she no longer smoked. "What, you thought I'd keep quiet? That elimination spell I gave your Rohan was basic, but very efficient. It should have drawn Lilith from your body. It didn't. I called them here to help us find out why."

"We knew why! Lilith was just too strong. We've been over this."

"Another reason to finish what Tessa started and get rid of hunters," Raquel said. "Rasha bumbling around above their pay grade, messing with spells they have no business casting. It's dangerous."

"Oh, good." I glared at Gelman. "You told them everything."

"They needed to know how, why, and who was involved." *Flick. Flick. Flick.*

"Yeah. Her Rasha boyfriend," Raquel rolled her eyes. "Real magical genius."

I exhaled to a slow count of ten. Witches and Rasha had

always hated each other, always been convinced that the team they played for had the best grasp on magic. Yelling at Raquel wasn't going to prove my point. An image of David with his slingshot flashed through my mind.

When faced with an impossible task, change the rules of the game.

"How do you kill a sakacha?" I asked, drumming my fingers on the table. "Any idea?"

"A what?"

I took the empty seat next to Gelman, also placing me next to Raquel. "A seven-foot tall wooden snowman demon whose kill spot is inside it. It's not on Google so you better know what you're facing, otherwise your death is going to be pretty painful. Because of its iron pincers. It totally has those. They can snap bone–" I snapped a gingersnap in half and Raquel flinched. "Like it's nothing. I'm getting the crash course on demons, but if I hadn't had some of those men in my corner, I'd have been dead in minutes. I respect that you have me and every Rasha beat on the magic front, but give them their due; they've trained their whole lives and studied like mad to kill these things so you don't have to."

"I've killed demons before," Raquel said. "Not that type, but all of us here have." She rolled her eyes at my stupefied expression. "Hello, witches. We're the original demon killers."

"I thought witches had no interest in killing demons anymore." I prodded Gelman's ankle with my foot.

"Tl;dr, they do," she snarked.

"Most don't slay." Elena, the Mad Max redhead was a lot more soft-spoken than I would have assumed. "Only a handful of us have kept to the old ways."

Raquel smiled good-naturedly at her. "Trust the Romanians to know all about the old ways."

"I agree with Nava that we need Rasha. I have no

interest in hunting." Shivani added some lox to her bagel and cream cheese. Her English was clipped in that posh way of the very upper class. "Not at this stage of my life. I'm happy to leave that to Rasha and younger witches who choose to pursue that path."

Catalina gently cleared her throat. "May we get back to the more pressing issue? Instead of pointlessly fighting Lilith, the spell redirected and went for the easier target to draw out."

"That's you," Raquel said. "The easy one."

Shivani raised an eyebrow at her. Raquel squirmed and looked away, but she didn't apologize.

"Lilith had cast your awareness into a magic box, had she not?" Shivani said. "The spell extracted you and put Lilith in there instead."

I laughed, spreading homemade raspberry jam on a scone. "Hoisted on her own damn petard. She made her prison. Let her rot in it. I'll live with her the way people live with bullets lodged in them."

"She's too strong to contain," Gelman said. "She's leaking out."

Cold washed over my body in a rush. "You said it was wisps."

Wisps were light, fluffy, almost invisible. They recalled dandelion puffs on a summer day and cotton candy at the fair. Leaks were how people described oil spills, disasters that irrevocably destroyed oceans and beachfront, speckling tides with fish floating belly-up and staring accusingly at the sky.

I slammed the table, rattling the china. "You. Said. Wisps."

Tea sloshed over the rim of Shivani's cup onto her saucer.

"Oh my," Shivani murmured, and grabbed a napkin.

When Gelman didn't respond, I snatched her stupid lighter, blasted one of its corners, and tossed it on the table.

She bristled, then deflated against her chair. "I didn't tell you because I wanted to be wrong. You were going through so much already. But yes, it's a leak. I've detected more and more traces of dark magic in you. If it keeps up at this rate, you'll have maybe a month before Lilith's box blows open."

A lot could happen in a month, couldn't it? Solutions could be found. Magic boxes could be reinforced. I shivered, reliving Lilith's seething flash of rage when I'd tried to negate our contract by breaking up with Rohan. She'd been terrifying back then, but that would be nothing compared with how she'd be if she got free now, furious from weeks of captivity and determined to exact revenge.

"How do I protect myself?"

A hush fell over the room, all the other witches suddenly very interested in adding sugar to their tea, refolding their napkins, or brushing imaginary crumbs from the tablecloth.

"Oh," I said, in a very small voice. "I don't."

I dropped my head in my hands.

A soft knit blanket was draped over my shoulders, but it didn't help. The warmth didn't soothe my ice-cold insides.

Gelman squeezed my shoulder, her shea butter and lavender moisturizer wrapping me in its calming scent. "I didn't bring everyone here for a public death sentence. We've found a way to remove her from you."

I lifted my head.

"Essentially, you tried to bypass the original deal you made with Lilith," Elena said. "That's why Esther can't get her out of you. That original magic is still rooted in place. You're like a clogged toilet right now and Lilith's magic is the sanitary pad jamming you up. Leaking bits into you."

"Are you—are you for real?" I spluttered.

Elena frowned. "Did I not say that properly in English?

Raquel poured herself some tea. "You said it perfectly, honey. Nava's a wadded-up pad. Go on."

Elena spoke enthusiastically, her hands madly gesturing. "We can plunge the box out of you."

"Like bringing the pad to the surface of the bowl with all the other gross stuff," Raquel added, squeezing some lemon into her frou frou cup.

"Thanks." I rubbed my eyes. "I got the metaphor."

"We can delicately extract the box before everything overflows and the situation is irreparable," Elena continued. "Then we transfer Lilith, while still unconscious, to a stronger vessel that will contain her indefinitely."

"Rivka is in London right now, getting that vessel," Gelman said.

"This sounds spectacularly repulsive, but if it gets her out of me?" I dug into my scone with the renewed enthusiasm of one who'd just had her death sentence lifted. "Unclog my toilet self."

"There's one problem," Catalina said.

I threw my hands up. "Of course there is."

"We need... punct ochit punct lovit. How do you say?" Elena tapped her finger against her lip. "Middle of target?"

"Bullseye," Catalina said. "It's an artifact rumored to cut through any magic."

"Rumored. Right. Which means you have no clue where it is or that it does what it says." Hysterical laughter bubbled up inside me, and I was scared that if I let it out, I'd lose myself to the madness of my situation. I added clotted cream to my jam-slathered scone and bit into it, willfully ignoring how the buttery, flaky biscuit choked my throat like ash.

Raquel arched an eyebrow, recoiling from my scone like

I'd shit on it. "That's like a thousand calories. What would your boyfriend say?"

I licked some jam off my finger. "He likes me well-fed." Regroup. Focus on what can be done. "Where's the Bullseye?"

"There's this demon. Baskerville," Gelman said.

I pointed my jam knife at her. "You're full of surprises today. A hunter, a consorter with demons. A very specific demon who happens to be my least favorite blue dude."

Gelman pushed the knife aside. "We're witches. We hunt demons or make deals with them as we need to."

I made a snarky face. "I know Baskerville. I'll get the artifact."

"Be careful with it. It's a single-shot deal," Raquel said. "Don't set it off."

"One attempt. Got it. And the highly trained person who's going to use this thing on me is?"

"Any idiot can use it," Raquel said. "Just press it to your skin."

"What's the downside?" It was a magic artifact. There was always a downside.

Catalina adjusted her scarf. "There's a fifty percent chance that it will extract your magic along with it."

"Really? My options are death or possible magic loss?" Funny, Rohan had been so mad at me for the deal that had restored his magic, but faced with these two outcomes? I'd drop to my knees and blow him in thanks if he could spring the same arrangement on me—one where some perv would get their voyeuristic kicks for a night, but I'd get to keep my magic.

I was working very hard on Regroup 2.0, but not gonna lie. It was a struggle. My scone fell from my hand to my plate.

"I won't let you lose your magic," Gelman said. "It's a

delicate operation but we have the combined abilities to extract her and contain her in the vessel with no harm to you."

I looked at each woman in turn. "And you've all agreed to this?"

"That's why we came. To meet you and decide if we'd do this," Elena said.

"Which we will," Catalina said.

Shivani nodded.

I looked at Raquel, who rolled her eyes. "I'm in, stop staring."

"Thank you." I put my hand on my heart, overcome at their generosity.

"I want more than thanks," Gelman said. "Stay on my good side for a change or fend for yourself."

"Your good side. Is that the one with your face or your ass?" I said, then took a delicate sip of my water.

"See what I have to put up with?" Gelman said.

Shivani burst out laughing. "Please let me be there when you meet Maya."

I choked on the sip I'd taken.

Gelman pounded me on my back, muttering encouragements like how if I died drinking water it would definitely solve the Lilith problem, but she'd never forgive me for denying her the thrill of trapping the most powerful witch of all time.

I coughed and shook my head at Shivani. "You're friends. With Maya Mitra."

"That grimace is a little much," Gelman muttered into my ear.

"My architecture firm worked with Dev's engineers many times over the years." Shivani pushed a strand of silver hair behind her ear. "Rohan's lovely."

Raquel reached for a napkin. The silky material of her

cream dress shifted enough for me to see her bra, a periwinkle, watered-silk push-up number studded with tiny
blue crystals. Jeez. Even her lingerie was epic.

"If you like that type," she said.

Whatever, honey. All breathing man-lovers liked that
type.

"Yes, he is lovely. What about Sienna?" I said. "I assume
you've been filled in on that situation as well?"

The women nodded.

"There's a deep schism in our community right now
over what happened with Tessa," Shivani said. "A lot of very
heated discussion about our place in the world. The only
good thing is that we've managed to keep Sienna's involvement a secret."

"For the time being," Catalina said. "How much longer
remains to be seen. It depends on what happens when we
find her."

"Or her next move," Shivani said.

"You're really not going to like my news, then." I filled
them in about Mandelbaum wanting a new witch. "Sienna
could do a lot of damage."

Gelman's hands paused on the teapot, then she smiled,
small enough that I almost didn't catch it. I didn't have to
share my Brotherhood information, sure, but if there were
anyone's friends I was going to trust, of course they would
be hers.

Catalina crossed herself. "We can't let him get her."

"We can't let certain witches get her either," Shivani
said. "She's playing with dark magic."

I slid the blanket off my shoulders and folded it.
"They'll try to stop her by any means necessary?"

"They'll try to join her," Raquel said. "We have our
share of Malfoy wannabes."

"Damn. I don't want to like you, McGonagall." I draped the blanket over the chair.

"Back at you, Luna."

"Excuse me. I always felt a certain kinship with the young Sirius Black."

Raquel snorted. "If I'm Head of Gryffindor, I should damn well know who's in my House, you starry-eyed Ravenclaw."

I doctored a bagel with a generous schmear of cream cheese and much lox. "Can you identify the most likely contenders? Watch them for any sign of contact?"

"Can and will," Elena said.

"I'll work on that with you," Catalina said.

"Raquel," Shivani said, "you compiled the dossier on Sienna. Where are you at with sussing out potential dark magic teachers or covens devoted to it?"

"A lot of rumors and nasty gossip. No useful leads. I'm working on it."

The landline rang.

"I'm going to speak with the older women in our community." Gelman headed for the phone. "See what I can learn about Millicent. She died when Sienna was very little so she wasn't the one teaching her, but she was her birth mother. It might be worth pursuing."

Raquel prodded me with the toe of her Louboutin. "Be careful with Baskerville. For all his smooth-talking ways, he's deadly. We've lost a lot of fine witches who underestimated him."

"Nava." Gelman held out the receiver. "It's Ari."

I wiped cream cheese off my fingers and took the phone. "Hello?"

"Why aren't you answering your burner?" he said.

"It's in my purse. Probably on vibrate. Why?"

"Ro was trying to get hold of you. Some radio interview he wants you to hear."

"Thanks, Ace." Despite my good intentions, I hadn't called Rohan last night. I'd been too raw after the call with Pierre. Maybe this interview would give me the opening I needed.

I made my apologies for having to rush out. Everyone was very gracious and Shivani even assured me that I'd do fine when I met Maya.

Gelman walked me to the door. "Your first witch play-date. Happy?"

Other than the shitty outcomes part, sure, but all that I'd learned about witches today made me feel like some of them at least, truly were my sisters.

"Very. It was a little much with the long toilet metaphor, but I feel better. Thank you." I paused, debating and then going for it. "Esther."

I braced myself, expecting a swat across the top of my head for presumptuously using her first name, but she trained a pleased smile on me, and blushing, I rolled onto the outsides of my feet.

"My pleasure, child."

6

I kept one eye on the light traffic and the other on the dial, tuning in the station Ari had given me where Ro was being interviewed. It was good to hear his voice, even if it was only the set up for the *Hard Knock Strife* theme song that he'd written and recorded.

Rohan bantered back and forth with the DJ and then they went into the exclusive first listen to the song.

Was this why he'd called? I'd already heard the entire thing, though I was happy to hear it again because he had a hit on his hands. His raspy growl perfectly captured the story of a man lost to the darkness, his voice smoothing to rich honey with the subsequent redemption.

I caught myself grinning and singing along. His Romantics were going to lose their shit. I couldn't wait to read the fan boards when I got home.

The interviewer came back on, essentially echoing my sentiment about Ro's fans, except with somewhat less profanity.

"I understand you've got another treat for us," the interviewer said.

"Yeah," Ro said. "I'm busy writing and recording a solo

album. A mini EP called *Ascending*. Six tracks that tell a story about my life these past three years."

My smile fell. Only six? There had been five leaked titles. Had "Slay" made the cut?

Had I?

"When can we expect this?" the interviewer said.

"Next month. September 27," Rohan replied.

A couple weeks after his twenty-fourth birthday.

"You're going to sing one of the songs, live, here today." Dude sounded like he was creaming himself. "Take it away."

Rohan strummed the opening chords. Chords I knew by heart, had sung myself to sleep to.

Hooooonk!

I wrenched the wheel, jerking the car back into my lane. He was playing the song he'd written for me? Why? Hands shaking, I pulled over to the side and parked the car. I didn't trust myself operating large machinery.

I turned up the volume and closed my eyes, pretending I was back in my bedroom the night of my birthday when he'd sung this to me. His voice curled around me, singing the story of us.

In the song he called me a cherub wrapped tight in barbed wire, and after he'd left I'd swear those spikes had taken hold deep in my flesh.

Falling for Rohan had been like slipping on black ice; I'd lost my footing hard and fast. That slide had been scary but exhilarating, and even with minor wipe-outs, one smile from him and I'd scramble back up and head his way. Until that horrible night when I'd crash-landed and could only lay there bruised and winded.

Singing "Slay" was Rohan's way of resetting us. Saying that all the hurt feelings over what had gone down were

69

behind us. Hearing him pour his heart into his words for me, for everyone to hear? I felt like I could dance.

No. I felt like I could soar.

I tried not to think about Icarus and flying too close to the sun.

By the time he finished those final ringing notes, the line "You know I've been slain" still hanging in the air, I had my phone out, waiting impatiently for the interview to end. This talk was happening now. We were going to clear the air between us and then move forward, stronger than ever.

"Sounds like there's a very lucky person in your life," the interviewer said.

I bounced up and down in my seat. Me. That's me.

"I'm the lucky one," Ro said.

Every organ inside my body turned to mush.

"Can you tell us about her?"

"She's amazing." The wonder in his voice, like I was a precious gift in his life, took my breath away. He cleared his throat. "Her name is Nava and she's incredibly special to me."

Something sunk in my chest. That sounded too rehearsed.

"I understand she was a fan first," the interviewer said.

"She was."

I bolted upright, cold sweat prickling my neck. No. Not this.

"In fact, I heard from the actress Poppy Wallace that she remembered the two of you when you were in Prague during the final few days of shooting on *Hard Knock Strife*."

"Yeah," Rohan said. "That was when I realized I wanted a more meaningful relationship with her."

Was that before or after Poppy's lips were on your dick?

The interviewer chuckled. "Apparently, you had a certain nickname for Nava? Lolita."

"I don't call her that anymore. It was a private joke, but it's over."

Oh, it was over, all right. I was going to rip Ro's balls off him and stomp them into pieces. I clutched my phone until the interviewer had thanked Rohan and signed off.

Ro answered on the third ring.

"Find someone else to be your fake girlfriend, asshole."

"Fake girlfriend?"

"Oh? Am I your real one? So hard to tell when the only time I've heard you say it in the past month was on the radio for this mission."

"What the hell, Nava? This was your idea." Ro had that silky menace in his voice I normally found sexy but right now found infuriating.

"No, it wasn't. Which you'd have known had you bothered talking to me."

"I tried. You didn't answer."

I checked my call history. Eight missed calls.

My eyes slid off the reflection in the visor mirror. A better person would have apologized for jumping to conclusions, but hadn't Ro done the same thing? I picked at the hem of my shirt, shame and anger both comforting and smothering. The Brotherhood had played Ro, but only because he'd been willing to go along with that script. Been willing to think the worst of me.

I couldn't bring myself to be the bigger person.

"My friend tweeted a stupid tweet about your love life that didn't even mention me. The Brotherhood, who've been monitoring all mentions of you by the way, decided this was a good in to find the demon that went after Gary Randall. Pierre asked. I declined."

"So they came to me and made me think you wanted to go public." Ro swore viciously.

"In what universe would I be having heart-to-hearts with the Brotherhood?"

"I dunno. If this made you happy, I'd do it. Even if…"

"What?" I said.

"Forget it."

"No. What?"

"It was odd you agreed to it without speaking to me first."

"Because I didn't."

"Well, I know that now," he said waspishly.

I laughed, slightly hysterically. "You thought I'd gone ahead and done this without your consent. Betrayed you again."

"No. I–fuck. I don't know. I wasn't thinking betrayal."

I rested my head on the wheel. "Oh, okay. Guess it was just Lilith controlling me."

I flinched, hearing him punch something hard through the phone.

"You want me to pretend she's not inside you?" he said.

"No. I want you to not make her the sum total of me."

Angry silence rolled down the line.

I closed my eyes. Rohan, this new development with Lilith, I was so very tired of it all. Couldn't I get the easy version of my life when all I had to worry about was demons and Mandelbaum?

"I'll call them and undo this," he said. "Tell Orwell that we refuse to make our relationship public."

I actually pulled the phone away from my ear and stared at it in disbelief. "Wow. That sounded like relief. Are we supposed to be a secret?"

"Now who's jumping to conclusions?"

"I'm not jumping to anything."

"Then why do you sound pissed?" he snapped.

"Because the only reason you mentioned us was for this

stupid assignment. Because you reduced me to your very special fan who fucked her way into your life."

"Part of the story," he growled. "How was I supposed to know the interviewer already talked to Poppy?"

"Even for the mission, you should have found a way to show you had a modicum of respect for me!" A family passing by in a Jeep stared at me, probably because I was red-faced and yelling. I lowered my voice. "I haven't seen you in a month, haven't had any indication that you plan on seeing me any time soon, haven't even heard an 'I miss you,' and now I've been reduced to a cover story. A *groupie* cover story."

"Back at you, sweetheart," he snarled. "You haven't exactly mentioned you were pining away for me."

I cranked the A/C, angling all the vents at my face. "What are we, Rohan? Because if we're done, then tell me."

"We're not done," he said.

My stomach unclenched, even as my brain picked up on what was being left unsaid. "But?"

"I don't know."

"That's some stellar enthusiasm," I said.

"Do you want us to be done?" he said, quietly.

I bit the inside of my cheek, not sure which answer I was scared I'd blurt out.

"I figured if we got some distance..." He sighed. "What do you want me to tell Orwell?"

Did I want to take on an assignment that might break us for good, but let me be around him a little while longer? Say no and cement the Brotherhood's disappointment in me and destroy any hope of respect I had, when the time was coming that I'd need to sway other Rasha to my side?

Or break up with him and walk away?

I started up the engine. "I have no idea."

CRAAACK. The black leather whip snapped the ground by my feet.

I jumped back. "Yikes, you really didn't need that second espresso."

Ms. Clara bounced on her toes. Since she was in six-inch, shiny stiletto boots, her head bobbed much closer to my eyeline than usual.

"I'm just so excited," she said in her breathy voice. "I never get to see demons, only do all the boring paperwork."

She twisted her wrist, flicking the whip in a complicated pattern before snapping it close enough to my face that its crack vibrated down into my toes. Only a handful of parked cars were witness to her lashing mastery on this Tuesday morning, which was too bad because she was impressive to watch.

I shielded my eyes from flying dirt. "I'm starting to regret my decision to bring you."

"You didn't. I blackmailed you into taking me because I have what you need. And Kane and Ari were busy." She clucked her tongue. "Though not getting busy, which would have been far more interesting with those two."

"No kidding. Aren't you hot?" I fanned out my tank top. There wasn't much shade here under the Granville Street Bridge, though the humongous chandelier art exhibit certainly jazzed up the joint, as did the cute sailboats moored in the small marina next to the red nautical-themed yacht club with its porthole windows.

"Eh. You get used to it. Ooh. Wait." She ran back to the car. Even if she hadn't been encased in a catsuit, there wouldn't have been any jiggle. Sitting on her ass as the Brotherhood Executive Administrator by day was counterbalanced by her exertions as a popular dominatrix by night. The woman was insanely toned.

The cars rumbling up top of the bridge were a comforting white noise, the bats zipping in and out of the struts overhead were cute, and it didn't smell like pee. All in all, a decent meeting spot.

"You like?" Slamming the trunk of her Mini Cooper, she spun around, now wearing a black leather face mask with oval eyeholes and an unzipped slash for the mouth. She stuck her tongue out. "So I can't be recognized."

"Like may not be the right word."

"What in good heavens is that?"

I spun at the molasses-smooth voice, tinged with a hint of the Deep South. "Hiya, Baskerville. How's tricks?"

The demon swallowed several times, his pronounced Adam's apple twitching. Using all three of his fingers and his linen handkerchief, he pointed at Ms. Clara. "What are you supposed to be?"

Again with the whip crack.

"Your worst nightmare," Ms. Clara growled.

Baskerville pressed his handkerchief to his face, the picture of a 1950's Southern gentleman in a linen suit with pressed cuffs. Well, except for his iridescent blue skin and a snout. "No, chérie. That's Frisbees."

"Says the dog demon," I said.

"Child, we don't need petty insults in our line of business. There is a robust market for these kinds of wares and you are by no means the only demand I have for my supply."

"How is that an insult? You have a whiskered, wet dog nose."

"I have a proud proboscis. I am not a dog, demon or otherwise. Do you see a tail on me? Floppy ears?"

"Not floppy, but they are pretty large."

75

Ms. Clara patted his arm. "Don't worry, sugar. According to the Japanese proverb, a powerful man has large ears."

"She can stay." He blotted the sweat at his temple with the handkerchief, frowning at her face mask. "Maybe."

"How's the demon world? Seen Malik lately?" I said. Last time I'd seen him he'd threatened to rain vengeance down on my ass. Then he'd gone M.I.A. and even Leo couldn't find him. So that wasn't worrying at all.

He sniffed. "I honestly cannot be expected to know the whereabouts of every demon."

"Like you don't. You're the most plugged in demon around. Come on," I cajoled.

He sniffed at my blatant butt-kissing, but didn't deny it. "Suffice it to say, you're safe from him. For the moment."

Small comfort.

I motioned between Ms. Clara and myself. "We both know you aren't going to hand over the Bullseye without wanting something in return, and my partner here is a master procurer. She's got a list of items to intrigue and delight."

Baskerville raised an eyebrow. "Such as?"

Ms. Clara coiled her whip around her wrist. Damn, she had badass down cold. "The Vashar."

She'd tapped into her admin network and discovered where the Brotherhood was storing the amulet capable of stopping a Rasha's induction. Sure, it was a risk handing it over to a demon, but if he used it on someone, I had a magic ritual that would make an initiate a full Rasha anyway, so it wasn't like anyone was going to be prevented from fulfilling their destiny.

I allowed myself only a small smirk at the look of surprise and greed that flashed across his face.

"It's true, that did intrigue back when I actually wanted it."

My smirk vanished.

"But I've got something else in mind."

"Let me guess, you want tears from a virgin guarded by a sleeping dragon. Or no." I snapped my fingers. "A unicorn dwelling up the ass of an ogre."

"One of Rabbi Mandelbaum's tzitzit," Baskerville said.

Ms. Clara frowned. Well, she gave off a frowny vibe. I couldn't really tell in that face mask. "Why do you want one of his knotted tassels?"

"My client wants it. I don't ask questions."

Mandelbaum wasn't going to hand over one of the tzitzit attached to the corner of his poncho-like prayer shawl, and given he wore this mini tallit under his shirt, would probably notice if I tried to cut one off.

"It's a really nice Vashar," I said. "Shiny, never used, brimming full of dark witch power."

"I think not."

It's not like tzitzis were rare. I could buy one and pass it off as the rabbi's.

"I'll know," Baskerville said.

"What?"

"I'll smell if it's the rabbi's. You humans are very easy to read." He glanced at Ms. Clara's mask. "Some of you."

"You know what Mandelbaum smells like? That's creepy, dude."

Ms. Clara cracked her whip at his feet, making the demon jump. "We could just take the Bullseye from you and give you nothing."

"I knew I was right to bring you," I said.

The demon crouched down and brushed dirt off his trouser hem. "You could. But you'd have nothing more than a paperweight. The Bullseye is a delicate artifact and I've encased it with a protective spell keyed to my touch."

Sparks flew off my skin. "Let me get this straight. I have a magic sanitary pad clogging my toilet body and to get it out, I have to handle Mandelbaum's fringe in order to get a demon to finger me so that Esther can blow my pipes?"

Baskerville turned to Ms. Clara. "Is she making sense?"

"Not a clue," she said. "But I wouldn't mess with her."

"Do we have a deal or not?" He spoke very slowly, over-enunciating each word.

"Just because you don't understand me, doesn't mean I'm communicationally challenged." I pretended to think it over, though with my options being steal off the rabbi's person versus die, it wasn't much of a choice. "Deal."

"Pleasure doing business with you."

"THEN I SAID, 'I hope a strix shits in your face' because like strix are these owl demons who eat humans and their shit is really naaaasty." The lamia demon gnawed on the femur of her former boyfriend, her lips smeared with blood.

"Sure. He shouldn't have cheated on you with that cock-atrice." Those were two-legged demons with the head of a rooster so I couldn't begin to imagine how that coupling had gone down.

I'd been driving along East 33rd Avenue, on the stretch that bisected the two halves of the city cemetery, mulling over how best to rob Mandelbaum, and failing that, looking for demonic troublemakers so I could pound my way to an answer on the Rohan front, when I'd spotted a woman slashing a guy's throat. I'd jumped out of my car, magic ablazin', until I'd seen that the guy in question was green and scaly with one arm too many and the "woman" had fiery red eyes and was screaming, "I'll give you head like nothing you've ever imagined, asshole!" before ripping his actual head off with her claws.

Domestic disputes didn't generally warrant my involvement, but tomorrow she'd be off feeding on small children, so she had to be stopped. I allowed her this last supper in sisterhood solidarity.

"I mean, you have to show them who's boss." She sucked his marrow with quiet snuffling noises.

I pulled my leg into my chest, trying to find a comfortable spot to settle back against the gravestone. "I'm not sure my situation warrants killing and eating my boyfriend."

"Your call, honey." She flung the femur over her shoulder and popped one of the eyeballs she'd been saving into her mouth, munching and making "mmmm" sounds. She picked an eyelash out of her teeth. "But if you're not gonna go with door number one, it seems to me that your only choice is to own it."

"I'm happy to own it. So long as I wasn't forced into it. So long as my boyfriend wants this for more than an assignment. Mandelbaum is behind this. He has to be. I swear that man was birthed through his mom's anus because no one is naturally that much of an asshole."

"Good one." She wiped her hands clean on the grass, pushing her luxurious fall of black hair over her shoulder. "You'll figure it out."

"Yeah."

Time to get this fight over with. Lamia were only moderately dangerous and in my mood, this was going to be a quick kill.

I got to my feet, but before I was fully upright the front of my chest was slashed open. The demon hadn't moved. Brushing aside the ruins of my shirt, I touched my fingertip to one of the three diagonal gashes across my boobs and hissed.

"Lamia can't attack from a distance."

"Yeah, demon daddy had some surprising genes. Gotta love being underestimated." Jumping to her feet, the lamia flexed her fingers.

Two of my ribs snapped. Her magic flooded me, a million spiky barbs ripping me up from inside. Paralyzing me.

"Let's wrap this up," she said. "I've got a date. Gotta get back on that horse. Literally. It's a kelpie." She slashed at the air in front of her...

...and sliced through my heart. I felt the pulpy mass goosh through her fingers, even though her fingers were nowhere near me. My heartbeat turned sluggish, trumpeting impossibly loud in my ears. The world buzzed in and out.

The lamia licked my viscera off her fingers.

Swaying, I crashed onto my ass. Blood streamed from my gashes; flaps of skin hung loose exposing my barely-connected fragments of heart muscle. I called up a red bloom of witch healing magic, trying to knit my mangled self back together.

I attributed the sharp stab and loss of breath to my dying and not any kind of regret at the life that had been within my grasp.

My witch magic pulsed faint pink and dimmed.

I collapsed onto my back like a sack of flour slipping out of someone's hold. My body was so cold, so heavy. My insides were fractured, my magic splintered like panes of cracked glass. So this was what death felt like.

Something dark and powerful, a black wisp of something other, drifted inside me.

Desperate, I hooked one of my magic splinters to it, and

visualized tying the two together
shredded chest began to knit itself
reached for another wisp of Lilith's 1
knotting faster and more furiously, my bc
at warp speed.

My magic re-up loosened the lamia's
reached overhead, grabbed her boyfriend's
the end, and hurtled the flaming bone at her li

Her hair caught fire with a satisfying whoos.., though it
stank like mad.

The lamia wasn't expecting that, shaking her head like a
none-too-bright puppy. Her mouth twisted, opening in a
soundless roar that sent a flock of little brown bats soaring
into the late afternoon sky like a rippling curtain.

She dove to the ground with a high-pitched shriek that
bottomed out into a ghastly moan, attempting to stop, drop,
and roll. It just tangled the tiki torch up worse.

I leapt on top of her, pinning her to the ground, and
fired my electric magic into her kill spot deep inside her ear
canal.

She disappeared, dead.

I beat the smoldering grass so the cemetery didn't go up
in flames, then marched back to my car, accidentally stepping on her ex's remaining eyeball. His femur winked out
of existence. Right. That meant he hadn't technically been
dead while she'd been eating him.

My stomach heaved.

Popping the trunk of my Civic, I got out the first aid kit
and cleaned up my wounds. Then I chugged a Gatorade to
replenish my electrolytes, checking in on my internal
injuries. All was well. Strong heartbeat, repaired ribs. The
dozen or so wisps of Lilith's magic had dissipated, and
while I didn't perceive any other new wisps, I also didn't
feel any lingering effects of having helped myself.

...d detected Lilith's magic before, but I hadn't. ...be able to sense and use it again? Because that had ...en a handy little trick.

I slid onto the hood of my car, soaking in the heat of the summer sun. Almost dying had given me some perspective. I'd spent the past month in limbo, waiting for Mandelbaum to make a move, for Sienna to show up, for Lilith to break free, and for Rohan to care.

I was done being the girl who waited.

The lamia had been right. I could be mad or I could own every fucking aspect of my life. If I was going to die, then I'd die trying for the version of my life that meant something.

Using a selfie of Ro and me, I fired off a quick post on Instagram to all the followers I'd amassed during my party days, trusting those gossipmongers to do the heavy lifting. *Can't wait to be reunited with my guy. One more sleep, baby. #thatsmyrockstar #RoMantic*

Go big or go home.

7

I drove directly to Rivka's house to update Esther on this new and exciting turn of events. She'd paused her light gardening to give me a quick check-up, then proceeded to subject me to a stern lecture about dark magic that essentially came down to "just say no."

My counterargument that my actions had been instinctual and I'd do the same again if it meant not dying failed to placate her. Neither did the fact that there was no spike of dark magic or any trace of Lilith that she could detect.

"Allow me to list all the ways dark magic will destroy your life." Esther pruned dead blooms off the rambling rhododendron in her sister's back yard. "It starts with paranoia-inducing voices, then you've got hallucinations of giant insects out of the corner of your eye and itchiness where you scratch yourself bloody." She jabbed the pruning shears at me. "And your growing debasement where you'll do anything for the high, forgetting to eat, and screwing over your loved ones."

I picked up the discarded foliage with the puffy gardening gloves she'd given me and dumped them in the compost bin. "Is that what happened to Tessa?"

"She skipped a couple stages and jumped right to the 'burning up from the inside' part."

I flicked an ant off my arm. "Lilith is inside me, which means, like it or not, this dark magic is inside me, too. Might as well use whatever is leaking out, assimilate it, and turn it into good magic by merging it with my own."

She snorted. "That's conjecture, not sound logic."

"Tell me with absolute certainty that doing nothing won't negatively affect me."

She pruned a branch with a hard snap.

"Exactly," I said. "You can't. I'm trying to make the best of this situation and I'm happy to follow any advice you have."

"Focus on getting the Bullseye and interact with Lilith and her magic as little as possible."

"I will." I lay my hand on her shoulder. "I've got a lot to live for. So I choose that."

It earned me a grumbled assent.

Being somewhat busy, I ignored my boyfriend's call in favor of a text that said we'd talk when I got to Los Angeles. We were doing things on my timeline now.

Twelve hours later, I'd bought my plane ticket, requested intel from Pierre after tearing a strip off him for manipulating Rohan and me, packed, and was currently headed to the airport.

"Emotions are going to be running high with you two right now," Leo said from the back seat of the Honda. "Better to be in the same room with Ro for your next talk."

I popped another extra-strength Tylenol, wishing I hadn't given in to my nervousness last night about this reunion and drank quite so much. Grabbing the bottle in the cup holder, I took a swig of water and swallowed it down.

"Roll down the window if you're gonna puke," Ari said.

"You are looking a little green," Leo said. "I told you not to add coolers into the mix. What are you, sixteen and trying to seem grown up and cool?"

I appreciated the teasing, since the coolers had been broken out at about 2AM. Why did the worst drinks always seem like a good idea at that unholy hour? As a result, my twin was still in pajamas, wearing the darkest shades he owned, and Leo was hiccuping softly, still tipsy.

She reached forward to pat my shoulder. "Kane should have come along for moral support so you could be distracted from how badly this could all crash and burn."

I shifted around to glare at her. "Your pep talk needs work."

"*I* don't think you and Ro are going to crash and burn. I just know that neurotic brain of yours is envisioning all those scenarios. Like a little worker bee." She hiccupped again and then stretched out across the entire back seat, singing some made-up song about bees.

Ari eyed her through the rearview mirror. "There's no room for Kane in the car."

I frowned at him. "Are you guys back to not speaking?"

I'd asked Kane to come out with us last night, but he'd mumbled some excuse about demons that needed killing and taken off.

Ari shrugged. "We'd have to be in the same room for that level of interaction. I'm refusing to buy into his issues, so Kane is avoiding me all together." He pulled up to the curb at Vancouver International Airport. "You ready?"

I unbuckled my seat belt. "Let's go with 'yes.'"

The good thing about spending the flight knotted up in anxiety at this reunion was that it distracted me from my broken economy seat, my shitty entertainment selection, and the fact that I had to sell a kidney to buy some Pringles and a sandwich.

I ponied up for the onboard wifi to see if Pierre had gotten the information I'd requested from him. It seemed likely that this demon had struck out at high-level people before Gary. Remembering the course my dad was teaching, I'd wondered if there were cold cases that fit its evil M.O. Other than the spawn possibly being attracted to cockiness, it was a fairly meagre demon profile, but I had to start somewhere and I'd bring a fresh set of eyes to it all.

Pierre had emailed a PDF that was close to a hundred pages long, filled with a combination of handwritten scanned documents and computer entries. I opened the file, but I was shallow and curious and I drifted over to Instagram instead. My post hadn't broken the internet, but it had cracked it. I ignored all the requests for details from my "very special friends," meaning anyone who'd apparently been in the same room with me for more than ten minutes.

Both #Rova and #Navan were trending on Twitter as possible celebrity names. Reaction over our coupledom was decidedly mixed. While some were happy Rohan had found love again, the nicest of the haters called me a small-town tramp.

Vancouver wasn't that small.

I could have called them out, but why get bitchy when I could get my boyfriend back?

I settled back against my seat, my knee jittering. As nervous as I was about this trip, I was way more excited to be winging my way to Los Angeles. Somewhere around my fourth hard lemonade last night, I'd had this epiphany about how amazing it was that I was going to get to publicly take my place as Ro's girlfriend.

I didn't want us to exist in the shadows.

I'd made a serious mistake letting him leave. He needed to remember how good we were together. And he would. It would have been nice had it been our choice, and given the mission, navigating our way to solid ground would not be without its challenges, but we could do it.

We *would* do it.

I'd been proud of my tap accomplishments and proud of how I'd handled becoming Rasha. Why shouldn't I be proud of my status in this relationship? I was gonna be the chick that tamed Le Mitra. Take that, haters.

But the best part of all?

I was gonna be the girl who got to have Ro.

HE'D SENT A DRIVER.

The driver was very distinguished with silver hair, a chiseled jaw, and warm blue eyes. He had a trim gold braid on his cap, white gloves, and the sign he held with my name on it displayed excellent penmanship. Had I been casting the role of driver, he would have been my number one pick, but it wasn't quite the "Nava runs across the airport in slow motion, jumping into Rohan's arms and crushing the bouquet he'd brought as he swings her around, lavishing kisses upon her" reception I'd fantasized while dodging fellow travellers.

Not even close.

Rohan Liam Mitra was a big fat coward.

I wrestled the suitcase with the wonky wheel to a stop, managing to run over my own foot in the process.

"I'm Nava," I said through gritted teeth.

"Very good. May I take your bags?" The driver relieved me of my two giant suitcases, wheeling them smoothly out the doors of LAX and over to a fancy-ass limo parked at the curb.

"Rohan sent a limo?" Fine. He was a coward with good taste.

The driver opened the door for me. "Also his apologies. He meant to be here but there was a last-minute issue with his painters." Painters? He was renovating? How permanent. "He decided it would be faster for me to get you and then meet him."

"Practicality. My favorite quality in a man." I scrambled into the limo and the driver shut the door, enveloping me in air-conditioned silence. A massive bouquet of multi-colored gerbera daisies tied with a red ribbon lay on the leather seats.

Guilt flowers. It was a start.

I pulled out the card, pressing the bouquet to my nose. *Welcome to L.A.* Nope, he lost points for the generic message, though he gained a few for having a chilled bottle of prosecco and a glass ready for my drinking pleasure. But I was still alone because he'd prioritized some painters over me.

His boyfriend karma was precariously in the red.

I took a couple of deep breaths, shaking off my annoyance. I was in Los Angeles. That's what mattered. Let the convertibles and palm trees commence.

Yeah, right.

Highway traffic was pretty much what I'd anticipated, though we bumped pretty hard along stretches of torn-up asphalt, and the trash caught in the scrubby brush along the edges of the highway didn't scream glamor. Neither did the graffitied off-ramp signs and overpasses. The street names like La Cienega and Hollywood Boulevard were familiar, but since that was only thanks to pop culture storytelling, I was starting to feel like I was on a giant film set, albeit one that didn't have very good production values.

This giant urban sprawl was fifty shades of brown. Much like my mood.

The city wasn't what I expected once we got off the highway, either. For one thing, there were a lot of strip malls. In fact, there were a lot of low-rise buildings in general. I hadn't expected so many places that were only one or two floors. It was weird. As were the black traffic lights (versus yellow) and yellow fire hydrants (versus red).

Where were all the cyclists and pedestrians? Weren't there supposed to be beautiful people keeping fit? Had TV and movies steered me so wrong? The surrealness of the situation intensified when the limo wound its way into the hills under the Hollywood sign along narrow, twisty streets. The houses followed a palette heavy on coral and sand, but as we climbed higher, there were more hedges and fences and less actual mansions to be seen. No sidewalks anywhere and still no people. Creepy.

The limo pulled up to a wrought-iron gate set into a long, curved white wall. Tall bushes had been planted for privacy, screening everything from view. The driver got out and spoke into the intercom, then the gates swung slowly open.

We drove up a wide, tree-lined lane and my mouth fell open. The property was secluded enough that there was no sense of any neighbors and so enormous that it required groundskeepers.

Groundskeepers! Had I stepped into Downton Abbey? Or, given Rohan's past, the Playboy Mansion lite? I'd had it in my head that Ro owned some modest place, so either I was wrong or he was deluded.

The limo pulled to a stop in front of a mid-century mansion, all white and natural stone accents with a flat roof, with nary a Bunny in sight.

The driver opened the door and offered his hand to me.

I sat there, paralyzed. What had I gotten myself into? I'd never seen Rohan in his natural element. Yeah, he was big game, but it hadn't hit me on a visceral level the way it did now, with the California sunlight winking off two levels of floor-to-ceiling glass. This home had probably been designed by some famous architect and cited in magazines and shit. You know who'd designed my family home? Neither did I, because normal people didn't know those things.

"Miss?" The driver prompted me to get out.

"You're sure this is Rohan Mitra's house?" I swung a foot onto the flagstone, waving off his assistance.

"No. This home belongs to Dev and Maya Mitra."

I whipped my legs back inside and slammed the door, making frantic "turn around" motions.

The door opened once more and Rohan stuck his head in. Gawd, he looked gorgeous. His hair was that slightly-too-long length that curled around his ears and was perfect to thread my fingers into. His brown skin was darker than I'd last seen and made his gold eyes blaze. "Seeing as I'm staying here while Dad is recovering, you getting out, Sparky?"

I crossed my arms, which worked to both bolster my displeasure and keep me from crawling up his body. I stared straight ahead. "I think not."

When he didn't respond, I glanced over at him. Mistake number one. No, he wasn't feasting on me, his eyes slightly wild. He was pulling out his tin of candy coated fennel seeds and popping one in his mouth. "You sure?"

"Guess I can." I shrugged. "Since I'm here already."

I got out of the limo like a goddess descending from on high.

We didn't touch, not while Ro collected my bags and brought them into the house, even though the small of his

90

back where his T-shirt pooled would have been an easy target for my hand. And we didn't touch, not while we thanked the driver and not while Ro shut the front door, his arms cording as he reached it, arms that had held me for entire nights, arms that I kept thinking it was okay to touch and having to stop myself like there was an invisible force field guarding him, exiling me from his space.

Here we were, in the same place for the first time in a month, and all I could do was stand there like a beggar at a feast.

"Hi," he said.

"Hi." We both kind of laughed and moved in for a hello kiss which ended with us bumping noses, our lips half on mouths and half on cheeks.

I squared my shoulders. At least he'd made physical contact. I guess that counted as a win. Had I made a big mistake in coming here without speaking to him first? I'd been positive he'd remember why we fit together so well and that we could work things out, but between the impersonal airport pick-up and this epic awkwardness, I wasn't so sure.

He held his arm out against mine. "Look at you, all tanned."

"Yeah. Gallery White is my spring look. I like to crank it up to a solid Eggshell for the summer." I danced out of reach, out of the foyer, and into the huge living room. Might as well stake out the dragon's lair.

For all the stark whiteness of the outside, the inside was alive with vibrant color, the coolest of which was this pop art painting of Maya hung over the stone fireplace. I recognized the purple dreads, nose piercing, and those startling gold eyes. "Love it."

"Yeah? You'll be interested in this, then." He took my hand. The calluses he'd built up from all his guitar playing rubbed like a gentle rasp. I stumbled over my feet, lost in the rush of being once more anchored by his warmth and strength coupled with a tingling anticipation of something about to happen. Hopefully not metaphoric missiles striking and everything safe obliterated.

I was so focused on the feel of his skin against mine that I didn't register what Ro had intended until he fisted my shirt in his hands and pushed me up against the wall, his face edging in close to mine. "Miss me?"

With every molecule. But I didn't understand his game, his proximity not aligning with the coolness of his words. I took my turn, polite and restrained. "Of course. You?"

He was unreadable as he studied me.

My stomach dropped into my toes. He shouldn't have been so poker-faced. Not after everything we'd been through. His expression should have been tight with anger, slack with relief, or, my personal preference, eyes blazing with hunger because he'd missed me so much.

There was one possible reason Rohan was so carefully neutral: all he saw when he looked at me was Lilith. And if I was right, we were over before we could even reboot.

8

"Rohan?"

Ro shook his head sharply as if to clear it, cupping my cheek with his hand. "Can I...?"

He brushed his lips over mine, and pulled back, his questioning eyes locking onto me.

My chest felt heart attack victim tight. I should have said no. One of us had to be the grown up and initiate the relationship talk before we gave in to our chemistry.

As much as I knew that intellectually, my body wasn't prepared to agree. My treacherous fingers gripped the front of his shirt like a baby with a security blanket.

Rohan's nostrils flared at the contact; his tongue darted into the corner of his mouth. He covered my fingers with his. The touch was pulsing, crackling, like an invisible current flowed between us, leveling our jagged edges, burning those immutable hurts and loosening the tangle of thorns we'd become for one electric second.

I nodded. Barely even a movement.

Ro's mouth crashed down on mine. I moaned because everything had gone dark and hot, his kiss fizzing through me. He sucked on my lower lip and my head fell back against the wall, hitting a framed print.

I twisted sideways so we didn't knock it down. Nope, not a print. It was one of Maya's platinum albums. Two minutes in my idol's house and I was pawing at her son and destroying personal property.

I squirmed in his grasp. "We can't do this."

Ro kissed down my throat and my good intentions turned into me grabbing him by the belt to press his body flush against mine.

"We can," he murmured. "We really, really can."

"Your mom will be home soon and me mauling her kid is not the first impression I want to make."

"*I'm* mauling *you*. But hey, if you want a turn just let me know and we can switch it up."

I waved a hand at the walls. "I can't behave badly in your mom's house surrounded by her platinum records."

"How about surrounded by awkward family photos?" He sucked on my ear and my knees buckled. Ro braced his arm across my back, holding me close. "Because if that does it for you, we've got a shitload in the TV room."

Yes, obviously, I'd be checking those out, but that wasn't the point. The fear of meeting Maya while grinding up on her precious son gave me the power to step away.

That and the fact that while sex had never been our problem, I didn't want it to be our solution.

"Stop."

Rohan stepped back. He dragged in a breath, his lips swollen, his eyes glazed. He ran a thumb over his lower lip.

"We need to talk." I placed my hand on his chest to keep him at arm's length.

Ro shot me a look of pure sorrow. "I know."

There was a brief pause during which neither of us moved.

"I want us," he said, his voice full of misery, "but I don't know what that means or how to get it."

I didn't visibly flinch, but a gut punch to the soul didn't have a physical impact. "I'll call Pierre on my way back to the airport. Tell him to put someone else on the Randall case."

I stepped past Rohan, desperate to grab my suitcases and bolt, but he caught my arm.

"Don't leave. Please."

Words I'd longed to hear that now left a hollow ache in my chest. "I'm sorry for how I made you feel, but I'm not sorry for making the deal and getting your magic back. And I don't know how to make you forgive me."

"I have a problem with forgiveness. I get that." He released me, but I didn't move. "Can we take things one day at a time? Try being together like a normal couple?"

I gave him a wry smile. "While enticing a demon to come after us and throwing our relationship into the spotlight for paparazzi and fans to rip apart?"

He screwed up his face. "Normal for us? We're not going to figure this out apart."

"True."

"So you'll stay?" His eyes darted across my face.

If we couldn't figure this out, losing Rohan would be as horrible as losing my tap dreams. I could cut and run and I'd hurt like hell and drown it out in hot guys in bars like I had before, but if I did that, I'd end up in an even worse place than where I started. And I'd never feel like this again: like everything was impossibly full of potential, like I could gamble and win it all. All I had to do was risk it.

I willed down the hot, tight panic urging me to flee. "I'll stay."

"Can I kiss you again?"

I stepped in close to him and tilted my face up to his. "Yes."

Rohan tasted like fennel seeds and home, his kiss rushing out to fill every inch of me. We tried to keep it sweet and light, but Ro and I weren't made for sunshine and honey. Our desire was tinged with shadow and dark cherry.

He gripped my hips, pulling me up onto my toes. Our tongues tangled and voltage thrummed through my lips under the onslaught of his kiss. My stomach dropped into my toes; it was that first plunge of a coaster, that long, fast slide of black ice.

Glorious free fall.

I wrapped my legs around his waist, tangling my fingers in his hair and–

A door slammed.

I flinched and tried to get down, but Ro clutched my ass, causing me to rub against his hard-on with every step as he walked us down the hallway, and really, how was a girl supposed to resist?

More importantly, why ever would she want to?

"Gardener's van," he said. "You'll know when Mom's here because she clomps up the front stairs. Also, she's out of town. I sent her and Dad away for a few days."

I rocked my hips, a slow grind. "You didn't think to lead with that?"

"Seeing you kind of scattered my thoughts."

It was a miracle we didn't break our necks up the stairs, making out like teenagers, our clothes flying and shoes kicked off. There was a precarious moment when we hit the top step and Ro's pants got tangled in his knees, sending us crashing into the bannister.

We careened off it, bouncing into Ro's doorjamb. He

laughed, sideways walking us through a doorway, and tossed me on a twin bed.

I snickered. "This is your old room."

It was plastered in superhero posters, except for the place of pride over the bed, which was dominated by a poster of a young Morrissey from The Smiths, prince of emo.

"Wow. It's everything I'd hoped for."

He spread his arms wide. "I have no secrets from you, baby. No shame."

I tracked the sheet music sitting on the bedside table, a pencil thrown over the top but I couldn't make out any actual lyrics.

He flipped the pages over, with a mock-stern shake of his head. Rohan's creative process didn't allow for other people seeing his work before it was finished.

"That and you want to get laid on your Batman blanket." I kept my voice light and teasing, like I wouldn't have given my right arm to know what that song was about.

"Fuck, yes." He climbed onto the bed.

"In that case." I crooked a finger at him and he fell on top of me, both of us laughing.

Suddenly, I winced and jerked sideways.

"Lilith?" he whispered.

"You caught my hair." I moved his arm.

He rolled off me and onto his side, propping himself on his elbow. "We can wait. For however long it takes to get her out of you."

I gave him a sad smile. "You look at me and you see her. You wonder–"

"No." His denial was swift and fierce. "When I said that to you on the phone the other night?" He rolled onto his back. "What if the reason she's trapped in you was because I did something wrong? Because my magic wasn't strong enough or good enough or I fucked up plain and simple?" His voice cracked with anguish. "And you had to pay the price?"

Oh, Snowflake.

I jabbed a finger in his chest hard enough to make him wince. "That guilt you've obviously been torturing yourself with?" I snapped my fingers. "Lose it. It's not your fault."

He hesitantly raised his head to look at me. "But–"

"No. It sucks that it happened, but we'll figure it out."

Now would be a good time for full disclosure about my potential demise and black magic borrowing. It would be a very emotional conversation, with lots of tears. In other words, a real mood killer.

"Sex isn't going to wake her." I reached for the waistband of his boxers, but he stilled my hand.

"Really." His voice was hard. Almost as hard as his rigid shoulders.

I replayed the past ten seconds. Oh. Was he freaking kidding me? I widened my eyes theatrically. "I have a confession to make. I've been with someone. The things he does." I whistled. "Buzzes, vibrates. He can go for hours."

Rohan ducked his head. "I didn't actually think you'd hooked up with anyone else."

"Yeah, you did, dummy. But I didn't." I swallowed. "Did you?"

"No." He unclenched my fists. "You've ruined me for all other women."

"Good." I gazed up at him through half-lowered lids. "Then where were we?"

His tender smile curled filthily and my pulse spiked up. "Turn off your brain."

I jutted out my chin. "Why? Because you're so amazing I don't need to fantasize?"

He pressed his hands to his heart. "She actually listens when I speak."

"Shut up and fuck me on your Batman blanket, Snowflake."

He put his hands together in prayer formation looking heavenward and mouthing, "Thank you."

Then he jumped me. My bra was slingshot and left dangling off a guitar.

Ro broke our kiss long enough to roll me over onto my belly, both of us naked, his hand playing with my clit. I pressed my ass against his erection, rubbing shamelessly against him as his lips against my throat kept time with his busy fingers. His teeth rasped against my spine as he covered me in all his naked glory. And I do mean glory.

Rohan played my body like a favorite instrument: quickening the tempo on my clit to elicit a moan, scraping his teeth against my skin to pull it hot and tight, rolling his hips slowly to leave me gasping and clutching at the blankets.

My blood fizzed under my skin. I squirmed, bending one leg to run my instep along his calf. "Ro. Please. I need to taste you."

"Since you asked so nicely." He rolled away from me, my body going cold at the sudden lack of contact. He stretched out on his back, one hand propped behind his head. With the other, he motioned at his erect cock. "Have at it."

I sawed my teeth over my bottom lip. I didn't want polite and bantery. I wanted him to lose his precious control, break down the walls still between us until the idea of being without me was unthinkable.

"Make me."

Ro's breath hitched, with a growl he tangled his fist in my hair, pushing me down his body.

I sucked his cock into my mouth, moaning at the musky, salty, utterly male taste of him. My magic hummed through my lips, vibrating up through his erection.

"Fuuuuck." He shuddered, his ass bucking off the bed. His fingers tightened on my locks and his eyes were two slits of gold under a dusky sweep of lashes.

My hair fell forward blanketing out the world, my entire existence reduced to the taste and feel of him. I scraped my nails along his inner thighs, licking down his cock to suck his balls into my mouth. I needed to be overwhelmed by him.

It was the only way to convince myself this was real.

He let go of my hair and I glanced up at him. The boy looked wrecked: pupils blown out, hands fisting the blanket, his mouth half-open, swearing under his breath, and canting his hips so I could take more of him.

"Stop," he groaned. "I have to fuck you. Now."

I gave one last saucy suck, before sliding off his dick. "That can be arranged."

"Can it?" He rolled me over, pinning my hands over my head.

"You got me where you want me, baby. Now what are you gonna do with me?"

"I can't hold back. This might be rough. That okay?" His voice was strained.

I cocked my head. "How rough?" Ro laughed, low and wicked, and I arched up under him. All the yeses to rough. A furious ache built up from Cuntessa, pulsing upward, muscles tightening in its wake. "Bring it."

He slid inside me and I sighed. I'd been scared I'd never experience that glorious sensation of Ro filling me again.

"Yes," he murmured. He teased Cuntessa with the pad of his thumb in small circles.

The room was silent except for the slap of skin on skin,

our involuntary gasps, and our forceful exhales. It wasn't tender, it wasn't sweet, and it wasn't enough.

I dug my nails into his ass, pulling him against me. "Harder."

Ro stood up, tugging my legs up into a ninety-degree angle and fucked me into the mattress. Hips snapping, he launched into this dirty patter about how every part of me felt on him. Around him. His voice wound me tighter and hotter and his musk and iron scent put me into a heady trance.

Delicious sparks of pleasure sparkled from Cuntessa all the way into my toes. With every sense, I drank him in, half-blind with lust, my eyes unfocused. I was writhing, the Batman blanket bunching up around me more and more with each thrust and the bed scraping the ground in rhythmic pounding.

My orgasm hit me with the force of a freight train. Blinding white light filled my vision and sparks crackled off my skin.

It set Ro off with a hoarse groan, his teeth gritted.

He collapsed on the bed beside me. "Lilith show up?"

"I told you, sex wouldn't wake her."

"Yeah, but that was using your piddly toy." He flexed his biceps, kissing each one in turn. "I'm all man."

"How do you live with yourself?"

He swatted my butt and I laughed, sticking my tongue out at him.

Much as I was mostly certain all this business with Lilith would be resolved successfully, if I was going to die, at least I could get fucked seven ways to Sunday in the good sense before I bit it. Round two, I was coming for you, but first, a small business matter to attend to.

I rolled off the bed.

"Come back."

Grabbing my phone, I flopped back down beside him, snuggling into the crook of his arm. "Selfie time."

I angled the camera to snap us from the shoulders up since I was too comfy cuddled up naked to bother getting dressed.

"We look like we've been having sex," he said.

"Exactly. The perfect photo to launch Operation Unbearable Girlfriend." I laughed. "Unbearable Girlfriend Hell. Code word: UGH."

Ro grudgingly played along until I added stupid hashtags like "#Blessed" and "#UGot2LuvIt" at which point he tried to choke himself.

"It's for the mission," I said. "You know how humble I usually am."

He started tickling me and I shrieked, getting tangled up in the covers as I tried to get away. I could have stayed there with him the rest of the day, joking, cuddling, fooling around, and crossing my fingers that we were building the foundation of normal, but his Brotherhood phone rang. Our idyll was over.

9

"Cisco, hey man. What's up?" Rohan said.

I got dressed so as not to prance naked through the house when I retrieved my suitcases.

Ro held up a finger for me to wait. "Yeah. She's here."

He winced, holding the phone away from his ears as a group of men whooped, calling out my name and for me to hurry up and come meet them.

"Got a sister?" one of them yelled.

"Brother," I said.

A bunch of "ooohs," and a "Bastijn, you're in luck."

"Kane? No?" Ro asked me over the good-natured ribbing bellowing out of the phone.

I shrugged and took the phone away from Rohan. "Boys, I'm flattered. We'll be there in a bit, so pretty up for me."

"Don't you have to pretty up for us?" another asked.

"There's one of me, and?" I threw a questioning glance at Ro and he held up five fingers. "Five of you. The odds are not in your favor."

Ro took the phone back. "Don't mess with my girl,

Cisco. She'll own you." He laughed, told the Rasha he was speaking with to 'fuck off,' and hung up.

"I need a shower first." I looked around the room at the twin-size bed and bookshelves packed with albums in trepidation. "Uh, am I supposed to stay here with you?"

"We're staying in one of the guest bungalows out back. More privacy."

"Not a pull-out couch. Not even a spare room. Entire bungalows. Plural."

"Mom had them built for musicians to stay in residence while they were recording. There are only three."

I patted his cheek. "It's good I showed up when I did, because you are clearly in need of re-connecting with how the little people live."

"You're a regular humanitarian."

"My compassion should be a model to all. A walking mitzvah. Where are my suitcases? I'll freshen up, we'll go meet the others, and then I want to pay a visit to Gary Randall."

"Billie put them in the bungalow already. Yes. We have a full-time housekeeper."

I mimed zipping my lips and waited for Ro to take a quick shower, after which he gave me a brief tour of the house.

There were a modest five bedrooms upstairs, each with their own bathroom that was spa quality. Maya's room was by far, the most shocking. The woman embodied rock-and-roll, yet her bedroom was pure old Hollywood glam, from its cream walls to the French vintage bed frame, its headboard and footboard upholstered in soft pink. A crystal chandelier hung over an art deco vanity table which held an assortment of glass perfume bottles and silver-handled makeup brushes.

I clapped my hands. "It's so girly. I love it."

Other than the colorful living room that I'd already seen on the main floor, there was a formal dining room with a table that could easily seat twenty whose top was a solid slab of wood, a kitchen that a professional chef would weep over, and the TV room, though there was no sign of these supposed awkward photos. There was, however, more comfortable seating than in V.I.P. movie theatres with higher quality screening equipment.

I sat in one of the leather recliners and pressed every button on the console, beaming when I was rewarded with heat and vibration. "Show me the bell pull to summon the butler and I may never leave."

"Mom got rid of that when she renovated ten years ago." I couldn't tell if he was joking. "Press that." He leaned over and indicated a green button next to a tiny speaker.

"We'll return to this later. Right now, I want to see those photos you promised me."

"They're in the TV room."

I looked from the giant white screen to the mounted projector. "This isn't it?"

"This is the screening room."

"Uh-huh." At this point, I expected the TV room to come complete with a stable of A-list celebrities to personally act out their filmographies for my viewing pleasure, so I was highly relieved to find a couple of beat-up couches, a normal flat screen TV, magazines and newspapers tossed on the coffee table, and family photos covering one wall.

I pretended to wipe a tear from my eye at the photo of a very young Rohan, maybe five or six, in a one-piece green spandex leotard, his hair in a mullet, and his two front teeth nowhere to be seen, standing in front of this cheesy solar system photo backdrop.

"There's just so much to unpack here, I don't know where to dive in."

"I was an asteroid in the school play."

"You were something. This is truly the greatest gift I've ever received."

"I'm adorable," he said.

"We've discussed this. You need to stop reading your fan boards. They're severely biased and not leading you anywhere good."

Ro tugged on my arm. "Enough. You've hit your blackmail quota for the day."

"Sweet deluded boy. You didn't honestly think you could show this to me and not have it be an ongoing topic of conversation, did you?"

I moved through the rest of the photos, some truly hilarious like an adolescent Ro, all goth attitude, others genuinely sweet, capturing Ro's life with his parents on beaches, at Disneyland, and in the studio with Maya. Even at his most teen emo, he was always smiling when he was with his mom and dad. Some might consider that nerdy. Not me.

The mid-afternoon heat scorched my skin as he led me outside. Not through a door. Please. Nothing so pedestrian. We stepped past the billowing sheer white curtains in the living room, and presto chango, we'd gone from inside to outside, thanks to the retractable wall.

Shielding my eyes with one hand against the glare, I looked from the sparkling blue pool and connecting hot tub with, oh yes, a waterfall, to the enormous stainless steel grill and the teak loungers with striped cushions arrayed in groups on the pool deck, and wondered if his parents cared to adopt me.

The charming yellow adobe bungalows with red tiled roofs were situated down a short path lined with spiky cacti and carefully raked rocks.

Ro stopped in front of the closest—and smallest—one. "I hope you like it."

It was cozy but bright, with a good flow from the living room to the open kitchen. Black leather bar stools were pushed up to the counter, while the long exterior wall was wallpapered in this 1970s-inspired, trippy purple iridescent pattern that should have been horrendous but was edgy and rock-and-roll. Kane could learn a thing or two from it.

There were fun touches like a beanbag chair with a space-age vibe, a Magic 8 Ball on the shelf which I may have squealed at, and a framed colorful painting consisting of geometric shapes, almost like a child had done it.

Hang on. I marched across the room and peered at the signature.

"This is a Kandinsky. A real Kandinsky. I saw his stuff in the Pompidou in Paris."

Ro jammed his hands in the pockets of his board shorts and rocked back on his bare heels. "Admittedly, this may be on a bit of a different scale from most people's homes."

"Stop talking. You're embarrassing yourself, Mr. One Percent. Prove you can get your hands dirty with the rest of us peasants and unpack my suitcases." They were visible through the bedroom doorway, sitting neatly in the corner.

"Billie would have done that already." He gave me his best innocent smile. "I can help you shower."

I only declined his offer because we'd never make it out of here otherwise, and stepped into the bedroom to grab the outfit I'd brought especially to meet my fellow Rasha. Not only was everything neatly folded, Billie had ironed a few key pieces before hanging them up.

I poked my head out the door. "Do your parents want to adopt me?"

"Incest is frowned upon in my family."

I scrunched up my face. "Billie ironed. I mean... I do have a really good vibrator."

Ro whipped a pillow at me. I shrieked, ducked, and went to take my shower.

All was well for the first couple of minutes but partway through shampooing my hair, my energy leached out of me. I slid onto the river rock shower floor and pulled my knees into my chest, letting the hot spray beat down on me. My skin felt itchy and ill-fitting. Everything seemed stuck in slug mode, from the water condensation streaking the walls, to the flat white noise of the spray, like the world had lost thirty percent of sound, motion, and color.

I guess lack of a good night's sleep, our emotionally-charged reunion, the sex, and gearing up to go meet new Rasha in potentially hostile territory had taken more out of me than I realized.

A couple of wisps had leaked out of Lilith's magic box since Esther had checked me out. Even in my inward-seeing magic vision, they were barely evident: fine, short, black threads drifting inside me.

My own magic presented as a spiderweb, stretching out from the crown of my head to my toes, and I mentally tied these threads into the heart of it, letting them fuse and evaporate, giving me an energy boost. Evil Willow may have been my favorite character on Buffy, but jonesing for dark magic to the point of destroying the world wasn't a life goal.

Holding my own at my first visit to the L.A. chapter, was.

Re-energized, I pushed to my feet and finished my shower.

Ro was waiting with a giant fluffy towel to wrap me in but I shooed him away so I could get dressed.

My fitted black crop top had hot pink glittery letters saying "Punches like a girl. Kicks your ass." I'd paired it with black hip hugger cargo pants that were cut off mid-calf. Thanks to a ton of gel, I'd achieved a sleek ponytail. I dusted gold eye shadow over my lids, with minimal mascara, all the better to let my red lips pop, and cat-walked into the living room in my black Doc Martins. "As the first female Rasha, am I appropriately representing?"

I got a thumbs-up and more kisses so I took that as a yes, and then it was out to his '67 Shelby Mustang that he'd had shipped back to Los Angeles. The two-door vintage muscle car had been freshly washed, midnight blue finish and white racing stripe glinting in the daylight.

"I hate to admit it, but I missed her."

Ro snickered. "You gave Shelby gender. I've broken you."

"Yes. You win. Mazel tov." I sank onto the passenger seat cooing, "You can't wait for me to drive you again, can you, baby?"

"Let's not get crazy." Ro reached across me to his glove compartment and handed me a flyer for a fundraiser for an international children's charity working with kids in Third World countries.

"Is this our debut as Navan?" I said. Ro scowled at me. "You prefer Rova? I can live with Rova."

"I prefer no stupid couple name."

"Celebrity couples get names and you count."

"Gee, thanks."

"Deal with it." There were a bunch of performers supporting this event. That meant press and probably fans. "Go big or go home. You're going to have to take me shopping, Sugar Daddy."

"Why? Want to look your best for Zack?" Rohan turned the key and the Shelby purred to life. He shifted gears, his bicep flexing, and roared down the driveway.

I looked at the paper again and squealed. "Zack is hosting this? You're letting me meet Zack?!"

"I'm letting you be in a room in which Zack will also be. Whether or not you actually get to meet him remains to be seen."

"Maybe he'll autograph my fanfic binder."

"You are not to discuss your adolescent sexual fantasies of the dude."

"Little bit, yeah, I am."

We kept the windows down and the music loud. At my request, Ro took a circuitous route along the Sunset Strip. The West Hollywood end of it was pretty swanky, with lots of boutiques and restaurants. Billboards advertising TV shows, movies, and concerts that I'd never heard of were everywhere. Sunset got less intense the farther along we drove. There were entire blocks where I could forget this was the entertainment capital. I even got the occasional glimpse of old Los Angeles with 1950s neon motel signs before Ro swung us back on the highway.

Any time he wasn't changing gear, he was touching me, his hand resting on my thigh, cupping the back of my neck, absently caressing my cheek. Keeping us connected.

I rolled down the window and turned up the music. "Going to Demon Club in the City of Angels. Ironic."

"Where do you think the Fallen Angels name originated? Go back. I like that song."

Making a face, I hit the button to return to the previous station playing the jangly indie guitar band song.

"You'd like this album," Ro said. "It's called 'Lolita Nation.'"

I gave him a tight smile and shifted in my seat to look at him. "So," I said casually, "from the interview you did it sounds like *Ascending* is coming together."

He made a frustrated sound, his hands tightening on

the steering wheel. "I have to release the tracks on September 27."

"Why? Are you under contract?"

"Something like that." He drove another block before he spoke again. "I finally believe that Asha wouldn't have wanted me to quit music, just be happy without losing myself to the industry, but I can't get back to where I was creatively."

I scrolled through the myriad of satellite radio choices. "You haven't forgiven yourself yet."

Ro braked at a light. He drummed his fingers on the wheel. "Maybe I can't until I find Asha's killer. Avenge her."

"You need to forgive yourself regardless because if you don't, you won't be able to move forward in all areas of your life."

Rohan was silent for a long time, during which I stared resolutely out the passenger window so he couldn't see me biting my bottom lip.

"Maybe," he finally said.

We crossed over a bridge.

"What's that?" I said, pointing out the window.

The thing was tall. It was skinny. It had fronds. It was not a tree.

"A cell tower doctored to look like a palm tree."

"Your hometown is weird, Snowflake."

The Arts District where the L.A. chapter was located was a mash up of reclaimed brick warehouses, trendy cafés, hip galleries, and works yards.

I climbed out of the car. "Look. Pedestrians! And cyclists!"

Cyclist, singular, but good to know there was at least one.

I stared at the ground for most of our walk along Mateo Street, Ro guiding me by my elbow, because there was all this great art stamped on the sidewalk, like "Wake the Fuck Up" or the "I Heart L.A." where the "I" was represented by a silhouette of a man standing and working on a laptop.

Passing a café with a profusion of planters out front, we turned down a side street and there it was. Demon Club La La Land was a two-story, brown brick building with arched windows and accent tiles in a deco wave pattern that occupied an entire block. Cameras encased in plastic bubbles monitored the exterior–discreetly–while a tasteful plaque next to the front door read "David Security International."

Rohan hit the buzzer and the front door unlatched.

I braced myself and stepped inside to a reception area with warm inset lighting, original brickwork, and white and steel furniture. The DSI logo was stamped on the concrete wall behind the reception desk.

The angular woman about my mom's age manning the desk smiled at Rohan, then held out her hand to me. "You must be Nava. A pleasure to finally meet you. I'm Helen."

We shook. "Nice to meet you, too."

"Helen manages DSI and our unruly bunch," Rohan said. "Los Angeles is the world headquarters of the security part of our organization."

"Usually you'll find me in the back," Helen said, "but Louis, our receptionist, had a final exam today. I expect Rohan is going to give you the grand tour, but if you're hungry there's a fully stocked kitchen upstairs."

I thanked her and followed Ro through the single door to her left.

"This floor holds everything DSI needs," he said. "Offices, conference room. They do double duty for the Brotherhood."

This part of the warehouse looked exactly like an international security firm should with its corporate veneer and various workstations. Rohan nodded at a few people, men and women both, as we passed. None of them seemed particularly interested in me.

"Not Rasha?" I said.

"The DSI support staff are Rasha-affiliated." Ah. They had family members that were Rasha or rabbis. "Some of our training rooms are also down here."

Ro slapped his hand on a sensor and a door swung open revealing a smallish indoor track.

"Running? Really? Exactly how much have you forgotten about me this past month?"

Rohan booped me on the nose. "Thought you might want to say hi."

A lone Rasha stood in the middle of the track in bare feet, a black Henley, and board shorts, his back to me.

"Treeeee Truuunk!" I ran for Baruch and jumped on his back, pressing a loud kiss to the side of his head while pretending to dry hump him, and that's when I saw the unfamiliar man.

Kippah wearing, no Rasha ring, fit but "gym fit," not killing-demons fit. Like he'd calculated the exact number of reps to get his lightly muscled physique, the perfect match to his tan, but not-overtly-so skin. This had to be the rabbi that ran this chapter.

I slid off Tree Trunk, he of the Zen expressions, whose twinkle of amusement could be construed as outright hysterical laughter, steeling myself for the rabbi's disapproval.

"Nava, hi." The rabbi extended a hand for me to shake. This was such unexpected behavior that I gaped until Baruch cleared his throat. "I'm Rabbi Wahl. Welcome to Los Angeles."

Everything about the rabbi was polished, from his business casual wear which projected a laid-back vibe of Mr. Reformed-Modern-Times-Jew, to his buffed nails. Overall, he presented the ideal snapshot of a shiny, attractive man who could have advertised modern California life.

"Thanks." I discreetly wiped my palm on the back of my cargo pants, positive he'd exuded an oily residue. "Happy to be here."

The rabbi made some small talk, offering up some sights I should take in if I had the chance. I kept my smile on my face, trying not to be distracted by the fact that I was hearing creepy clown music and imagining him offering cotton candy, all with that used car salesman smile of his.

Baruch and Rohan chatted with him so familiarly that they were a breath away from breaking out a guitar and rocking out together to "This Land is Your Land."

Were my instincts that wrong?

One more welcoming statement and the rabbi excused himself.

I raised my eyebrows at Ro in question.

He shook his head. "Keep your guard up around him."

"And the hand sanitizer close. So, Tree Trunk," I said brightly. "How's life? How was Ms. Clara's visit last month? How come you're in Los Angeles? How much did you miss me?"

"Where's the recording you made of Ilya's confession?" Baruch packed a lot of displeasure into those eye blinks of his.

"Your absolute disinterest in any type of small talk is one of your most charming traits. Also, a very specific question for someone whom I haven't told anything to yet."

Baruch snapped an elastic off his wrist, tying back his shoulder-length black hair. He still looked like a surfer Special Ops. "Another thing to discuss," he growled.

Was Tree Trunk genuinely mad at me? Had my mentor become my enemy?

"Nava!" Two unfamiliar men poured through the door.

Baruch's expression didn't soften and the newcomers obviously had some kind of expectations around me. All this on top of today's already ragged emotional journey. I wanted to back into a corner and take a freaking minute to regroup.

Instead, I waved a hand at them, a teasing smile firmly in place. "Relax, boys. There's more than enough of me to go around."

Rohan snorted, the men swept me away, and my talk with Baruch was thankfully put on hold. For now.

10

These two dudes were a riot. First to introduce himself was the cocky, Native American Cisco with the chiseled cheekbones and short ponytail, the oldest of the L.A. group in his early thirties. Then there was wisecracking Danilo from the Philippines, totally tatted up with a shaved head and built like an MMA fighter.

As they toured me around upstairs, the men peppered me with questions: which demons had been hardest to kill, what my first gig as lead Rasha had been, and what I'd been doing when my power manifested.

Cisco was bent double over the kitchen counter, howling with laughter at my hand job story, while Danilo rooted through the fridge proclaiming that we were going to need more beer.

"Chama, you're going to fit in fine with this bunch," said a male voice with a Spanish accent. A dark-skinned man in jeans with ragged hems lounged against the doorframe, his black curls damp against his scalp. His startlingly green eyes were alight with amusement as he looked over the room.

"Thank you?" I said.

Rohan barked a laugh.

Cisco straightened, wiping a tear from his eyes and pointed at the newcomer. "Bastijn, if Nava's brother is anything like her, you'll want to move in on that fast."

I wrinkled my nose. "Yeah. Sorry. He's not exactly single."

"Isn't that always the way?" Bastijn grabbed a beer from Danilo's hand.

I tried not to track his ass, but damn, was it tight.

"Where's Zander?" Danilo asked.

Bastijn mimed smoking a joint.

Cisco and Rohan shared a concerned look, then Cisco suggested we move our party to the living room.

Unlike in Vancouver, only Zander and Danilo lived here. The others had their own places. Considering this floor looked like a giant mancave, I was thrilled I'd landed a spot in the bungalow.

We settled in and the guys asked me more questions, but from the darting glances they kept shooting at the door, I only had half their attention.

I was about to suggest that we wrap this visit up and go see Gary Randall when Cisco clapped his hands. "Enough small talk. Give up the goods on Ro's sexual prowess. Is he as good as he posts on his fan boards?"

I grinned and took another handful of chips from the snacks they'd set out for my interrogation.

"Coño. For a guy who claims to be straight, you're awfully fascinated with Ro's dick," Bastijn said.

"Exactly what I keep saying." Ro had seated me on his lap, idly playing with my hair. I snuggled back against him.

"For a guy who claims to be gay, you're awfully uninterested in Ro's dick," Cisco fired back at Bastijn.

"Also, exactly what I keep saying." Ro stole my last chip.

I smelled Zander before I saw him: a total surfer dude

about my age with shaggy blond hair and red-rimmed eyes, reeking of pot.

"Hey man," Danilo said. "You good?"

Zander blinked twice at him, like he needed the time to process Danilo's words. "Yeah. Seen Ethan?" He had that Southern Cali drawl, way more pronounced than Ro's.

"He'll be here soon," Cisco said.

Zander nodded and shuffled away.

Bastijn watched him leave, frowning. "It's out of control and he won't talk about it."

"We're gonna have to force the issue," Cisco said. "He can't keep this shit up."

The men fell into a contemplative silence.

Gary could wait a bit longer. In order to buy Ro some time to speak with his friends, I stood up, brushing chip dust from my shirt. "More beer, anyone?"

Danilo asked me to bring another couple of six-packs from the fridge.

I made a note to ask Ro if any of them were aligned with Mandelbaum, though unlike with Rabbi Wahl, I didn't get any bad vibes off them. Team Mandelbaum radar, though useful, was not yet a skill set I'd nailed, unlike my stellar gaydar.

I rooted through the fridge, choosing one six-pack of pale ale and one of Guinness, and popped the tab on one of the lighter beers.

A black-and-white blur smashed into the white cupboard next to me.

"Shit!" I jerked, splashing beer at my feet. I grabbed some paper towels to mop it up.

"You're a girl." A very young, Asian Harry Potter looka-like in a grubby Batman sweatshirt scooped up his soccer ball, tucking it under his arm as he regarded me gravely.

"Yup. I'm also Rasha."

The Kindergartner sucked on his top lip as he digested this.

I dumped the soggy clump of toweling paper in the trash. "Are you an initiate?" He nodded. "I'm Nava. What's your name?"

"Benjy."

I shook his pudgy hand while he stared at me with the fascination usually reserved for meeting an alien species.

"You're the first initiate I've met since I became Rasha," I said, "so I'm very pleased to meet you."

All Brotherhood members in Western Canada, whether initiate, hunter, or rabbi, came through my Vancouver chapter. I'd been warned that sometimes we might have a handful of initiates training and studying for years or go months at a time without anyone there.

It was weird and cool to meet a mini Rasha-to-be.

The kid continued to stare at me.

"You like Batman?" I asked, motioning at his shirt, and wondering if he and Ro had bonded.

Not a big talker but he'd perfected his "d'uh" look. "I'm gonna *be* like Batman one day," he said. "Helping people." His eyes lit up. "Like Rohan."

Yup. They'd bonded.

"Do you know him?" he asked.

"He's my boyfriend."

Benjy scrunched up his face in universal little boy "ick." Whoops. I'd lost Ro some cred. "Are you going to be here long?"

"Not sure." I picked up my beer, cradling the other unopened cans.

He gave a long-suffering sigh. "Okay."

Speak of the devil. Ro poked his head in the door. "We have an email from Orwell."

"Rohan, I printed all my letters properly." Benjy held out his hand.

Ro scratched his chin. "I dunno. Which way does the small 'd' face?"

"Round part goes left of the stick."

"Good job." He pulled out a tub of sour keys from a cupboard and dropped two into Benjy's hand. The kid immediately sucked one into his mouth, thanking Ro through a mouthful of candy.

Danilo called out for Benjy to hurry up because his dad was double-parked outside.

"See you soon?" I said.

"Uh-huh." He turned to Ro with an expectant look.

Ro crouched down to his level and fist-bumped him. Two dark heads bent in towards each other in total focus.

"R-E-S," he began.

"P-E-C-T," Benjy finished.

Ro mussed up his hair. "All right, little dude. Be good."

Benjy nodded and flung his soccer ball out the door, running into the hallway after it.

"You okay?" Ro said. "You look weird."

Just unclenching my ovaries. "Cute kid."

I dropped the beers off for the rest of the guys and followed Rohan into a computer room, equipped with a couple of laptops and printers. One of the printers was chugging pages out.

"What's with this doc they sent?" Ro asked.

I explained about cross-referencing these incidents with Gary's to form a profile and narrow down which potential demon we were dealing with. Pierre had already sent me one batch of cold cases and these were the last ones he'd found.

Rohan straightened some pages before they slipped off the printed stack. "Good idea."

"You know it." I held my beer up in cheers. "Wait! Selfie!"

"Jesus," he groaned.

I handed him a beer. "Okay. Clink. Again. Yeah, that did it. Now one for us and not the public."

We clinked cans...

...and were rocked off our feet.

Foamy liquid sprayed like blood across the white wall.

We bolted from the room and sprinted down the stairs. It took us less than a minute to get there, but all was already chaos and bloodshed.

And screaming. I'll never forget the sounds of Helen's keening. I peered over a desk to see what had set her off and gagged. It was a blackened lump, an adult burned past all recognition.

My heart clawed its way up my throat. "Benjy!"

I ran to Helen and tripped. Over another burned body, this one recognizable from his blond hair. Zander. I stumbled to my feet, trying not to hyperventilate. "Helen. Please. Where's Benjy?"

She'd pressed her fist to her stomach, rocking with low cries.

I threw an arm around her. "Ro!"

He couldn't hear me over Helen and the panicking DSI support staff, who he was trying to herd to the front foyer.

Danilo grabbed my arm. "Benjy's safe. I helped him into his dad's car five minutes ago."

I pressed a hand to my thundering heart. "Help me with her?"

"The rabbi," Helen sobbed. "He killed him."

Before I could ask who, Baruch crashed into our room through an enormous, jagged hole in the wall that had not been part of the decor when I'd first arrived. It would have been comical, had he, Cisco, and Bastijn not been battling a flaming creature.

"Turn it off, Ethan," Baruch growled.

Not a creature. A man.

A Rasha.

Baruch whaled on him with a flurry of punches, ignoring the burns to his skin, but his super strength didn't even slow Ethan down. Neither did smashing his fist into Ethan's nose. Ethan's head jolted sideways, blood spraying out in an arc, but he kept grappling.

I held up my hand against the splattering drops.

Helen's head lolled back like she was about to faint.

"Stay with me," I said.

Danilo and I ushered her toward the front door. I kept one arm slung around her, rubbing her back as she sobbed into my chest.

Cisco flexed his fingers and the cement under his feet cracked. Vines slithered up, tiny at first, but growing into fat ropes in the seconds they took to wrap around Ethan's legs and bring him crashing down.

Ethan flared brighter. Bastijn squatted down and touched the bare earth that Cisco had exposed. The floor rumbled.

Danilo and I each seized one of Helen's arms and ran as dirt geysered up, burying Ethan's body. Smothering the fire.

In all the video games I'd played or watched Ari play growing up, earth was weak to fire. It burned. But now I saw how wrong that was. Plants burned, but earth suffocated. The still-visible flames on Ethan's head flickered and died under an avalanche of soil and stone.

There was a collective sigh of relief, then Cisco stepped forward. "Listen, man–"

Eyes rolling back in his head, Ethan bucked so hard

that a bone broke with a sharp snap. Dirt trickled off his half-exposed body.

Helen fainted. I'd lost my hold on her because I was shaking violently.

Rohan ran in from the front foyer. "Everyone is outside..." Ro charged a half-dozen steps in my direction, then stopped. He kept a careful eye on me, but didn't treat me any differently from the other Rasha who'd been in the room.

I appreciated that, willing down my trembling with a steely control.

"What the fuck?" Danilo pressed a soot-streaked fingertip to his scorched side and hissed.

Cisco had lost a shoe somehow, staring at his sock like he couldn't compute its existence. "Ethan went rogue."

A pulsing throb started up at the nape of my neck. My skin prickled from head-to-toe, like it had shrunk in the wash.

"He killed Rabbi Wahl," Bastijn said, his gaze hollow. He checked Helen's pulse. "Zander, too."

"We're sure that was actually Ethan and not a demon?" Cisco said.

"Were the wards breached?" Ro said.

The pulsing ran down into my shoulder and along my arm. I turned my palm over, drawn by the smear of Ethan's blood along one side.

"I'll check," Baruch said. "What about the rest of the staff? Bystanders? Do we need to set up some kind of perimeter? Deal with a possible police presence?"

"From outside there was no sign of anything odd happening," Danilo said.

"Most of the staff hadn't actually seen anything because it all went down so fast," Rohan said. "I sent the calm ones home and the others I put in a taxi to Dr. Ramirez. He'll take care of them."

The room went hazy and gauzy, the only clear image Ethan's blood on my skin. I sniffed my palm. *Yessssssss.*

I touched my tongue to it and stiffened, an electric jolt snapping through me.

Eww. No. I wasn't some weird vamp wannabe.

I flicked my tongue against it again. Just the tip.

Then a longer lick, its taste as intoxicating as the finest wine.

Ro strong-armed me, muscling me toward the stairs. He shielded me from the others, whom I could only see through a milky cloud tinged at the edges with red. His mouth was working but I couldn't hear him, deafened by the slow glug of my heart.

Tick tock.

The beat of my heart.

Blood to rule the might.

Ethan's blood.

Freezing water sluiced over my head. I blinked, shaking like a wet dog, and jerked my head out from under the bathtub tap, sputtering.

Ro held himself in check, his mouth a flat line. "You said Lilith wasn't controlling you."

"She's not."

"I was calling you for twenty minutes. Smacking your cheek. Pinching you. You didn't react. And that was after your eyes had gone cloudy and you stiffened up like a board. We barely got out of the room in time." A muscle jumped in the hard set of his jaw.

I sank down against the white floor tiles, my back against the tub. Water ran from my hair down under the neck of my shirt. "Snowflake, I'm fine. I promise you she's not awake."

"You might not know. And if I'm talking to Lilith right now, she's hardly going to admit to running the show." Ro wrenched off the cold water with such force I half expected the tap to snap off. He'd probably broken about seven California bylaws letting it run that long.

Ro's guilt wasn't going to ease up if I explained exactly what was going on, and he wasn't going to get any less angry at me, but how could I hope for us to move forward if I left him in the dark?

Full disclosure sucked, but not having Rohan in my corner was worse. I nudged the bathroom door shut with my foot, and using my shirt to blot myself dry, told him about the lamia, drawing on Lilith's leaking magic, and my looming one-month deadline before she broke free. I did it as quickly and succinctly as I could, praying that our fragile re-connection held.

Ro had gone full-body knifeman by the end of my story, gauging deep slashes into the bathroom floor tile, his fingers tensed like claws.

"The black magic called to me downstairs," I said. "Not like 'come to the dark side' or anything, more in recognition."

"Because it's part of you!"

"Let's not overreact. Is Lilith shitting her magic into my body? Yes. But I'm hardly the Wicked Witch of the West."

"You are literally using dark magic. It kills people." He yanked his blades out of the floor, retracting them with visible effort. "One month."

Even after our time apart and our choppy emotional waters, it seemed I still couldn't handle Rohan being in pain. I was the one at risk, and all I wanted to do was soothe his hurt. I patted his leg.

"The witches are working on it and meantime,

absorbing it like I am may be the best course of action. I've become my own magic purification system."

He scrubbed a bladeless hand over his face. "You're acting like you've solved it, but you're just hoping for the best."

"Is letting the magic float around inside me the better option?"

"I don't know."

"Neither do I. Neither does Esther. We're in uncharted territory here. The fact of the matter is that the dark magic is inside me and I can't just sit here and do nothing." I'd lived my life feeling helpless and at the mercy of the universe's cruel whims for too many years. Fuck that.

"And what if you hasten along your death because you're messing with things you don't understand? Or you hurt some innocent person because this dark magic has totally screwed with your ability to see right from wrong anymore and you think you're infallible?"

Caring a little less about his feelings right now. "My moral center is intact. You don't know what you're talking about."

"Addiction and fucking up because you think you know best?" He barked a harsh laugh. "Yeah, sweetheart, I do. I also know exactly how easy it is to pull the wool over the eyes of the people closest to you."

Rohan had lived that path and it had cost him Asha. Much as I wanted to wrap my anger around me in a cloak of self-righteousness, I appreciated that this situation had to be a living hell for him and I refused to flashback him into the worst time in his life.

I pushed to my feet. "I'm doing what instinctively feels right, and I'm being open and honest with the people I trust to watch my back on this. But I can't swear that the magic won't tip me into a bad place. And I understand if you can't be around that. I really do."

There were only a few feet between me and the door. If I blinked my eyes really fast and moved right now, I could get out of here with my dignity intact.

"Jesus, Nava. Did I say that?" He stood up and wrapped me in his arms, holding me with his cheek pressed to mine, until the tension left my body, and his racing heartbeat slowed. "You can't drop this on me and then expect me to roll with it. I want to destroy her. I can't..." He swore under his breath, his arms tightening around me.

"You won't have to put me down like a rabid dog."

Rohan gave a pained laugh. "Don't you dare joke right now."

I smiled against his neck.

"Lilith can't have you, okay?"

"Okay." And in that moment, surrounded and secure in the arms of the person I cared so much about, it was.

We sat side-by-side on the edge of the tub, Ro holding tight to my hand. "What happened downstairs?" he said.

"Ethan."

"What about him?"

"He didn't go postal. He was bound. Just like the demons. Dark magic. 'Blood to rule the might.'"

"Ethan's blood. What did you learn?"

"The recognition. Right. I was able to put my under-standing in context because of the first part of the zizu prophecy."

Rohan mimed wiping his brow. "Oh, good. Wouldn't have wanted that creepshow to fade into obscurity."

"Ro." I kissed his knuckles.

He sighed, but looked at me. "The attack. Was it Sien-na's doing?"

"I couldn't tell, but I'm gonna go with yes. The wards weren't tampered with, were they?"

"No."

"How's Helen?" I said.

"Danilo took her to Dr. Ramirez as well."

"What happened? Because that was a shit show."

"From what we could piece together," he said, "Ethan asked to speak with Wahl and Zander, then soon as they were in the same room, fried them. Didn't care who saw. That's when Baruch broke through a wall to tackle him and pull him away from everyone else, and you were there for the rest."

"Why those three?"

Ro shrugged, his expression tight with frustration. "You want to go back to the bungalow and get cleaned up? There's not anything more we can do here."

"Yeah, but one other thing. When I–" I coughed, but it was reflex, not the magic silencing I'd experienced up until now. "The first time I met Lilith, she'd asked for permission to experience a memory. There wasn't blood exchange involved and I gave my consent, but once it had started, I couldn't have stopped it or refused her taking as much as she wanted off that memory. Whatever Sienna did to compel Ethan, there's no chance he could have fought it."

I was actually able to articulate details of my interaction with Lilith. What if drawing on her magic was allowing me to regain control of my words, my body, my life?

"The others need to know that," I said, "but I'm not sure how to tell them without sharing all the backstory. I'm sorry, Ro. I don't know who to trust here."

Ro stood up. "I don't either. We'll clear Ethan's name somehow. We've been friends for years. He's a solid guy. No way he went rogue." He extended a hand and pulled me up.

"Meantime, the first order of business is to figure out why Sienna used Ethan to go after those two."

"No," Baruch said, having eased the door open and stepped inside. "The first order of business is: who's Lilith?" He crossed his arms, puffing up his chest and pretty much obliterating any view of the hallway behind him. "And why is there a zizu prophecy helping you understand dark magic?"

Ro hadn't shared the *entire* story with Baruch, and the big, unhappy man didn't let us go until he was satisfied that he'd wrung every last detail from us. Including what would happen in a month if I was lucky, and sooner if I wasn't.

Tree Trunk had gone Nava Red.

I bounced nervously on my toes. "Baruch?"

He stood there, scarily still and scarily silent, but the most terrifying part was his blinking that gave away nothing.

I tugged on Rohan's sleeve, my eyes anxiously darting to Baruch.

Ro squeezed my arm in reassurance, then stepped forward, partially shielding me, and clapped Baruch on the shoulder.

"Mandelbaum has extra tzitzit," he said in a calm voice. "Baruch, you got someone you trust back at HQ who could get one for us?"

Baruch pinched the bridge of his nose and I held my breath that he didn't go nuclear. That I hadn't lost him. I'd barely found a way to live without Drio and we hadn't even been friends for much of our relationship. Losing Baruch was an ache I wouldn't be able to staunch.

He exhaled slowly and deeply. "The witches are confident they can keep you from losing your magic?"

He was worried about me, not angry. My shoulders

relaxed down from my ears as I considered how best to answer him.

The witches had been optimistic when my chances were still fifty-fifty, before I'd drawn on Lilith's magic. Had I decreased my odds? Maybe, but if I let myself go down the rabbit hole of despair, I'd lose my shit entirely. I needed to stay strong; the fate of the world and my happily-ever-after depended on it.

"Yes. They're confident."

"Then no problem," Baruch said.

"That's it? It's that simple?" I said.

"Is there an alternative?" Ro said. I shook my head. "Then, yeah. It is. But take me along for back-up when you deliver it to Baskerville."

"Of course. Though I did have back-up the first time." I dug my burner phone out of my pocket with grimy fingers. I'd be sanitizing it later. "See?"

Baruch's eyes darkened somewhat at the photo I'd snapped of Ms. Clara in her latex glory. Minus the freaky mask.

"She used the whip?" His voice sounded rougher than usual.

"Oh, yeah. Ever seen her do that wrist-wrapping trick? She's balletic with that thing."

"You're a menace," Ro murmured, his eyes twinkling.

Baruch stole one last glance at the photo, then smoothed down the front of his shirt. "Have you told us everything?"

Everything except Ilya's memory wipe, but I wasn't about to drop two bombs on Rohan in a row. "Yup."

"Why can't you find Sienna?" Baruch asked.

"She's shielded herself from any location spells and gone off any technological grid. Her place was cleared out. Dr. Gelman couldn't even find a hair to trace back to her."

My hand flew to my mouth. "I have to tell Esther what Sienna's done."

Just once I'd like to be the bearer of good news. I was never getting my rugelach.

"May I leave the bathroom now?" I asked.

"We'll reconvene back at the bungalows," Ro said. "Baruch is staying at Mom and Dad's."

Normally I would have been overjoyed. Now, I nodded in resignation, and answered my phone.

Before I could even say "hello," Ari was freaking out on the other end, asking if I was okay. "Ace. Calm down. I'm... uninjured." I couldn't lie and say I was all right, because I still had Ethan's blood on me and I was holding on to my sanity by my fingertips.

There was shouting on Ari's end and then Kane was on me, demanding I answer the same question. He had the phone wrestled away from him by Leo who bombarded me with yet more concern.

Baruch plucked the phone away. "Who is this?" he barked. He held the cell away from his ear as Leo yammered at him, her voice cutting off with a shriek as Ari reclaimed the phone.

"Nava is holding up," Baruch said. "Rohan is taking her home. You can speak to her later. What? No. Ari. No. I–Ben zona!" He blinked at the phone, stupefied. "He hung up on me. Your brother is as annoying as you are. He's also coming to Los Angeles." He tossed me my cell back, suddenly looking incredibly weary. "We need a strategy."

A text from Ms. Clara lit up my phone. *Mandelbaum coming to L.A.*

"I'd say this was the last straw, but..." I gave a harsh laugh, handed Rohan the phone, and walked out the door.

11

I didn't call Esther until I'd showered and burned my clothing. Okay, not really. Billie had promised to dispose of them. Being clean and Ethan-free, plus the sandwiches and shot of whiskey that she'd brought, helped dissipate my shell-shock a tiny bit, as did the chocolate chip cookies, warm from the oven. Not one or two either. Like a dozen of them. And she told Ro they were all for me.

"You look like you need the chocolate, lovely." She tucked an escaping strand of blonde hair back into her bun.

"You are the best human being in the history of the world." I was wedged into the corner of the couch in the bungalow living room with pillows stuffed around me and a bright knit blanket thrown over my legs.

She smiled at me, all grandmotherly. "I like this one, Rohan. She's a fine judge of character."

He planted a kiss on her plump cheek. It was a sweet maternal tableau made sweeter, though decidedly less innocent, by the fact that Ro had also showered and was only wearing boxer shorts, his chiseled abs on display. "I like her, too. But I'm glad you approve."

"Billie, do you have stories of Ro as an irrepressible child?"

"Dozens, dear."

"Can I come help you make cookies some time and can you share them, starting with the most embarrassing?"

"Any time." She tucked the bundle of dirty clothes under her arm, told me to call if I needed her, and left.

I took a photo of Ro munching on his second cookie and posted a nauseatingly cute caption to go with it. "Yo, cookie thief. I didn't even hear you ask for the first one."

"It's for the mission," he said, spraying crumbs.

"Funny boy."

"Funny boy who let you wear his clothes."

"True." I was enveloped in a pair of his sweats that were too baggy, an old skater T-shirt, and a Fugue State Five sweatshirt that he'd dug out of the depths of his closet especially for me.

"I guess that entitles you to two cookies."

I picked up the top of a pair of Sienna's nurse's scrubs that I'd grabbed from Raquel on the way back to the bungalow. She was back home in Los Angeles after our meeting in Vancouver, having used the scrubs to do a location spell on Sienna without success. I hoped to have better results with my dark magic boost.

Trusting Rohan and Esther was one thing; I didn't know Raquel well enough to predict how she'd react to me drawing on Lilith's magic, so I'd swallowed my retort to her snarky "good luck finding her."

Location spells were tricky, requiring a personal item—blood and hair worked best—as the cornerstone to the whole procedure. I had to cast my awareness out along an invisible thread of belonging that connected the item to its owner. The complicated part was making that thread magically tangible using infusion magic. It was a delicate procedure, and easy to lose track of the thread at any point. Though once the connection was secured, the person's location would be immediately revealed.

Sienna had managed to erect a big fuck-off magic barrier between herself and anyone doing the spell which the other witches hadn't been able to breach.

My turn.

Closing my eyes, I took a moment to center myself. I reached out for the couple of wisps inside me, knotting them onto my internal visualization of my own magic. My magic had always presented itself in my mind's eye as a kind of whitish blue, emblematic of electricity. Now, however, it was morphing into a marbled grayish-black.

I opened my eyes after the third failed attempt.

Rohan handed me a glass of water. "You gave it your best shot."

I stilled his jittering leg. "Thank you for trying to contain your freak-out that I'm using Lilith's magic."

"I'm a master of serenity. Desperate times, but fuck, I hate this."

"It's not ideal, but Sienna has amped things up in a horrifying way. If I can find her, then it's an acceptable risk." I gulped the liquid down greedily. "One more try. I'm hitting that same barrier, but I have one final section to probe for a weak spot."

Rohan took the empty glass from me with a kiss. "Do it."

I shook out my neck and shoulders and closed my eyes again, clutching Sienna's shirt to my chest. Once more I slid along the thread and crashed into the enormous black barrier looming up in front of me.

I carefully sussed out every inch of the bottom third but couldn't get through. If I couldn't change the barrier, could I change my magic? I'd been like a hammer, perhaps I needed to be like smoke. Or water. My magic sank into the barrier, burrowing deep down like rain in the root system of a tree. I allowed myself to fall into Sienna's magic, becoming one with it.

Her magic collapsed in on me, burying me and filling my lungs like I was drowning.

I wheezed, panicking. The magic buffered and bashed me against the barrier, until I had no idea if I was still physically upright, my lungs screaming with a burning need for air.

Blackness wove itself around me, pulling tighter and tighter.

Fighting didn't work so I surrendered to it, allowing it to sweep me away like the tide. I broke through the other side, blinking at a harsh light. Death?

No, sunlight. And a very familiar wall thronged with praying crowds seen in the distance through an open window.

I opened my eyes, grinning. "I've got her."

"You're going to give me a heart attack," Ro muttered and swiped another cookie.

I checked Lilith's magic box. A pinprick of light now emanated from one corner. Not bright, welcoming light. Gloomy, oppressive light that wasn't much better than monster-hiding shadows, but I'd successfully completed the location spell, so I was counting this as a win.

Esther skipped the "good job, Nava" part and went straight to the downside. "So she's in Jerusalem. Where am I supposed to hide *you* so she doesn't come after you for breaching her barrier?"

"How's she going to know it was me? You said yourself there's no way to determine who casts magic. No magic forensic chemist. Besides, any signature I had as Nava is changing due to my forced proximity with Lilith." I

135

explained about the color change and the pinprick of light.

My poor boyfriend looked like his head was going to explode. He stomped into the bedroom.

On the other end of the phone, Esther flicked her lighter at warp speed.

"Sienna's attack changed the gameboard," I said. "If she's using us as weapons, then we need to use everything at our disposal to fight this war. That means Lilith's magic. It might be the only edge we have."

"Remember the part about dark magic being addictive? That's what you're sounding like. An addict, justifying what you want." Esther said.

"I'm using it to help us!"

"Are you sure?"

"Positive. Also, I want to talk to her when you catch her."

"We'll discuss it after we've brought her in. Focus on the mission that brought you to Los Angeles."

"Speaking of which, Mandelbaum is coming to town."

"The rabbi is going to investigate the attack," she said, "which means it's only a matter of time before he learns about Sienna. I'll let the others know. Be careful."

The image of Ethan on fire rose up before me, the stench of burned flesh still seared in my nose hairs. I scratched the phantom blood on my skin.

"Will do." I tossed the phone onto the sofa with a shiver and hurried into the bedroom.

Rohan stared at his sheet music, his pencil between his teeth, but at my entrance, he shoved all of it into the bedside table drawer and patted the mattress.

I slipped between the cool sheets. Even the linens in this place were deluxe: the softest Egyptian cotton that rich-people-money could buy. "Can I hug you like a teddy bear tonight?"

"No." He snapped off the light. "I have a headache and it's your fault." He snuggled up against me, pulling me into his arms.

"It's Sienna's fault."

We lay on our backs staring at the ceiling for a few moments, both of us fidgety. Were we really still on the same day as the attack? I felt like I'd aged five years.

"Do you want to cry or rage or something?" I said. "I mean, my strategy is 'denial to exhaustion,' but that's not generally how you play it."

"I don't know how to play it. I'm furious at Sienna, gutted over Ethan, and some combination of both about Zander." He rested his head on his bent arm. "I don't know how to play it," he repeated, more softly.

"Ah, babe." I hugged him.

"Next Thursday," he said after a while.

"What about it?"

"That's my strategy. I keep my shit together until Thursday next week. Far enough away to have dealt with everything. Then I'm going to crack." He lay his cheek against my chest. "I don't want to lose more friends."

I kissed the top of his head, inhaling the tang of citrus shampoo on his still-damp strands. "Whatever you need. I'll be here for you."

"I'm counting on it. And back at ya. In case the denial wears off. Whatever you need."

"FYI, Snowflake, I consider blanket statements like that legally binding."

"It's always 'check the fine print' with you."

More staring at the ceiling. More restless limbs. More lack of sleep.

Rohan flipped on the bedside lamp. "Cards?"

I pushed the covers aside with a sigh. "Gin. The drink and the game."

I REACHED for my fourth cookie of the morning, having a sliver of tummy space left to cram it into. Mouth full, I pulled the cold case print-outs from my enormous purse and thunked them on the table.

Rohan rifled through a few pages. "You sure you want to do this?"

"If it silences the instant replay my brain is stuck on? Positive."

My phone buzzed with a text from Esther. *Sienna got away. Locked up a couple of witches for a few hours but didn't harm them.*

I slammed my palm down on the table. "Damn it! We lost her."

I texted back. *Want me to try again?*

No! I'll come after you personally if you do.

"What happened?" Ro held the shirt from Sienna's scrubs out of my reach.

"I'm not trying again. Esther forbade it."

He tossed it on the sofa. "And you're listening to her? Does that mean you'll listen to me?"

"Situationally." I shoved half the pile of cases at him. "Get working."

We created a subset of cases that mirrored what had happened to Gary. The cases were very, very mind-numbingly detailed. Most of the day later, by which point I was reading while hanging upside down off the couch, we had a plausible trail.

"Who do you like for it?" I said.

Rohan flipped between the various demon entries he

had open on the Brotherhood database. "Hybris. A Unique demon specializing in insolence, hubris, violence, reckless pride, and general arrogance. It fits the pattern. Give the victim their heart's desire, then take them down in a very public humiliation." He clucked his tongue. "Very few one-on-one Rasha encounters with her. Some supposition that the kill spot may be in her trachea."

"Let's phone it in." I shuffled the relevant cases into a pile, my hands only mildly shaking at the Ethan flashback that hit in the quiet.

Pierre answered on the first ring. "Are you all right?"

"I'm dealing. We found a pattern starting back in the twenties. Al Capone. Bootlegging, gambling, prostitution, racketeering. He had the gall to claim he was doing a public service for the people of Chicago, since ninety percent of them drank and gambled. Said he was just furnishing them with those amusements. Feds couldn't make anything stick. Not even the St. Valentine's Day Massacre. And then he's brought down by tax evasion?"

"Who else?"

"Richard Nixon in the 1970s and his belief in his infallibility during Watergate. Colton Bannister in the 80s. Bannister was a business tycoon, who did a brutally ruthless takeover of this small mining company."

"Gold, right?" Pierre said.

"Yeah. They'd found a gold mine and predicted they stood to make billions. After the takeover, the founder of the mining company was so devastated by the loss of his family's company that he killed himself. The tycoon didn't care. His exact quote?" I flipped through to the back page of that particular file. "'If he didn't have the balls, he shouldn't have been in business.'"

"Oui," Pierre said. "I remember. The mine was in some

country that had had peace and prosperity for two hundred years."

"Except as soon as Bannister owned the mine, the country was plagued with every kind of natural disaster: floods, hurricanes, mudslides." I checked the file. "And civil unrest. Things got vicious and desperate. He had sunk a large part of his own fortune into the mine. Not only did he lose his shirt, his own family was killed in a plane crash en route to the mine. Colton was the only survivor. Awful, but it hadn't been tagged as the result of demon activity at the time."

"We missed it," Pierre said.

I named a few other incidents then said, "Case number 230DDX."

Ro smirked at me, shaking his head.

I heard Pierre type the number in.

"That actress about ten years ago?" he said. "The imprisoned one. Big international scandal?"

"Yeah. What was her name again?"

"It's written at the top of the file."

"Kinda smudged on my end," I said.

"Tabernac, you know who I mean."

"Yeah. I just want you to say it, Frenchie."

"'Annah 'Utton. Colisse, you suck."

I snickered, happy for any humor, juvenile or otherwise, today.

Hannah Hutton shot to fame playing a CIA agent in a series of films. Off the popularity of that, she'd bragged she could get an audience with the dictator of a fractious Third World country during a very tense time with the United States. That she'd be the peacekeeper to tone tensions down, just like her character did. Surprisingly, she managed it–the invite part at least, as it turned out the dictator loved the franchise.

Had Hannah stuck with chatting about the movies, all would have been well and she might even have calmed things down as a good-will ambassador, but she'd decided that playing a CIA operative had somehow made her an expert on foreign policy. Poor Hannah didn't even get to the end of her lecture on how the dictator should behave on the world stage before she'd been arrested. She was still rotting in prison.

"Any chance of getting to her?" I wasn't risking portalling into an unknown and extremely dangerous environment, but Hannah was the only victim on my list who was still alive besides Gary.

"Unlikely."

"Maudite marde." I swore, earning a snort from Pierre at my exaggerated Québécois accent. Once I'd hung up, I turned to Ro. "Want to go see Gary Randall with me?"

"Now?"

"Better than sitting and dwelling on horribleness until Baruch comes back. Besides, with Boris Badenov coming to town, we need something to report on." I clapped my hands. "Can we have code names? I can be Moose and you can be Squirrel."

Rohan gathered up the laptop, carefully winding the plug. "You wanna be an ugly beast with knobby knees? Knock yourself out."

"Moose aren't ugly. They're majestic Canadian animals. Anyways, why does it matter to you? You're Squirrel. The sidekick."

Ro tipped my chair sideways, knocking me on my ass. "Again with the sidekick designation? If anyone's the sidekick, it's the moose. Rocky and Bullwinkle. Squirrel goes first."

I scrambled to my feet, my arm punch failing to wipe the smirk from his face. It was very important I had higher status in this code name designation. We'd be revisiting this once I'd had a chance to think through my argument. "So, Gary?"

"Are you up to portalling to Tampa with a passenger?" Rohan said.

"No need. He's still here. Even though his contract was signed, he hadn't yet flown out to Florida for training camp. Pierre got me his apartment details. If you'll drive us over, I'll beam us up." I nudged his leg with my foot. "You cool with that?"

I'd been with Ro the first time I'd ever portalled. Accidentally. To say it had been a shock was an understatement.

"I'm cool with any magic you've got." His posture was relaxed and his expression sincere.

My stomach unknotted.

"Does he have bodyguards? Nurses?"

I shook my head. "No bodyguard, but a nurse in shifts. We can handle a nurse."

"Sienna's a nurse," Rohan said.

"A Muggle nurse," I amended. "We got this covered."

12

The nurse in question was a bearded, six-foot-four lumberjack of a man whose biceps were bigger than my thighs. The only reason we got the jump on him when we portalled into the thirtieth-floor suite was that he was busy changing Gary's morphine drip.

Rohan injected the nurse with Methohexital, a fast-acting sedative with a brief window of action that we'd picked up at Demon Club La La Land on our way over. I'd made Ro go in and get it without me because I wasn't ready to revisit the scene of the tragedy.

The chemical kicked in, and in seconds, the nurse went limp.

Ro slid him to the bedroom floor and set an alarm. "Five minutes."

I ran over to the closet, flipping through Gary's clothing for the jacket he'd worn the night he was injured.

Gary shifted, groggily opening his eyes. "Erik?"

The jacket wasn't in the bedroom. He might have tossed it, or sent it to be cleaned, but events were so recent that I doubted he'd had a chance to do either.

I stood over the bed. "Not Erik."

"Are you an angel?" Gary slurred.

Rohan snorted and I stepped on his foot.

"Check the hall closet," I said quietly, then turned my attention back to Gary. "Yes. I'm an avenging angel."

I checked Gary's drip. High was good, tripping balls high was better, since he'd never remember us. OD high, however, if we'd accidentally interfered with something Lumberjack Nurse Erik had been adjusting, was not how I wanted this to play out. His drip didn't seem to be flowing too fast or have an air bubble and I had to trust the dosage was correct.

Gary nodded, like that made perfect sense. "Kill the person who destroyed my career."

"That's right, Gary. I'm going to smite them."

"Because I was the best hockey player ever."

"Let's not go that far," I said. "You were grandstanding on your breakouts, rarely passing the puck to better positioned players."

"You're a mean angel." Gary frowned.

Rohan entered the bedroom, jacket in hand. He unscrewed a mason jar with a mix of Snowdonia Hawkweed, salts, and water that we'd doctored up.

"Three minutes." He painted the mixture on Gary's jacket in order to do the magic signature spell.

"The best hockey player ever," I repeated with forced enthusiasm. "Back to the night you got hit–"

"Where are your wings?" Gary flapped his arms in slow-motion.

"I left them at home. Stay with me here. On the video, you spoke to a woman. Right before you tripped off the curb. Who was she?"

He crossed his arms. Missed and whacked himself in the chest. "No wings. You're not an angel."

I blinked, suddenly backlit by a harsh white light. "Seriously?"

Ro shrugged, the flashlight of his phone trained on me. "Try speaking in a more Heavenly voice."

He held the jacket up to me, now pulsing blue. Demon magic. Gary's fall hadn't been an accident.

"You're loving this, aren't you?" I said, squinting.

"Who are you speaking to?" Gary said. Ro was in the shadows and Gary couldn't see him.

"God," Ro boomed out.

I mimed gagging.

"Ohhh." Gary's eyes bugged out. He also drooled a bit.

"Gary Randall, you must cooperate," Ro said in that same stupid voice.

Much as I wish Ro's egomania had spectacularly back-fired, it did the trick because Gary nodded at me eagerly. As eager as possible given he was moving slower than molasses. "I'll help you smite them, angel. What's your name?"

"Angelika," I said at the same time that Ro said, "Charlie."

"Hi, Charlie."

"You're not helping," I hissed at my dumb boyfriend, who was silently snickering and holding up two fingers. Great. "Hi, Gary. Who was the woman? What was her name?"

Even if we got an alias, it might be traceable.

"Tia. She was so excited for me." His head lolled back.

We were losing him to the drugs. I slapped his cheek. "Stay with me, dude. Can you describe Tia? How'd you meet her?"

"Met that night. Headed to different bars so texted later to meet up."

"One minute," Ro murmured.

"Do you still have the texts? Or a photo?"

His eyes fluttered shut.

"Thirty seconds," Ro said.

Gary grabbed my arms and I jumped. "Angel, make me better. Miracle me to play again." There was such sorrow in his voice.

I'd been so focused on what a douche he'd been in his hockey career that it hadn't hit me that his dreams were dead. And as awful as that was, I couldn't lie and pretend I could fix this. It would be too cruel when he realized that nothing had changed.

"I'm sorry," I said gently. "I can't."

The alarm beeped, but Lumberjack Nurse Erik didn't stir.

Gary sighed, his shoulders slumping. Then he perked up. "S'okay. Once I get through rehab, I'm gonna act. I'm hot."

My sympathy leeched away.

"Good for you, buddy," Rohan pronounced.

I grabbed Gary's phone off the nightstand. "Give me your password."

Erik rustled at Ro's feet.

Ro crouched down, ready to administer a carotid sleeping hold to buy us a few extra seconds if necessary. "Hurry."

Four times I asked for and was given a wrong numeric code for Gary's phone. Apparently, he changed it a lot. It wasn't his birthday, wasn't his home address, wasn't some part of his phone number.

Two more tries before the phone was disabled. "Focus, Gary."

His reply? A loud snore.

What could it be? What did I know about him? He was arrogant and the code was six digits. "What day was he signed to Tampa?" I said. "Do you remember?" Luckily, Rohan did. I typed the day, month, and year in. "Fuck."

"Your Canadian is showing," Ro said. "Gary's American. Month then day."

I typed it in and was rewarded with his home screen. No photos but there was a text chain. I fired off a quick text wanting to chat. It was delivered, proving the number was still in play.

Erik snorted back into consciousness, slowly blinking up at us. "Who are you?"

"God," Ro boomed, shining the light in the nurse's eyes. "We are the glory you are not fit to gaze upon."

I rolled my eyes and portalled us out of there.

Seated in the Shelby once more, I emailed Pierre the phone number I'd texted, asking if he could track the phone's location since no one had responded to my text.

We drove back to Casa Mitra in silence. I rolled the Shelby's windows down, drinking in the city at night. I preferred L.A. this way with all her lit-up signs competing for attention and telling her story.

Back at the bungalow, we made a fresh pot of coffee and rolled up our metaphoric sleeves. Rohan propped a pillow under his head and stretched out on the couch with a laptop balanced on his chest.

Curled up in the comfy plush chair I'd pulled up beside him, I yawned, taking a swig of my lukewarm java. "Look at that." I yawned again. "Sorry. It's Hybris's Roman name."

"Petulantia. Tia. Nicely done, witch girl."

"Imagine how amazing I'd be with sleep."

Pierre texted that Tia's phone had been located in a dumpster in Burbank. Dead end.

Rohan paged through Gary's file. "Let's check his friends' social media accounts. Maybe one of them got a photo of her."

Gary had been with two buddies that night, also players from his junior hockey team. One of them had no social media presence other than a pretty sparse Twitter account with some game results, but the other one's Instagram was a shrine to his own shirtlessness combined with snaps of himself with every girl he'd ever wanted to bang. Or, in many cases, given the follow-up pix of them in bed, had.

"A douche, but a predicable douche, which works for us." Rohan showed me the photo he'd found. Captioned #wingman, it was a photo of this friend, Gary, and Tia, recognizable in the same clothes as from the video footage.

Tia was about five-foot-ten, willowy, with long, black hair.

"Celebration selfie," I said, smushing my cheek up to Rohan's.

Right as I snapped it, he kissed me. The phone tumbled from my hand and hit the carpet with a gentle thump. My arms snaked around his neck and my world fell away under the taste of him, like every bad thing had been erased, like it was just us, forever.

There was a knock on the door.

"Hello?" Baruch called out.

Ro mimed shooting himself in the head. "To be continued. Coming, man."

Ro let Baruch in while I posted some more smug bullshit. Come and get me, Tia.

"Greetings and salutations, Tree Trunk. Whoa. You look terrible." I'd never seen him with bags under his eyes, a stoop to his shoulders, and smelling a bit rank in clothes he'd obviously slept in. At least they weren't the same ones he'd fought Ethan in.

"This is the first time I've left the chapter since the attack," he said.

Ro arranged for a late supper, which Baruch gratefully

accepted. He unwrapped the foil from the plate Billie had brought him, thanking her for the steak and potatoes and picked up his knife, sawing away at the slab of meat.

"Witches. Tell me everything you know about them."

"We use elimination and infusion magic but Rasha only got the bit pertinent to killing demons."

"Elimination magic is negative?" Baruch said.

"Not at all. There's no value judgment either way." I squirted ketchup onto the French fries that Ro had thoughtfully procured for me. "Portalling is elimination magic. So is healing if it's killing disease. A lot of witches work in medical research." I explained about how there was one magic pile and the more Rasha drew from it, the weaker the witches were. That was why they couldn't just magically cure AIDS or cancer, but they could look for magic-infused chemical cures.

"Sienna was a nurse," he said.

"Could that be relevant to her agenda?" Rohan said.

"Which one?" Baruch said. "Attacking Rasha or binding demons?"

"Sienna being a nurse is relevant because by all accounts, she was dedicated and great at her job. Everyone at the hospital adored her." I munched a fry. "It's hard to reconcile that person with someone who would unleash demons."

Baruch swallowed the half a steak that passed for a bite in his reality. "Table it until her motives are clearer. Infusion magic. Examples?"

"Witches infuse the earth. Heal toxic land, repair blighted crops. A lot of us work in agriculture, medicine, engineering, geology, all types of sciences geared toward keeping the earth and her inhabitants as healthy as possible." I dragged a fry through the ketchup. "I keep circling back to Tessa. That whatever the reason Sienna did this, it's tied to Tessa."

"Sienna used dark magic to kill three people," Rohan said. "She's out for revenge."

"I'm not excusing that, but it was three specifically targeted people who are probably guilty of something. DSI was full of employees–if she wasn't being careful, she could have easily taken out a dozen people. She didn't. Nor did she hurt the witches that went looking for her in Jerusalem. She's incredibly dangerous, but not bloodthirsty."

Baruch snorted. "That remains to be seen."

"Binding demons is dark magic, but it's still elimination magic," Rohan said, snagging a couple of fries. "Taking away free will. That's what Sienna did to Ethan with this attack, which means we're all vulnerable. It would be a point in favor of telling Mandelbaum what we know, except it's countered by the hell-no negative that he'll then do whatever it takes to find her."

"Could you contain a witch with dark magic?" Baruch said. "I couldn't. From the sounds of it, I would have trouble taking down a regular witch."

I threw a couple air punches at him. He swallowed both my fists with one of his and pushed my hands down.

"A witch in *full* possession of her powers," Baruch said. "The rabbi will fail."

"The good rabbi is hardly going to be that logical about it," Ro said dryly.

"How's your moral flexibility, Tree Trunk?"

He pushed his empty plate away. "Is this a trick question?"

"Sadly, no," Rohan said. I elbowed him and he threw up his hands.

"What if you told Mandelbutt the wards *had* been tampered with and you've determined that Ethan was compelled by a demon? We'll pick a plausible type. It's not far off the truth and he still comes out as another victim in all this. Then you could issue a warning for all Rasha. Put everyone on high alert and let them know you suspect this isn't an isolated attack."

Baruch placed his left palm face up. "We tell Mandelbaum about Sienna, it doesn't stop the attacks, he knows there is another witch capable of carrying out his plans, and perhaps more Rasha die attempting to find her." He placed his right one up. "Don't tell him? Rasha die because they don't know the real danger to watch for."

"Doesn't matter if they know about her. They won't see her coming," I said. "But at least we could get them on their guard without handing Sienna to Mandelbaum."

"Moral flexibility wins," Rohan said.

I pressed my hands against my heart. "The words I've longed to hear you say."

Rohan shook his head. "Really need to think before I speak around you."

"Don't forget that the witches are actively looking for Sienna as well," I said.

Baruch stood and cracked his neck. "I have to sleep on all this." He wished us goodnight and left.

Ro stretched out on the couch. "It occurs to me that there's another point to be made about infusion and elimination."

"Yeah? What?" I cleared the dishes. Not a big hardship since all I had to do was put everything back on the cart it had been wheeled in on and place it outside the bungalow like room service.

"You and Mandelbaum."

Leaning against the doorframe, I breathed in the night-blooming jasmine scattering its heady, fragrant scent. It was after midnight and still warm. Crickets chirped away in a call and answer song and a beetle buried into the cool earth at my feet. I stared up at the hazy light pollution in the night sky. "Meaning?"

"The rabbi could very well destroy us, but you? You've infused new life into the Brotherhood. For better or for worse," he added with a cheeky grin that I caught over my shoulder. "Forcing a new balance between Rasha and witches."

"I'm the new hope."

"I wouldn't go that far," he said.

"I'm basically Princess Leia and Han rolled into one." I shrieked as Ro grabbed me around the waist, swinging me around.

"Not anywhere in the galaxy."

I stuck my tongue out at him, then stopped and slid to the ground. "Ro? Did we speed the clock? The prophecy?"

As prophecies went, it was frustratingly short and vague. *Tick tock goes the clock, blood to rule the might. Tick tock, speed the clock, the lovers reunite.*

"We reunited and Sienna launched that attack," I said. "Are we responsible?"

I wanted so badly for Rohan to laugh and tell me I was crazy, but from the troubled look on his face, he was wondering the same thing.

13

The makeup I put on Friday morning was less cosmetic enhancement, more war paint. My eyeliner was black and heavy, my mascara spiky, my lips blood red. I wore all black, every inch the kickass warrior.

If only my twisted-up insides had matched my outward appearance, because I hadn't been able to eat breakfast. Ro kept offering to find a drive-thru as we sped toward Demon Club, but I shook my head every time, not even wanting coffee. I'd fiddled with my hamsa ring so much that I was gonna have a permanent groove in my finger and the inside of my cheek was bleeding from gnawing on it.

"Hey." Ro took his hand off the wheel to squeeze my thigh. "Badenov isn't going to know what hit him, Moose."

"Changed my mind. I'm Squirrel," I said. "Height-wise, it makes sense for you to be Bullwinkle. Gender-wise, too. Moose is a guy."

"Squirrel is a guy," he said.

"Don't think so. Gender nonspecific. He has a pretty high voice."

"You literally just used 'he.'"

"To make it understandable for you. Also, Rocky was

the smarter of the two. I'm Squirrel. No take-backs." I put up my dukes. "You gonna argue with me?"

Ro's grin turned wicked. "Depends where it lands us."

Sadly, it landed us at the chapter. I trudged toward the entrance, pausing when my phone beeped.

I sighed. "Selfie time. Do something cute. Pick me street flowers or something."

"Bored of cataloguing the incredibleness that is Rolita already? You kids and your pathetic attention spans."

"I'm annoyed that it's fake work moments instead of the two of us making actual memories. And don't even joke about that name."

"Check the webs. It's trending."

I opened Twitter. "Nooooo!!!"

Ro kissed my brow. "Sorry, sweetheart. But hey, you have your reunion with Mandelbaum to look forward to." He chucked me under the chin. "How fun will that be?"

"So fun that we'll immortalize my joy with a damn selfie."

This was my first face-to-face with the rabbi since he'd sent Ferdinand after us. I didn't know if he was going to play coy or have me killed the moment I stepped through the front door.

From the assessing look Mandelbaum gave me when I entered the DSI foyer, he hadn't made up his mind yet. I'd dressed my part as the loveable-yet-not-to-be-messed-with underdog, but he hadn't dressed his. He'd left off his suit jacket and his shirt was misbuttoned, the right side of his collar jutting up higher than the left. One of his tzitzit had come untucked and was sticking out the bottom of his black vest.

The skin at the corner of his eyes was pulled tight, like clamping down on the grief reflected in their depths was taking up most of his energy. It didn't detract from his aura of undisputed power, though it made me want to try to be friendlier.

Sort of.

The moment stretched on, the world falling away to the black void of his dark eyes boring into me. I kept my hands jammed in my pocket. One breath in, one breath out, I held his gaze, refusing to cower. Refusing to look away.

He was just a man. Flesh and blood and heartbeat. I saw beyond his physical form to his life force, a pale orange light. A flicker, easily extinguished.

Extinguish it. My voice. Not Lilith's.

I blinked and the rabbi once more stood solid before me.

"Conference room in twenty," he barked in his Russian accent and strode off.

The wiry man who'd been trailing the rabbi scurried behind the reception desk, looking as if he was trying to make himself invisible as he dropped into the chair.

I reached behind me and took Ro's hand, because my heart was racing, and my legs were questionably stable.

"You good, Louis?" Ro asked the man, holding my hand tight between our bodies.

Louis, the receptionist, nodded. "The rabbi's in a mood. Can't blame him, but..." He looked up at us with bleak eyes. "If a daeva compelled Ethan, what hope do *we* have? Tell me straight, is it safe for me to keep working here?"

"I don't know," Rohan said. "Do what you need to and don't feel guilty either way."

Louis nodded, biting his bottom lip and looking down.

Ro clapped him on the shoulder and we headed through the door into the main DSI area.

"He won't last to the end of the day," Ro murmured. "You okay? You look a bit shaky."

I was going to brush it off with an excuse about seeing

Mandelbaum, but the very fact I wanted to brush off what I'd seen worried me. I wasn't an addict and I wasn't going to start lying. I told Rohan about the pale orange light and wanting to snuff it out.

"I wasn't drawing on her magic, I swear."

Rohan ran his hand up my back. "I believe you, Sparky. Do you want to call Dr. Gelman?"

"No. Let's see if anything else weird happens. I mean, I've pretty much wished I could murder Mandelbutt since I met him, so it might have been all me."

"True. We'll go with that for now."

Probably about 70% of the staff that I'd seen yesterday had returned, which was pretty amazing, all things considered, but the mood was understandably subdued. Not much work was getting done, and mostly people grouped together to rehash events.

Helen wasn't back yet. Her assistant informed us that Dr. Ramirez still had her under observation.

The carpet had been removed and the walls cleaned of all blood and gore, but the broken floor and jagged hole in the wall were a taunting reminder of yesterday's events.

I dragged in a shuddery breath, closing my eyes against the desperate look on Ethan's face before he'd died.

Ro spoke quietly into my ear. "Tell me what you need."

I opened my eyes. "Email. Let's see if Orwell sent anything."

They had: a single line stating that the photo of Tia didn't match anything in their archives of confirmed demons. It would have been nice to be delivered Tia's address wrapped in a shiny bow, but if we couldn't go to her, we'd have to make sure she came to us. We'd have to make a huge splash tonight at the charity event.

Ari crushed me in a hug just outside the meeting room. "Fuck, Nee."

"Ace." I lay my head on his chest. My twin was here. It was as good as leveling up.

"Don't hog her." Kane rolled his eyes at my brother, but I didn't miss how close he stood to Ari, with no thrumming hostility. Between that, the fact that he looked rested, and the atrocious polka dot shirt with striped sleeves that he wore, I launched myself into his arms with relief.

Baruch showed up, took in our assembled team, and nodded. "Let's go."

Our little show of solidarity was lost on Mandelbaum, because he wasn't in the conference room.

Cisco, Danilo, and Bastijn were.

Cisco raised his eyebrows at the sight of us entering all posse'd up.

"Is this the cavalry, Hoss?" he drawled at Rohan. He leaned back in his chair, hands laced behind his head, but behind the carefree attitude was a sharp glint of anger. "You think we're all going to go rogue like Ethan, so you're strutting in here to pop our asses?"

"We suspect that Ethan was under a daeva compulsion," Baruch said. "Your chapter had reported new activity in the past few weeks."

Sometimes the anal-retentive paperwork that the Brotherhood demanded came in handy.

Danilo snorted. "Not on this scale. The fuck is going on? You people waltz into our city like some kind of Tarantino squad and what? We supposed to be impressed? Scared?"

He curled his fingers lightly into his palm.

A gust of wind danced around my group, tightening like a lasso around us. My eyeballs strained against my closed lids. The invisible pressure grew and grew, my breathing labored.

"Stop!" Bastijn knocked the Rasha off his feet with a localized earthquake. Very localized.

It broke Danilo's hold on us. Instantly, every single one of my friends and I had accessed our magic. Rohan's body was outlined in a wicked-looking blade, Kane's skin was purple, the sharp tang of salt watering my eyes. Ashy-smelling shadows wove and bobbed around my brother, while metallic-tasting electricity crackled off my skin.

All Baruch had to do to look scary as hell was drop into a crouch with his fists up and his eyes flat.

Ropy vines swayed behind Cisco like cobras. "We drawing lines in the sand now?"

Danilo pushed to his feet, murder in his eyes, and a small tornado dancing around his stocky form.

The tension ratcheted up, the air thick with it. The next move, the next word could unleash destruction galore.

A sharp whistle cut through the room. Bastijn looked at each of us with disdain. "We're not going to play into the hands of whoever or whatever did that to Ethan. Everyone sit down."

None of us moved, our two groups eyeing each other warily.

"¡Coño de la madre! I said 'sit.'" The ground rumbled.

We sat.

That's when Mandelbaum walked in.

I gasped at the cadre of Rasha he'd brought with him. Four of them. Including Ilya.

"Fuuuck," Ari breathed on my left side.

Kane was absolutely deadpan, careful not to touch anything because his skin was still coated with the remnants of his magic poison. Neither of them knew about my memory wipe, they were just worried he'd recognize me.

I tipped back on my chair, brazenly watching Ilya enter. Ilya glanced at us, but other than a nod at Baruch, he paid us no attention.

Ro's eyes flickered from the new arrivals back to me. He raised an eyebrow.

"Ilya," I muttered, subtly jerking a chin to indicate who I meant.

Ilya clearly didn't remember me and he couldn't rat me out. My witch magic had worked because I was just that good. The only thing that concerned me was why Mandelbaum had also brought a posse with him. Were they people he trusted in the face of this attack? Or was it a subtle warning to me?

One thing I was certain of, if I ran the names of the posse, they'd come up as deceased on all official records, just like Ilya. Mandelbaum had his own ghost squad.

The rabbi frowned at the table and despite everything, I clamped my lips together to keep from laughing out loud. The conference table was round and it was obvious he really, really wanted to sit at its head like our lord and master.

He yanked out a chair and sat down. He'd fixed his clothing, but sorrow still pulsed off him, his mourning painful to behold.

"Rabbi Wahl was a friend of mine for twenty years."

"I'm sorry for your loss," I said.

"Thank you." Something flickered in the depths of his gaze and then his weary expression was wiped away. "Every chapter is on high alert. No one works solo until given the all clear." He rubbed one of his tzitzit between his fingers, absently. "This attack wasn't a daeva. It was witches."

The room erupted in an uproar.

Baruch pounded his fist on the table. "Sheket!"

Silence fell.

"You're joking," Danilo said. "I mean, witches are fun to date because some of those women are hella freaky, but they're hardly a threat."

Wait? What? He knew about witches?

"Jeez, man," Cisco said. "TMI."

Mandelbaum tapped the table twice with his finger. "This is priority one, gentlemen. Find those responsible." He pointed at me. "You stay on your current assignment."

"Why? Because I'm female?" Please let that be his reason. Did Mandelbaum know I'd met with witches?

Did he know I *was* one?

"Yes, it's because you're female. Don't make a scene. I don't want you feeling sorry for them and not doing what has to be done."

I sat on my hands, magic sparks jumping off them to shock my poor butt.

"Which is what?" Bastijn said. "What do you want us to do when we find whoever compelled Ethan?"

"Bring them to me," the rabbi said in a dark voice.

It was a brilliant, nightmarish countermove. Sienna's attack allowed Mandelbaum to search for a witch possessing dark magic using all his resources, while pretending it was in the name of justice.

"Where do you want me?" Rohan asked. "Stay with Nava or on the witches?"

"The witches, but unfortunately, I'll have to keep you with Nava since she's dragged you into the public eye with her idea."

I leaned forward, ready to argue that it had been Orwell's grand plan, but Ari grabbed my wrist under the table, yanking me back.

Interesting that the rabbi was keeping Ro away from the witches as well. Ferdinand had come after us warning us to back off our investigation into his activities, which meant Rabbi Mandelbaum knew what we'd been up to. Was this yet another good cover story to get what he wanted–keeping us far away from further investigation?

Ari half-raised his hand. "Rabbi? Since Kane and I aren't familiar with the city, we're going to put together a timeline of Ethan's last few days."

Bastijn nodded. "Another way to track these witches."

"Not quite. See if Ethan was really compelled or if he made a deal with them," Ari said.

The entire Los Angeles contingent, including my boyfriend, bristled.

Ro's finger blades flickered out for a second. "You didn't know him."

Some of Cisco's tension left his muscled frame at Ro's reaction.

"Even good Rasha can find themselves addicted and willing to do whatever it takes to get their fix," Ari said. "I would know." A Rasha had done that exact type of deal, allowing Asmodeus to kidnap and torture my brother. "If Ethan had any problems that would have led him to willingly partner up with these women, we need to find out."

Opening an investigation into a Rasha/witch partnership, again under the pretense of justice? My brother was kind of a genius, too.

"Ethan didn't have any problems," Danilo said.

"That's precisely the kind of person who has problems. The one who doesn't want you to see them and who can hide them well enough so you don't," Kane snapped.

Cisco wore a thoughtful expression and I couldn't read Bastijn. Mandelbaum's contingent looked politely alert, except for Ilya who stared down at his lap, his brow furrowed.

"Rabbi?" Ari prompted. "I really want to contribute somehow."

Don't over act, golden boy.

"Good, Ari," the rabbi said. "Agreed. If Ethan's attack

was a result of some deal, we need to know. Betrayals will not be tolerated."

Hypocrite, thy name was Mandelbutt.

"Can I see Ethan's body?" Kane said.

Rabbi Mandelbaum said something in Hebrew. "Ilya."

Ilya jerked up his head at the rabbi's sharp tone, blinking rapidly like he'd been momentarily disoriented. "What?"

"I'll call the Chevra Kadisha representative," Baruch said, picking up Ilya's slack. "They're performing the Tahara on Rabbi Wahl and handling the transport of Ethan's body, but we can get Kane in before Ethan is sent home."

Rabbi Wahl was being prepared for Jewish burial with the ritual washing and prayers, but Ethan's burial would be handled once he was in Switzerland.

Rabbi Mandelbaum said he was staying here in Los Angeles until this situation was resolved. He demanded a quick update from Rohan on our current assignment and upon hearing that the charity event was tonight, his lip curled. "Have fun," he sneered at me.

Ro took my hand, out of sight under the table. I thought it was for support until I felt something tickle me. He was drawing on me. A tiny rough sketch of a squirrel in goggles.

I snorted a laugh, doing my best to turn it into a cough.

The meeting broke up after that. The four Rasha the rabbi had brought ushered him out in tight formation, but Mandelbaum paused at the door.

"This was a tragedy and those responsible must pay." Did he linger on me longer than the others? "Be'ezrat HaShem."

I prodded my brother. "What did he say?"

Ari watched the rabbi leave. "God willing."

14

The door slammed before the rest of us could go anywhere. Cisco leaned against it, arms crossed. "Why does the rabbi need bodyguards?"

"How did he even know it was witches that compelled Ethan?" Bastijn raked a hand through his curls. "The attack happened yesterday and we'd never had any issue with them before. I didn't even know they existed until Danilo revealed his weird-ass tastes."

Danilo stretched and grinned. "You just wish there were dude witches, man."

"I'm good," Bastijn said. "Anyway, what's with the rabbi? A day later he shows up with bodyguards because they're priority one?"

"You know something," Cisco said to Ro. He sat back down at the table, studying each person in my group with a shrewd look. Then he cocked his fingers like a gun at me. "But I think you know more."

He was one Rasha among eight, all shoulder-to-shoulder at a round table, like King Arthur and his knights. If that wasn't a sign to go a-questing together, then I didn't know what was.

"Give me your cell." I held my hand out to Cisco, who drew his phone out of his pocket, but held on to it. I blasted the phone out of Cisco's hand and it hit the ground, smoking.

All the L.A. Rasha froze, wearing identical "Oh shit, crazy chick" expressions of wide-eyes and slack-jaws.

I turned to Danilo. "Phone. Now."

When he didn't move, I blasted his chair–between his legs–with a single lightning strike.

Hand over his crotch, he jumped up so fast, his chair toppled over backward. He tossed me his cell.

Bastijn didn't need to be asked. He slid his over immediately.

Scooping up Cisco's phone, I took them all, opened the window, and tossed them outside. I slammed the window shut.

"Mandelbaum was working with a witch who had dark magic to unleash demons on the world and make the Brotherhood a big savior. She's dead and he's looking for her replacement. Ta da." I threw jazz hands. "Pick a side."

"Go big or go home?" Ro said to me.

"Playing coy was yesterday's reality."

Kane tilted his head, studying the other group. "No protests that he'd never do such a thing. Interesting."

"Walk us through what you've learned," Cisco said.

"And how you learned it," Danilo said.

I'd told this story so many times, I could take it on the road as a one-woman show. Thing is, I'd never had to fudge a version that got me to the witches without Ari's involvement. I was deep into a fascinating and totally plausible story about running into a coven on a full moon in Prague when Ari interrupted me and told them the truth about his induction.

No one seemed to care, though Bastijn looked intrigued.

Kane shifted his chair closer to Ari's.

"Fine," I said to the group at large. "I met Dr. Gelman because of the induction." I included Sienna in the story though I kept my witch status, Lilith, and Ilya's memory wipe out of it. They seemed trustworthy, but I was holding off on those details until I had absolutely no doubts about them.

"So we're looking for Sienna," Cisco said.

"You can try," Kane said. "Most likely won't find her until she wants to be found."

"Ferdinand Alves," Bastijn said. "Guy shows up out of nowhere and is treated like a V.I.P. He was a part of all this, wasn't he?"

The L.A. Rasha told us about Rabbi Wahl assigning Zander to work with Ferdinand on some classified gig a couple months ago. Cisco had heard Zander and Ferdinand arguing about something, though he only heard the raised voices, not the topic. They'd subsequently disappeared for a few days, and when they got back, Zander stayed stoned-to-the-point-of-catatonic for a week.

He'd also had deep scratches all over his hands that he'd refused to explain.

I stopped pacing. "When was this?"

Cisco turned to Bastijn. "What night did you get back from Caracas? It was then."

"June twentieth," Bastijn said.

"That's around when Ferdinand died," Rohan said. "Shedim killed him."

"Shedim controlled by Sienna," I said.

Danilo cursed. "Are you sure?"

"Yeah," Ro replied. "I was there. Ferdinand was trying to kill me. Though we didn't know about Sienna until later."

"Well, fuck," Cisco said.

I drummed my fingers on the table. "The timing of the fight also fits for when Tessa died."

"Ferdinand's wife," Ari clarified for the others. "And the witch with dark magic that Mandelbaum was using."

I'd taken a snap of the photo Ro had found of Tessa and Ferdinand at his apartment and put it on my burner phone, along with one of Sienna. I passed the cell to the men.

Danilo whistled. "I saw her once. Pegged her for a witch in about three seconds."

Bastijn took the phone from him. "You think they killed Tessa?"

"No. Dark magic killed Tessa," I said. "It's not a sustainable hobby. But there's some connection with the timeframe of the fight that we're missing."

"Rabbi Wahl?" Cisco said. "Not-so-innocent bystander?"

"Seems likely," Rohan said.

There was a loud crack. Baruch held a chunk of the wooden conference table in his hands and was glaring at it. "This runs too deep into the heart of the Brotherhood."

"So let's find out where everyone's loyalties lay," Ari said.

"Quietly." Baruch pinned the L.A. Rasha with his steely blue gaze. "Find out how far Rabbi Mandelbaum and his friends' tentacles stretch. Contact those you trust. Rohan, can we commandeer my bungalow to set up a war room?"

Rohan nodded.

War room. I swallowed. Then I broached the unpopular topic still unresolved. "Why Ethan?"

Danilo stood up with a scowl. "This again?"

"If Sienna didn't care about using an innocent person, why not just make him into a magic bomb and take everyone out? This was a precise strike. None of the staff were hurt and the Rasha that tried to stop him weren't hurt because of Sienna. They got hurt in the fight. That means Sienna didn't want them hurt."

I was starting to sound like a broken record, but the distinction was important. It would be too easy to paint Sienna as an archvillain, see her in terms of black-and-white absolutes. That would be to our peril.

"You didn't know him," Bastijn said.

"No, I didn't. My thinking isn't clouded by personal sentiment, either." I'd effectively split us back into us and them and I wasn't sure which group Rohan fell into.

"It all must be considered," Baruch said.

Before I could lay out a plan, Ro cut me off. "Get burners. No Brotherhood cells anywhere near you when you're discussing this assignment."

Cisco stood up, cracking his knuckles. "Love a good dose of paranoia."

Danilo jabbed a finger at me as he strolled past. "Stirred shit up." He looked pleased to have a fight on his hands.

Bastijn clapped Ari on the shoulder. "Good to see you again, chamo."

Damn, his accent was hot. I cut a sideways look at Kane, who scowled at them. That's right, son. Man up and appreciate my brother.

"You too, Bastijn." The tips of Ari's ears were pink but there was no awkwardness, so while they'd totally slept together, it was quite a while ago.

"Hussy," I whispered to my brother.

"What a touching reunion," Kane said.

"It is." Ari exchanged a warm smile with Bastijn.

Bastijn smirked at Kane and left.

I poked Kane with a pen, since he still wasn't touch-safe. "You're an idiot."

"For what?" Kane said.

"Put your razor-sharp mind to it for five minutes and see if you can puzzle it out."

Ro checked the hallway. "Sorry for cutting you off, Nava. They weren't going to listen. I'm having trouble believing it of Ethan and I know you're probably right."

"He wasn't working with Ferdinand," I said, "because the others would have noticed. Maybe some side job via Rabbi Wahl or reporting directly to Mandelbaum?"

"Follow the money," Ari said.

"You think that applies here?" I said.

He shrugged. "Dad always says in nine out of ten cases if you follow the money, you get motive."

"I can do that," Kane said.

"Ace, you'll cross check the timeline to whatever Kane finds out?"

"On it."

"Last thing," I said. "I need to search Mandelbaum's room."

"Why?" Ari asked.

Ugh. Did I really want to go into the details? My brother did not need to know about my clogged toilet situation.

"Long story," I said.

"Rohan lost his magic," Baruch said. "Nava made a deal with Lilith, yes, that Lilith, who is alive thanks to dark magic, to get it back. Now she's trapped inside Nava and if we don't trade one of Mandelbaum's tzitzit to a demon for an artifact to remove her, your sister will die in a month."

"Okay. Maybe not that long," I said.

"Are you fucking kidding me?" Shadows slithered around Ari's body like snakes. I could taste the charcoal. "Why didn't you tell me she was trapped in you?"

"I didn't want to upset you."

Ari went apoplectic.

Kane went to put his hand on Ari's shoulder and

stopped himself, his skin still faintly purple. "Freak out later, help your sister now."

"Did you know?" Ari demanded.

"No, calm down." Kane said, then arched an eyebrow at me. "But we'll be having words about this secret-keeping of yours, babyslay."

"Good. All our secrets can come out at once, then." I looked pointedly from him to my brother.

Kane jutted out his chin with a huff. "Curiosity killed the cat."

Ari was struggling to get his magic under control. It filled more of the room, careening wildly.

"Shut it down, Ari. She'll get through this," Baruch said.

"You can't promise that!" Whoa. Ari was snapping at his idol.

"Esther is working on it," I said. "I'll be okay, I swear, but right now, I need your help."

He drew his magic shadows into himself with visible effort. "Everyone is too paranoid right now. Wait until later to search."

"Now's the perfect time. Mandelbaum is busy. Distracted."

"He's got bodyguards," my brother shot back.

"All of whom probably have special instructions where you're concerned," Kane said.

"Tell me what you really think," I said.

"Sure." Ari said. "Not now. No."

"Great. I'm gonna take that as a 'go for it.'"

"Nee."

"One month, Ari. How about I don't put this off?"

He flinched like I'd hit him. "I'm telling Mom and Dad."

"Before or after I'm dead?"

Ari glared at me.

"Go," Rohan said. "We have your back."

I portalled upstairs. All was silent as I crept to the deluxe guest suite where Mandelbaum was staying. The door was wide open and the room was empty.

It had to be a trap.

I searched all of his drawers with a cutthroat efficiency. Jackpot. I slid a tzitzit into my pocket.

"Not now, Baruch," Mandelbaum said, his footsteps drawing closer. At Baruch's protests he said he'd meet him downstairs in five. "Oskar, with me."

I might never get an eavesdropping opportunity like this again. I wriggled under the rabbi's bed. It was not badass and super spy. It was me crammed in with the box spring digging into my sweaty back, nervously straining to hear every sound, while getting too intimate with the dust bunnies tickling my nose.

Two sets of feet entered and the door closed.

"Well?" Mandelbaum said.

"You were right," said a male voice with a German accent. "He was tight with Ethan."

The hair on the back of my neck stood up. I shimmied as far forward on my belly as I could without being seen, but it only got me a view of their legs.

"I don't trust him," the rabbi said. "He's acting cagey, disobeying orders. I warned him to sever that relationship."

Ro. I pressed my palms into the carpet to smother the sparks flying off them.

"You want to keep an eye on him for a bit longer?" Oskar asked.

"No," Mandelbaum said. My heart stuttered a dozen times. "He's run out of chances."

I reached for the hem of the blanket to move it out of the way and stop them, when Oskar said, "Too bad. Ilya was a good guy. But you're right. Every time I checked in with him about whether he'd found out what Ferdinand planned to give us the night he died, he claimed to forget."

"Something happened on his trip up north," the rabbi said. "Something changed."

My stomach dropped into my toes with a queasy lurch. The memory wipe. Ilya was no innocent but he didn't deserve to die because of my actions. I portalled out, landing behind the reception desk.

I ran toward my friends.

"Ilya. Find him." I clutched Baruch's arm. "Please."

Had I anything personal of his, I'd have done a location spell.

"Why?" Kane said.

This was it. The last moment that my friends and family ever looked at me without disgust.

"I memory wiped him meeting me, but I guess I screwed up and Mandelbaum thinks he's gone off-book and ordered him killed."

They sprung into action. We scoured the building, but he and the German were gone and I had my first human death on my conscience. Too bad it wouldn't be my last.

15

———

The last thing I wanted to do was doll up and attend Zack's charity event, but I couldn't back out. Not after all my posts of the past couple of days, each one more self-satisfied and entitled than the last, shoving this relationship in everyone's face, and setting the stage for first contact with Hybris.

I'd tried calling Baskerville but it went straight to voice-mail. I put the tzitzit in my underwear drawer, then moved it to my T-shirt drawer because, nope, too weird.

Since I had to look my part for the evening's festivities, I channeled my impending nervous breakdown into a total destruction of Billie's fine unpacking.

"I have nothing to wear!"

"The mound on the bed suggests otherwise."

I rounded on Rohan with a feral snarl.

"But you're right. Also perfect the way you are."

"Say it." I jabbed him in the chest. "I killed Ilya. I'm a monster."

"You didn't kill Ilya."

Demons disappeared when we killed them. Humans didn't. I may not have had the firsthand visual of Ilya's lifeless eyes like I did with Ethan, but I could picture his dead body all too easily.

Actually, what I couldn't stop picturing was that damn bright pink pastry box that Mischa had brought for the two of them. They'd had their final birthday together and for the rest of his life, his twin would manifest as a phantom ache, a deep-seated loneliness Mischa would never be able to escape.

Stories liked to toss around the old "it takes a monster to stop a monster" trope. It sounded so guns-blazing and sexy. So very "I'm gonna be the biggest badass on the block." The truth was that becoming a monster wasn't a grand jump into darkness, but a small step sideways: walking past a homeless person asking for change, ignoring the food bank appeals while standing in line for your second latte of the day.

The scary thing about becoming a monster was that we all had the potential in us, and with Lilith trapped inside me, I had it more than most. If I needed to keep using her magic to help our side I would, but I was going to fight tooth and nail to keep my humanity.

Thing was, had it already changed how Rohan saw me?

"Everyone was too focused on finding Ilya to say anything, but it's you and me now." I laughed bitterly. "Don't hold back."

Rohan pushed my pile of dresses aside and sat down on the bed. He patted the mattress beside him, but I shook my head, rooted to my spot, my arms wrapped around myself.

"Six months ago, I would have agreed with you. You practiced magic on a fellow Rasha, magic that you didn't have a handle on, and as a result, he's dead or whatever they've done to him."

I hoped for Ilya's sake he was dead. "Now?"

He clasped his hands between his knees, elbows braced

on his black tux pants. His tux jacket fell open and his tie was loosely knotted.

"Montague took down wards so Asmodeus could get to us. The head of my Brotherhood is planning to unleash the very creatures we're sworn to kill on an unsuspecting public to feed some kind of messiah complex. Ferdinand tried to kill Drio and me, I almost lost my magic, and as a result, you've got the most powerful witch in the history of mankind locked inside you. I would have killed Montague if I could have, and I sure as hell tried to kill Ferdinand." He pulled me onto the bed, drawing me into his side. "You're not a monster, sweetheart. You're fighting a war."

I rested my head on his shoulder. "Our world is filled with shadows and we Rasha possess our fair share, but I'd have sworn that *this* shadow, harming a human, was one I'd never cloak myself in. I'd been so certain."

"Ilya would have killed you at the cabin. That memory wipe was the least injurious self-defense you could have done and ultimately, Mandelbaum gave the order. Not you."

"It was a lot easier to deal with moral quicksand when it didn't involve actual loss of life." I rubbed the heel of my palm against my chest. "How am I supposed to keep going?"

Ro kissed the side of my head. "Same as we all do. One breath at a time."

Touching as it all was, his words didn't solve the immediate problem that everything I owned was unwearable crap and in two hours I was supposed to magically transform from my oversized ratty bathrobe, snarled hair from running my fingers through it anxiously, and no makeup, into my half of Rolita to incite fans' wrath and attract a demon's attention.

I fell backwards onto my clothing. "I need a fairy godmother."

"Oh. I have the next best thing. Mom's stylist. Let me run up to the house and call her."

"Wait." I beckoned him closer until he stood over the bed, then pulled him down to me by his tie and kissed him. "Thank you."

"No thanks needed."

I enjoyed the view of his fine ass walking away until he'd slipped out the front door, then I hauled myself off the bed. Buck up, camper. I padded into the living room and headed directly for the small liquor cabinet, do not pass Go, do not collect $200.

The civilized thing would have been to pour the whiskey into a glass but there was barely two fingers left, so I put the bottle to my lips and gave 'er. I wiped my mouth with the back of my hand, shaking my head at the burn and raising the empty bottle in victory. "Fuck yeah!"

"I've never seen Macallan consumed quite like that."

The bottle hit the carpet, bouncing twice, and scattering tiny drops of sticky booze on my feet. I clutched my obscenely gaping housecoat. I'd envisioned every first meeting scenario possible, including one involving poodles and arson, and yet missed the one where I looked like the cover model for a Kid Rock album.

"M-Maya. I mean, Ms. Mitra."

"Oh, good. You know who I am." Her accent was even more SoCal than her son's.

Rohan got his gold eyes from his mother. On him they were my barometer to his emotions. On Maya, they were as implacable and unreadable as the sun. Add that to the total picture of her purple dreads, bindi, nose piercing, and black studded leather tunic thing that made her so much cooler than I could ever hope to be, in addition to being the woman who birthed Rohan and probably had some definite opinions about the type of girl her son should date?

I was fucked.

"Lox!" I yelled like a crazy person.

Maya rightfully stepped back.

I gave a kind of strangled eep and ran to my suitcase, returning in record time with a vacuum-packed box of smoked salmon with a bow on it that I pressed into her hands.

"I brought you lox. Because you're Jewish." I laughed, flapping my hands like I was trying to fly. "Which you know. Did I say how much I respect your career?"

Maya flipped the box over, taking in the glossy photos on the back. "Were you trying to bribe me into liking you? With fish?"

"Is it working? Because if not, it's a hostess gift. Contrary to how it seems, I wasn't actually raised by wolves."

I was getting nothing from this woman, except Baruch-worthy impassive blinks. I gnawed on a cuticle until it was ragged, contemplating my next move, but I'd just caused a man's death. My ideas, unlike the whiskey I'd just slugged back, were not top shelf.

There were running footsteps and Rohan skidded to a stop in the doorway. "Don't scare her, Mom."

Maya didn't even turn around. "Go check on your father, beta."

"Dad's fine."

"Rohan."

My badass, human-blade of a boyfriend nodded meekly and slunk away. "Okay."

"Coward," I yelled. Maya turned that look on me. "He's a fine boy," I amended.

She sank onto the arm of the sofa, all languid elegance and black nail polish. "Sit."

I sat.

"Before you say anything, I have a few points to make on why I'm an excellent girlfriend for your son." I reached into my pocket.

"Those are index cards."

I pulled off the elastic securing them. "I wasn't sure I'd remember all my points."

"How many are there?"

I flipped through the cards. "One hundred and seven. Though I might have rephrased a few in different creative ways to pump up the content."

Maya threw her head back and laughed. "Holy fuck, you're even funnier than Ro-Ro said."

Ro-Ro? Oh, revenge would be sweet on the scurrying bastard.

Cautiously optimistic, I stuffed my cards back into my bathrobe pocket. "Did you like the song he wrote you for Mother's Day? I thought it was beautiful, but I'm not a professional."

I was totally planning to claim all the points for being the one to convince him to write it.

Maya jabbed a finger at me. "This album mess is all your fault. I never would have worked with my stubborn-ass kid if he hadn't written me that cute song. That's on you."

I reached for my cards again, but she snapped her fingers at me, stopping me.

"Did I say I didn't love it? That I didn't want my son writing music again?"

I eyed the door, mentally calculating how I could make a quick escape if need be, because she was scary. "Uh, no?"

"The depth and maturity of the songs on *Ascending*? It's his best work." She shook her head from side to side. "Or will be when he finishes it."

I relaxed a fraction. "He's punished himself for Asha long enough."

"He has." Maya slid off the arm so that she was sitting beside me. "Rohan is extremely proud and stubborn. He gets it from his father."

Don't laugh. Don't laugh. "Uh-huh."

She raised an eyebrow. "Sometimes his pride is a good thing, but sometimes..." Her face etched with sorrow. "My son went down some dark roads. But you keep bullying him back into the light."

"I wouldn't call it bullying. A gentle encouragement."

Maya snorted. "I know the two of you haven't had it easy, but you're good for him. Is he good for you?"

As evidenced by Exhibit A, the index cards, I'd been ready for Maya to hate me. The woman had a fierce reputation and didn't suffer fools. Best case, she'd be indifferent. But this? This wasn't just expectations of me, it was expectations of her son *for* me.

"He really is."

"Okay then." She stood, the salmon tucked under one arm.

"Out of curiosity, did the bribe help?"

"I'm deathly allergic to salmon."

"Next time don't lead with the lethal toxin. Got it." I picked up the whiskey bottle, checking if by any miracle, some booze had survived.

There was a sharp rap on the door.

"Hello?" said a French-accented female's voice. A tiny bird of a woman, with a severe jet-black bob, her arms full of garment bags and a massive cosmetics kit, edged inside the bungalow.

"Cristianne." Maya rose, kissing her friend on both cheeks. "This is Nava."

Cristianne carefully lay the garment bags over a chair,

then crossed the room and pulled me to my feet. "Oui. I can work with this."

"Merci de m'aider si rapidement," I said.

"Vous êtes Francaise?"

"Canadian, but educated in French."

The stylist beamed at me, chattering away in French about how she'd hadn't been certain but now she had the perfect dress.

The next hour was a whirlwind of pinning and hair and makeup. Maya had left ages ago, mumbling some excuse about a pressing issue in the studio.

Cristianne sprayed hairspray on my wave of hair falling over one eye and pinned a large crimson flower behind my left ear. "Et voilà."

I turned to the full-length mirror she'd had brought in and beamed.

She'd put me in a midnight blue, satin, retro glam number with a sweetheart halter, fitted to my every curve and then sweeping out at the bottom in a fishtail. I looked like I'd stepped out of the 1940s.

Someone wolf-whistled. "My son has excellent taste," said a man with an Indian accent.

"Dev!" I shuffle-hopped over and hugged Rohan's dad. "I'm so glad to meet you properly. How are you feeling?"

He danced a couple of jig steps. "Never better. Cristianne, exquisite work as always."

She gave a very Gallic half-shrug, her arms full once more with all her supplies. "Mais, bien sûr."

After some last-minute instructions and an order to dazzle, she winked at me and left.

Dev and I chatted for a bit. His recovery was going well, though he was frustrated with everyone handling him with kid gloves. I thanked him for his hospitality with the bungalow and after five minutes, inexplicably found myself invited to a cricket match, a sport I always confused with croquet. I had the good sense not to ask which one Alice had played in Wonderland using flamingos.

"Look at you." Ro stepped inside and motioned for me to turn.

"I'll leave you kids alone." Dev clapped his son on the arm and left.

Ro swept a very slow, very thorough gaze over me and I preened.

"Lox?" Ro said.

"Thank you, I feel beau—Wait. What?"

"You gave my allergic mom salmon?"

I planted my hands on my hips. "And thanks for the heads up, Ro-Ro."

He grinned at me, his white teeth gleaming. "Only Mom calls me that, so if you're ever planning on having sex again?" He made a slashing motion across his throat.

"Noted. Do I look good enough for a demon?"

"You look beautiful, but you're missing something." He pulled a robin's egg blue box out of his pocket.

"That's from Tiffany's."

"If you say so."

I grabbed the box and opened it. "Tell me that goose egg isn't real."

The oval sapphire on a long, slender gold chain could have been used as a weapon.

"It's real." He slid the chain over my head. The jewel nestled in my décolletage, catching the light in a million fiery prisms. "You want to attract a demon, right? Go big."

He slid his arms around me, turning us to face the mirror. While there was no doubt this couple could stand on any celebrity stage, truthfully, I liked the private version of Ro and me best. The one where he was wearing one of my tap T-shirts, or we were dancing around and singing, being goofs.

"This isn't us," I said.

"I know." His arms tightened, his chest rising and falling in tandem with my heartbeat. "Speak now or forever hold your peace, because there's no going back. You ready to step into the spotlight?"

16

After a quick glamouring of our Rasha rings so that Hybris wouldn't know we were hunters if, no, *when* she showed up, Ro ushered me to the limo he'd rented. He'd stocked it with champagne and chocolate-dipped strawberries.

Limo ride 2.0 was way better than the first one.

I bit into a large berry and licked chocolate off my lip, watching refracted streetlights slither over the tinted windows. "I'm rethinking the definition of us, because I could get used to this. Also, Rolita is damn hot."

"You'd get stabby if you had to wear Spanx on a regular basis."

I held out my champagne flute to be filled. "Who said I was wearing that?"

"No one is that smooth under form-fitting satin. Seen a lot of women in evening attire."

"More like you've removed a lot of evening attire."

He winked at me and tipped his flute back.

"Little less hot now, buddy."

He ran a hand along his body. "I'm the ultimate hotness."

"Eh."

"Take it back." Ro pulled me to him and rained smooches on my cheek.

"Watch the hair." I squealed and batted him away. Feebly, because let's face it, even his cheek kisses were worth having.

When the limo pulled up to the curb outside the upscale lounge where the charity event was being held, I scooted closer to the window. I couldn't see the front doors for the paparazzi. In fact, I could barely see the red carpet.

I did a couple of breathing exercises from my tap days to center myself.

The door opened and the driver extended his gloved hand.

"Allow me." Ro got out to assist me.

I stepped onto the red carpet and the world exploded in a flurry of flashbulbs. My vision was a blur of white dots and I couldn't hear myself think over the dozen reporters yelling at us.

Most of the crowd jamming the barriers on either side of the red carpet was female, many holding signs professing their love for my boyfriend, and all of them shrieking with near-hysterical fervor.

Honestly? It was madness and I reveled in it. When it came to performing, my attitude was the bigger the audience, the better. With each step, my spine grew straighter, my chin notched up just that much more.

Ro kept one hand on the small of my back, ushering me along the carpet, as he waved at his fans, totally at ease. Another day at the office. "Well done."

I couldn't have wiped my smirk off my face if I'd been paid.

Nothing I'd seen or read had prepared me for the tangible current of his fans' adoration. It was that live-wire hum that one wrong spark could turn into an all-consuming inferno. And from the hate shining out at me from many of them, I was that spark.

I'd dealt with so much shit since becoming Rasha. I'd had demons try to kill me and go after my people, I'd had my very sense of self challenged and tested and remade via the same kind of force that turned carbon into diamonds, and on top of all that, I was trying to stave off the apocalypse. So apologizing for daring to be the woman on Rohan's arm? I wanted to throw back my head and laugh. That's right. Take a good look.

I swaggered into that club like I had a cape and theme music.

The frosted glass doors didn't mute the clamoring much. If anything, the crowd seemed to swell in a disappointed chorus once they closed behind us.

To get inside the main room, we had to pass a wall of colorful photographs featuring youth of all ages in different impoverished countries that this charity had helped get off the streets and into affordable housing and jobs. The stories mounted under the photos were incredibly moving. I was especially taken with one physically disabled young girl who'd been abducted by a gang in South China and forced into slave labor, begging on the streets and giving whatever she earned to the criminals. Now in her early thirties, she oversaw the charity's operations in that entire country.

"I want to donate," I said. I couldn't give my time, but I wanted to contribute something.

"Sure." Rohan turned from the profile he'd been reading to smile at me. "I'll put you in touch with my contact."

"You're already familiar with this organization?"

"Zack and I learned about them at the same time on

our... second? Yeah, second world tour. I've been supporting them ever since."

A knot of people had gotten bottlenecked at the photos, so Ro and I moved on to the main space.

It was an enormous circular room with a dazzling stained glass ceiling in blues and greens that gave a dreamy underwater effect. Dozens of crystal chandeliers cast a cool white light and the air was thick with perfume and entitlement.

Old money was represented by distinguished men in conservative suits and their much younger trophy wives. New money was the flashier, younger set in designer wear that ran from chic outfits I'd seen on the covers of fashion mags in the airport on my way to Los Angeles, to a dress whose ball gown skirt was an explosion of feathers and twigs, to the guy wearing a powder blue tux jacket with pants that seemed to be made of balloons.

"Is that?" I tugged on Ro's sleeve, flicking my eyes to the superhero star deep in conversation with the squeaky-voiced singer of this week's number one Billboard pop hit.

"Yeah. You wanna meet them?"

"You know them?"

"No." He shrugged. "What does it matter? They're just people."

"No, they're your kind of people. Famous ones. The rest of us can't casually saunter over and engage in conversation. We accost, beg for scraps, and are pathetically grateful when they deign to take a picture with us."

"Rohan always took celebrity as his due," a mellow voice said from behind me. "Even before he was famous."

I whipped around and crushed his Fugue State Five band mate Zack in a hug. "It's you." I sniffed him. "You even smell good. My fanfic was bang on."

Rohan had covered his face with one hand, as if trying to distance himself from me, but Zack was laughing.

"Oh, good," he said. "I was worried when you met me you'd be disappointed."

"This conversation is weird," Rohan said.

"Hush. This doesn't concern you." I took in every inch of Zack's wiry six-foot frame, from his short afro and neat goatee to his soulful eyes, black skin, and those beautiful pianist hands of his. "No. You never disappointed me. Except for the gay part, since even *I* had a tough time justifying your fictional interest in me."

"Life is disappointment," Rohan said.

He pulled Zack into a hug, both manbro slapping each other's backs. The only other close friends of Ro's that I'd seen him with were Lily, which as an ex had a different vibe, and Drio, which given their shared guilt over Asha, also had a different vibe. It was nice to see him interact with someone with such ease and genuine warmth.

And it was positively delicious hearing the two of them gossip like moms on a playground about half the people in this room.

After Rohan had shared some juicy tidbit about what really went down between the two actors pretending not to know each other over by the bar, I nudged him. "And I'm the starfucker?"

He snickered like a twelve-year-old boy. "You are. It's even in the job description."

I shook my head, with an aggrieved sigh.

"Amazing that you ever get laid." Zack smoothly stepped in between us and slung an arm over my shoulder. "Come with me. I have to talk up the charity and sadly, even important causes go over better with beautiful women."

I struck a saucy pose. "He thinks I'm beautiful."

Rohan grinned. "You're okay in certain lighting."

"So underappreciated."

Zack watched us in blatant amusement. "I have a cousin you might like. He'd appreciate you just fine."

Ro raised an eyebrow while I pretended to consider the offer.

"Nah, I'll stick with this one." I shooed my boyfriend off. "Redeem yourself and fetch drinks, good man."

"Will you pay for them later?" he murmured into my ear.

Heat flared hot and bright in my belly. "Put them on my tab."

His eyes darkened, then he headed for the bar.

Not gonna lie. Being ushered around and introduced to celebrities for the first hour was fun, helping Zack by recounting some of the stories about those kids was even better. Most of these people hadn't bothered to read the profiles so my excellent memory from years of having to quickly pick up dance steps came in handy. The only sucky part was how many people interrupted us to ask about Rohan and me. It was good on the assignment front, but bad for the charity and made me feel like fresh meat.

I took a sip of my vodka cranberry, parched from all the talking I'd been doing. "Sorry. I think I was more distracting than useful."

"Naw," Zack said, his slender fingers tapping against his glass of sparkling water. "They'll all be dishing about how they were here with you two and the charity will get mentioned. All good press."

Rohan joined us from his sweep of the room. Since Zack knew what Ro did, we didn't have to keep things hidden from him. In fact, we'd given him the demon's description to have another set of eyes on the lookout for her. "No sign of Tia."

"Luna!" Raquel air-kissed me. "Who'd have thought you clean up so well?"

"McGonagall, darling. Nice hand towel."

Her silver sequined dress was très mini but she rocked it and the matching sequined bra that winked out from beneath the dress strap was to die for.

Zack and Rohan clutched their drinks, eyes darting between us.

Raquel burst out laughing. "Oh, you poor puppies. They can't tell if we like each other or not. Relax, gentlemen. We're all good." She nudged me. "Introduce me."

"Rohan and Zack, meet Raquel."

They all shook hands and then Raquel asked if she could borrow me for a minute. "You okay?" she said. "I heard about the attack."

I shrugged. "Have you found Sienna?"

"She's moving around a lot. We almost had her once but..." She shook her head. I guess Esther hadn't told the witches that I was the one behind the location spell.

"Question for you. What did Tessa do for a living?" I said.

"She was a de-clutter and positive energy consultant."

I laughed. "No, really."

"Really."

"Wow. That's very Californian."

"Mock all you want, but Good Vibrations was pretty successful. She had clients consulting her from around the world."

Taking flakiness global. Maybe Ari and Kane could do something with the information.

"I met the head of the Brotherhood," Raquel said, casually steering me to a quieter corner.

"My condolences."

"Right? What a major dickhole."

"What'd he want?"

"To threaten me into turning over the witches responsible for the attack on his chapter. I told him that my witches weren't responsible and to go fuck himself. Then I threatened to set his junk on fire if he so much as looked at any of them funny."

"I'd have paid good money to see that."

"Yeah, he ran like a little prison bitch. One other thing."

"That already doesn't sound good," I said.

"When Tessa was found, I called in a favor from a witch in the coroner's office and asked for an autopsy. Off the record. They were backlogged and I just got the results."

My hand tightened on my glass. "And?"

"Tessa was tortured before she died. It's not what killed her, that was definitely the dark magic, but she had cracked ribs, broken bones in her hands and feet, and a cracked skull. Someone worked her over a few days before she died. If Sienna knew this somehow?"

"How? If Tessa had told her, Sienna wouldn't have waited this long to go ballistic."

"I got the call Wednesday morning."

The day Sienna attacked. "Shit."

"Everything okay?" Rohan slid an arm around me.

"No," Raquel said. "I'll let your girlfriend tell you. I've spent too long talking to this nobody." She swiped my drink, took a sip, and throwing a finger wave over her shoulder, sashayed back into the crowd.

While it was all well and good that we had Sienna's motive for the attack, it sucked that Zander had most likely been part of the torture, as evidenced by the scratches on his hand that he wouldn't explain.

Rohan's foul mood over that soured further as our primary mission was turning out to be a bust. The evening was winding down with no sign of Tia. There were a number of performances, including one by the pop star, and one from this middle-aged soft rock artist whose saxophone use resulted in evil and insidious ear worms. I wished he'd been a demon, but alas. Needless to say, Dad adored his stuff. I recorded the two songs he performed and emailed the video to my father, before going into the designated green room with Rohan.

He and Zack would be closing out the night with a song they'd written together years ago and recorded as a one-off track.

"You're a rock god." I slipped off my heels, sitting on a lumpy sofa.

In front of the mirror, Rohan closed one eye, applying his eyeliner with a steady hand. "Which you knew."

"Knowing and experiencing are two different things. Those fans outside were crazy. Let's do something really bold to get Tia's attention."

"Like what?" He turned from the mirror and struck a pouty model pose. "Whaddya think?"

Ro had changed out of his tux into an outfit he'd told me was called a sherwani. Made of soft velvet with a stiff collar, this long, olive green jacket shot through with gold thread had a militaristic feel with its row of buttons down to the knee. He wore the traditional garment over a camouflage tank and olive green skinny jeans rolled carelessly up at the ankle, his bare feet stuffed into burgundy leather runners. His gold eyes popped against the eyeliner and he'd gelled his hair into bedhead spikes.

I beckoned him close with the crook of a finger. "This may be the sexiest I've ever seen you."

He scrunched up his face. "Are you exoticizing me?"

"I believe I am, yes. However, in the interests of fair play, I can break out the shtetl garb and headscarf should you wish to fulfill some Jewess roleplay fantasy." I batted my lashes at him. "I know how much you like roleplaying, baby."

"Not with you dressed like your grandmother. I'm good."

"Please. Bubbe only wore Chanel."

Rohan cocked his head. "How do you feel about Chanel? One of those tweed mini suit things?"

"You wanna play naughty student and sexy teacher, don't you?"

"I didn't until two seconds ago, but now I'm thinking I could get behind the idea." He prowled toward me.

My heart kicked up. "The door isn't locked."

His grin turned wicked as he straddled me. "I know."

Rohan sucked on my neck.

Knock. Knock.

"The door," I mewled, my chest rising and falling in ragged breaths.

"Whoever it is could just walk in." His lips vibrated against the pulse in my throat.

"That would be bad."

Another knock. More insistent.

"Rohan?" Zack said.

Rohan untied my halter top, the silky fabric slipping down to my waist. He set his mouth to one breast. "Hmm-mmmm."

I clutched his shoulders and moaned.

"Five minutes, Rohan. Don't make me come in there and see something we'll all regret."

"Nothing to see. All good," I called out in a shaky voice.

Zack laughed. "Right." He walked away, his footsteps growing fainter.

Ro canted his hips, pressing his hard-on into me. "Five minutes works for me."

I ground up against him. "Ooh, fast sex. Can we make it shitty and dry, too?"

"Ask nicely and I'll give you the entire regret trifecta."

My laugh turned into another moan as Ro kneaded my breasts. "Do you have a condom?"

"We covered this," he said.

"We covered the 'nobody cheated' part. I'm not having you splooge my dress. Really don't need to be the stain seen 'round the world."

"Grr." He slid off me.

"About my bold idea?" I retied my halter straps, resigned to being sexually frustrated for the next little while.

He twisted the cap off a water bottle. "Yeah?"

"How do you feel about getting married?"

Rohan choked on the water.

"Snagging you as my boyfriend and being a dick about it isn't enough. Make me the luckiest girl in the world, Snowflake."

"Tonight? For the mission?"

"Yes. After your number. Publicly declare your love. Tell the world you can't live without me."

I didn't show the slight thrill I got at that idea, because this was about work.

"I've done a lot for the Brotherhood, but standing up in front of everyone with a fake proposal? Are you kidding?" His hands tightened on the bottle, sending water cascading up over the lip. He swore, wiped his hand on his pants, and slammed the bottle onto the counter.

"It's a groupie's ultimate coup. Don't you want to stop this demon?"

"Yes. By tracking her down, not taking something that means everything and reducing it to nothing for an assignment." He poured himself a shot of bourbon. "How could you be so angry about going public for this assignment and then suggest this?"

"That was the Nava who assumed we had the luxury of time. We hadn't found Sienna in a month and look how that escalated. What if it takes us that long to find Tia? Are you willing to live with the collateral damage because we didn't try everything? Because I can't."

And I might not have that long.

He slugged the booze back, shaking his head, his jaw tight.

"It's just another act," I said. "Another performance. You're a performer. A good one."

"A good one because my performances come from a place of truth, not an utter fucking lie. Do you hear yourself? This is totally mercenary. It's something Lilith would do."

"No, it's not." I forced a smile. "There are a lot of things to worry about when it comes to Lilith affecting me. This isn't one of them. Trust me, Ro. Please?"

He finally gave me the barest nod.

"You won't be sorry. It's a brilliant idea."

17

It was a terrible idea.

Their performance was incredible. I had a front row seat at one of the linen-covered bistro tables by the low stage. While Zack played a mournful tune on a baby grand, Ro sat on the piano bench, shoulder-to-shoulder with him, keeping time with his foot. His voice was raw and soulful, singing a ballad of a young man seeing the pain and suffering in the world and realizing all his privilege.

The music swept over the audience like waves over sand, a shared journey that held us spellbound. The melody changed from a minor key to a major one, the lyrics reflecting a hope not usually found in Ro's older emo writings.

He gave a small secret smile, gaze trained on the crowd, before launching into the final chorus. His voice rose in a rich velvety crescendo around the bold chords, and the audience turned toward the two of them like flowers to the sun.

The final notes crashed over us, the song over with a suddenness that left the audience bereft. There was a second of silence and the room erupted in applause.

Rohan blinked back from whatever blissed out place he'd been in while singing, grinned, and nudged Zack's shoulder. They stood up and bowed.

Zack took the mic to thank everyone for coming and speak a bit more about the charity and how people could donate or, even better, get involved. He conferred quietly with Rohan, then handed the microphone over.

"I'd like to echo Zack's thanks for coming out and supporting this worthwhile cause. The song you heard tonight was written shortly after we learned about this incredible organization, and any sense of optimism is all due to them. It's really important for us to remember how lucky we are. I've experienced fame and fortune." He gestured to Zack standing off to the side of the low stage. "I have long-standing friendships with men that are like brothers to me."

Zack patted his heart and pointed at Ro.

"And now I've found the woman who makes me the best version of myself. The one I want to spend the rest of my life with. Nava?" He dropped down to one knee and the crowd gasped. "Will you marry me?"

He pulled out the fake diamond ring we'd borrowed off Raquel.

A spotlight swung onto me.

I'd had it all planned. I'd practiced a quick "who, me?" look of surprise in the mirror back in the green room and how to squeeze out a few tears.

So much for best intentions. I stood there frozen, his words leaving a metallic taste in my mouth. I wanted so badly to go back and smack the me of a half hour ago upside the head. I didn't want to hear a proposal and see that sweet, goofy, besotted smile, knowing it was all an act.

Rohan and I had had a lot of firsts together; I didn't want this to be one of them. Not like this.

"You've overwhelmed her, Mitra." Raquel pinched my hip. "Don't blow it," she hissed.

I have no idea how I made it on stage, wishing for once that all eyes weren't on me. I uttered some Hallmark platitude about how happy I was, convincing everyone my breathy acceptance and wide smile were real.

Everyone except Rohan. I was close enough to see his small furrow of concern.

Close enough to see it wiped away in favor of his own blinding smile and cold eyes.

I bit the inside of my cheek so I wouldn't cry. I was sacrificing the one thing I meant to cherish and protect in order to nail a demon.

Except, I wasn't doing that either because I was going to lose my cool and blow it. And wouldn't that just be ironic? I'd strong-armed Rohan into this stupid plan and if I couldn't cut through my mounting hysteria, the sobs I was barely biting back would give our charade away.

I cast about inside myself for a wisp, a boost. There was nothing. The box was as still and impenetrable as ever, except for that pinprick of light. I worked on the hole until I'd turned it from a pinprick into a hairline fracture.

Dark threads floated out and I tied them to my magic.

My smile grew brighter. I stood up straighter and held out my hand. Every inch the queen awaiting her due.

Rohan slid the rock onto my finger and once more the room erupted in applause. He dipped me and kissed me. It was void of any emotion or chemistry but from the wolf-whistles, the audience bought it.

Rohan and I were nothing if not consummate performers.

I endured the steady stream of well-wishers as long as I could; those beady-eyed scavengers were practically salivating at the rumor currency they'd accrued being here at ground zero. Even though we liked to pretend we were secure in our finery and first-class lives, we were all the same kind of liar as Los Angeles itself: glamorous until you went too far past the studios and saw the rundown parts desperate for cash and glory.

We were all starfuckers in the end.

The need to flee with Rohan and fix this overwhelmed me, but I stood my ground. This farce had to count for something, but no demon approached us.

Hollowed out, yet not numb enough to endure another second, I shot Rohan a manic look, that I was drowning and needed out. The only people I said goodbye to were Raquel and Zack.

Ro gave some instructions to the driver then bundled me into the limo where we spent the ride in silence, both of us staring at the ring. I'd pulled it off, twisting it this way and that between my thumb and forefinger.

He grabbed it and flung it. It bounced off the leather seat and rolled to the ground. "Ask me to go through with the wedding and we're done."

My eyes filled with tears. "It's not how I want us. I messed up."

Rohan swore and slid over to me. He brushed the pad of his thumb under my lashes.

I ghosted my hands up his biceps, raking his locks back before laying my palm on his cheek. My restraint was a living breathing thing. "Can I...?"

He nodded. Barely a movement.

I brushed my lips against his. "I'm sorry."

Our kiss was slow, exploring, unraveling us only to rebuild us with an increasingly frenetic tempo. I shifted against him and his breathing picked up, his hands flexing on my ribcage before his fingers bit into me as he hauled me into his lap.

I nipped at his lower lip; our tongues tangled in a dirty, reckless kiss. Rohan groaned and pressed me back against the leather seat, his kiss almost bruising.

A honking horn and voices yelling out on the street cut through my haze of desire.

I pulled back, trying to catch my breath. Rohan ran his thumb over his lip, all hard muscle, messy hair, and swollen lips.

The limo was parked at a curb on a quiet street.

Rohan helped me straighten my clothes. "Come on. You need Corn Man."

It was after midnight in a deserted neighborhood and that sounded more like a threat than a treat, but, leaving the sapphire necklace on the seat and the ring on the floor, I scrambled out of the limo. I stopped short at the smell of roasted corn and the line-up of people twisting through the darkened parking lot behind a discount store waiting their turn at the tiny cart staffed by an older man and his son.

Rohan joined the end of the queue.

"Where are we?" I asked.

"East L.A. Lincoln Heights. Corn Man makes the best elotes ever." He rose onto tiptoe as if counting how many people were ahead of us. "He's here till about 2AM but if he runs out of corn, that's it. Too bad. So sad."

A car slowed down as it drove past, the driver hanging out the window and yelling "The wait is worth it!" before zooming off into the night.

The customers were of all ages and all ethnicities, dressed in everything from the two girls in pjs wrapped in a huge purple blanket, to us in our evening finery. Rohan was still in his sherwani.

Ro was recognized in stages: a muttered debate in Spanish and English from the two couples behind us on whether or not it was him, the decision that it was, the person anointed to get confirmation.

"Hey man, you Rohan Mitra?"

"Yeah."

The skinny speaker nodded. "Cool. I hated your shit. So depressing." He punched Ro in the arm. "Lighten up, homie."

"Yeah, Ro," I said. "Lighten up."

The next hour and a half was spent sharing beer and chatting with this group about our chances of getting to the front before the corn ran out and the best foods to eat when you were plastered. That turned into them prompting me for weird Canadian words when I mentioned being drunk on a mickey of vodka and learned that Americans had no clue what that flask-like bottle was.

It was a weirdly carnival atmosphere.

The closer we got to the front, the tenser I got, more and more determined that I had to have my elote. I didn't even know what it was, but damn, it smelled good and the people walking away with their orders looked like they'd won the Super Bowl. I'm not saying I would have busted out my magic if it got me to the food, but I'm not saying I wouldn't have.

My feet were throbbing and I was huddled into Ro for warmth when we finally, mercifully reached the front.

"Bowl or cob?" the older man asked.

Ro looked at my dress. "Bowl."

The man scooped a bunch of corn from a water-filled blue cooler into a styrofoam bowl. His movements were economical, an ease born of repetition: the dollop of mayo, the heavy sprinkle of cheese, the squirt of lime juice, the dusting of chili powder.

Ro bought corn for the couples behind us as well: the

last four cobs. Our new friends cheered, while a collective groan went up from the rest of the line.

We got into the limo. Rohan had also bought a bowl for the driver.

The elote was sweet, spicy goodness that I fell on like a starved wolf, humming in joy between bites. Rohan wasn't eating with any more dignity. We basically ignored each other until all had been licked clean.

I patted my belly and refastened the sapphire around my neck. "You told the driver to come here when we first got into the limo. When you were still mad."

He shrugged. "I knew you'd like it."

My heart palpitated in my chest like a distressed old woman fluttering her hands, but for the first time ever, my brain didn't scream at me to run away. It dug in with an "I'm good."

I was so shocked that I actually twitched. "Tunes," I sputtered. "Put on some music."

"Uh, okay." He punched on the stereo, fiddling with the song choice until Michael Franti's "I'm Alive" came pouring out of the speaker. Ro had introduced me to this song and it had subsequently become a happy place.

Just like he had.

I checked back in with my brain, but it was still perfectly content where it was, phonetically mangling song lyrics, so I tentatively relaxed into the moment.

We zipped along the highway, the moon roof open to let in the Los Angeles night, with our bellies full of corn, belting out this song about just wanting to be with a certain person.

Since I had no clue where in the city we were at any given moment, I didn't realize we hadn't gone back to Maya and Dev's place until we turned onto a leafy street that curved up a hill, ending in a cul-de-sac.

"Now where does my midnight adventure lead?"

"My place," Ro said. "I want you home with me tonight."

"Where else would I have been? Had you been planning to kick me out of the bungalow and only just changed your mind?"

"*My* place. My home."

"Oh." I pressed the heel of my palm into my chest to keep my heart from bursting free and jumping out the window.

The limo pulled partway into the driveway, blocked from getting to the gate by the half dozen people clustered there.

Ro sighed. "Reporters."

I peered out the window, though it was hard to see much more than shadowy figures huddled in the darkness between the sparse streetlights like the light might burn them.

They swarmed the limo, bulbs flashing in through the tinted windows, yelling questions at us.

"Way to disturb the peace," Ro snarled.

I eyed the ring on the floor of the limo, wishing I could just get inside and put some distance between myself and this sham engagement, but I'd made my bed, now I had to lie in it.

"Let me handle this." Ring back on my finger, I opened the door, squinting into the gloom. I only got vague impressions of them: the Dracula-esque slicked back coif of one, the shlubby baggy sweats of another, the red leather trench coat of the sole woman in their midst.

"Is it true?" Dracula-dude asked. "Are you engaged?"

I held my ring finger up like I was flipping them off. "You tell me."

Flashbulbs popped in my eyes.

The shlubby one edged forward to get a shot of me, but was pushed back by the woman.

"Are you pregnant?" she asked.

I ran a hand along my body. "Do you really think the only reason he's with me is obligation?"

"Groupies don't tend to have staying power," she said.

Most of the others laughed, but the shlubby one sent me an apologetic smile from the pool of light he'd been pushed back into.

Something about the woman's comment was off. Too pointed.

"If you're gonna insult me, at least have the balls to show your faces." I studied my ring like I couldn't care less.

They shuffled forward.

"Let's get a shot with you and Rohan," the shlubby one said.

I smiled at him. The brief glance I'd spared for the woman had confirmed it.

Tia.

I'd been all wrong about how the fake engagement would affect me, but in terms of finding the demon, my instincts had been bang on.

Hiding my triumphant smirk, I ducked into the limo. "Come take a photo."

"Okay." There was nothing in his expression as we posed together to indicate he'd recognized Tia, but he squeezed my waist in signal to me.

"Thanks, babe," I said to Rohan. "You can get back in the limo."

One of the reporters made the sound of a whip cracking.

"Hey." I motioned Tia over. "How would you like an exclusive?"

"Why me?"

"Because you're the only woman here and if I give it to one of the boys, I suspect you'll be merciless towards me."

"You want to control your press? It doesn't work that way."

I wrinkled my nose. "Direct my press. What do you say?"

She'd set up a cover persona and having gone this far had to play her part. The only thing that might blow it was if she suspected I was Rasha. I glanced down at my Rasha ring, but it was still glamoured to look like a funky titanium band.

"All right. Tomorrow." She gave me a time and a place in the late afternoon.

"See you then."

I got back into the car and slammed the door, the reporters grudgingly moving so the driver could get behind the security gate.

"Tia Lioudis," I said. "Wants to meet outside the Museum of Modern Art."

"Not ideal, but we can find somewhere to take her down." Rohan high-fived me. "Go big or go home. You made the right play."

18

High off my success, I relaxed enough to enjoy the tour Ro gave me of his place. His house, though much smaller than his parents' mansion, was more in line with what I'd expected.

Sort of.

"Didn't you own an apartment?" I said.

"I did, but I sold it when I came back before we went to Prague. I wanted something in a quieter area."

The house was still rock star appropriate with floor-to-ceiling windows and interesting touches in every room from Ro's travels like the glass Moroccan lanterns in the living room or the black lacquer cabinet carved with Chinese dragons that housed his alcohol.

A stunning mahogany-colored baby grand piano dominated the living room, next to a stand of acoustic guitars.

Beyond the wide porch with the lattice roof was a panoramic view of the city. A long fire pit ran the length of it, while cozy patio furniture made it an inviting space.

"The painters did a great job with all the cream walls," I said. "I mean, they didn't get any on the floors and it doesn't even smell like paint. Good thing you were here to oversee them instead of meeting me at the airport."

"You're such a brat." Rohan tugged me down a hallway and flicked on the light in a room. A room that was painted my favorite shade of royal purple, not too lilac and not too blue.

My mouth fell open.

He'd installed a tap floor. The wood planks, warm and smooth under my feet, were even sprung, all the better to absorb the shock from my percussive dance and prevent injury.

"You did this for me?"

"Nah. I did it for my other girlfriend. Just thought I'd get your opinion."

I hopped into the middle of the floor in my bare feet and started tapping. This was insane. He'd had this whole thing installed for me. Who did that? Was it a normal rock star thing or was it something else? And if it was something else, what did it mean?

I could see myself dancing in here with the early morning light streaming through the large windows, Rohan coming to kiss me good morning and bring me coffee. The two of us jamming, late at night, like now, with crickets adding their song to ours.

There it was again, the hard fast slide of black ice, my heart surrendering to gravity. I was falling hard for him and with everything still so fragile between us, did I need to put on the brakes before I got hurt?

I stopped dancing and sat down in the middle of the floor. "Do you know how to be us yet?"

He folded himself onto the floor next to me, shrugging out of his sherwani and laying it beside him. "It's not a one-person decision."

I toyed with the sapphire pendant. "You forgiving me is."

"I forgive you."

"Doesn't sound like it."

He met my eyes steadily. "I've lived my life in absolutes and it's been hard to come to a place where I can forgive you instead of walking away. It's not so much about you as about me."

Quit poking at painful wounds, my brain ordered. *Thank him for the tap floor and ride the bliss.*

No, my heart countered. *No matter how hard this is to hear, you have to have this talk. I can't take all this second-guessing.*

Ugh. My heart was right. We had to grow up and face our fears and our baggage and do this right. We deserved that.

I deserved that.

"Do you think you'll ever get there?" I said.

He rubbed his jaw. "Zack made me shave and get a haircut before you came because he said I was starting to look like a mopey homeless dude. It's not going to be easy being back together and in the public eye, but I want this. I want us." His expression turned soft and open. "You make me want to share, Sparky. My thoughts, my dreams, my life. And I'm an only child. I don't like to share. Or, I didn't before you. So, yes, I forgive you. Do you forgive me? Do you want this?"

The clear depths of his eyes shone with a raw vulnerability.

Rohan had been the driving force in us becoming a couple, and while the arrogance of it was breathtaking, there had been something compelling about his certainty that we would end up together. Even our break and superficiality of the past month had felt like a course Ro had set with no hesitations, which was why it had devastated me.

He rubbed his index finger and thumb together rapidly, the rest of him rigid as he waited for my reply. How very wrong I'd been. Ro was fumbling through this as much as I was, with all the same fears.

My heart slowed to a normal tempo. The metaphoric rope I'd been bound in that had cut off my circulation for the past month had finally fallen away, my body sagging in relief and my lungs capable of taking a deep breath.

"I want this, Rohan. And I won't go behind your back, try to save you, or decide what's best for you. I won't break us."

"I won't either. But this has to go." He took my hand wearing the ring and gently pulled it off. "If I give you a ring, I want it to mean everything."

I may have eeped.

Standing up, he swung me into his arms.

I draped my arms around his neck. "You abducting me? Because I'm fine with that."

He strode down the darkened hallway. "I want to make love to you in my bed. I never wanted anyone in there. Not until tonight. Not until you."

I cradled my cheek in the crook of his neck. "I'm glad you waited," I said softly.

We were pressed heart-to-heart, a single racing beat.

He set me down on the throw rug in the middle of his bedroom, raising his arm so slowly, I could barely tell he was moving until his fingers grazed the side of my neck. He untied the ribbon holding my halter together. My gown puddled to the floor in a silken wave. I was naked, outlined by night and distant lights through the floor-to-ceiling window.

He trailed a finger down my side. "I was wrong about the Spanx."

"I forgive you. See how magnanimous I am?"

Rohan snorted.

I went to pull the sapphire necklace off, but he stopped me.

"Wear it," he said in a thick voice. "I want you draped in jewels like the goddess you are."

I had to remind myself to keep breathing, because otherwise I'd black out and not get kissed by him and I needed to be kissed by him in this moment, with all our barriers down, and the two of us choosing each other, as much as I'd ever needed anything.

I rose onto my toes and leaned in.

Rohan's expression was serious, his eyes that molten gold that made my belly do flips. He clasped my hips, his fingers squeezing and releasing.

I tilted closer, closing my eyes and inhaling his spicy iron musk. My lips parted.

I was left hanging. I cracked an eye open.

Rohan stood there, watching me.

"Problem?" Please say no. Please say no.

"I'm nervous." He briskly rubbed his hand over his stubble. "It's stupid, but I feel like this is our first time and I don't want to disappoint you."

I kissed his jaw. "I'm nervous, too. So we'll just take care of each other, okay?"

"I'd like that."

I helped him shrug out of his tank top, rolling the fabric up to run my hands over the delicious planes of his abs. I scraped my nails along the fine dusting of hair on his brown skin and Ro hissed.

He picked me up and deposited me onto the bed, a

massive wooden platform bed that made me think of pirates and plundering.

I bounced on his divine mattress with a squeal, the sapphire thunking against my chest, and scooted back as Ro prowled on all fours toward me. Giggling, I grabbed a pillow and swatted him with it.

He knocked it away, grabbing my sides and dragging me down so I lay on my back underneath him. His jeans hung unbuttoned off one hip, his erect cock pressing into me.

I wrapped a leg around him. "Oh no. You caught me."

"Mwahaha–"

I leaned up and kissed him, my tongue dancing with his.

Ro groaned into my mouth, grinding his hard frame against me.

I wormed his jeans down. "Too much fabric." He kicked them off and I wriggled out from under him, swinging a leg over to straddle him. "And I want to be on top."

"You've got me where you want me, and now you're just going to boss me around?"

"Pretty much." I rolled my hips against his hard-on. "Did you want to register a protest?"

"Depends on what comes next."

I stretched myself out over him. "Kiss me."

He really did follow orders beautifully.

Our lips tangled in a long, deep kiss, Rohan's hands bracketing my face and his legs intertwined with mine. Lips moved to shoulders and were pressed to ears with whispered endearments. I buried my head in his neck, sucking on the sweet skin there, marking him, making him mine.

Rohan let me set the pace as I relearned the planes and contours of my boyfriend. His right little toe was bent outward and sucking on it made him groan. If I kissed him behind his knee, he gave this sweet half-sigh, half-giggle, and if I rasped my teeth over the divots in his hips while stroking him, his cock jerked, hardening further.

He pushed my thigh aside with one hand, sliding his fingers in and out of the wet heat between my legs. With each thrust of his finger, I fell further apart.

"Ride me," he said in a gravelly voice. "I want to watch you come undone."

I sank onto him. Strands of hair clung to my damp brow, spilling over my shoulders.

His hands flexed on my thighs. "My fallen angel."

"Kickass in a hot package?"

"That too. But radiant. Indomitable."

"I can take on the world, so long as I do it with you."

"Always." He moved his hands on my hips, encouraging me to ride him, then laced our fingers together. "Mine?"

"Yours." I kissed his sweat-damp brow.

We moved in a slow slide, the bouncing necklace keeping time. Our eyes locked on each other. Did he see the same reverence in my gaze that I saw in his? The same tenderness?

I ran my hands over his powerful body as he lay sprawled under me, entirely at my mercy.

"Touch yourself." Rohan moved my hand to my clit, rubbing his thumb over mine. "You have no idea how beautiful you are when you come. Show me."

I rose halfway up on my knees, only to sink fully down on him. My skin tightened, feverish. My moves grew faster, sloppier, Rohan's guiding hands more insistent.

My thighs clenched, that hot spiral of desire tightening its coils deep within me.

He cupped the back of my neck urgently, dragging my lips to his, swallowing my cries as I rode him harder and harder, lost to this mindless urge.

Lost to him.

Rohan canted his hips, changing the angle of his cock. He gasped; the muscles in his back tensed and he pushed against me one final time.

"Nava," he groaned, shuddering in the grip of his orgasm.

I tightened and shook, my whole body clenching as I came, hard.

"Fuck," he growled, and kissed me like his life depended on it.

A crack of thunder rattled the windows then the world lit up with a blinding flash of light.

Rohan tugged me off the bed. He pushed open the sliding door to his balcony and the two of us ran outside, laughing as warm rain sluiced down over our fevered skin.

He pressed his forehead against mine. "If I ever get mad and leave, know that I'm just cooling off for a couple hours and I'm coming back. I promise you." Thunder raged above us, Rohan raising his voice to be heard. "I'll always come back."

"Me too." I wrapped Ro's arms around me. "I'm not letting anything tear us apart again."

I vowed to remember this moment for the rest of our lives, standing here soaked, skin to skin, watching Mother Nature's fireworks dance in the sky while thunder provided the percussive soundtrack carrying us to our future.

The two of us flawed but unguarded. Bowed but not broken.

Together at last.

19

I was woken up by the blaring of Leo's assigned ringtone to find myself laying half-sprawled over Rohan. He gave me an absent smile, his focus on the sheet music balanced on his knees.

Blearily, I reached for my phone, almost knocking over the Tiffany's box with the sapphire necklace stashed once more inside. "Hello?"

"Have you been online this morning?" Leo asked.

Scrambling out of bed, I searched both of Ro's closets until I found a housecoat to borrow. "Not yet. Why?"

I blew a kiss at him, closed the bedroom door behind me, and headed downstairs into the living room.

"Good. Don't. Preferably ever, but definitely not for the next several weeks."

I put her on speaker, typing my name into Google as fast as I could. The articles with the most views were the ones featuring me giving the finger with my sham engagement ring on. They were all headlined with some variation of "Rohan's new fiancée doesn't give a damn what you think of her."

None of them were written by Tia. Fingers crossed that meant she was planning on showing to our rendezvous today.

"It's not that bad," I said. If this was the sum total of carnage as a result of our engagement stunt, I could live with that.

"If you really want to see the worst of it?" Leo sighed. "Go to page two of the search."

"They dug up Stefan?" I shook the phone like I was wringing his scrawny neck. "That bastard. *I* was the one sleeping my way through campus? Hey, pot." Sparks flew off my skin. "Did Cole say anything?"

"No. They asked him, but he's keeping his mouth shut. Too much respect for you, he said. Speaking of respect, thanks for the bare minimum warning text, by the way. TMZ called me twice this morning."

"I'm really sorry." Leo could handle herself, but my stomach cramped up in a knot at the idea of reporters poking into who she was.

"The good news," she said, "is that you're even being gossiped about on the demon dark web. So this Tia is bound to hear about you."

"Already meeting her. Wait. There's a demon dark web and you didn't tell me?"

"I didn't know until today. Harry showed me. There is some deeply disturbing shit there." Awesome. Even Harry, Leo's ancient, curmudgeonly boss was keeping up with my bad press. On second thought, eh. That slander wasn't great, but it wasn't like his opinion of me could go much lower.

"Sleeping with me and Samson, were you?" Rohan stood in the living room doorway, naked, holding up his phone. "Poor guy. So devastated he killed himself over you."

"Come oooooonnnn." I buried my face in my hands.

"Hi, Ro!" Leo called out. "Don't let her go any further down the social media rabbit hole, okay? It's vicious."

"Too late," he said. "She's looking for my–nope. Found my laptop."

Leo made a "grrrr" sound. "Nee, please don't take this personally."

"Yeah, yeah. It's totally impersonal. Love you. Schmugs."

"Schmugs," she said and hung up.

Ro gently closed the laptop. "She's right. Don't do this. There's no way not to feel hurt by the vitriol. Believe me. It's part of why I quit doing my own social media."

I moved his hand and pushed the lid up. "If I don't look, I'll sit here imagining way worse."

Nope. I was wrong. I hadn't come close to the bullshit being said about me.

Reading about my explicit starfuckery and gold-digging ways wasn't the most pleasant experience, though I was stunned at how badly I was being slut-shamed when no one said word one about all the people Rohan and Samson must have slept with.

@MainMitraMistress led the charge against me on Twitter. She was one of Rohan's superfans who had posted photos of Ro and Lily back in Prague and had thoughtfully reposted them now, along with a detailed opinion piece about why those two were the One True Pairing because Rohan could never be happy with someone whose vagina had more unique visitors than Google.

I abruptly shoved my chair back. "I'm taking a shower."

I stood under the water, a sharp spray drumming down over my bowed head. I had to move past this because the only thing that mattered was stopping Tia. My stomach remained a pretzel until the water ran cold, but at least by that time my spine had stiffened the fuck up.

I bundled myself back into Rohan's housecoat, following the scent of freshly cooked bacon. Sitting on one of the bar stools at the counter, I snagged an extra-crispy, curled piece from the plate. "Is this pity bacon?"

He leaned across the counter and kissed me. "It's breakfast."

I could have handled him making a joke, but his quiet compassion undid me. "I feel like dog shit on the bottom of humanity's shoe."

"Been there." He pushed the bacon toward me.

I choked down another bite. "How did you deal with it?"

"I gave the finger to the world and became the biggest asshole I could. I doubled down on the emo, hit the alcohol hard, and topped it off with a callous disregard that got my cousin killed." He munched on a piece of bacon. "I don't advise it."

"Wasn't exactly my plan." I padded out through the sliding glass door and curled up on the rattan loveseat, staring out at the city.

Even in my misery, this view was insane: all glimmering edges and bright sunlight, beauty that cut you like a knife.

Rohan sat down behind me, pulling me into his arms.

I wrapped them around me. "This bites."

"I know you're amazing. Your friends and family know it and the Rasha that matter know it, too."

I laughed despite myself. "Nice qualification."

"Made you laugh."

I snuggled back against him. "Yeah. You pretty much make me happy on a regular basis."

"I try."

I elbowed him. "So this is the part where you tell me how happy I make you."

My phone rang.

"Better get that," he said.

I boffed my snickering boyfriend across the top of the head and went back into the living room to grab my phone.

"Hey, Mom."

"Do you know what you're doing?"

"In theory." Rohan and I had both texted our family and close friends last night about the plan so they didn't wake up and have a heart attack about our fake engagement.

Esther had replied to my text with *Don't get hurt, idiot child.* She wouldn't have bothered if she didn't care.

"Okay," Mom said.

"Really? You're not mad?"

"Well, I was worn out after yelling at three different news vans to stay out of my azaleas, but your father is in his element. He's been out there for half an hour, all 'no comment' and 'we love our daughter and ask you to respect her privacy.'"

"I'm sorry you're being harassed." For someone I'd spent so long at odds with, this protective instinct to keep her safe was weird but welcome.

"I'm sorry you're being vilified. Remember that no one who matters believes any of the awful things they're saying about you."

I blotted my damp eyes. "Thanks. I love you."

"I love you, too. Be careful. Hug your brother for me and tell him to phone."

"Will do."

My Saturday went further downhill after that auspicious start. Baskerville still wasn't answering his phone and I waited for Tia by the crazy metal sculpture outside the red tiled building housing the Museum of Modern Art for over an hour while Ro patrolled the surrounding neighborhood. She was a no-show.

I stomped back to the Shelby, my foul mood made worse by the fact that we had to gun it to get to Zander's funeral.

The funeral was an oddly strained affair in a cute yellow church with an understated decor. All the better to feature the enormous Jesus on the cross behind the pulpit.

Talk about fire and brimstone. It was a private service with Zander's immediate family, Rabbi Mandelbaum, all the Rasha, and many of the DSI staff in attendance. Even Helen had come, her impeccable attire failing to hide her air of sorrow. She confessed she'd started seeing a Rasha-approved therapist.

The Evangelical pastor had an exceedingly low opinion of Zander, droning on about his numerous sins–mostly involving sex and drugs.

"Does he know Zander was out there fighting evil?" I whispered to Rohan. I wasn't excusing what he'd done to Tessa, there was no excuse possible for torture, but he'd also done good in the world.

He shook his head. "Even his family didn't know. They'd kicked him out years ago and hated that he was working for a Jewish security company."

His prune-faced parents and older brother didn't even look sad that he'd died. They nodded along with everything their pastor said while my group quietly fumed.

None of us were asked to get up and eulogize, but Rabbi Mandelbaum got up anyway. "I'd like to say a few words."

The pastor hesitated a fraction of a second too long.

Mandelbaum took it as assent, barreling his way up to the pulpit to speak about this young man who'd had his troubles but who also had a deep well of compassion. Zander had volunteered helping socialize scared pitbulls rescued from illegal dogfighting rings to get them ready for adoption. Even at his lowest, struggling with addiction and cutting people out of his life, he never failed to write back to this seven-year-old-girl he'd saved once on a DSI job. Rabbi Mandelbaum had had to call the girl's parents earlier today to explain why Zander wouldn't be sending letters anymore.

The Rasha and DSI staff looked gutted; his family remained unmoved.

The anti-semitic distaste the pastor had for the rabbi was evident by how he looked like he wanted to sanitize his pulpit when Mandelbaum stepped down.

There had been many occasions illustrating shades of gray for me since I'd become Rasha, but none more so than this funeral.

A life riddled with challenges, where ultimately I couldn't tell if the good outweighed the heinous.

A comrade, brother, and son, mourned and yet not.

A rabbi willing to hurt the many for his own gain, but with such compassion for a single person.

I twisted the program in my hands.

The weirdest part was when the pastor announced that only the family would be moving on to the cemetery. We were then expected to shuffle past the family offering condolences, while they stood there stiffly, barely deigning to shake hands.

If most of us looked baffled when we got outside, Rabbi Mandelbaum looked furious. "Tonight we memorialize Zander as well."

Ethan's body had been shipped back to Switzerland, but his memorial service was planned for this evening.

"You gave a beautiful eulogy," I said to him. It somehow

seemed important to acknowledge how much the rabbi cared about his Rasha. Most of his Rasha.

The rabbi studied me like I was a riddle he couldn't figure out. "Thank you," he finally said. "I appreciate how respectful you've been about our fallen brothers."

"Of course. I may not have met them, but Ethan and Zander were my fellow Rasha." What they'd done was awful too, but they hadn't deserved the fates they'd met. I shook my head, helplessly. "I'm deeply sorry we lost them."

A frown marred his brows. "You really feel that way, don't you?"

"Why is that so hard to believe?"

One of his bodyguards called him over. Rabbi Mandelbaum threw me another puzzled look, then with a slight shake of his head, left.

Our memorial service for the murdered men was definitely more upbeat. Someone at DSI had booked the courtyard patio in an upscale restaurant nestled in the canyon. Twinkling fairy lights were strung through the branches, the food was simple and flavorful, and wine flowed freely.

There was a lot of laughter and, yeah, tears from even these most alpha of men in remembering their fallen fellow hunters.

Kane was behaving oddly, pricklier than usual and barely on this side of respecting the departed, cracking jokes that were neither appropriate nor funny.

Baruch approached Ari at our table and told him to keep an eye on Kane.

"I'm not his keeper," Ari growled and stalked off.

Baruch cocked an eyebrow at me.

"On it."

I dropped into the chair beside Kane, now sitting alone at a back table. "Hola, chamo."

Kane glared at me. "Really? You're parroting that Venezuelan asshole?"

"Bastijn is lovely. And not remotely the one being an asshole." I smiled broadly and pointedly at him.

Kane poured us each a glass of crisp white wine, perfectly chilled and tapped his glass against mine in cheers. "To being an asshole. Takes one to know one, babyslay."

There was no talking to him in this mood and while I wasn't about to start a fight at a memorial dinner, I wished I knew how to help him through his hurt. "I'm over there if you want to sit with us."

Kane glanced where I'd pointed, his wan smile faltering at Ari doing shots with Bastijn. "Pass. I'm not great company tonight. I've got to work later."

"Okay. Thanks for the wine." Picking up my glass, I kissed his cheek and made my way back to my boyfriend.

None of us could forget the circumstances of the Rasha's deaths, but there would be plenty of opportunity for recrimination tomorrow. Tonight was about celebrating their lives and even though I hadn't known these men, I was really glad to be included.

The meal and the memories lasted until well into the night, which probably wasn't the best idea, given we had to be sober and presentable at Mount Sinai Cemetery in the Hollywood Hills for Rabbi Wahl's service the next afternoon.

Rohan and I spent another night at his house but on Sunday morning we headed back to the bungalows in ample time to get ready, more bleary than bright-eyed.

I made Rohan swing by Demon Club en route in hopes of having something to contribute to the strategy meeting before Rabbi Wahl's funeral.

Zander had been assigned to work with Ferdinand and

he'd stayed extremely stoned after Tessa was tortured. He'd obviously been deeply upset by what he'd had to do, and unhappy, angry people often kept journals detailing their woes–or blackmail material.

While we heard people talking at Demon Club, we managed to avoid everyone until we got upstairs and peered around the corner to the short hallway where Zander's room was located.

A Rasha stood guard outside the closed door. Not Oskar.

We flattened ourselves back against the wall.

"Bingo," I whispered.

Mandelbaum wouldn't post a guard if he wasn't worried about what people might find in there. Possibly like whatever Ferdinand intended to hand over on the night he'd died, but hadn't.

"I'll distract him," Rohan said. "You go in." He crept down the stairs, this time whistling as he approached. He winked as he passed me. "Yo, do you know where at the cemetery the funeral is being held?" he called out.

I portalled into Zander's room, letting my eyes adjust to the dark instead of opening the blinds or cracking a window to air out the stench of old socks.

On the other side of the closed door, Rohan was still chatting with the guard, though it was more a one-sided monologue punctuated with brusque answers.

Zander's clothes were piled on the floor in heaps. Some looked flatter and ranker than others, so I checked pockets in those piles more quickly. With all this clothing strewn on the carpet, there wasn't much left in his drawers. Some ratty T-shirts and a healthy stash of pot paraphernalia, including a couple of resin-caked pipes.

His few books didn't reveal any secret documents.

Mandelbaum would have already searched the room

but if the guard was there, he must not have found what he was looking for.

There was nothing under the bed or between the mattress and the frame.

I flung open the closet door, listening to Rohan being ordered away despite his best efforts to keep the guard engaged. I pushed the clothes aside and examined the walls for any indication of a hidden compartment. Zilch.

Next, I stepped into the center of the room, trying to think like Zander. He's got hold of something that he shouldn't. He's worried. Paranoid? He's definitely stoned.

I eyed the large carved hookah sitting on his dresser. The plastic pipe and mouthpiece had fallen off.

The bedroom door opened.

As the slash of light from the hallway washed over me, I snagged a couple wisps of Lilith's magic from the hairline fracture, called up an electromagnetic field, and deflected the fuck out of that light to create an invisibility cloak. I refused to portal out before I'd checked the hookah.

The overhead light snapped on.

I didn't dare to breathe, didn't dare to move my eyes and check if it had worked. I could see Mandelbaum's Rasha, but could he see me?

He looked around the room, but didn't spot me.

Whoa. I was freaking invisible. Wait until I told Esther!

However, I didn't know how to move around with the cloaking intact and I still took up space. In about six more steps, he'd knock into me.

Five...

Four...

He was wearing Old Spice.

Three...

I sucked in a breath, making myself as tall and thin as possible as his arm almost brushed mine.

Two...

"Pietr?"

The Rasha stopped and turned towards Mandelbaum's voice. "In here."

Rabbi Mandelbaum stepped into the room. "Why did you leave your post?"

Sweat ran down my back. Yay me for pulling this trick off, but I had no idea how long I could hold it.

I counted off the seconds while the Rasha told the rabbi he'd heard something, Mandelbaum told him he'd been imagining things, and they then discussed a few details about the funeral.

Ohmigod, shut up already.

At the forty-two second mark, my shield started to fail from my feet up.

It was dumb luck that they didn't look down before leaving the room and closing the door.

I collapsed against the dresser, my entire body trembling as I shook the hookah. It was heavy and water sloshed around inside it. I held it up by my ear and shook it again. The water wasn't just sloshing, it was quietly slapping against something.

I unscrewed the base, breathing through my mouth at the rank bong water, and flipped the carved body over. A tightly rolled paper encased in plastic had been stuffed up the hollow section. I didn't bother examining it there, portalling out to Rohan's car.

His hands were tense on the wheel. "Trouble?"

Other than using Lilith's magic?

"Nothing I couldn't handle." I clicked the seatbelt in and sank back against the seat, gripping the roll of paper. "Let's get out of here."

After I'd showered, changed into funeral-appropriate clothing, and chugged back a bunch of electrolytes, we sought out Baruch. The larger bungalow where he and Ari were staying had been transformed into the proverbial investigation HQ. I suspected my brother's hand in the set up because Ari was mad for crime dramas.

War was in the air. A sharp bite in the wary looks and tense conversations, along with a gut-twisting certainty that Sienna's attack had set a snowball of events in motion.

One wall had been cleared of artwork to make room for a giant whiteboard upon which was taped photos of all the major players, divided into one of two columns. Either they sat under Mandelbaum's photo or Sienna's, though most everyone was posted under the rabbi's photo as confirmed or suspected Rasha or rabbis. My brother had written "zealot minion" for each of Mandelbaum's posse in his neat printing.

Sienna's associates were limited to Ethan and Tessa.

String and magnets were used to connect various people, like Tessa to Ferdinand or Ethan to Mandelbaum.

Any known motive had been written down in dry erase marker under the photo. While there was a detailed agenda for Mandelbaum, only the word "revenge?" was ascribed to Sienna. It wasn't enough to find Sienna before Mandelbaum did; we also had to untangle how everyone fit together.

Danilo and Cisco were on their phones, checking in with trusted Rasha and getting flight details.

Bastijn stood next to a large map of Los Angeles hung on another wall, consulting a list of places pinned along the side and marking off the ones where they'd already searched for Sienna. They'd combed the city, even intimidating various demons, hoping for any bead on her whereabouts, but she was a ghost.

Baruch was on his phone as well, deep in a rapid-fire

Hebrew conversation. Rabbi Mandelbaum's screaming voice was bellowing out of the other end.

It had to be killing him to be stymied by the witches.

Ari waved us over to the large conference table that had replaced the sofas. He dug through a stack of color-coded files, each one neatly marked with the name of one of the players.

"Check it out." He slid an orange folder with Rabbi Wahl's name over to me. "Oh, and hey, Nee?" He tugged on his earlobe. "Fuck those reporter scum."

"Thanks, Ace." I scanned the top sheet summary and whistled. "Wahl is ex-Mossad?"

"Part of an assassination cell," he said.

"How did you get this?" Rohan asked. "It's got to be classified."

My brother jerked his chin at Baruch, his eyes gleaming in fanboy adoration. "Dude has friends in high places."

Rohan tapped a date typed on the paper. "Wahl came to L.A. two years ago, but he left the Mossad ten years ago. What's he been doing all that time?"

Ari dug out another couple of pages and laid them on the table. "Not proof, just conjecture. This is a list of everywhere we could place him. And this?"

It was a half-dozen news clippings about the deaths of politicians, high-ranking military, and behind-the-scenes powers players around the world. They matched up with Wahl's travel.

"*Mandelbaum has a hit squad?*"

All activity screeched to a stop. Like I heard the record scratch. Everyone stared at me.

"Care to repeat that? I don't think they heard you in the main house," Rohan said. "Do you think that all of his crew was involved in shit like this?"

"Yeah." Ari tapped the pages into a neat line. "You know

what this means, Nee? Ilya was no innocent. With every-thing he's done, Mandelbaum wouldn't have had him taken out for just being spacey the past few days. This isn't on you."

He meant well.

"It's a clusterfuck out there." Cisco tossed his burner phone on the table. "All the chapters are edgy. Rumors are floating around of attacks that never materialize."

"Sienna is playing cat and mouse," Bastijn said.

"I hate being the mouse," Danilo grumbled.

"Anything on the coroner's report?" I'd passed on the information Raquel had given me the night of Zack's event.

"The estimation of when Tessa got those bruises matched up with the fight Zander and Ferdinand had," Ari said. "We spoke to the witch that handled the autopsy for Raquel and she admitted that Sienna had contacted her soon after Tessa's death for the same autopsy request. When she heard that the head of the coven here had already asked for it, Sienna thanked her politely and said she'd get it from Raquel. But here's the thing. The witch said that when she was doing the autopsy, she had the strongest sensation of being watched."

"She probably was," I said. "Either Sienna was there cloaked somehow, or she'd put something in place to alert her. Magical tracking wouldn't be tough for her."

Baruch clapped his hands to get everyone's attention. "Rabbi Wahl's funeral has been postponed until 3PM. They're expecting a large turnout and want it to be the last funeral of the day."

There went my Sunday.

"Next item," Baruch said. "Rabbi Mandelbaum has called the Executive and the other rabbis to Los Angeles for a meeting on Tuesday. We don't know if his men have found Sienna, but everyone needs to be prepared for an acceleration of events."

"Are we going to be present at this meeting?" Cisco asked.

"We haven't been invited, which doesn't mean I'm not going." Baruch's blue eyes darkened in menace and my heart leapt into my throat.

I held the folder up like it could protect me if he raged out.

"It's my chance to see who his allies are," he said. "The second we have hard proof of what he's done, we're forcing him and the Executive out. No more rabbis in leadership and Rasha on the street. The Brotherhood needs to be more collaborative and hunters need to take a more active role."

He got my vote for leader. The other men nodded at his words.

I half-raised my hand. "I checked Zander's room. I was hoping for details about what they were up to or even where Wahl and Ferdinand had been conducting their business. Mandelbaum's men were modifying demons, but we still don't know where."

"There has to be some kind of base," Rohan said.

"I looked as well," Bastijn said. "I never found Zander's laptop and his phone got destroyed in the attack."

Mandelbaum must have confiscated the computer the second he got to Los Angeles.

"I did, however, find this." I pulled two sheets of stapled paper out of my pocket, unfolded them, and smoothed out the crease. They smelled faintly of bong water.

Cisco peered over my shoulder. "A lease agreement. Who's Millicent Daniels?"

"Millicent is Sienna's birth mother. Someone went to the trouble of continuing a lease in a dead woman's name.

Probably Tessa, and now likely where Sienna has been hiding out." I explained about Tessa and Sienna growing up in the same foster home. "I bet this was what Ferdinand wanted to give to Mandelbaum. We dodged a bullet."

Cisco put his two fingers in his mouth and let out an ear-piercing whistle. "Heads up, people. We have an apartment to check out."

"You can't go," I said. "It's too dangerous."

Danilo kissed each of his massive biceps. "Bring it."

"I'm serious. You guys are no match for a witch with dark magic. Not to mention there could be deadly wards on this place that none of us can sense. Don't underestimate Sienna. We need to be smart about this."

"How?" Cisco said.

"Let me call in my friend. Dr. Gelman."

"The one that helped induct Ari?" Bastijn crossed off the last area on the list of possible Sienna hideouts. "Can she be trusted on this?"

"I trust her with my life. She can check out the apartment with me and if need be, we'll call in reinforcements." I'd need the other witches here for my Lilith extraction anyway.

"You don't mean us, do you?" Bastijn said.

"Nope. Ladies-only on this one." Stepping outside for a bit of privacy, I quickly updated Esther on what we'd found.

She agreed that she should be there with me. Apparently, Rivka had gotten back from London with the vessel to contain Lilith, so Esther would bring that along. Afterwards, we'd meet with the other witches and we'd get Lilith out of me once and for all.

Oh... good. "When can you get here?"

"Hmmm." I heard the clacking of a keyboard. "I can get a flight tomorrow afternoon. I don't want to portal because I'll need all my strength."

"Fair enough. I'll see you then. And, Esther?"

"Yes?"

"I'm really glad you're coming. I miss you."

"Sentimental nonsense," she said. "You just saw me days ago."

She totally missed me too.

20

The moment I stepped back inside, Cisco stuffed me into a chair next to Rohan. I sent Ro a questioning look and he shrugged.

Cisco opened the fridge. "Happy engagement!"

The L.A. contingent broke into hoots and whistles as he set a cake shaped like a semi-erect penis down in front of me.

Ari merely shook his head while Baruch looked profoundly disturbed.

"You people are children," Baruch said.

"Tree Trunk, do the naughty edibles upset you?"

Baruch scowled at me and decamped into his bedroom.

"I mean, he's not wrong to flee." I grimaced at the cake.

It was a flesh-colored atrocity, complete with chocolate sprinkles on the balls for pubes. The words "To Have and To Hold" were written in icing script along the shaft.

"You really shouldn't have," Rohan said. The guys knew perfectly well that it was a fake engagement.

"I know." Cisco looked smug. "That's what makes me so great."

"Putting the ejaculating in congratulating," Danilo said.

Bastijn snickered. "Chevere."

Danilo and Bastijn fist-bumped.

"Pucker up." Cisco knelt down with his mouth close to the tip. "You'll get a special surpriiiise," he sang.

"Herpes?" I said.

Danilo laughed. "We should have had it rigged with those spicy cinnamon schnapps."

"Gross." Ari stood up. "I'm out. I can't unsee my sister getting jizzed."

"Fair point," I said. "But I'm not planning on—whoa. Okay."

Cisco had shoved Rohan's chair directly in front of the blowhole. "No offense, kiddo, but you are not the photo opp that I ponied up big bucks for."

"Yet you still insist you're straight," Bastijn said, musingly.

Rohan rolled out his shoulders. "When you guys are lying awake at night lonely and depressed because you will never find anyone whose mouth is a marvel like mine, don't come crying to me."

"A marvel, huh?" I said.

He winked at me.

"That's the spirit." Cisco got his phone ready.

"Wait." I got out my phone, too.

"So predictable." Rohan bent over and opened his mouth.

Cisco hit the little pump. The cream stuttered out like penile dribble. "Huh."

He pumped it again. Nothing.

Once more with feeling.

The pump rumbled.

Rohan ducked.

The cream jetted out over Rohan's head, hitting Danilo in the stomach.

Bastijn hooted. "I knew you liked it messy, chamo."

Danilo didn't miss a beat. He swiped his finger through the cream and licked it off with relish.

Then Rohan one-upped him and did the same.

Cisco pretended to wipe tears from his eyes. "I can die happy."

I checked the burst of photos I'd taken. "Me too."

"Had I known we were having this kind of party, I'd have come back sooner." Kane lounged in the doorway.

I was hit with three unassailable facts. First, Kane was drunk, swaying on his feet and reeking of booze.

"Fucking hell," Ari said, having left the bedroom at the sound of Kane's voice.

Second, Kane was dressed in all-black. No fashion nightmare, just pure badassery. Had the apocalypse started?

Ari examined Kane with a similarly wary look.

And third, from his messy hair, post-coital glow, and oh yeah, the giant hickey on his neck, he was freshly fucked.

"What did you find out?" Baruch strode out of his room.

Kane blinked because he'd just seen Ari come out of there as well. He grabbed an unopened bottle of beer from the table, twisted off the cap, then dropped into a chair and plunked his feet on the table.

"Raise your hand if you knew Ethan was part of the swinger community." No one did. "Did none of you ever see the tattoo on his inner thigh? Male symbol with two female symbols?"

"Oh," Ari said.

"Really? You're the one that gets it?" Kane chugged some beer.

"Wasn't looking at his thigh," Danilo said.

"Is that why you wanted to see the tattoos?" I said.

"Tattoos and scars can tell you a lot about a person. If you know to look." He shot a scathing glance at everyone.

"How is poking around in the man's private life relevant?" Cisco said.

"Kane." Baruch took his beer away. Kane swiped for it, but Baruch held it out of reach. "You've had enough."

"I trolled the local scene," Kane drawled. "Your boy had some interesting tastes." Danilo bristled at him, but Kane just rolled his eyes. "Calm down. I'm hardly one to judge."

"No kidding," Ari said.

"Heard that," Kane sang. "I found Ethan's preferred hangout and that he'd gone to play there the night before the attack, then I charmed the security footage out of the bouncer and–" At Ari's snort, Kane raised his eyebrows. "You want me to continue or not?"

"By all means," Ari said.

Kane tipped back onto two legs of the chair. "The footage isn't monitored and luckily, I got it before it reset and was recorded over. Guess who brushed past Ethan on the street when the club let out that night? One touch and bam. Sienna."

"That's hardly earth-shattering." Bastijn waved a dismissive hand at him. "We know she forced him."

"Not enough for you?" Kane thunked his chair back onto the floor. "Then how about this? For the past couple of years until about four months ago, your boy was making himself a nice little witchy side income to the tune of two grand a month."

Baruch wrote everything Kane said under Ethan's photo.

"Doing what?" Rohan said.

"No clue? But whatever it was, he was doing it for Tessa."

"You're lying," Cisco said.

"Don't take this the wrong way, hot stuff, but I'd have to give a shit about your friend to lie. Plus, I traced the deposits back." Kane rose and bowed sloppily. "You're welcome."

He swaggered out of the room back to the bungalow he'd snagged for himself. Or was exiled to.

"Pendejo," Bastijn said.

Baruch watched him go. "Has he seen his father lately?"

"Yup." Ari followed Kane, with me hot on his heels.

We barged into Kane's bungalow as he was pulling his shirt over his head. He sniffed it, then pitched it from the living room into the bedroom. "Ever heard of knocking?"

"Your dad is a dick," Ari said. "Get the fuck over it. We need to act like a team, not have you parade around like a giant asshole."

"That's not you, Kane," I said.

He crossed his arms, his eyes blazing. "You should both mind your own business."

"You are my business, idiot," I said, "because you're my friend. I get that your relationship with your dad is tough."

"Don't try and psychoanalyze me, babyslay. It's not your strong suit. Stick to stirring shit up and screwing your boyfriend." He notched his chin up.

"Put your chin away. If anything goes wrong, I'm not spending this time fighting with you."

"Fuck you. You don't get to play your death card. Nothing is going to happen."

I spread my arms wide. "Anything could happen. Ethan walked in and took out a Rasha and a rabbi. This is a whole new gameboard."

Kane scrubbed a hand over his face. "I'm sorry. Bring it in."

I hugged him.

Ari tsked me. "You always were a soft touch."

Kane stepped away from me. "Why don't you take your judgy face and go somewhere else? I don't know what you want from me, but I have a funeral to get ready for." He headed into the bedroom.

"You know exactly what I want from you," Ari said. "A relationship."

I snapped my mouth shut.

Kane froze in the doorway. Then laughed. "No. You definitely didn't want that."

Ari grabbed his shoulder, forcing him to turn around. "Don't tell me what I want. After our mission in Osoyoos? Didn't you want more of that closeness?"

Kane knocked his hand off. "Don't confuse pity with intimacy."

"Last chance," my brother said. "Keep playing the same script or stop letting your dad's opinion win. The ball's in your court. But this is it, then I'm done."

Ari spun around and walked out.

Kane inhaled sharply like he'd been punched in the gut, before he stomped into the bedroom and slammed the door.

I tapped my index finger against my lip looking between the opposite directions they'd taken, then I strolled into Kane's bedroom without knocking.

He grabbed his unbuckled pants before they slid off his waist. "You didn't bring ice cream or booze so, sorry, not discussing your brother."

"This isn't about Ari. We're at go big or go home, Kane, and I need to know if you can go big with me without imploding because of your dad."

"Hey, I was the one who solved what Ethan was up to."

"Mazel tov." I pointed at the hickey on his neck. "And you managed to do it with a massive fuck-you to your team members. Way to go."

Kane rolled his eyes. "Spare me the dramatics."

"Takes one to know one. I mastered the art of keeping people at arm's length and you know what?"

"You found true love and realized the error of your ways?"

"No. I got tired. Living down to people's expectations is exhausting." I planted my hands on my hips. "I always thought your poison magic was because you were toxic in relationships, but that's not it at all."

His mouth curled in a sneer. "Do tell."

"You hate yourself."

Kane flinched and shoved past me.

I jumped in front of his bathroom door, practically hip-checking him in his angry stride.

"I don't know what number your father did on you, but Kane?" I clasped his shoulders, forcing him to look at me.

His breath came in harsh pants and his nostrils flared.

"You are a good man. And you're allowed to be happy."

He struck my hands off him, his skin turning purple and my eyes stinging from the bitter stench of salt.

Still, I grabbed his wrists, ignoring his poison corroding my skin, needing him to hear me through the wild-eyed panic on his face.

"I know how bad it sucks to have people always think the worst of you. It took me way too long to figure out that I didn't have to be that kind of person, that I could be someone else. Because fuck those haters. Why should the people who want you to suffer have a say in your life? They're not worth destroying yourself over. You're allowed to be happy," I repeated in a gentle voice.

His expression went scarily blank. "You might want to wash off."

I turned my palms up; they were covered in raw angry blisters that prevented me from fully opening my hands.

236

Kane brushed past me and locked the bathroom door with a click.

I ran for the kitchen sink to rinse off, hoping my healing kicked in soon, then went looking for my brother.

Ari was sitting out by the pool.

I kicked off my shoes, and sat down next to him, dipping my feet in the cool water. "Does super bitch always make an appearance after he sees his family?"

Ari swung his foot back and forth, watching the ripples. "It can take weeks for the toxic cycle to run its course. Kane's mom died when he was young, and when Mr. Hashimoto remarried and had Ren he got the son he'd always wanted. A manly sports kid, unlike his gay, computer-loving older son."

"But Kane was destined to be Rasha and he's a great hunter. That's got to count."

"Being Rasha was his one redeeming quality, but his father kept on about how his Rasha ancestor's genes had been passed to the wrong child."

"I hate him."

"You don't know the half of it. It's why Kane's so rigid about people betraying him. One strike and you're dead to him." Ari kicked up a spray of water. "He's so fucking hard on himself and everyone who gives a damn."

I put my head on his shoulder. "Whatever happened in Osoyoos, it's why you got that lion tattoo, right?"

"Sometimes I hate having a twin," he said, resting his head on top of mine.

He didn't elaborate and I didn't push. Ari and I would always be close, always have that twin connection, but we both had other people who were our number ones now. As it should be. Or rather, as it could be if Ari and Kane worked things out.

"It's all good," he said. "I'm fine. Better than fine."

"Strong like the lion for whom you're named."

Ari roared lamely and we both snickered.

I was about to pat his arm but my palm still hurt a bit from the poison, even though the blisters were shrinking.

"Don't give up on him. If Ro hadn't patiently knocked down all my issues one-by-one, we wouldn't be where we are." I trailed my fingers through the water in slow ripples.

"Yeah, but Ro had issues of his own."

I flicked water at him. "You have issues."

"Name one."

"Don't you get my yearly email listing of your many faults?"

"I tend to delete anything from you."

"That explains a lot. All kidding aside, ask him again. Kane's hurting right now. Don't let your pride screw up your long-term happiness. You two are good together."

"Kane needs to come down a few notches on the douchebag scale before I'm willing to have that conversation." He knocked his shoulder against mine. "When did you get mature and shit?"

"Our last birthday. It was like boom! I am a sage Zen mistress. A deep well of wisdom."

"With such a lack of ego," Ro said from behind us. He pulled his car keys out of his pocket, twirling them around his finger. "Wanna go for a ride?"

"Rawr. Lead on, baby."

Rohan laughed. "In my car for an errand, but we'll come back to that."

"Nope." Ari scrambled out of the pool. "I'm having dick cake flashbacks."

He jogged off, leaving a trail of wet footprints.

Rohan and I drove down out of the hills and past a stretch of low-slung houses that bumped up against an overpass. Yes, Los Angeles had a glitzy side to her, but she also had parts that were more "tired morning after." Like she'd woken up and staggered outside in her now-wrinkled party clothes, her makeup smeared and her hair tangled, blinking blearily into the sunshine and wishing once more for night to make her glitter.

I kicked off my demure navy sandals and propped my bare feet up on the dashboard, my back pressed against the sun-warmed leather seats and a cool breeze rolling over me from the window.

"How did Ethan know Tessa? Even if he dated a witch like Danilo had, Tessa was older and they wouldn't have traveled in the same circles. And I doubt he used her consultancy services."

Ro shifted gears, his bicep flexing with the motion. "Could DSI have subcontracted out to her and he met her on a job?"

"Not unless you subcontract out for feng shui. She was a de-clutter and positive energy specialist."

A truck rumbled past, its bed stuffed with rainbow-colored, star-shaped piñatas. Their tassels blew in the wind, leaving multicolored tracers in their wake.

Tracers? I was neither drunk nor high. I rubbed my eyes and the world darkened, like a total solar eclipse. I rubbed them again and this time, the world went black.

I gripped the sides of my seat.

Breathe. Logic this out.

The car was still moving and there were no screams, screeching brakes, or crashing metal, so Rohan was fine. I cast deep inside to examine the box, still leaking that black light along the hairline fracture.

Since I couldn't seal the box back up, I sent healing magic into my eyes with a steely focus.

The world cleared but I'd been too pre-occupied to notice we'd stopped and were now parked in front of a cute olive green adobe house with a bright red door and cool rock and cacti garden running under the front window.

Rohan watched me intently; he'd shredded his poor seat belt with his extended blades. "Lilith?"

I nodded, dropping my head in my hands. "She blinded me."

"You need to stop drawing on her magic." He tilted my chin up. "Nava, promise me."

"What if it's too late for that promise to matter?" I whispered. "What if this is the beginning of the end?"

He held up a hand, his expression thunderous. "It's not."

There was that arrogant absolute certainty about something he couldn't single-handedly dictate.

I clung to it with everything I had.

Rohan reached into the back seat and grabbed a large, cellophane-wrapped gift basket with a bright gold bow. "Baskerville is out of chances. Text him and say you want to meet around five and to bring the Bullseye. That's enough time for the funeral. Tell him if he doesn't, he loses that warehouse he's so fond of."

"What warehouse?"

He slammed his car door. "I investigated the slippery fuck after we first met. He's got a sweet stockpile of artwork presumed missing. Caravaggio, van Gogh, a Rembrandt. The Irish Crown Jewels and the Faberge egg in his possession are priceless."

"Why didn't you take it away from him?"

"Saving it for when we needed it most."

The threat did the trick. Baskerville responded in seconds with: *Olvera Street. 5PM sharp.*

Rohan rapped on Helen's door.

She opened it, took one look at us, and tossed the oven mitt she held at Rohan's head. "Last time you showed up with a gift basket I had to spend three days on the phone with the Executive convincing them you and Drio had nothing to do with Rabbi Moishe's rental car being hung off the roof of DSI when he visited."

"I was fifteen."

"With Rabbi Moishe asleep in it."

"See? We didn't even wake him." He waggled the basket overflowing with items from Lush Cosmetics. "Can we come in?"

"You're a pain in my ass."

She led us through small bright rooms in warm colors to the kitchen. Cheerful hand-painted tiles backed a massive gas stove with a copper vent, pans hung from a rack in the ceiling, and garlic braids and a carved spice rack hung on one wall.

My stomach heaved at the moist, rich scent rising off the carrot muffins cooling on the stove. If Lilith's magic made me queasy, I'd be so pissed. A Nava who couldn't eat was a Nava no one wanted to experience.

"About the Executive–" Rohan began.

"Hi, Helen. How are you doing today? I know it's Rabbi Wahl's funeral and you're probably pretty upset," she said.

Rohan ducked his head, placing the basket on the counter. "Sorry. It's just... This is about Ethan."

"We're really sorry to bother you about this. Especially today." I actually had no idea what "this" was, since Ro hadn't told me, but barging in here like that had been rude.

Helen scooped a fat pug off one of the kitchen chairs and motioned for us to sit down. "Good. Teach him some manners."

She insisted on serving us coffee and muffins before we discussed business. Normally, I'd have been all over that, but the one tiny crumb of muffin I tried under her encouraging smile sat like lead in my gut and the smell of the coffee made me want to puke.

She pulled her apron over her head and tossed it on a chair. "What do you want?"

"Remember a few months ago how a couple of the Executive rabbis showed up and were all over your ass about something?" Rohan said.

"If Rabbi Wahl hadn't gone to bat for me, I would have been fired."

"What happened?"

She wagged a finger at him. "You know I can't tell you."

Rohan pushed the gift basket closer to her. "I bought all four of your favorite soaps."

I scratched at my arms under the table, marveling at his unmitigated manipulation.

"You don't have clearance," she said.

"And bath bombs."

She peered through the cellophane. "I can't."

Rohan pulled out his rock fuck grin. "I also got a cute bunny-shaped sponge."

"Shame on you, Rohan. That smile hasn't worked on me since the last gift basket."

"Helen, you are a rare and precious woman." I fanned my shirt. Was it hot in here? "But we need your help. This might help us figure out why Ethan did what he did and give some peace and closure to the tragedy of losing Rabbi Wahl."

"Why didn't you say so in the first place?"

I smirked at Rohan.

"I'm keeping this." Helen placed the basket on the ground beside her chair.

The pug waddled over to sniff it then grunted and toddled off.

"The Brotherhood discovered that a number of sensitive documents in the archives, as well as some powerful artifacts in lock-up had gone missing," she said.

"Why would they suspect you?" I said. "Did you have a key to them or something?"

"No. They were located in different places around the world. That's why it took them a while to realize the thefts were connected." She picked at a corner of the cellophane. "All scanners require handprints, you know that."

"And they had a record of yours?" Rohan said.

"In every place the theft had happened. If Rabbi Wahl hadn't sworn I'd been here the entire time, I shudder to think what would have happened. He really cared about us all." Eyes damp, she took a Kleenex and blew her nose. "Sorry, I get overcome."

She hurried out of the room.

I made a quick call.

"Well?" Rohan asked when I'd hung up. "Is it possible?"

"Raquel said she couldn't do it, but a witch with dark magic could. All Ethan had to do was get Tessa into Helen's office and give her access to the scanner. The residual oils from Helen's skin would have left a print that Tessa could use to infuse over top of her own. Abracadabra, she'd have Helen's handprint and be able to walk in the front door of any chapter. Retrieve any document that Helen had clearance for. Any magic artifact. If Tessa had her own agenda to bring down the Brotherhood, it was a pretty good place to start."

"And Ethan was helping her." Rohan kicked one of the chairs, then caught it before it toppled and carefully set it to rights. "But why?"

21

The answers to that question took us the next forty minutes and a minor B&E into Ethan's apartment. His place was bare–like one plate, one mug, and a mattress on the floor, bare.

"Did he just move in?" I said.

"No. I was here six months ago. He had furniture." Rohan roamed from room to room, but there was nothing to see.

I pulled out the trash can from under the sink, but the bag was empty and the junk drawer only held stained take-out menus.

My joints ached. The sooner Lilith was out of me, the better. I raided the medicine cabinet and helped myself to a couple of extra-strength Ibuprofen from the bottle next to the half-empty tube of shaving cream and a bag of disposable razors. My last search was the bed itself. A handful of poker chips had fallen between the mattress and the wall.

"Ro?" I headed back into the living room with the chips.

Rohan looked up, a smear of gray dust on his cheek. He'd sliced open the wall above the baseboard in the corner with one of his blades. "Fresh drywall."

He pulled out a metal box from between the joists and flipped the lid open. It was stuffed with bundled bank notes and poker chips.

I tossed him the chip I'd found. "Gambling addiction?"

"Ethan liked poker, but I had no idea. Tessa's money must have been keeping him afloat."

"Until the Brotherhood killed Helen's clearance everywhere outside the L.A. chapter and Tessa stopped paying him?" I guessed.

"If this cash didn't come from Tessa, where did it come from?" Rohan said.

"Finder's fee for connecting Mandelbaum to Tessa?"

Rohan counted the money. "Depends if he willingly sold her out or Mandelbaum smoothed over Ethan's dried-up extra income with a bonus to keep him loyal."

"He'd already sold Tessa out, how loyal could Mandelbaum have thought he was?"

"There's ten grand here. If Ethan had blown the money from Tessa, the rabbi was pretty confident he'd bought his man." Rohan put the money back in the box and slammed the lid shut.

As for where Ethan had met Tessa, the answer was Switzerland.

Ro found a photo of Ethan visiting his mom at their family home, taken when she'd been recovering from a bout of pneumonia. The date on the back lined up with shortly before the payments had started. Ethan had told Ro about his mom getting rid of everything, believing her stuff was harboring dangerous bacteria that had contributed to her brush with death. She'd cleansed her space and purged the bad vibes out. He'd joked about her calling in the professionals.

Tessa.

Ro was grim on the drive over to the funeral, hating that

he had to tell his friends what he'd discovered. "I can't believe I never knew."

There was nothing I could say to make him feel better. Ethan had been undermining the Brotherhood for Tessa, sold Tessa out for the Brotherhood, and then paid for his actions by killing his friends and dying.

Was that justice?

We were definitely in the right mood for a funeral, but this was Hollywood. Even the cemeteries here were epic on a whole other level. The Jewish cemetery back home was located in a suburb and overlooked by a Skytrain line. This place was more like a museum than a final resting place.

There was artwork. Artwork! Everything from a massive Heritage Mosaic mural to fountains and sculptures, not to mention beautiful gardens.

Rabbi Wahl's funeral was much better attended than Zander's had been. The place was packed to overflowing. All the Rasha were sitting together on the left side of the chapel. Except Kane, who sat on the other side.

I slid in next to Ari. "Really?"

"His choice." He did a double take. "You okay? You look kind of sweaty."

Ever since my temporary blindness, my body had been aching with the desire to get a magic bump. I don't know if my decision not to use her power was somehow contributing to these amped up detoxing symptoms or not, but I grit my teeth, popped another couple painkillers, and hoped my natural accelerated healing abilities would kick in soon.

In addition to all of us that had been at the restaurant holding the memorial yesterday, Rabbi Mandelbaum's posse was in attendance–minus Ilya–as well as Rabbi Wahl's family and friends. He'd had a large social circle and everyone was devastated to have lost him in a security attack from a disgruntled client.

The rabbi conducting the service spoke warmly about his friend, and there was a long line of extended family and close friends wanting to eulogize him.

It made sense for Rasha to say they worked for an international security firm, but I'd never understood how rabbis got away with it. Baruch whispered to me that even non-Brotherhood rabbis worked as security consultants for secular firms.

DSI may have been Wahl's cover story, but by the way that Rabbi Mandelbaum greeted the widow and surviving children it was clear they knew the truth about Rabbi Wahl's job. The chapter head truth, not the hit squad one.

Other than the giant lie surrounding the circumstances of his death, it played out like every other Jewish funeral I'd been to.

The widow and Wahl's children all tore their shirts over their heart to symbolize their loss. Then the pallbearers carried the plain wooden casket from the chapel out to the freshly dug gravesite. Since there were more than ten Jewish men present, the minimum number required to form a minyan, they said Kaddish at the grave, and as a final way to honor the departed, people were asked to shovel dirt onto the casket. Every single Rasha came forward.

Even Benjy was at this service. Ro explained that they didn't shield the initiates from the hard truths of being in the Brotherhood, no matter how young.

After the service, I gave Rohan space to tell his friends about Ethan, and ambushed Oskar, the German who had been in Mandelbaum's room. So, you know, most likely Ilya's killer.

"Where's your friend Ilya?" I still harbored a stupid

hope that Ilya had been chastised and sent away, but Oskar hesitated a fraction of a second too long before replying that Ilya had left the country on DSI business.

I clasped my sparking hands behind my back and gave him a faint smile and a non-committal "oh."

Oskar went to confer with Rabbi Mandelbaum, who gave me another assessing look.

The sheen of sweat on my face was edging into gross territory so I locked myself in the women's washroom and splashed cold water on my face and hair, blotting myself dry with one of the folded hand towels laid out in a rectangular basket for my convenience. My eyes were clear, and aside from a splotch of heightened color on my cheeks, I looked normal.

My body, however, throbbed in a dull ache. I was cold and I wished I had some ginger chews.

Rohan was waiting for me when I emerged. He placed his hand on the small of my back. "Walk with me?"

He looked uncharacteristically solemn, so I accompanied him in silence, reading some of the names on the gravestones as we cut through one section of the cemetery.

"You holding up okay?" he said, turning us onto a tree-lined path.

I rubbed my arms. "I feel like I have the flu. Esther will be here tomorrow. We'll get Lilith out and all will be well."

After another few minutes' walk, Ro squatted down by one of the graves on the lawn. He pulled a smooth pebble from his pocket and placed the rock on the corner of the gravestone. "Hi, snake."

I knelt down as best I could in my pencil skirt.

Asha Sarah Patel. Beloved daughter and cousin. The inscription, along with the dates of her birth and death were set into a heart in the marble gravestone that lay flush with the ground.

Rohan sat down on the grass next to the grave and placed his palm in the center of the heart.

"Hi, Asha." I sat down beside him. "Why did you call her 'snake?'"

"A.S.P. Her initials. It started when I was little and since it annoyed her, I kept it up."

"Asp! That's why the song title. Some of the track names were leaked," I said.

He gave me an odd look. "Nava, you don't have to read my fan boards. If you want to know something, ask me."

"I wasn't sure I had the right."

He tucked a curl behind my ear. "Sweetheart, you have the right."

I leaned in to his touch, savoring it. "I thought the title was some metaphor about me being the death of you."

He raised an eyebrow. "Not everything is about you."

"But mostly it is, right?" I grinned at him.

He rolled his eyes then leaned in and stole a quick kiss.

"The song," I said. "Is it about a specific memory?"

He plucked a handful of grass out, systematically shredding the blades. "It's the last remaining track I have to write and I can't get it right."

"Could you release the album without it?"

"No. Asp starts my story. It has to be there and *Ascending* has to be released next month on the twenty-seventh."

"Why?"

"Because Asha's favorite artist was Prince and he wrote *Purple Rain*, her favorite album, when he was twenty-five."

"Did he release it on the twenty-seventh?"

He smiled and tapped the gravestone. "It's her birthday. Asha made me promise that since she couldn't write music and release her own album at twenty-five, that I should immortalize her at that age."

"I like her logic."

"You would." He lost his smile. "I can't let her down again."

I scratched at my arms. "You'll get it."

Rohan caught my hands. "Tell me how I can help you, but stop hurting yourself."

My skin had red nail marks slashed across them. "Distract me. Talk to me about Asha."

He laughed softly. "You'll love this. When we were little, she'd dress me up in her mom's clothes because she wanted a younger sister."

"Did she make you have tea parties?"

"I wish. She'd make us pretend we were TLC and perform their albums."

"That doesn't seem so bad."

"And Destiny's Child."

"Right."

He ducked his head. "And Spice Girls."

"Tell me you were Scary."

"Baby."

"Did she put you in a blonde wig?"

Rohan scrunched up his face and I lost it, howling with laughter. "Shut up." He nudged me. "I've never come here with anyone."

I stopped laughing and squeezed his hands in mine.

"Not even my family since her funeral. It's too hard to be here with them, so I come by myself."

"I'm honored you brought me."

He jumped up, pulling me to my feet. "I wanted you to meet."

He said it so matter-of-factly, granting me the same importance in his life that she'd had. My bones unstitched and knit back together with the shattering simplicity of a single thought:

I love him.

I thought I'd been in love once before with Cole, but that was puppy love. Sweet and young and light and short-lived. My feelings for Rohan were anchored in every atom. We were each other's best friends, lovers, protectors, and confidants. There was a strength and a surety and a completeness to it. He was the one I wanted to wake up to and fall asleep with, the heart of my heart, my one and only.

The moment I'd seen him standing in the alley those many months ago, I'd been intrigued. The moment he'd first kissed me, I'd been besotted. The moment he'd trusted me with Asha here, I'd fallen head-over-heels.

I pressed a hand to my side like I'd run a marathon and couldn't quite catch my breath, but the bliss of this new-found knowledge was better than any runner's high.

He was my person and I loved him with everything inside me.

Was it tacky to tell him here? Standing at his cousin's grave? Maybe when we got back to the car?

We needed to get back to the car.

"Ro–"

"It's him!" A dozen women cut through the row of trees lining the nearby walkway. Forget any semblance of privacy and respect in this place of mourning. It was like the running of the bulls as they charged us. They were led by Tia, who'd forgone her red leather trench for a demure sundress.

Bitch shouldn't have stood me up.

"Can I have your autograph? I know it's rude, but I'm your biggest fan." Tia's voice quivered. Oh, she was good. As she spoke, she drew closer and closer to Rohan, away from the rest of the group who'd hung back waiting to see how he reacted. She reached into her black purse and pulled out a pen and photo of Ro from his Fugue State Five days.

"Quite the secret identity, Rasha." Only we could hear her. "I had no idea."

"Now that we both know where we stand." He trained a glittering smile on her.

"You could kill me." She glanced back. "But do you really want to replace the adoring look in their eyes with the fear that nightmares exist? You're supposed to keep them safe, not terrify them."

She held the pen out to him.

Rohan's mouth flattened and he snatched the pen away to autograph the picture. The move was the starter pistol, the other women rushing him.

Tia took her photo and disentangled herself from the mini mob. "Do you get off on being with the big bad hunter, sweetheart?"

This demon piece of shit was fucking with the man I loved. Defiling Asha's grave with her presence.

I gripped her hip, letting my magic flare between my palm and her dress. "I get off on *being* the big bad hunter, sweetheart."

She jerked away, her pupils dilated. "Fascinating. I suspected something was up with the interview request, but I never imagined this."

Adrenaline flooded my system, but I'd only used my magic, not Lilith's. My rage blew away some of my achiness. The hard part was not eviscerating Tia on the spot.

"Tia!" A petite Asian woman held up a signed photo, triumphant.

I jerked my hands behind my back, shutting my magic down.

"Way to go, D'arcy!" Tia said. "Told you he was a class act."

"Holy moly." A woman in a dress patterned with cats

was standing on Asha's grave. "Is this your cousin that died?"

"Please get away from there," Rohan said, his voice strained, but still attempting to be gracious and finish signing autographs.

Tia raised her eyebrows and went to look. She stared at the grave for a very long moment, then started laughing. Doubled over, uncontrollable, gasping for air, belly laughter.

"What's so funny?" he snarled.

"Ask Desiderio."

Rohan froze, confusion morphing into horror. "No."

Why would Drio know? Had this been a demon he'd hunted? But no, that was dumb. Drio always made the kill. After the demon who murdered Asha escaped, he'd honed his tracking skills and ruthlessly dispatched his assignments. His record since her death was flawless. I'd even creeped on his Brotherhood stats via Orwell one slow day, just to see it for myself. Every single demon he'd tracked, he killed. Every single demon he'd hunted was gone.

Every single demon except for one.

Oh. My. God.

The other women were murmuring and exchanging odd looks.

"Everyone needs to leave." I clapped my hands together. "Yo! Now!"

"We don't need to listen to you," one snarked.

"Get out of here," Rohan roared.

The women fled.

"She didn't scream in the end. I'll give her that." Tia knelt down and petted the grave like she was complimenting a precocious student.

We were screened from prying eyes by the trees, plus,

she had to die, so I blasted her, but she vanished before I hit her, reappearing behind Rohan and wagging a finger at me.

"You weren't the demon Drio was tracking." Rohan looked perilously close to short-circuiting, his left eyebrow twitching, and his body trembling like he was battling both shell shock and nuclear rage.

"No. But he was on *my* radar. The ultimate hunter. The pride of the Brotherhood." She wrinkled her nose. "It was such fun to take Desiderio down. And look! I got two for the price of one." She leaned toward Rohan, inhaled and shivered. "You are going to be a delight to destroy."

Rohan lunged for her, stumbling off-balance when he swiped at empty air.

She was gone.

"Nee!" Ari and Baruch were sprinting our way. My brother skidded to a stop and grabbed my arms. "What happened?"

"The demon we're tracking. She killed Asha."

A howl of unendurable pain ripped from Rohan's throat. He stared into the distance, his eyes blazing with a fanatical intensity. "We're going to burn her world to the ground."

22

It was a tense and silent drive into the downtown core, and even the cool art deco buildings around Olvera street didn't lighten Rohan's stormy mood.

I met Baskerville in a wide-open plaza featuring a massive twisted tree with exposed gnarled roots situated across the street from this beautiful little church called La Placita, Our Lady Queen of Angels.

Hispanic families dressed in church finery poured out the front doors, headed for the parking lot next door. Chic parents held the hands of little girls in white poufy dresses and young boys in white suits. Even the grandmothers set a gold standard of working it, sporting dresses in bold colors that showed off their every curve.

Baskerville had glamoured his blue skin and snout and as a result, looked more like a bespoke Wallace from "Wallace and Gromit" than ever.

The two of us strolled along Olvera Street, a tree-lined pedestrian zone, flanked by Mexican restaurants pumping out hip-shaking salsa. Two long lines of red painted stalls in the center of the street hawked a variety of products: Frieda Kahlo T-shirts, gold jewelry, sugar skull printed wallets, Los

Luchadores masks, candles with photos of the saints, embroidered dresses, and miniature guitars painted vivid blues, reds, and purples.

Too vivid. The riot of colors hurt my eyes, the music set my teeth on edge, and the scent of churros made my stomach rumble in disgust.

I presented the demon with the tzitzit I'd stolen from Rabbi Mandelbaum. "We good?"

He tucked it into a suit pocket. "It's satisfactory."

I jumped out of the way of a little girl barreling down the street on a ribbon-bedecked scooter.

Baskerville handed me a hinged pendant covered in engraved symbols, dangling from a silver chain. He stopped me from opening it. "Not until you're ready to use it."

I slid the chain over my head, but could sense nothing magic about it. It was heavy for its size and cool against my skin. "If you're faking me out with some dud, I'll kill you. Ooh. Avocado sauce. Let's try that."

"Thank you, no. I'm not hungry."

"Don't be rude," Rohan fell into step with us.

"Hiya, babe. Good timing," I said.

Rohan still had that feral quality from our Tia encounter, emanating the off-kilter energy of a man on the verge of going postal.

I hustled us all into the shack of a restaurant that Ro and I had scoped out before the meet-up as the best venue to conduct our business. Aside from the galley kitchen there were maybe eight square wood tables with benches. A family of six squished in together around a table at the front eyed us warily, but other than that, the place was empty, the dinner rush not yet begun.

Baskerville glared at me but he didn't disappear because one of Ro's finger blades was jammed in between the demon's shoulder blades. One wrong jostle, even to portal out, could kill him.

Ro maneuvered himself and the demon so their backs were against the wall, facing out to the stalls.

I sat across from them and ordered the tacquitos with avocado sauce, thanking the waiter for our tortilla chips and salsa. My stomach turned over at the smell of food, but if it meant keeping up "all is well" appearances in front of the demon, I'd muscle the food down with a smile on my face and ask for seconds.

Rohan popped the tab on his iced tea. "Gotta hand it to you. You're excellent at ferreting things out."

"What on this green and vibrant earth could you possibly want?" Baskerville frowned minutely at the tortilla-chip-and-salsa sandwich I stuffed into my mouth. "And please, spare me the posturing and the theatrics. I've already moved everything of value in the warehouse, so it's no good threatening me with that."

"Lots of on-call minions, huh?" Rohan said. "I want information. I get it, you live."

"Information such as what?"

"Hybris." I thanked the cook who'd placed a paper container with my two tacquitos drenched in avocado sauce in front of me, swallowed down the taste of bile, and cut off the smallest piece imaginable. "Where is she? We want every known hiding place of hers on earth, and a way to find her in the demon realm, too."

"Oh, now I have no idea."

Rohan jerked his hand on the kill spot and the demon flinched, all color draining from his face.

"I'm telling you the truth," Baskerville insisted.

"Then who does? And think faster."

"There's an ooliach who frequents a, shall we say, less-than-top-notch establishment on Seventh Avenue called Deke's. Go bother him."

Something slithered against my leg and I yelped.

"Ah, yes. You might like to know that those are the poisonous barbs extending from my limbs. Pain upon pain, hellfire for days before you die. All if I so much as break the skin." Baskerville smiled at Rohan pleasantly. "So it comes to you. Will you remove that very annoying knife or will poor dear Nava meet a slow and drawn-out end?"

Rohan retracted his blades.

"Bless your heart." Baskerville stood up and straightened his cuffs. "And if it wasn't already abundantly clear, please never call me again. My business is closed to you."

I could only nod, busy forcing the tacquito down, but the moment the demon's back was toward me, I nailed his kill spot with a thin current.

Buh-bye, Baskerville.

No one noticed the demoncide. The family had left, the cook whistled along to the mariachi music playing on his radio while he washed dishes, and the pedestrians were too pre-occupied with shopping to pay attention to what was happening inside the tiny restaurant.

Rohan raised an eyebrow.

"What?" I wiped sauce off my finger. I felt bad about killing him, but I wasn't an idiot. I'd left Malik alive because he was too powerful and I was too drained at our last encounter to kill him. I'd pay for that when he next came after me, so I wasn't about to look over my shoulder for another angry demon. "We couldn't let him walk away. He would have retaliated and I've got enough on my plate."

"No shit," Rohan said, "but I thought I'd have to rationalize that fact to you after *I'd* killed him."

"Yeah, we're skipping the rationalizations now."

Ro bussed our table, throwing out the garbage and

placing the pop cans in a bin set out for recyclables. What a mensch.

My heart swelled two sizes. Maybe I could tell him now after he cleaned up my trash? Was that too weird? I mean, we'd change places before I said it. Hit the gazebo at the head of the street–that would be perfect. The thick ropy trunk of the sprawling tree with its deep roots would wave its leathery, dark green leaves at us in benediction and whatever mariachi tune floated over to us from the market would become "our song," the one Ro would sing to me as he twirled me around the room, leaving me breathless with love and laughter.

I could tell him then.

When Ro came back, his features were grim. "I paid. Ooliach time."

Or not.

SEVENTH AVENUE RAN through some nice areas but the closer we got to Matteo Street over in the Arts District near DSI, the more depressed it became. Various tent-cities occupied trash-strewn sidewalks in front of empty warehouses vying to be leased for film productions. Homeless people lay on the street watching planes rumble overhead, while the stench of grease wafted over everything from a nearby fast food chain.

Deke's was down a couple blocks from the Greyhound Terminal, not far from the huge salmon pink factory that anchored the corner at Alameda. It was dark, dingy, and smelled like old Ripple chips. And that was on the outside.

The bartender looked surprised to see us enter, probably because the closed sign and locked front door were grimy with disuse. Also because he had two heads and, I'm betting, didn't see a lot of walk-in human clients.

Sorry. Portal-in.

"Greetings and salutations, assorted spawn. We're looking for an ooliach," I said.

The various fanged, horned, and snarly creatures rose as one to their feet, hooves, and crab legs.

Ten minutes later, I'd decimated the bar's pool of returning clientele with good old-fashioned magic lightning, discovered that kishi, these two-faced hyena demons were fucking batshit but would conveniently rip each other to shreds when they bled, and determined that yes, there was in fact booze too foul for human consumption.

While I'd single-handedly dealt with the rest of the demons, Rohan had tracked the ooliach. Okay, found him face-down drunk on the bar. Given his human form was about five feet tall and a hundred pounds soaking wet, the two empty glasses in front of him constituted a bender.

The weaselly little shit–did I mention they were weasel demons?–took one look at Rohan and his Rasha ring, and sneered. "Go away. I've had a really bad day."

Then he lost his balance and almost fell off the stool.

Ro steadied him–by the scruff of the neck. "It'll be your last day if you don't talk."

The ooliach hiccuped, wafting pickles.

I took a large step back.

"Whaddyawant?" the demon slurred.

"Where's Hybris?" I said.

The demon held up one of his two furry, twig-like fingers, then passed out, hitting the bar so hard, he snapped two whiskers off of his snout.

Ro grabbed his arm. "Portal us back to DSI."

"What about your car?"

"Fuck the car."

Fuck the car? Yikes. I portalled us.

We landed in a supply closet on the main floor. My best option for using portal magic undetected.

I was half-jogging to keep up with Rohan, hell-bent for the iron room, when he swung us into the stairwell and almost collided with Rabbi Mandelbaum.

"What's this?" the rabbi snapped. Dude's kippah was half-off his head and his bloodshot eyes looked one more sleepless night away from total unhingement. He turned to me. "Deal with your mission so I can have Rohan back helping me."

Rohan bristled. "The demon on *our* mission killed my cousin. So I'm going to take as long as I fucking have to to find her. Got it?"

"Watch your tone, Rohan. Your disrespect has gotten out of hand." Mandelbaum cut a sideways glance at me, before stepping aside to let us pass.

Yeah, yeah. I'm the bad guy for leading your precious hunter astray.

Dragging the limp ooliach by an arm, Rohan flung open a door, and tossed the demon inside.

Torture time had begun.

It was obvious Rohan didn't want me to participate (and honestly neither did I) and his movements with the blade made it clear he took no joy in this, not like Drio had when I met him. I would have left Rohan to it, but when I reached for the door he stopped, words on his lips I didn't need to hear to decipher: please don't leave me alone, not in this darkness.

My ass went numb from the iron floor, plus weird green demon fluids that had missed the drain had soaked my shoes, but I stayed. If my boyfriend was going to lose it, I needed to be there.

We never got Tia's location in the demon realm, and by

the time the ooliach gave up the address of her son's place in the valley, Rohan was bathed in sweat and there wasn't a lot left of the demon.

Rohan pulled out his phone and hit a number, ignoring the twitching creature at his feet.

"How were the funerals?" On speakerphone, Drio sounded uncharacteristically somber, the usual sexiness of his Italian-accented English muted. I couldn't help the small stab of loss at hearing his voice for the first time since he'd become, if not my enemy, no longer my friend, either.

There was a rustling on Drio's end. "Say something, paesano. What's up?"

"The demon Nava and I are tracking? Hybris. She killed Asha. It wasn't the one you were after."

Dead silence from Drio.

The ooliach jerked and splooshed out some more gross fluid.

"I need you here," Rohan said.

"No. *You* have to kill Hybris."

"Fuck, Drio." Ro raked a hand through his hair. "You don't need absolution. You have as much right to take her down as I do."

"It's not that." Drio exhaled sharply. "If I come back, I'll lose myself to the hate. I can't keep living that way, Ro. It's killing me."

I closed my eyes against the quiver in his voice. Drio didn't quiver. Drio was one of the deadliest people I'd ever met.

"It doesn't mean I love Asha any less," Drio said.

"I would never think that." Ro sounded fierce enough to convince even Drio who gave a quiet, "okay."

"Come back anyway," Ro said. "You need to move on. There doesn't have to just be one person."

Drio's laugh was harsh. "I wouldn't go that far. I can't

stay stuck in the past, but maybe the present is good enough. Take that bitch down."

"I swear it." Rohan tucked the phone away. "Let's go." His eyes burned with a feverish gleam.

"Rohan." He didn't stop, so I put the ooliach out of his misery and followed, Robin to Ro's totally psycho Batman.

Two months ago, I'd have fought Rohan about his behavior, but with my new in-love realization, it was hard to tell him he was wrong. He wanted to kill Hybris and get closure; I just wasn't sure that was going to let the ugly gash he bore from Asha's death heal cleanly.

Rohan needed to forgive, himself most of all. I didn't know if he'd be receptive to my insights in his current frame of mind, so I supported him by portalling us.

Hybris wasn't there but we found her son Koros in baggy pants, lounging by the pool and surrounded by succubi in thong bikinis. Maybe this was normal for the valley?

I machine gunned the females with my magic in their tramp stamps. I mean, yeah, the tattoos were offensive, but those glittery butterflies and hearts were also their kill spots.

Koros was so high, it took him a moment to notice that no one was grinding up on him anymore. "The fuck are you?"

Of course he had one of those stupid gold dental grills. I itched to kill this walking travesty so badly, but who was I to deprive Ro of the pleasure?

"Where's Hybris?" Ro said.

"Not here."

"I'm going to say this one more time. Where's? Hybris?"

Koros shot him the finger.

And when Rohan left the note saying "sorry we missed

263

you," on the lounger, the gold dental grille kept it from flying away.

BARUCH PEERED in through the bungalow's window back at Dev and Maya's, an actual worried expression on his face at the sight of Ro sitting on the floor with his knees drawn up to his chest and his shoulders slumped.

I shook my head.

Baruch turned to speak to Ari who bobbed up behind him.

Ari tugged on his ear lobe, our twin code for "I have your back."

I gave him a sad smile. There was nothing he could do for me if there was nothing I could do for Rohan.

"How do I tell my family that I let her go?" Ro's words startled me. He hadn't spoken since he'd killed Koros an hour ago.

I fingered the pendant containing the Bullseye like it was a talisman. "You couldn't have killed Tia at the cemetery. Those women had their phones out. You would have caused mass panic. You can't beat yourself up about this."

"Still, I should have been able to do something more than just let her walk away."

"No." I hugged him, his head resting against my chest since he was seated on the floor and I was on the sofa. "Remember when we found out that it was Asmodeus who'd taken Ari? You told me to take what I was feeling and let it fuel me not consume me. You gotta do the same. We'll get her. I promise you. I promise Asha. But you need to let yourself out of this guilt prison you've built. Because if you don't, then Tia wins. She becomes this specter that ruins the rest of your life

264

and I can't imagine Asha would have wanted that for you."

His arms tightened around me and he dragged in a shaky breath. "Okay."

"Go. Talk to your parents."

"I don't deserve you." He stood up.

"Au contraire, baby. I'm exactly what you deserve."

"Back soon." He kissed me, then left wearing a troubled expression.

I called Leo from the bedroom, flopped on the bed. I squirmed over to lay on Rohan's side. Sniffing his pillow may have been involved.

"Where are you?" I said. "I hear muzak."

"Grocery shopping. I'm glam like that."

"Can you go sit in your car or something?"

"Why?"

"Ro spoke to Drio."

"Good for him. Debit please," Leo said to the checkout person.

I had half her attention at best right now, but as I told her about Tia and Asha, the silence on the other end grew more focused.

"He doesn't want to come back from Rome to avenge the great love of his life." Leo slammed her car door. "And?"

Why was I surrounded by stubborn people? Soon as this mission was over, I was going to get a group of easy-going friends. "Did you hear the rest of it? The part about the hate killing him?"

"You know what I didn't hear? Any mention of me."

"Leo."

"No," she growled. "I can't go there."

"He's not going to kill you. He won't even hurt you. I really believe that."

"He already hurt me. I didn't expect him to be in love

with me, or even get over Asha. If I'd had someone like that, I'd love her forever, too. But all he saw when he threatened me was a PD. After everything that had been building between us, he looked at me and saw scum."

"To be fair, we kind of dropped a bomb on him."

"Are you taking his side?"

"I'm always on your side. I just think that if you have a chance at love you should take it."

"I'm living the Cole years all over again."

"What's that supposed to mean?"

"You have Rohan who's stupid for you. Yay, you. You were exactly like this when you were with Cole, trying to get everyone else around happily settled. Don't, Nee. You can't expect us to find that just because you suddenly did."

"Maybe you would if you actually put yourself out there."

"You of all people cannot be saying that to me."

"And yet, here I am. Yes. Drio was a big idiot and walked away while Rohan gave me chance after chance. But I almost lost Ro and I don't want you losing out. So you get me pushing you because I've watched you find reasons not to get involved with lots of great people."

"I was involved with Madison."

"You used Madison. Mutually used," I amended. "You said it yourself. You and she had sexual chemistry and a solid friendship and it was never going to be more than that. Which is fine but there was no need to commit and that's why you didn't run from her."

She made a noise to interrupt me, but I barreled ahead.

"Think about it. Drio wouldn't have even given you a warning if he wasn't stupid for you, too. Call him. Text him. Make contact." The quality I'd sensed in Drio's voice was now painfully clear. "He sounded so lonely."

"Have you spoken to him?" she said.

"No."

"Have you told Le Mitra you love him?"

"Who said I did?"

She waited me out.

"Okay, yes. I totally love him, but how did you know?"

"Know that you love him or know that you haven't told him?" she said.

"Both. Either."

She waited me out again.

"Whatever. Are you going to call Drio?"

"No chance. You're incredibly irritating, but I love you. Schmugs."

"You're incredibly annoying, but I love you, too." I sighed. "Schmugs."

I tossed the phone on the bed right as the front door to the bungalow opened, grateful I was spared having the most important three words of my life being overheard like cheap gossip.

"In here," I called out.

Ro lounged in the doorway, looking a tad emotionally frayed.

"How'd it go?"

"Shitty, but cathartic, if that makes sense."

"It does."

We went back to his house for the night, because as Ro said, he had good whiskey, and between learning about Asha and Ethan, he was drinking himself into a stupor. "Tonight is my next Thursday, Sparky."

"Rage away, Snowflake. I'll keep you safe."

I cut him off when he had to be cut off, covered him with a blanket when he passed out, and held him tight all night. And I may have whispered that I loved him a time or two, hoping it made it into his dreams and took away some of his pain.

23

R ohan was up early on Monday morning, seated at the piano determined to nail Asha's song. "After I kill Hybris," he said, "I'm going to write a reprise to 'Asp' that will go after 'Slay,' the final song. *Then* the story will be finished."

It would be wonderful if he could write his way into closure, though I doubted it was that simple. Hmm. This wasn't the moment to gloat that my song was on the album, but was it the moment to tell him how I felt?

"Ro?"

He was lost to me, testing out chords.

Apparently not. I kissed him goodbye and portalled to the address I had for Millicent's apartment in West Los Angeles. Portalling was a fairly gentle sensation. A slight tug from my core propelling me forward as I popped out of one place and appeared in the other.

I started strong. I'd had a good night sleep, and my detox symptoms had subsided. I fixed the address in my head, closed my eyes, and eliminated the spaces in between. Why hello, gentle tug... and whaaaat?

I stopped dead, yanked backward like someone had grabbed my waist with a giant hook.

I landed on my feet, none the worse for wear, though that would change in approximately four seconds when the big rig bearing down on me splattered me all over the California highway.

I tried to flash out.

Hoooonk!

Three seconds.

The semi's brakes screeched; burning rubber filled the air.

Two seconds.

I was a deer in the headlights, frozen in place in the second-to-left lane of an eight-lane highway. Nowhere to run. Nowhere to hide.

The driver's face contorted in horror. I was going to be dead, but she was going to have to live with the consequences.

Gritting my teeth, I dug deep.

I flashed out with a millisecond to spare. The truck whipped past, its rush of wind propelling me through my portal. Better for that driver to think she was seeing things than live with a death.

Trust me.

I tumbled onto the side lawn of Millicent's place. It was another hazy, smoggy morning, already very hot and very dry, but I was shivering, bathed in cold sweat. There was no way I'd miscalculated that badly.

I checked Lilith's prison.

The box pulsed, that oily black light spilling out from all the seams. Lilith actively trying to get me killed was bad. Was it the end of the world? Not if the familiar thin woman stepping out of a taxi had anything to say about it.

Esther had refused my offer to pick her up at the

airport, saying she liked to have alone time to decompress after the stress of flying.

I bounded over and threw my arms around her, crushing her giant purse.

She pressed a hand to her heart. "You never heard of waving?"

"Yeah, but I wanted to hug you." I took her suitcase, my adrenaline jitters from the truck episode smoothing into a warm mellow buzz at her presence.

This stubborn old witch was one of my favorite people in the entire world and having her here was a shot of hope. With the Bullseye hanging around my neck in its pendant, the sun shining merrily, and Sienna within reach, I practically skipped along the flagstone path.

Even the clatter of Esther's suitcase wheels tapped out an up-tempo staccato.

Millicent's apartment was actually one of two buildings on the property, each vaguely Spanish-looking, that flanked a long rectangular pool. An abundance of trees cast dappled pockets of shade and kept the complex cool. The place in question was located at the far end of the north building, with a private staircase leading to the second-floor apartment.

The gauzy curtains were cracked open wide enough to see that no one was in the living room or kitchen.

Esther pushed me behind her. "The doormat has a pressure sensitive ward on it. And that door." She rummaged in her oversized purse for a pair of reader glasses and slid them on. "The ward on it is a thing of beauty. What a waste of talent."

I sat down on the top stair, but didn't even have a chance to get comfortable, before she announced, "Get up, lazy bones."

The front door now stood open.

I stepped into the humid foyer. "What if Sienna shows up?"

"She won't kill *me*."

"How reassuring."

"Fine. I won't let her hurt you either." She pushed her glasses into her hair. "Don't let me forget these are here."

"Does that happen a lot?"

"Getting old is the pits."

The apartment had sponged yellow walls with stenciled ivy paint around the doorframes. It was an interesting choice with the red and blue modular furniture. The walls were bare, not a single personal memento in the place.

I reached for a blue glass vase filled with blue marbles. "It's so clean in here."

"*Stop.*"

I froze, bent forward, my hand hovering in mid-air and my fingertips barely touching the glass.

"Get under the dining room table."

I did as I was told, scrunching up into a tight ball under the heavy wooden table to make room for Esther and the suitcase. "What's going on?"

"This is an old building. They're not well sealed. Even the tidiest housekeeper can't prevent dust motes floating in the air. The room is glamoured."

"Booby trapped, too?"

"I can't tell. But better safe than sorry. I need to remove the glamour from inside the room, but we don't want to be exposed when it happens."

"Why not?" I said.

She flexed her fingers, pushed them slowly outward, and then snapped them sharply down.

The air splintered, falling around us in translucent shards. They shattered against the wooden floor with a loud crash, melting into the wood.

I snatched a shard out of the air before it hit. Solid and deadly sharp. I tossed it out onto the floor. I was totally learning that trick.

"All clear," Esther said.

The glamour hadn't replaced the questionable interior decorating, but it did reveal that the walls weren't bare at all.

They were covered in photos.

I helped Esther to her feet. "Damn, lady. You're good."

"You should have seen me before the cancer." She turned in a slow circle. "I don't sense any dark magic or other wards." She removed the purse she'd been wearing messenger bag-style and dropped it on the sofa. "Let's contact Sienna."

She pulled something out of her bag.

"Whatcha got? Eye of newt? Toe of frog?" I snatched the Tupperware out of her hands and opened it. "*Rugelach*?!"

Esther grunted, heading into the kitchen and placing the Tupperware on the counter. "That stupid Shakespeare play set our community's reputation back millennia."

"That's your takeaway? You're bribing the Wicked Witch of the West." I contained my pout that she never made me those stupid cookies.

"A goodwill gesture, in case she shows." Closing the container, she dug into her pocket and pulled out a black rubber bracelet with "Fuck Cancer" in white on it. "Sienna bought this when she heard about my diagnosis. Wore it in solidarity." She traced a finger over the embossed letters then handed it to me. "Ever since Sienna disappeared, I've been trying to contact her. Magically."

"Are we talking magic voicemail, magic FaceTime, or magic email?"

Esther mimed for me to zip my lips. "More like a magic tap on the shoulder. They are fairly gentle and wouldn't have worked to contact her before, but now that I have this?" She pulled out a Ziplock bag filled with small, spiky, olive green leaves. "It will amplify the tap to a punch. Hopefully, she'll answer."

"I'm not sure I should be part of this."

Esther's eyes narrowed.

I blurted out about the side effects I'd been having and my reluctance to use any more of Lilith's magic.

"Hallelujah," she said. "The girl sees sense. You didn't go far enough down that path for there to be lasting effects. Once she's out, you should be back to normal in a couple days. No magic rehab for you."

"Is that a thing?"

"I'd make it a thing." She unzipped the baggie and removed a leaf. "And I wasn't planning to involve you anyway. I don't want Sienna sensing the dark magic and coming after you." Esther placed the leaf under her tongue, held the bracelet cupped between her palms and sent out her magic punch.

Sienna didn't respond.

Esther prodded me back into the living room. "Give her some time to answer."

"Here." I tossed her a set of latex gloves that I had stuffed in my pocket, my attention drifting between examining the dog-eared paperbacks for hidden documents and examining Tessa and Sienna's lives unfold in photos.

There were even faded pictures featuring a slight brunette that must have been Millicent. A few showed her pregnant, but none showed her holding Sienna.

It was weird seeing a young Sienna goofing around with Tessa, who was maybe ten years her senior and as much a sister as if she'd been blood.

I'd have meted out worse on the Brotherhood if they'd taken Ari from me, so it's not like I didn't understand why

Sienna had attacked the Los Angeles chapter. But what if in taking her revenge Sienna unleashed the apocalypse? She had to be stopped.

I multitasked, going through the contents of the apartment while summing up everything that had happened with Mandelbaum and Lilith since Esther and I had last seen each other.

I pulled the pendant out of my shirt. "These symbols are protective, not destructive, right?"

"Yes. They're keeping the Bullseye safe." Esther ran a thumb over the front, then dropped the pendant lightly against my chest. "I want Lilith out of you today. The vessel is in my purse and the others are on stand-by to portal in. Raquel said we could go to her place when we were finished and get it done."

I carefully replaced the books I'd searched through and hugged her again. Shouldn't this dark magic leaking into me make me want to get all destructo, instead of wanting to put on my sweats, watch Super Bowl commercials, and cry?

"Don't get weepy." She stepped back with a pat to my shoulder. "Isaac and I were on the same flight. That man snores like a stuffed-up elephant. He was vibrating my seat at the back of the plane."

"Don't mock Rabbi Abrams."

"I've known the man for over forty years. I'll mock all I want."

"He must be here for Mandelbaum's big meeting."

"Mandelbaum." Esther examined the entertainment cabinet. "He's been harassing Raquel."

"Raquel held her own. But yeah, he's on the warpath for witches."

"He's on the warpath to find one he can use. He doesn't give a damn about us other than how we can serve him."

"If Sienna targeted the Brotherhood because of what

happened to Tessa, she'll go ballistic if he hurts any innocent witches," I said.

"I hope it doesn't come to that."

We had no luck in the living room, so we moved into the kitchen, methodically searching every drawer and cabinet.

I rummaged through the junk drawer. There were old chopstick packages, a cloth measuring tape, a tiny battery-operated fan, and a rolling pin.

"As soon as Lilith's out, I'm going to take everyone out for a fancy dinner. All the witches, and Rabbi A, and Ari, and Rohan, and Baruch, and Kane and the L.A. Rasha. Oh, and Maya and Dev."

Esther opened a drawer revealing pots and pans inside. "How are you going to pay for it all?"

"Rohan obviously. We're celebrating his girlfriend being alive."

"He's a lucky man," she said wryly.

"Right?" I opened the freezer. There was a freezer-burned bag of corn and a cloudy tray of ice. "This is pointless."

We hit the jackpot in the bedroom.

"It's like conspiracy central." I whistled at the grainy photos of an Area 51-esque compound in the desert that were tacked to the walls. All the angles were covered: from aerial views to shots from every side taken using a telephoto lens.

A huge map of the California desert was also pinned up, with sections crossed out in marker. It was exactly what Bastijn had been doing to find Sienna and would have been funny if it wasn't a hunt for a powerful witch mirroring a hunt for a secret compound.

"Fuck." Esther picked up a crescent moon pendant from the dresser.

I scurried over because she didn't drop F-bombs.

"Is that the necklace Tessa was wearing in the photo I have of her and Ferdinand?" I sniffed the air. "I smell bitter lemon."

She pressed down on one of the points of the pendant and it popped open, revealing a narrow hidden compartment filled with a pale yellow powder. The smell of bitter lemon intensified.

"Erocine powder," she said. "Its organic base is a mild toxin, but according to lore, witches would combine it with dark magic and let it sit, growing in potency until it matured to full power on the summer solstice. It would have been bright yellow at that point and instantly fatal."

"Does it lose its strength? Because it's almost white again."

Esther closed up the pendant. "Yes. Erocine powder was banned by our community about a hundred years ago. Tessa may have been planning to use it on Ferdinand."

"Or Mandelbaum. It would make sense. She hated Rasha and here was the leader. She could have gone along with his plans as a way of getting close enough to take him out. Pity."

"Condoning murder now, are you?" she said.

"Meet the man and then get back to me." I photographed the compound photos.

"Finish up and we'll head to Raquel's. I'll meet you in the living room."

"On it." I sent the photos to Ari, with a short note explaining where I'd found them and that we needed to know where and what this place was.

"Where are my damn glasses?" I heard Esther say.

Chuckling, I headed down the hallway after her and stepped into the living room doorway. "On your..."

Esther pressed one hand to the bloody gaping gash across her throat, blood spilling through her fingers like silk. She reached out for me with the other, her fingertips grazing mine before she crumpled to the ground next to her purse.

"...head."

I shook my head, not computing. Not Esther and not Oskar, standing in the open front doorway.

Esther gave a gasping wheeze like a slow pressure cooker decompressing. Her eyelids fluttered and she fell still.

"Stop it." I fell to my knees, shaking her.

Oskar flung green magic at me. It passed over my head to hit the wall, eating through the plaster.

I blasted him into the kitchen, clamping my left hand against Esther's throat and attempting to use my healing magic to fix her.

To get her to breathe.

Blood coated my hands, viscous as molasses. Its hot sickly stench turned my stomach. I sealed her flaps of skin together and pressed my lips to hers to give her mouth-to-mouth.

Breathe.

She refused to obey. I fixed the image of Lilith's box in my mind and swiped inside the hairline fracture to grab a metaphoric fingerful of Lilith's magic straight from the source. Like stealing batter from a magic cookie bowl.

I couldn't get into the box. I could only access those wisps that were doing fuck-all.

Breathe.

Oskar jumped me, knocking me sideways. He grabbed my head and slammed it onto the ground, face first.

My vision doubled and a tinny ringing sound overpowered everything else. His acid magic sizzled through my scalp, hot rivers of lava burning their way into the side of my head. My hair fell to the ground in charred clumps.

I'd barely pushed myself up before he yanked my head back again.

My electric magic exploded over my skin, crackling away like a bonfire.

"Shut it down." Still standing behind me, he clamped my jaw, twisting my face up to his. "Or I'll melt that pretty face of yours before I kill you." His flat, expressionless eyes belied any promise of compassion.

I snapped his hold, twisting out from under him to slam my palm against his heart that beat strong and steady.

He didn't transform before my eyes to a flickering life force. No, Oskar remained flesh and blood, reminding me how human he was. Should I memory wipe him? Or should I cross that one remaining line and purposefully take a man's life?

Keep my last vestige of humanity or enact the only justice Esther would ever see?

I was breathless, caught between these two versions of myself, swept away by loss and hurtling toward the unavoidable. The inescapable.

I flooded him with my magic. This was worth becoming a monster for.

Oskar twitched and danced; his flesh bubbling from a light pink sunburn to black ash.

I poured more power into him, blinking against the electric magic pouring out of me, and then against the split-second image of Sienna standing there poker-faced.

His life drained from his body. I drank it in like an elixir until my puppet on a string thrashed one last time and his heartbeat stopped.

I hadn't even needed any of Lilith's magic to do it.

Outside, a car blasted The Beach Boys' "Good Vibrations." Light glinted off the photographs and dust motes danced through the air, beautiful, fat, silvery dots lazily bobbing in a sunbeam like it was an ocean.

I retrieved Esther's purse from under Oskar's body. Something jangled inside. "If those are her glasses, you're in so much trouble," I sang.

I fished around in the contents, finding the oval, clay vessel to contain Lilith.

"Silly me. Your glasses are still on your head." I smiled at Esther.

She smiled back, but not with her mouth, with the second set of smeared red lips Oskar had given her across her throat. The ones made deeper red and black by the acid burn that had torn her flesh apart and still hissed, dully.

I grabbed a raggedy tea towel from the kitchen and tied it around her neck like a scarf.

"Very jaunty." I kissed her forehead. Closed her eyes.

Once upon a time, I'd killed my first demon and called my brother to come save me. I knew better now. A phone call that could fix everything was a lie because there were certain things that could never be saved.

Esther's life.

My innocence.

Funny, what you didn't realize you had until it was gone.

I looked back at the mess, knowing it was my duty to clean up, that this was part of my job and that I ought to be able to do it alone. Then I shucked my burner phone out of my pocket and punched in Ro's contact with shaky fingers.

"Clean up on aisle nine," I said and began to laugh hysterically.

24

————

"You're not leaving that note." Rohan tossed a corner of the triple-layered, blue plastic tarp to Ari which they unrolled on the living room floor.

"That's incredibly short-sighted of you," I said.

He and my brother dragged Oskar's body on to it. "Are you seriously criticizing my decision-making skills in front of the man you just massive coronary'd to death?"

"Don't you dare define me by the one time I killed someone."

The guys tied off the corners so Oskar lay in a little tarp packet like fish in aluminum foil.

"One murder, one assist," Ari said. "As you didn't pull the trigger on Ilya." He kicked the dead man in the gut. "And you had no choice with this one."

"Oh, I had a choice," I said. "I could have memory wiped him and he'd never have remembered I was here."

"He still would have tried to kill you," my brother pointed out.

"Regardless. I *wanted* him dead. Still believe I'm not a monster?" I said to Rohan.

He sliced the Rasha's head off with a savage blow. "Still believe you are?"

"Nice thought, Snowflake, but catch-up decapitation doesn't count. Your hands are clean."

Could you regret something and still not want to change it?

I ran to the bathroom and threw up, heaving until there was nothing left inside me but the dark taint on my soul. I slammed on the tap, rinsed out my mouth, then squeezed half the bottle of aloe vera soap over my hands, furiously scrubbing my skin like I could wash away the symbolic blood as easily as the real stuff. *Out, out, damn spot.*

I scrubbed until my skin was red and raw and would have kept scrubbing except Rohan yanked my hands away, gently encasing them in a towel.

"Stop."

I pulled my hands away from the compassion in his touch, avoided the sympathy in his eyes.

Did it count as regret if, despite feeling like I'd lost an essential part of myself, I'd kill Oskar all over again if faced with the same choice? Would I have killed him if it meant Esther would survive?

I threw the towel on the vanity and marched back to the living room, locking down all my horror and disgust. Next Thursday. I'd collapse under the weight of what I'd done then. Right now, I had a war to win.

"Esther's death is not going to be in vain."

"I give up," Rohan muttered, right on my heels.

Kane stepped inside the tarp with the body. He'd arrived, glared at me, then wrapped an arm around my shoulder, and stayed by my side. "This entire system has broken down into utter fuckery."

"I wasn't the one to unleash the slaughter." I placed the note for Sienna with my burner phone number on the dining room table. "That's on Mandelbaum. And Sienna. I just embraced the bloodletting."

Kane's hands turned iridescent purple. Grimacing, he rubbed them over Oskar's naked chest. "I'm talking about the fact that I've been relegated to some kind of marinade. You're lucky I'm a good person, babyslay."

Ari froze. "What?"

He didn't speak with snark or sarcasm, just disbelief. Like Ari had grown up constantly being told by someone that the world was flat, and no matter how many times he patiently tried to prove otherwise because it was an important basic concept, it had been to no avail. But now that flat earther had done a 180 and Ari couldn't wrap his head around the fact that maybe he wouldn't have to fight this battle anymore.

"Babyslay. It's been my nickname for your sister for literally months now, catch up."

"No," Ari said slowly, "the other thing."

"I'm a good person," Kane repeated. "Obviously. No one but a good person would melt an entire unsexy evil henchman for a friend."

Rohan gathered up Oskar's clothing and stuffed it into a trash bag. "You're not leaving your phone number for Sienna. Stay away from her."

I watched my brother for a moment longer, but he shook his head at me and moved over to the window. "I thought you gave up," I said.

"I gave up trying to get you over your warped self-image," Rohan said. "I'm not half-done on this."

I frowned at the smear of blood I'd left on the edge of the note. "It's not ideal, but I have to tell her about Esther."

Or had I really seen her for a second and she already knew?

"She doesn't deserve that consideration," Rohan said.

Kane rolled the body over. "Could his ass be any hairier? This is not how I like my men."

"But dead and headless is okay?" Ari asked.

"If you're going to be all logical about it." Kane massaged his poison onto the body with sulky vigor.

"Think practically, then," I said. "Sienna might know where the compound is. If it's faster to ask her than have us track it down, we have to try." I left out that I had a magic back-up plan in case the note didn't work.

"And you think that after you tell her the Brotherhood killed her friend that she'll be in a sharing mood?" Rohan tied the bag of stained clothes closed.

"The enemy of my enemy is my friend." I crossed my fingers that having killed Esther's assassin would buy me some goodwill.

"Done." Kane stood up, cracked his neck, and stepped out of the tarp. His poisons were already kicking in, eating away at the Rasha's flesh.

"How long for the bones to dissolve?" Ari zipped up the protective chemical suit he'd brought and slid on the gloves.

"About a day?" Kane said.

"That works." Ari sealed the tarp with a ton of duct tape before slinging the body over his shoulder in a fireman's carry.

"Careful." I pointed to a spot where Kane's poison had eaten through.

"Back in a sec." Ari jumped into the shadows and entered the Emerald City, where he was going to leave the body. We didn't know if anyone else had the ability to access the shadows like Ari did, but in case someone did, we didn't want proof of this crime to exist, hence the poisonous finishing touch.

Nothing like body disposal to show you who your true friends were.

Kane went into the bathroom to scrub the poison off.

I moved the area rug back into place. "Crime scene cleaned. I'll grab Esther and we can get out of here."

I entered the kitchen and crouched down beside the body bag Rohan had put her in. I reached for her shoulders, but pulling her to her feet when she couldn't stand on her own wasn't going to work. I attempted to scoop her up, but that was weird, too. Maybe the answer was to sling her over my shoulder.

"Do you want me to take her?" Rohan said.

I love you for trying to spare me.

"She was my friend. I'll carry her." I stared down at the black body bag. "It looks like a garment bag, doesn't it?"

"Not really."

Esther's unseeing eyes.

"Hangers are vaguely people-shaped, so I'm right. I could unzip it and find a beautiful ball gown."

Her throat, eaten away by magic.

I gripped the counter.

"Nava?" Rohan clasped my shoulders.

"I can't..." I clawed at the neckline of my tattered and acid-burned shirt, hyperventilating.

"Sweetheart, you're in shock. You can breathe. You're not a monster. You saved yourself and you've suffered a huge trauma with Esther. Watch and breathe with me." Rohan planted himself in front of me, taking exaggerated deep breaths. "Your body knows what to do."

Yeah, it did, but it wasn't in control. I tried to tell Rohan, but the world and my oxygen supply fell away and all was black.

I CAME AROUND at the tug of my pendant being pulled off.

"You've got the fucking Bullseye. Use it!" Rohan held me in his arms, the only part of him not outlined in sharp, deadly blades.

"Wait." Raquel retrieved the vessel from Esther's purse. "The others will be here within the half hour. I need them all."

She wasn't blinged out and dressed to kill. She wore a denim mini, with a measuring tape slung around her neck and a handful of pins stuck haphazardly to the front of her green cap-sleeve shirt that brought out the red in her puffy eyes.

She wiped her eyes with an already soaked tissue, then stared at it, like she had no idea why it was in her hand.

"No Bullseye," I croaked out. I pushed against Ro's chest to make him put me down and when he ignored me, I wriggled onto my feet.

"You can't even stand. Stop fighting." Rohan retracted his blades, slid his arm around my waist and held me close. My wobbly legs had no issue with that.

I snatched the pendant back. "You're not using the Bullseye."

Rohan and Raquel gave me identical "yes, we are," scowls.

I needed to buy myself a couple of minutes to formulate my plea deal. I had one shot to convince these judges. "Where am I?"

Bolts of fabric from rich hand-dyed silks to the palest laces leaned up against walls, while one wall was essentially a giant corkboard, filled with sketches. A red dressmaker's dummy stood in one corner, with dials to adjust the bust, waist and hips. The long table against the wall underneath the cabinets exploded with fashion magazines and spools of thread in every color.

"In my studio." Raquel laid a cool hand on my forehead. "You're not blue anymore. That's a step up from how you were half an hour ago. And you'll be in perfectly good health, *when we use the Bullseye on you.*"

I stroked a half-stitched corset in black satin, draped over the sofa next to me. "You're a lingerie designer? Don't you run a coven?"

"That's not exactly a paid position and stop changing the subject. How do you not kill her?" she said to Rohan.

"With great difficulty," he ground out.

"Do you want some clean clothes? I've got some sweats you can wear and you could help yourself to some lingerie samples." She sounded as muted as I felt.

It was a generous offer, and yesterday I would have jumped at the chance to get my hands on all these pretty, girly bras. Periwinkle and pink, silk and lace, I would have put them on and paraded them for Ro.

Now, they'd chafe as badly as the still-healing burns on my skin.

"Thanks, but I'm good." I clutched the pendant. "You'd have sold that bribe if you hadn't glanced at the Bullseye. I'm keeping it and you're not using it."

"Really? Can you sense how close Lilith is to breaking free?" Rohan pinned me in his laser focus like he was trying to invoke X-ray vision.

I shrugged. "It won't happen today."

"Do we have a day? A week? Nava, your throat was rippling like something was trying to strangle you from the inside."

I sat down. "Oh."

Kane and Ari strolled out of a back room. My brother's eyes were red as well.

"What's wrong?" I said.

"I never got to meet Dr. Gelman when she was alive and if it hadn't been for her?" He shook his head.

Kane stepped closer to my brother and draped an arm around his shoulder.

"We took her body back to her sister," Ari said. "EC transport."

"When's the funeral?" Raquel said.

"Rivka is going to let us know," Kane said.

I pressed my index finger against my lips, shoving my grief back inside. Allowed myself three breaths.

"Talk sense into your sister," Rohan said. "She's refusing to let us do the extraction."

"Have you asked her why?" Ari said.

Raquel and Rohan exchanged guilty looks.

"Thank you." I stood up briskly. "Mandelbaum and Sienna are going to throw everything they have at us. Help me figure out how I can access Lilith's magic without waking her, because right now, I can only tap into the wisps she discharges and it's not enough. Let me be the weapon that tips the scales in our favor. I've said from the start that we needed the advantage Lilith's magic gave us. It's time for me to stop dancing around the issue and embrace it."

Ro's blades slid out again, but words were beyond him.

"And if taking on that much dark magic destroys you?" Raquel said.

"Then I go out in a blaze of glory."

Ari started to speak, but Rohan jerked up a hand to cut him off. "Do you hear yourself?"

"Even with my regular magic I could die. Not like Rasha have long lifespans. I want to make a difference. I want to matter."

Ro slammed the side of his fist onto the table. "You matter."

"I want to matter to the world."

287

"That's Lilith's ego talking, not you," he said.

"Maybe mattering is where this path started for her. Maybe she and I aren't that different. I promise you, I don't have a death wish. I want to be around for years." I cut a sideways glance at Rohan. *I want to tell you I love you.*

"You have a plan?" Ari asked.

"My own magic allows me to manipulate brain waves and make people unconscious. With Lilith's magic amplifying mine, I could do it in one giant wave that would take all of Mandelbaum's men out simultaneously once we find this compound. Then our Rasha could secure them without any fighting. Without any loss of life."

"We can take them," Kane said.

"But why should you have to? Why risk even one more person when I can do this without anyone else getting hurt?"

Why force anyone else to have human death on their conscience? Why force anyone else up against their monster-self? If I could fully embrace Lilith's magic, I could allow my friends, my family, my love to keep their moral compasses intact. I could embrace the worst to allow them to show off their best.

"And don't forget, we've got Sienna who can turn any one of us against each other," I said. "She's proven that. I need magic that's stronger than hers to take her down."

Raquel fiddled with the end of her tape measure. "Okay."

"Really?"

"Okay, I'll talk to the others and see if it's even possible for you to dip into the box and access the magic without releasing Lilith. Just don't hold your breath. We discussed a lot of possibilities when Esther first mentioned you to us, and this never arose as one of them. If none of us know how to do it, I don't know who would."

She started crying again, muttered, "fuck" and reached for a tissue.

I bit down hard on my lip so I wouldn't do the same, because if I let my anguish over Esther out I wasn't sure if I could stop. I had to keep it together until Sienna was contained.

"Is there some kind of test run?" Ari said. "How will we know you've solved how to keep Nava safe versus letting her access magic that immediately kills her?"

I glanced at Rohan, standing rigidly on the far side of the room, refusing to make eye contact. Hopefully, he was taking some much-needed processing time. A cooling off and any second now he'd come back to my side like he'd promised.

Raquel blotted her eyes. "Accessing the magic is simple. But we won't know if we've found a way to protect you until you actually do it." Raquel gave a thin smile. "If you don't drop dead, we're good."

"How is that any better than doing nothing and Lilith waking up and killing her in a couple weeks?" Kane demanded.

"It's my choice," I said. "I'm willing to risk it. My life versus all of humanity. Isn't that essentially the Rasha code?"

Rohan had come up behind me and put his hands on my shoulders. "What are you going to do with Sienna?"

He had my back and was respecting my choices. I allowed myself a spurt of hope at how far we'd come.

"There's got to be something that can imprison her," I said.

Kane flicked a finger against the pendant. "Could you use the Bullseye to put *Sienna* in the vessel?"

Raquel tossed her tissues in a small trash can. "It would kill her. Lilith is, well, we don't know what she is anymore, but she can't be alive in the normal human sense and we can contain her. Sienna is still very much human."

I nodded. "No killing Sienna. Plus, if I become a danger or this somehow all goes sideways, then you need to use the Bullseye. Oh. What happens if Lilith wakes up and breaks free of the box before we extract her?"

"She'll still kill you," Raquel said. "Your only chance to stop Sienna and make it out alive is to tap into Lilith's magic in a way that doesn't kill you when you overpower Sienna, find something to imprison her in, and then use the Bullseye to extract Lilith from you before she breaks out of her magic prison. Any of those things don't happen in the correct order, either Sienna or Lilith will eviscerate you."

"When we win, you'll let us use the Bullseye on you immediately afterward, right?" Rohan said.

"Fifty percent chance I lose my magic, Snowflake."

Raquel cleared her throat. "Not anymore. You've been tying your magic to Lilith's. We pull her out, you lose your magic for sure. No ifs, ands, or buts."

My hand tightened on the pendant.

"But you live," Rohan said. "Promise me. You get through the battle and you allow the extraction."

Without any magic, I'd be an ordinary girl. Rohan wouldn't be an ordinary guy. Would we still be able to have a happily-ever-after or would I resent him for his magic?

"I promise," I swung my gaze between them all. "Provided you find a way for me to get Lilith's magic that also doesn't kill me in the process."

Raquel sent off a text. "I've put the others onto it."

"You still need something to contain Sienna once you take her down." Kane looked at Ari. "Remember the night we broke into the Brotherhood library in New York?"

"Ari Katz, you scoundrel," I chided.

"I was drunk," he said.

"Even better." I wagged a finger at him. "Share, so I can repeat your failings as an upstanding young man at our next family dinner." The wobble in my voice betrayed my attempt at pretending all was normal.

My brother, bless him, didn't show any pity or sympathy. He knew it would undo me.

"You're thinking of the Tomb of Endless Night," Ari said.

Kane fired a finger gun at him. "Got it in one."

"That sounds promising," I said.

Raquel sniffed. "I've never heard of it."

"You don't know everything? Le gasp." Kane smirked at her.

"It's a cage that nulls all magic," Ari said. "Even dark magic."

I started laughing. "Esther."

The dam broke. Tears were pouring down my face and I couldn't catch my breath, but whether from the manic laughter or the sobbing was anyone's guess.

"Babyslay?" Kane inched closer. "You cracking up?"

I gasped for air. "Esther kept threatening to throw me in a Faraday cage that would do exactly that."

"This isn't the same thing," Ari said. "And it's a sarcophagus, not a cage. The Tomb is coated in dark magic. Lilith created it centuries ago."

"Built to take out the competition?" I grabbed a tissue and dabbed at my eyes, while Rohan rubbed my back.

Kane shrugged. "Who knows? But the demons got hold of it about seventy years ago."

"Which means there is only one demon who would have deigned to get it for you. Baskerville." Raquel stared pointedly at Rohan, who glared back at her.

"Fuck off," he said. "We didn't know."

"Damn," I said, my voice still watery. "Seems I was a bit

too clever tying up that loose end. You've got to have other demon leads. Try them. I'll try my contacts as well. The Tomb sounds like our best and only way to contain Sienna."

"What a bunch of dismal options. Damned if you do and damned if you don't," Kane said.

Or just damned.

Ari smacked him.

"Like we weren't all thinking it," Kane said.

He wasn't wrong.

THERE WAS something about being immersed in water, be it stretched out in a bathtub or floating in the ocean, that was intensely calming. The fact that this comfort zone had an infinity edge and an epic view of the city didn't hurt. Too bad I could barely see it with my swollen, damp eyes.

I drifted across Dev and Maya's pool on my inflatable lounger, the early evening shadows lengthening. The waterfall in the connecting hot tub had been turned down to a mere trickle.

"Is it my fault Esther's dead?" I shook the Magic 8 ball I'd taken from the bungalow. "*Reply hazy. Try again.*"

Ari jumped in, splashing me.

I paddled backward.

"Quit asking it that question," Ari said.

"Fine. Are more people going to die?" I shook the ball. "*Signs point to yes.*"

Ari swiped the ball away.

"Ask it if I need to moisturize." Kane floated past on an air mattress, wearing mirrored shades despite the sun almost having sunk below the horizon. He also wore a

292

hideous cheetah-print speedo that left nothing to the imagination.

Generally, I was all for realities as impressive as his, but this was the dude I wanted for my brother, so nope.

Ari shook the ball. "*Without a doubt.*" Kane whipped the glasses off to glare at Ari, who shrugged. "I'm just the messenger."

My brother tossed the ball into the water, where it bobbed, floating.

I turned my lounger around to face the view once more. "I'm tired."

"Take a nap." Kane slid gingerly into the water.

Ari snagged Kane's mattress and hefted himself onto it, laying on his stomach. "She meant existentially, idiot."

Kane pushed him halfway across the pool. "Save me from angsty twins. What will be will be, Katzes. There's no point worrying about it."

I hooked my foot onto the pool deck to keep me anchored in place. "I'd been so certain I had this all under control. That I could outwit and outplay everyone."

"That only works on game shows," Ari said.

The ball floated by. I grabbed it and shook it. "*Ask again later.*" I tossed it back in the water. "Stupid ball."

"Divination tools ain't what they used to be," Kane said.

"Ask what again later?" Ari asked.

"The prophecy. I keep circling around to whether Ro and I being together has sped up the timeline. Not like I'd have stayed away from him even if it had, but there's the first part of it. Blood to bind the might."

"The blood used to bind demons," Ari said.

"What if it has another meaning?" I pulled the pendant back and forth on its chain. "Blood's been spilled. Is the Brotherhood in a stronger position because they killed Esther? She was a powerful player and they took her out.

And what about Sienna? She spilled blood and hurt the Brotherhood. Did that make her stronger? What about when she finds out about Esther?"

"You're assuming she cared about her," Kane said.

"She loved her. Just like I did." My heart ached but I'd cried myself dry.

Kane headed for the stairs. "It's war, babyslay. There are going to be casualties and shit is going to get dark. Your only real choice is how you want to live your life in the face of that."

"Yeah?" Ari said. "How do you want to live yours, Kane?"

Kane bowed his head, his shoulders rising and falling on a deep breath. Then he slammed a sheet of water halfway across the pool and marched up the stairs, his back ramrod straight as he got out.

Ari watched him leave. "Guess I got my answer."

"Ace."

"Don't." He jumped onto the stairs and left.

I glanced over at my bungalow, lit from within with a warm, candlelit glow. What did I want? I wanted to reaffirm life and prove that the darkness didn't get to win.

25

I stepped inside and was hit with the mouth-watering aromas of sizzling garlic and wine.

Ro stood at the stove, his jaw all stubbled and his damp hair tousled, dropping fat white prawns into a pan while Ella Fitzgerald sang about being bewitched, bothered, and bewildered on the stereo. A cut-up crusty baguette was arrayed on a wooden cutting board on the table next to a big colorful salad. "Wine's chilling in the fridge."

My breath caught at the cozy picture of domesticity. *This.* The world was exploding around us but tonight we could have this bubble.

We could have us. And then I'd tell him I loved him.

I hugged him from behind. "You're the best."

"I am. But that's old news."

"Are we going to talk about earlier?"

He shook his head. "I respect your decision. Hell, I understand your decision. But I can't talk about it. Not tonight, okay?" He squeezed some lemon onto the prawns. "Shower off and come get comfortable."

I ran a hand down his abs and under his shirt. "What if I'd rather eat and then take a bath with my boyfriend?"

I teased him for a good minute before he relaxed and turned to me with a grin that was so sinful, I surreptitiously checked my red polka dot bikini bottoms to ensure they hadn't spontaneously combusted. They were still there but what little dryness they'd achieved had just suffered a serious setback.

He captured my lips with the sweetest tease of a kiss.

Seriously. It lasted all of two seconds. I stood there with my mouth puckered but he'd already turned back to the stove. I poked him in the back and he chuckled.

"Pour us both a glass and let me finish, or we won't eat."

"I can wait."

"You'll need the stamina."

I shivered at the promise in his voice. "Dinner first it is."

I still planned to bathe with him later, so I just threw a wrap over my bikini.

Dinner was lighthearted, filled with delicious seafood, a Moscato that went down like fruit punch, and a confessional about words we'd misunderstood as kids.

I wiped a dollop of salad dressing off my upper lip. "My turn. When I was about seven, Ari and I were playing Monopoly and he was being a total brat."

Ro swiped a piece of bread through the buttery wine sauce from the prawns. "He was winning."

"Exactly. So, to insult him and prove I was smarter than my science nerd brother, I decided to call him an organism. Except I couldn't remember which was the single-celled life form and which was the sex thing and, well, orgasm it was."

"He must have had a field day with that one."

"He knew I meant organism but he wasn't too sure what an orgasm was either, so being the curious child he was, he had to find out."

Rohan shook his head, his expression half-amused, half-fearful.

"We were staying with my bubbe that summer who didn't have internet. Imagine this perfectly coiffed woman nervously twisting her diamond ring while her twin grandchildren peppered her with questions about orgasms. I think she tried to answer the first one, then she gave us ten bucks and told us to go buy candy."

"Why do I sense an extortion scam?"

"Because you know me. To be fair, Ari was just as bad. We must have raked in a couple hundred bucks that summer. Just stayed high on Gummi Bears and Chupa Chups. Mom had to detox us when we got home." I speared a piece of avocado. "That was also the year Ari broke his ankle rollerblading off a homemade ramp and I ended up with a really bad case of road rash trying to ride my bike on one wheel." I picked out the lone candied pecan left in the salad bowl and tossed it in my mouth. "There may have been a correlation."

"At least your story had a happy ending." Rohan covered his eyes with his hand. "I can't believe I'm going to tell you this."

I pried his hand away. "But you are."

"I used to think that hot and bothered meant annoyed."

"When was this? When you were seventeen? Eighteen?"

"Funny. No, I was six. I walked up to my mom and Asha and said, 'You know what gets me hot and bothered?' Mom got this weird look on her face like she'd swallowed something the wrong way, but asked me what."

"And you said?"

"People picking their toe nails."

I snorted, my fork clattering to my plate. "That poor woman. Thinking she had a little foot fetishist."

"It gets worse. Years later, when I was dating Lily, unbeknownst to me, Asha dropped that little tidbit into a conversation with Lils without saying I'd been a kid when I said it. And she did it on the very night Lily and I were planning to sleep together."

I tried to keep a sympathetic expression on my face, but my shoulders shook. "Your cousin was an evil genius. Please keep over-sharing."

"I had this whole romantic night planned."

"Dude, you were sixteen when you lost your V-card. How romantic could you have been? A black candle, a hotel room, and Morrissey crooning sweet nothing matters on the CD player?"

"Morrissey is more post-organismic." He smirked at me. "Did I use that correctly in a sentence?"

I shot him the finger.

"So Lils comes in and things are happening and then she asks me if I want her to take off her socks. Thinking it was go-time, I said yes, super enthusiastically, and took off *my* socks. I also took off my pants and my shirt and when I turned around, naked, she was trying to trim a toenail with this determined look on her face."

I choked on the mouthful of wine I'd taken.

"Probably jumping back in horror and yelling 'What the fuck, Lily?' wasn't my finest moment."

"*You think*?!"

He knocked my leg with his knee under the table. "She yelled back that I was the one who got hot and bothered with toenails to which I really cemented my chances of never getting laid by telling the A.P. Honor Roll student that she was an idiot because hot and bothered meant aroused, not grossed out."

I put my foot in his lap. "Wow. And yet she did eventually have sex with you."

"After two months of me groveling." He massaged my instep, exactly how I liked it.

I sighed in delight. "Did you get Asha back for that?"

"Hell, yeah. I left a herpes test kit in her open purse for Drio to find." His smile faded and his massage stilled. "Did killing Oskar help?"

"In the moment. But taking a life for a life didn't give me any closure." I brushed some crumbs off the table into my palm, sprinkling them on my plate. "What a stupid idea. Taking his life isn't going to heal my heart. It isn't going to bring Esther back." I stared out into the indigo night. "It hammered home one thing though. I finally understand on a visceral level that this is war. The first shots have been fired and they won't be the last. And even though I feel like I have this permanent taint inside me, guilt isn't going to do me any good."

"What is?" Ro asked.

"Winning." I gathered the plates, but Rohan shook his head, motioning for me to stay seated. "It'll be different for you," I said. "Hybris isn't human."

"Human or not, you killed a monster." Ro stacked dishes. "I'm not sure killing Hybris will bring me any peace around losing Asha."

"What will?"

Rohan kissed the top of my head. "Finish your wine. I'll draw a bath."

This may have been a guest bungalow but even the bathtub was deluxe, wide and deep.

I sank into the steaming hot water with a sigh, leaning back against Rohan. For a while, neither of us spoke. He played with my hair while I raked my nails along the soft dusting of hair on his inner thigh, our legs tangled together.

"I'm sorry about Esther," he said. "But it wasn't your fault. I heard you in the pool. No. Wait." He put his hand over my mouth for a second. I nipped his finger and he pulled it away, playing with my hair once more. "You think that you brought her into this fight, but you didn't. The witches were never going to be passive bystanders."

"I only just got to know her and there's this giant hole in my heart. What if..."

His arms tightened around me. "I'm terrified of who I could lose, too."

I flipped over to straddle him, my arms draped around his neck, falling into the sensation of being wrapped around his hard body with the water softly lapping against my back. Our gazes locked.

He rocked into me ever so slightly, rubbing himself against my clit, his eyes never leaving mine.

Deeper and deeper I fell.

My heart jumped into my throat. We'd hit a point of intimacy that would usually have me making a joke or reframing the action into something I could handle.

I didn't want to "handle" anything. I wanted to be lost in him, let that undertow drag me under and revel in how gloriously deep this went.

I stood up, water sluicing off my body, and held out my hand, catching sight of myself in the partially fogged up mirror. Hair in wet curls, eyes glassy with a drugged dizzy need, I looked like a sex-crazed Botticelli.

No. I looked like a woman deeply in love with the man before her.

From the way Rohan's eyes darkened, making a very slow and very thorough sweep of me, it worked for him. He rose and twined his fingers with mine, letting me lead him into the bedroom.

My hand shook slightly as I pushed him back on the cool sheets.

Rohan reached for the small lamp, but I stopped him, my eyes adjusting to the dark enough to see.

Reverently, I traced his jawline, his stubble prickling my

fingertips, following up with kisses pressed to the softness of the underside of his jaw. That secret vulnerable spot that Rohan exposed with no hesitation to me.

He raked one finger blade slowly up and down along my spine, pressing my chest against his.

"Do you have any idea what you mean to me?" I said.

His mouth found mine with an urgency I matched kiss for kiss, our lips sliding together messily, tongues dancing.

I pulled away. "Final frontier."

"What? You want to watch Star Trek? Now?" He glanced down at his very hard cock with a pained expression.

"Yes. It gets me hot and bothered. Did I use that correctly?"

He barked a laugh.

I slid off the bed, opened my suitcase, and pulled out the object I wasn't sure I was going to have the nerve to try. I tossed it on the bed, along with a small bottle of lube. "Final frontier."

Ro's brows wrinkled then his eyes lit up and he reached for the butt plug. "Is this for me or for you?"

"Me for now, but we are definitely coming back to that statement. I, uh, thought we could start with this and work up to larger things." I flicked a glance at his hard-on.

"Oh yeah, we will." Ro held the plug in one hand like he was weighing it. He chewed on his bottom lip, studying me. Then he shook his head. "Not yet."

My eyes darted from the plug to him. I wasn't sure if the hollowness in my chest was relief or disappointment. "Why not?"

"Because even the Enterprise didn't just rush out to the furthest reaches of space on their first go. It's a journey."

"Yeah? How's this work then?"

He smiled widely, slightly impish. "First, I'm gonna make you see stars."

He put his mouth to the side of my neck, his lips cool on my flushed skin.

I tangled my fingers in his hair, pulling him closer to me as I fell to the mattress. I sucked on his lip, then did it again, just to elicit his low growl once more.

He cupped my face. "I love that I get to look at you whenever I want. Touch you." He caressed my breasts and I arched into his touch. "Taste you."

He suckled my stiffened peak.

My breasts grew heavy and sensitive and I let out a breathy sigh.

Rohan trailed kisses down the length of my body, nudging my knees apart so he could show Cuntessa some love. He lavished attention on every inch of me, bringing me to the brink time and time again until I was trembling beneath him.

He grabbed the lube. There was a squirt and then he slid his finger into my ass.

I dug my heels into the mattress, coils of pleasure rippling through me under his stellar multitasking and highly talented tongue.

"This is lovely," I gasped, "but I'm not seeing stars."

Rohan lifted his head. "Demanding much?"

"I was promised stars. Shame if it was false advertising."

"I'm gonna enjoy making you beg."

"Oh no. Please don't threaten me with mind-blowing sex." I fluttered my hands. "Scaaaary."

He squirted out a very generous handful of lube, oiling up both me and the butt plug. "Get on all fours."

I eyed the friendly green plug that suddenly seemed way too large to fit into me, even though it was a slender starter model.

He slowly inserted it, letting me catch my breath through the stretching burn. "Should I stop?"

I exhaled and shook my head. Except about five seconds later, I was ready to pull the plug myself, so to speak.

Before I could, Rohan said, "there" and things started vibrating.

A wrecked moan tore from my throat.

Rohan's face popped up upside down in my field of vision. "You like?" he purred.

I could barely nod, awash on a sea of intensity. Every pleasure-inducing nerve ending had lit up.

"We can stop here," he said. "Or—"

I stretched my neck forward to kiss him messily. "I want 'or,'" I panted.

The answering grin he trained on me, the tip of his tongue sticking out the corner of his mouth from between closed teeth, had me reaching for him again, but he ducked away to stand behind me. He gripped my hips, sliding inside me with a powerful thrust.

Rohan fucked me hard, his hips slapping against the base of the plug. I was so full and everything was vibrating and then he brought Cuntessa into the mix and holy fuck.

Sweat trailed down the back of my neck. I dropped onto my bent elbows, rubbing my breasts against the blanket, my right cheek pressed to the mattress and my ass in the air.

"You like that?" he said.

"Ohgodohgodohgodohgod."

The Bullseye pendant thunked against my collarbone with each thrust. My inner thighs shook. A spark caught in my core, detonating outward in shockwaves.

I growled deep in my throat and fell face first onto the bed, decimated by the most explosive orgasm I'd ever had.

Ro came at the same time, then fell on top of me. He moved my sweaty hair aside to kiss my neck.

My body was all pleasantly throbby and warm and boneless. I checked the hairline fracture on the box, because talk about big bang, and if anything could have woken Lilith it would have been that orgasm, but all was well.

Squirming out from under my boyfriend, I pulled the plug out with a slippery and vaguely uncomfortable pop and put it on some tissue. "Next time we scale up."

I expected a chuckle or a fist bump, but Rohan was uncharacteristically silent. I propped myself up on one elbow to look at him. "You okay?"

He caressed my cheek. "Killing Hybris isn't going to heal me, because being with you already is."

In that moment all was clear. I'd be fine without magic if it meant having Rohan like this for the rest of my life.

Tell him.

I smoothed a lock of floppy silky hair back from his still blown-out molten eyes. "Ro. I–"

Pound! Pound! Pound!

"Open up!" Baruch roared.

Rohan jackknifed off the bed. We each grabbed a blanket to cover ourselves and sprinted for the front door.

I threw it open and stepped back at the fury twisting Baruch's features. "What's wrong?"

He clutched the door frame hard enough to crack it. "Benjy's been taken."

26

The way Ro blew through every light en route to the chapter, it was a miracle we didn't end up being chased by a line of cop cars. Baruch and I held the Shelby's "oh shit" handles, careening into our doors and praying Ro didn't flip the car.

We ran inside to the conference room where Bastijn was keeping a close eye on Benjy's parents.

Cisco motioned for Baruch to come into another office.

Benjy's mom Eun Ha was pale, her eyes glassy. Jung, his dad, wasn't doing much better. He stumbled when he tried to get to his feet at Rohan's entrance.

Rohan hurried over to them, giving each a hug and vowing that we'd find their son unharmed.

Bastijn came over to me.

"How are they?" I asked.

He launched into rapid, agitated Spanish, but caught himself mid-tirade at my look of confusion. "¡Discúlpeme! ¡Cristo!" He took a breath. "We gave them sedatives. I tried calling Ro the second I got off the phone with Jung, but it went to voicemail so I called Baruch."

"What do we know?" I said.

"Pustema!" Baruch roared from the other room.

"You need to see this." Danilo poked his head into the room and motioned for Ro and me to come into the other office.

A kitten with a snapped neck lay on a blanket on the desk.

"Their place is warded," Danilo said, "but the kid's only five. The demon lured him out with the kitty."

Cisco held out a note. "This was stuffed in the collar. We're not sure what it means."

It was a rough sketch of a square with a heart inside it. The words "sorry I missed you" were scrawled inside the heart.

"Asha's grave. It's Hybris." Rohan crumpled the note and dropped it on the table.

"You sure?" Danilo said.

"We're sure." I twisted my hands together. What had we brought about?

"I'm not losing anyone else to her," Ro snarled. "Nava, portal us."

"You want back up?" Cisco said.

"No. We've got it." From the icy menace in his voice to the rigid line of his shoulders and the deadly glint in his eyes, Rohan was a lethal predator, hell-bent on taking Hybris down.

I snapped the men a small salute, took Rohan's arm, and portalled.

Cemeteries were creepy in the middle of the night. The artwork and gardens in this one only made for more looming shadows and places for monsters to hide.

Hybris was filing her nails, carelessly sitting cross-legged on Asha's grave. Her red hair flowed around her shoulders and her red trench coat billowed out behind her.

Rohan bladed up instantly.

"Ro–" I reached out to stop him, but he was too fast for me.

He strode toward her. "Get your filthy ass off her grave."

"You're more worried about ancient history than a little boy who'll be dead within ten minutes?" Hybris cocked an eyebrow. "You're no hero, Rohan. Not to anyone who matters."

"Just–" Rohan visibly tensed, trying to calm himself as Hybris flicked another shred of fingernail onto Asha's gravesite. "Where is he?"

He grabbed her by the collar of her trench coat, tracing the curve of her neck with the blade of his index finger.

She laughed and flicked her hair off her shoulder to give him better access.

My eyebrows shot up into my hairline.

Rohan jerked her head back. "Tell me where Benjy is."

Tia was too unconcerned. Too certain he wouldn't find her kill spot. Some demons literally did have to be taken apart to get at their kill spot, but while Rohan was more than capable of ripping her in half with his bare hands right now, the demon just looked bored.

She flashed out, far away from us. "You'll never get me, Rohan, and do you want to know why? I'm not your worst enemy. You are. Your self-destructive streak after Asha died, your inability to finish your album. You've framed yourself as the wounded hero determined to save the world. Do you know how much power I draw off all that lovely pride? I'm going to feed off you for your entire, pathetic life, and when the end comes, my face will be the last thing you see."

Rohan flinched and stumbled backwards. "You're wrong."

Hybris laughed. "What? You thought you could escape by quitting music? That you'd beaten all the perils of fame? How sad. There will always be more temptations, and there will always be more ways for me to make you fall. Eventually, you'll give in."

His eyes were wild with panic. "No."

Hybris spread her hands. "You're only nervous because you know you won't be able to last forever against me. At the end of the day, you're the same person you were at fifteen."

To me, her words merely sounded like typical head games. Ro had heard worse, so the only reason he was acting this way had to be because of some magical influence.

Was this how she'd gotten Gary to step in front of a car?

I fired a series of lightning strikes at her, attempting to hit her flickering form as she dodged from tree to tree. "Let him go."

"I'm not doing anything. He's fine. Alone with his thoughts."

Given the stark bleakness etched on his face, he was drowning in them. Neutralize Tia, snap Ro out of it, find Benjy.

"Yeah, right," I said. "You want to destroy him."

"True, but..." She stopped suddenly, her trench coat swirling around her legs and widened her eyes theatrically. "You think Rohan is my endgame?"

"I know it. You have no idea how much compassion and love this man is capable of."

"Do you?" She looked genuinely curious. "Or do you just want to believe that because it makes you the person who saved him? Newsflash. You're no savior either."

Her words lashed me, slithering inside me with an insidious whisper.

I clapped my hands over my ears.

Tia stood over Ro's prone form. "He'll never be able to destroy me, because he'll never be able to forgive. I will always win where Rohan is concerned. Him and his revenge fantasies, trapped into believing that if he stamps out the offender, he'll finally feel good. That his world will be this happy little place." She caressed one cheek, crooning at him. "You lost your cousin, you lost your creativity, and now you'll lose that kid."

"He won't lose me," I said.

"No. You'll do that all on your own."

She was right; I was a fuck-up. Why continue to live and torment myself with my existence?

A choking rage bubbled up thick and black inside me. *No.* Hybris was nothing. She was no match for the righteous babes I was descended from and she wasn't going to take me down.

Standing tall, I reached inside me for all the wisps I could access, bound them to my magic, and poured all of it out toward her.

My gold lightning was flecked with darkness, closing around Tia like fingers. "Where? Is? He?"

"What are you?" she wheezed, her body spasming.

"I'm your worst nightmare. You worried?"

"Worried about you damaging some fragile business relationships of mine with this harassment."

"Then kill us," I taunted.

"Maybe that would damage some fragile business relationships, too." She winked at me and slipped my magic net.

Ro shook himself, coming to. He pushed to his feet, shaking with the effort, like he was being pressed against the ground with a heavy weight.

"I'll make you a deal," Hybris said. "Stop chasing me for good and I'll show you to the kid. Come after me and no matter where I am, I'll drop everything immediately to make sure the little snot dies horribly. Your call. Tick tock."

Rohan hesitated, busy tormenting himself about who to let down: Asha or Benjy.

I clamped my lips together so I wouldn't yell our decision because there was no real choice here, but Rohan had to say it, not me.

"Benjy," Rohan said between gritted teeth. "I'll kill you later."

Hybris laughed, seeming to grow taller. "Keep going. I'm getting such a rush off you."

Ro and I exchanged a look. I flicked my gaze to the demon and he gave a tiny nod.

I slammed Hybris with the full power of my electricity. Her body bucked and flew up into the air, bowed over backward like a string pulled taut.

The second Ro reached her, I crashed her to the ground, but even scorched and brain rattled as she had to be, she blinked out a full second before his blades whistled past empty space.

"Not even close." Hybris popped up, standing on Asha's grave, her left stiletto leaving a muddy smear on the stone.

She was cut off with a strangled croak, Ro's finger blades jammed through her throat.

I'd portalled us to her.

She cupped a hand to her ear, completely unconcerned with the blood burbling out of her. "Do you hear his little cries? Back off for good, or no kid."

She wasn't anywhere close to being dead. The trachea kill spot was, sadly, simply a rumor.

Rohan ripped his blades free with a curse, his features stark.

Hybris flicked her fingers and, with a whisper of wind, opened a portal. A cluster of jagged, sawed-off stalactites hung down at the entrance like teeth in serious need of braces.

"Have fun," she said and vanished.

We ducked under the stalactites and headed into the gloom. The farther we descended, the steamier the air grew. It smelled like rotting vegetation.

I called up a ball of magic so we weren't stumbling around in the pitch dark, but something in the air kept sucking the light out to the barest flicker.

I'd never seen Rohan so grim, his body locked in some kind of death-march. He was still lost to his emotions, and I needed his rational brain back in control if we were going to get Benjy out unscathed.

"Did you like the 'I'm your worst nightmare' bit?" I kept my words light, straining to see any release of his tension. "Because Hybris was pretty terrified."

Not in any reality.

He remained silent for a moment before coming out with, "You realize that's Batman's catchphrase."

"Like I'd know that nerd trivia."

"You've Googled everything about him. And you know why?" He paused and then clapped his hands to the side of his head like the Bat cowl. "Because I'm Batman."

"No, you're a majestic moose."

His look promised retribution. That I'd probably really enjoy so, there was that, plus he no longer was walking like he was about to snap. Those were the only upsides because the rest of this journey plumbed the depths of sucking balls. A ticking clock hung over us, the going was slow, and my portal magic didn't work.

The passageway narrowed. Fat drips fell on our heads, running under my neckline and leaving a slimy trail down my spine.

Algae coated the floor. Ro skated along one particularly slippery patch, almost wiping out and taking me with him.

We slid our way deeper and deeper underground. The

wind turned phlegmy, the raspy, wet gusts reminding me of my breathing when I'd had pneumonia, while the ground beneath our feet rose and fell unevenly.

I held my weak ball of light up to the wall. It had the squelchy consistency of mud, not rock, but was pink and fleshy.

"Ro," I hissed. "This isn't a tunnel."

Rohan pressed his palm against it, the fleshy surface Hoovering it up. After a brief struggle, he freed himself with a wet gurgle.

"What is it?" I whispered.

He sucked in a breath. "Alive."

We crept forward, literally making our way to the belly of the beast. Every footfall sank into the spongy ground. Warm liquid rose until it swirled around our ankles.

We threw our arms over our noses to block out the smell of half-digested food.

My magic light cast a hazy glow over the stomach. The walls were soft pink, fleshy coils that glistened with a thick film of mucus. They pulsed with a faint pink light.

There was no sign of Benjy. Had we fought with Hybris for too long?

A rumbling noise vibrated up from our feet. The stomach walls contracted, the coils spasming and pulsing. Ro and I hung on to each other for dear life, trying to stay upright and ride out the convulsions. When it had settled down, except for the continued bronchial breathing, a weak whimper reached our ears.

Ro froze, his eyes darting around.

Most of Benjy's tiny body had been absorbed into one wall, though his right leg from the knee down was still free, as was his bony left shoulder. The outline of his face pressed up against a filmy covering like he was wrapped in saran wrap.

Rohan sprung forward, carefully slicing away the thin film.

The second his face was free, Benjy started coughing, trickling milky mucus.

I wiped his eyes and mouth with my sleeve.

Benjy's eyes were totally dilated. "It hurts, Rohan."

Rohan smiled. I hoped Benjy couldn't see how forced it was. "I know, little man. You've been so brave. I'm gonna cut you out."

The ground bucked.

Ro and I staggered backwards.

My shoulder hit the stomach lining, sticking to it like velcro. My head was yanked back as my hair was sucked into the wall and gelatinous, slimy flesh slithered over my arms and legs, trapping me.

A flood of pink liquid gooshed from the walls, soaking my feet and ankles.

Rohan roared, thrashing. Every time he cut himself free, the flesh wrapped itself around him, grappling with him.

The liquid rose to my knees.

Benjy screamed.

I let my magic loose. I was so tightly trapped that it rumbled around like a pinball on tilt between me and the wet flesh before the monster cave spat me free.

I landed on my ass, in the warm, tingly goo, utterly drenched.

Ro ripped himself free, jumping away from the wall and grabbing my hand to pull me to my feet.

The entire stomach convulsed.

Benjy's face and shoulder were sucked deeper into the walls.

"No!" Ro stumbled his way over the bucking ground and grabbed Benjy's foot before that last part of him disappeared. He slashed at the walls, but the flesh had hardened into some kind of adamantine rock and his blades bounced uselessly off.

My first blast rebounded off the rock and almost took us out. New plan.

The liquid rose to our waists, swirling around us and trying to drag us under.

I planted my feet wide, one hand on the slick walls desperately trying to keep my balance.

Rohan kept at the rock, iron chips flying as his blades lost the battle, his face contorted in pain.

Our magic wasn't going to work. We were going to lose Benjy for good.

Unless...

My hand crept to the Bullseye pendant around my neck. Guaranteed extraction. No training required.

I clutched the pendant. The Bullseye was a one-shot deal.

So that was it, huh? Save Benjy now or save myself later.

At the wall, Rohan was bloody and his blades were mangled, still not any closer to making a dent as the digestive enzyme liquid rose higher. Any second now the way out would be underwater.

It was easy to be cavalier about the value of one life in the face of all humanity. But what about when it was one life versus another? When it was the life of a thin, pale child, whose glasses lay broken on the ground and whose foot was no bigger than my hand, against my own life?

If I didn't use the Bullseye before Lilith broke free, I could kiss my happily-ever-after goodbye.

The stomach convulsed again.

Rohan lost his grip on Benjy's foot.

Time slowed down to the naked desperation on my

boyfriend's face, a dirty Batman sneaker with blinking lights in the heel, and the solid weight of the pendant.

Rohan was trying to regain his footing, though it's not like I would ask his advice on who to save: his girlfriend or a little kid.

It would be so easy to walk away. Say we'd done our best to help Benjy and keep this safety net in my pocket. I indulged in a brief second of a world saved and a long life fully lived at Rohan's side, though ultimately, it was innocents like Benjy, like that little girl in Prague eating chocolate that I was doing this for. Embracing the darkness so they could have the light.

Fumbling the clasp open, I dumped the Bullseye into my palm.

Weirdly, it looked like a penny.

In for a penny. I pressed the artifact to the rock right about where Benjy's chest was.

The Bullseye flared bright and shriveled in on itself, winking out of existence with a quiet pop. Failing to do anything.

"No!" I beat at the wall. How the hell could it do nothing? What kind of bullshit magic artifact was that and how, in every goddamn possible way for this to have gone, had I managed to choose the one path where everybody died?

All of a sudden, the stomach was silent and still. Even the air seemed to hang motionless. Then the world split apart.

Benjy flew from his fleshy prison.

Grunting, Ro caught him like a football to the gut.

A hole opened at the opposite end from the passageway out and the floor tilted. Everything was being flushed out.

Rohan hung tight to Benjy, who was sobbing but breathing, while I hung tight to Ro.

We fought the liquid and the backwards pull, heaving

ourselves toward the way out. No way was I going to be expelled from some demon ass. For every torturous inch we won, we lost two. I cursed whatever magic was keeping me from portalling us out of here.

Sweat poured into my eyes and I felt like a brined turkey in this stomach fluid. I slipped, splashing down.

Ro grabbed my collar and hurled me up into the passageway, slogging up behind me. Finally clear of the stomach, we sprinted for the mouth.

My heart was in my throat, uncertain if we'd find a dead end with no way out, trapped by those jagged teeth. I was so slick with fear, that when I saw the pinprick of moonlight up ahead, my knees buckled.

I tripped over my feet but kept going.

The stalactite teeth pounded down with arrhythmic, bone-jarring thuds.

With those deadly gnashers just missing taking a chunk out of the back of his head, I could barely watch Ro jump through with Benjy. I wasn't worried for myself. I had my death sentence and this wasn't it.

I easily cleared the teeth, collapsing onto the cemetery lawn next to Ro who was holding Benjy, rubbing his back while he vomited mucus, but I scrambled up immediately at the sound of slow clapping, my magic at the ready.

There was no physical sign of Hybris and every sense of her presence.

Rohan hefted Benjy into his arms, the child hanging limply on him like a little monkey. "He's safe," Rohan called out. "We won."

"Oh. You thought Benjy was the endgame?" No demon, just her disembodied voice. "So many assumptions you both make."

A phantom finger traced the pendant.

"You knew about the Bullseye," I said.

"I make it my business to hear the whispers in the wind," she said.

I spun around, but she was still nowhere to be seen.

"The bigger the ego, the more delicious the fall." Her words drifted on the breeze.

"Nava?" Ro looked at me, confused, his eyes searching. He went still, reaching out to touch the open, and empty, pendant.

A strangled noise punched out of him.

"You guys saved me." Benjy's voice was hoarse.

I pasted on my brightest smile. "Sure did."

"Like we'd let anything happen to you." Rohan ruffled Benjy's hair, but when he looked at me over the top of the boy's head, his eyes were damp.

Using the last of my energy, I portalled all three of us back to DSI.

Benjy's parents let out cries of relief, running to take him from Rohan, and crush all of us in hugs.

Snuggled close to his mom, Benjy reached for me, winding his thin little boy arms around my neck and pressing a kiss to my cheek. "I'm gonna be like *you* when I grow up."

"I can't wait to see it."

I managed to keep up my happy facade until Ro took me into the other room and crushed me to him. "We'll find another way. I swear to you," he said. "You're going to live."

I lay my head in the crook of his neck.

Esther was dead, Hybris was gone, and I had no way to get Lilith out of me before she broke free and took me down in the process. Not to mention, I hadn't told Rohan I loved him.

Not my best Monday. Even if it was potentially the last Monday I had left.

27

Ro left to make up one of the spare beds because we were too exhausted to leave the building. The chapter head rabbis that had flown in had opted to stay at a nearby hotel, and Mandelbaum had moved there as well, so we had our choice of rooms.

I collapsed on the couch, yawning like my jaw was about to disengage and swallow someone whole, and called Leo.

"Fuck you," she mumbled.

"Did I wake you?"

Another slurred curse.

"Wake up, sunshine. I need instructions on how to get to the demon dark web."

Silence.

"Leo!"

"Mmmgh. Fine."

I smiled through the gaping despair hanging over me, picturing her doing her little wake-up wriggles.

"Harry is extremely pissed off at you for killing Baskerville," she said.

"Boo hoo. Baskerville would have killed me otherwise

and I'm full up on being a target. Harry can get over himself."

"Yeah, well if you want access to the dark web, you need Harry's password."

"Which I'm sure you have. He'll never know and even if he does," I said, "you'll still help me because you're a good person."

"I'm really not. Good talk. 'Night."

"Hybris kidnapped a little kid tonight, Leo."

"Tell me." Leo was fully alert.

I explained my plan and she gave me very precise instructions involving four different router websites, Harry's login, and balsamic vinegar.

"Everything about demons is stupid," I said.

"Agreed." She yawned. "Can I sleep now?"

"One more thing." I told her about the Tomb of Endless Night.

She groaned. "That would have been a job for Baskerville. I'll talk to Harry, but don't hold your breath."

My stomach twisted because I needed that tomb to contain Sienna. I needed to stop her in the little time I had left. "Do what you can. Schmugs."

She mumbled something that may have been schmugs and hung up.

Rohan met me in the hallway, holding two laptops. He handed one to me. "Got it?"

"Yes."

We didn't have the printouts of the cold cases with us, but I still had the original emails. We each took half of the cases we'd connected to Hybris.

"Check who broke the stories," I said. "What photos do we have of the victims' moments of humiliation? Is she in any of them?"

"Your hunch was right," Rohan said, a half dozen empty

Coke cans later. He'd been crowded up against me the entire time, but I hadn't complained.

I'd memorized the feel of him: the flex of every muscle with each tiny movement, the way that the more he focused, the more his posture went to shit, making him slump against me, and how he couldn't go more than a couple of minutes without rubbing my shoulder or laying a hand on my thigh, almost as if assuring himself I was still there.

Rohan showed me the list he'd compiled.

Hybris, in her Tia Lioudis persona, had reported on all the cases that had made the news throughout history. She was even present in some of the photos of the main events like Capone's arrest and Nixon's impeachment. She didn't care if she was seen, because even once the internet was a thing, she figured we humans were too stupid to put all this together.

"All the judgment I've faced over the past few days got me thinking about how Hybris fancies herself the ultimate judge," I said. "She preys on our pride, but what's the one thing she's prideful about? What's most important to her?"

"Getting to judge without being judged herself," Rohan said.

"Hybris believes herself infallible and you know what word is in 'infallible'? Fall."

"Nice one, Sparky."

"I'm on-the-fly clever that way."

Using the copious demon intel I had access to, a fake profile, and a few well-placed, thinly veiled rumors about various dangerous spawn on the demon dark web that any demon with half a brain would attribute to Hybris, I slammed back a disgusting shot of balsamic vinegar, logged in with Harry's password, and started rumor-mongering to set my trap.

Let the other demons track her. Rohan and I would follow that trail after she'd been smoked out of hiding.

Let her feel what it was like to be the one being judged. The one being hounded.

Hunted.

By the time we crashed, both of us were tapped out, physically, emotionally, existentially, you name it.

I peeled myself out of Rohan's embrace and into something vaguely resembling a functioning human being late Tuesday morning. Fumbling for my phone, I fired off an impatient text to Raquel. I didn't mention the Bullseye; it would just distract her from the more pressing task.

She texted back that they had a solid lead on the Tomb and were working on a safe way to access Lilith's magic, but it didn't look promising so did I have a Plan B?

I was a lot farther down the alphabet by this point, but yes, I did have someone else I could reach out to. I crept outside to Rohan's car, grabbed Esther's purse from the trunk, and crawled into the backseat. After rummaging around in her bag for a bit, I found Sienna's bracelet, then I placed one of the spiky leaves under my tongue and tried to replicate the steps Esther had taken yesterday to magically call Sienna.

I infused my essence into the bracelet, but I couldn't get it to latch. Without that subtle snap into place, I couldn't push the magic out, letting it ripple back to her. If I pulled it off, she'd experience it as a sudden shiver, that "someone walking over your grave" feeling. It was the origin of the expression. Witches had made up the term as code and it had taken root in the non-magic consciousness.

Thanks to the amplification properties of the leaf, it was more someone stomping over her grave. Stomping sounded pretty good right now, my frustration rising with each failed attempt.

I spit out the leaf and set the bracelet to one side, taking ten minutes to run through a series of meditation and centering exercises that I had used back in my performing days. Stage fright had nothing on the looming end of my life.

I rubbed my eyes. I had to make the time I had left count.

With a fresh leaf and a fresh attitude, I tried again. This time, I felt the snap. I think. It was either incredibly subtle or a figment of my imagination. I'd try again after I'd dosed myself up with java.

I tucked the Ziplock bag and bracelet into my pocket and headed bleary-eyed into Demon Club's kitchen, ready to rip the balls off anyone standing between me and caffeine.

Fingers crossed I'd find Mandelbaum.

But no, it was Rabbi Abrams standing in front of the small TV on the counter, speechless, his tea going cold in his hand.

"What's wrong?" I said.

He raised the volume on the remote.

"We don't know why the plane suddenly lost thrust." The sleek-haired reporter stood on the beach, choppy waves crashing behind him.

"A plane went down?" I said. "That's too bad."

It didn't explain the rabbi's stricken expression.

Rabbi Abrams sank into a chair next to his half-drunk mug of tea, hunched in on himself. Everything about him drooped: his shoulders, his beard, even his masses of facial wrinkles seemed to puddle around his jawline. "Navela. It was the Executive."

"What?"

"...about eight hours into the flight from Jerusalem to

Los Angeles, going down in the North Atlantic," the reporter said.

Back in the studio, the Asian American anchor with the carefully modulated facial expression cut in. "Ken, we're getting reports that the crash was caused by seagulls flying into the engine. This is an incredibly rare occurrence. Can you confirm this?"

"Yes, Samantha. The black box has yet to be recovered from the private craft, but that is the speculation at this moment." He touched his earpiece. "We're receiving word that search and rescue teams are being called back in and recovery and retrieval teams are being dispatched instead. Our thoughts are with the families of the six men who perished."

"Thank you, Ken. As our listeners may know, in emergencies, black box recorders..."

I snapped the TV off, white-knuckling the counter. I'd never met any of the Executive and had only briefly spoken to Rabbis Simon and Ben Moses, but I couldn't wrap my head around the fact they were gone.

Rabbi Abrams rocked back and forth murmuring Hebrew prayers for men who had fallen from a great height and would not return home again.

Planes had extra fuel tanks, signals, all manner of technology that could save them. We were supposed to have engineered our way out of emergencies. But when it came to emergencies consisting of birds in the engine of the plane that happened to be bringing the Executive to Los Angeles?

There was no way to engineer our way out of magic.

I should tell someone, but who? Esther was gone and I couldn't leave Rabbi Abrams here alone, praying. I poured myself a coffee, in order to feel like I was doing something.

The rabbi finished his prayer and motioned for me to join him at the table.

We sat in silence for a while, Rabbi A holding my hand in his gnarled old man ones. Water dripped from the tap into someone's discarded oatmeal bowl.

"Rivka called me." He spoke the words so quietly, I barely caught them.

Sienna had been there when Esther was killed. Rabbi Abrams and Esther had been friends for decades–he deserved to know the truth.

"Sienna was retaliating for Esther."

"I've told Boris about Sienna," Rabbi Abrams said. "It seemed likely she'd attack again."

I struggled to find the right words that wouldn't snap his head off. "Mandelbaum killed Esther and you've alerted him to the presence of a witch with dark magic?"

He stroked his beard. "I overheard one of his men speaking with him this morning. My Slovakian is rusty but apparently, maybe a month ago, Boris distributed photos of women who are leaders in the witch community. Esther was recognized when Boris sent one of his Rasha to pick me up and the Rasha saw her. Apparently that Rasha is now missing."

I choked down a strangled sob. If I hadn't asked her to come to L.A. she would never have been recognized. Wouldn't have been murdered because of a stupid chance encounter.

"You took precautions? With whatever may have been left at the crime scene?"

I dumped more sugar in my cup, even though the coffee was already cloyingly sweet. "Wasn't there."

He'd made his choice and as much as it killed me, I couldn't trust him anymore.

Rabbi Abrams pounded his fist on the table. Once. Hard enough to rattle the honey spoon in its ceramic pot. "Those men on the Executive were my friends. Esther was my friend. This madness must stop before we destroy each other."

I crossed my arms on the table and lay my head on them. "This is a disaster."

"Sienna has to pay for what she did and Rasha are best equipped to apprehend her."

"No, the witches should do that."

"You can't protect her," he said.

Wearily, I lifted my head. "I'm not trying to protect Sienna. I'm trying to protect the Rasha who are the good guys. Sienna isn't using demons against us. She's using animals and, well, us. If she knows we're coming for her, she'll throw everything, everyone, at us. How do we protect ourselves when any living creature could be a threat? I can't–"

I shivered, my entire body breaking out in goosebumps. I rubbed my arms briskly against the shuddering that I couldn't stop. Sienna was calling me, but I had no way of magically picking up the phone.

The shivering grew worse, more insistent. My teeth chattered.

Rabbi Abrams maneuvered himself to his feet, holding tight to the table's edge for balance. "Navela?"

"Quit it! I heard you!"

He stepped back in alarm. Great. Now he thought I was crazy.

"I have to go," I said.

Nodding, he shuffled out of the room. "There are calls I need to make. The families..." He stopped in the doorway and turned back. "Maybe you should go home."

"Is that a threat or concern?" I flinched at the hurt flashing across his face.

He glanced out into the hall and pitched his voice low. "I'm worried Rabbi Mandelbaum suspects you're a witch."

I froze. "Why? What did he say?"

"Nothing. But a month ago you and Rohan were looking into Ferdinand and Tessa and that's when the rabbi put witches on some kind of hit list. Including Esther, a witch you were connected to."

I sighed in relief that Rabbi Abrams hadn't heard something on this visit. "Mandelbaum would never have let me remain free if he knew I was a witch. And he certainly wouldn't have kept me working with Ro when this would have been the perfect excuse to rid himself of me once and for all. I appreciate your concern, but he doesn't know."

Not yet.

Rohan came in, clapped the departing rabbi on the shoulder, and offered his condolences for the Executive. "You want to go get breakfast?" He glanced at the clock. "Lunch? Anything to get us away from here right now?"

"Sienna wants to meet." I stuffed my spasming hands into my armpits. "It's not optional."

"You want me to come with? I don't like the timing of this."

"No. If she wanted to hurt me, she would have."

He kissed me hard, his hand clasped on the back of my head. "Be safe. I'll wait for you at the bungalows. Our out-of-town guests have shown up and everyone is getting busy finding the perfect spot for our reunion."

Ah. The trusted Rasha contingent had arrived and were working on finding the compound.

Sienna portalled me out before I could say goodbye.

I landed on Sienna's front porch and peered in through

the windows at all the photos still visible on the walls. That meant Sienna hadn't reset the wards, so I probably wouldn't be fried for stepping on the doormat.

The door swung open before I had a chance to knock. I needed a full minute to psych myself up enough to enter, and in the end, basically flung myself inside, although I couldn't stay in the living room. Even though Kane, Ari, and Rohan had removed all visible traces of what had happened, the room was permeated with a dark, twisted energy that pressed in on me.

I hurried into the kitchen.

The Tupperware was sitting on the counter. I chuckled softly, remembering Esther's prickliness at my eye of newt comment. We'd taken turns poking at each other during our friendship, her with a wit so dry it was practically gallows humor.

I opened the container and breathed in the aroma of buttery, flaky rugelach. She hadn't stinted on the raspberry jam filling; it gooshed out of the crescent-shaped cookie in a dark red seal.

This tiny woman with her sharp mind and her giant heart was gone and it was so fucking unfair. Bringing the Tupperware with me to the glass-topped kitchen table, I saluted Esther's memory with a rugelach and bit into it.

My teeth snapped closed on empty air.

"Those are mine."

"Jesus!" I scrambled back, my hand on my heart.

It took me a second to recognize Sienna, dressed as she was in jeans and a blouse instead of scrubs. Also, she'd lost weight since our last meeting. Her black skin hung gauntly on her narrow frame and her brown eyes had lost some of their fire. She'd cut off her dreads, her hair now barely a couple of millimeters long. Sienna reminded me of when

Esther had been in her chemo treatments. Dark magic had killed Tessa. How much longer did Sienna have?

She munched on the cookie with a moan of delight. "Damn, that woman could bake. Oh, stop making those puppy dog eyes at me." She pushed the container at me. "One."

I swallowed half of the rugelach in a single bite because, wow. They may have been the best ones I'd ever eaten. I blinked away the thought that Esther would never make them again.

"How'd you tag me?" I said. "You don't have anything of mine."

"My magic is way beyond that."

We ate our way through the cookies.

I braced myself in case I had to emergency portal out, but I had to ask. "How could you take down that plane?"

"Wise up. All of the Executive was in on Mandelbaum's plans. None of them were innocent."

"Esther didn't want Rasha gone," I said. "She wanted hunters and witches to work together."

"You talk a big game, don't you, but when it comes down to it, where's your loyalty? Is it to the Brotherhood who killed her?" She turned her palms outward and the air shimmered.

An image of Rohan, Ari, Kane, and Baruch in the bungalows with some unfamiliar Rasha popped up, like I was looking into a scrying mirror. There was no sound, but it was live.

She said something softly under her breath and everyone in the room froze. One of the men was partially squatting, not having quite sat down. Ari was about to catch a pen thrown to him by Kane, while Baruch tacked a photo up, his hand extended to Rohan who ripped off a piece of tape.

The image narrowed in on my friends and twin.

The hair on the nape of my neck stood on end. "Don't touch them. Mandelbaum's group is one corrupt element. These men are innocent."

"There is no innocent when it comes to the Brotherhood," she sneered. "The last innocent person was Esther and she's dead. You think we have demon problems now? If we don't rid the world of Rasha, the witch community will grow so small and so weak that the wards we're propping up between our world and the demon realm will fail entirely. Then you can kiss humanity goodbye. But if we get that magic back, in fifty years not only will there be no more demons, we'll have the power to cure disease, end hunger."

"Esther didn't think we'd grow stronger. She said that maybe in the beginning we could have reclaimed our magic by stopping the creation of Rasha, but too many years have passed. Rasha magic lives in the bloodlines and there's no going back. Killing off hunters won't transfer all the individual grains of magic into one big pile for us, it'll simply mean that our small pile will be bunched with a large heap of magic gone bad. Magic that's become unstable and unpredictable without its host."

"Don't act like you knew her better than I did." Sienna choked me, lifting me off the ground without laying a finger on me.

I scrabbled at my throat, but there was nothing tangible to pry off me. My magic pulsed off my skin, rippling outward at Sienna.

It bounced harmlessly off an invisible shield, dissipating in the air a foot away from her.

"That entire organization is our enemy," she said. "History has taught us time and time again that the men will not allow us to sit at the table. The Brotherhood doesn't want harmony. They want war. Their entire existence is predicated on it. Maybe they'll throw us a conciliatory bone and let us be healers. Keep the wards up. But let us have a say in our world? In our magic?"

My lungs were on fire and my vision kept swimming in and out of focus. "Then help me, in Esther's memory, so I can do the right thing," I croaked.

She closed her fist and I crumpled to the ground, dragging in shaky breaths.

I rubbed my throat, barely managing to stay upright. "When I... killed Oskar, his magic did something to me." My eyes pooled with tears. "He blocked me somehow. You have to release it because it's killing me."

I placed my hand over my breastbone. Over the box.

Sienna stared at me suspiciously, then placed her hand over mine. Her brow furrowed. "There's something there."

I was enveloped in a warm light. It started as a tingle: in my toes, in the crook of my elbows, and the jut of my hips. I bound my own magic to Sienna's as fast as I could. She gasped and tried to break free, but I was also drawing on Lilith's magic.

Sienna screamed, her head thrown back and the tendons in her neck straining.

I fired all the magic inside me at whatever invisible barriers kept me from accessing the magic inside Lilith's prison.

And that's when I felt Lilith's eyes snap open. Awake at last. Still trapped, but very much present in whatever plane she existed in.

The tingle became a trickle, a river, a rush of pure power.

I'd experienced a lesser version of this, when Lilith had amped me up to heal Rohan, but now? I canted my head back, bathing in the magic like it was rainfall.

My heartbeat mingled with the delicate patter of a bird's heart on the windowsill outside. I scouted the savanna through the night vision of a tiger and blinked slowly at fuzzy light through a newborn's eyes on the other side of the world.

I was a mote in an infinite spiral, fully alive and aware and rooted and universal for the first time in my life. I gasped, spinning around. Dorothy in Oz, seeing life in Technicolor when it had only ever been flat Kansas brown.

Sienna wrenched free, physically and magically. "What have you done? How is Lilith inside you?"

"Long story." I laughed in wonder. "This is why you practice dark magic, isn't it? Not to be evil. To return to this kind of power. The power our foremothers had before the Rasha took it."

"Stole it," Sienna said. "The way you stole my magic." She blasted me.

I raised a hand, drawing on Lilith's magic and yet still straining to keep Sienna's power at bay. "Seems we have a stalemate."

I'll kill you, Lilith whispered. *You dare claim my magic? You nothing. You human. I'll be strong enough to be free in days and you'll suffer. You'll beg for death.*

My arm wobbled, allowing a burst of Sienna's magic to slash across my side. I grit my teeth, visualizing swiping inside the box for more of Lilith's power.

"You really want to use that up on me, knock yourself out." Sienna didn't even look winded.

My magic flared brighter with the Lilith boost. "Scared you can't hold me off?"

"As if. You have no idea what you're dealing with. So long as Lilith is trapped inside you, her magic is static, which means you can drain her like a battery. No sweat off my back if you drain her dry."

Was this true? I had no way to tell and Lilith wasn't volunteering anything other than a pulsing hatred.

"Damn, you're stubborn," Sienna said. "Fine. Let's stand here while you waste all the magic."

I powered down, as did Sienna. "Why would you give me the heads up on that?"

"Esther cared about you and I'd rather not see you dead if there are other options. Though you've got a death wish. The human body wasn't designed to get this much dark magic this fast. It's going to kill you."

"I don't have a death wish. Quite the opposite." I spread my hands in entreaty. "Can't we find a way to work together? What if it's a new regime of men who want to work with women?" My head reeled with the possibilities of women with this level of power ruling the world. We could be transformative. Usher in a new age, a new way of being with our male allies.

Humanity needed all of us, and I could show them the way.

"That will never happen. Don't you get it? We witches render Rasha obsolete."

"We kill them and we're no better than the men who tried to do that to us."

"We're infinitely better, but you won't believe me until you see it for yourself." Sienna led me to the photos of the compound. She ripped a corner off the map and scribbled down a string of numbers. "Latitude and longitude."

I clutched the paper tight. "The compound? If you know where it is, why haven't you stormed it?"

"I can't deal with all the variables inside on my own."

"Sucks for you." I stuffed the paper with the coordinates in my pocket. "Why would you give this to me?"

Her eyes flashed silver for a second. She took a deep breath, exhaling slowly and her eyes returned to their usual dark brown. "You have no idea how to manage the magic inside you. You want to save humanity? You want to live? You need me. Make the right choice."

She vanished.

I cast my awareness around the magic box. It shuddered under the force of Lilith's pounding, a constant buzz against my sternum. My brain throbbed with her sneering certainty that I'd be letting her out soon and then I'd face eternal torture.

"Bring it."

Sienna said I needed her to live. Could she get Lilith out of me, even without the Bullseye?

I washed out Esther's Tupperware, because it seemed rude to her memory not to. The water was steaming hot as I soaped up the plastic, turning my skin red, but it couldn't thaw out the block of ice that my body had become. I'd amassed a lot of regrets in my life, like pushing myself too hard in dance after I was first injured, and how I'd pushed people away, but I didn't regret doing the deal with Lilith to give Rohan back his magic.

Don't get me wrong, I didn't want to die for Rohan; I wanted to live with him.

I thought I'd destroyed that dream last night when I saved Benjy and used up the Bullseye. But what if I hadn't? What if Sienna could help me?

Ro and I could take a road trip, staying in cheesy motels, or eat our way through Europe. We'd have a million more of our flirtatious, silly, hilarious conversations, and every night, I'd fall asleep beside him, his hand holding mine, and his even breathing a steadying presence.

I'd tell him I loved him for the first time and then tell him again every day for the next ninety years.

I shut off the tap, the container long since clean, and my fingers wrinkled prunes.

I didn't regret having finally tapped fully into Lilith's magic because I still believed that this was how we'd stop all the bad shit from coming to pass. It was just that faced with a dream of quiet, full intimacy, go big or go home had lost its appeal.

28

I popped back to our guest bungalow to grab Rohan and a pair of binoculars.

He was standing outside on the path, but at the sight of me waving at him from the window, abruptly ended his chat with a couple of other Rasha and bolted inside.

He shoved me back into the bedroom.

"Not exactly the time," I said.

He grabbed my shoulders and spun me to face the mirror.

My eyes were obsidian black. Shadows danced and slithered in my irises.

"What the fuck happened?"

"Oh." I leaned in, kind of fascinated. "The short version is that I can now tap into all of Lilith's magic."

Rohan let out a stream of Hindi curses, while I held strands of hair up to the light. My curls had gone from dark brown to black.

"The good news is Sienna may be able to get Lilith out of me," I said.

"Yeah, I'm sure she'll be really receptive once you foil her plans."

"She will if I've got her stuffed in the Tomb and am holding her magic hostage. Here." I dug in my pocket for the co-ordinates. "I know where the compound is. Wanna check it out with me?"

"All I ever wanted was a peaceful life," Rohan said. "And then I met you."

I grabbed a pair of sunglasses and slid them on. "You're welcome."

We landed along the side of the compound next to a chain link fence complete with signs proclaiming it was electrified and that this was private property and trespassers would be prosecuted.

"There." Ro pointed to the high ridge of rock about a hundred feet from the back of the compound.

In a blink, I repositioned us. Crawling on our bellies in the fine yellow dust, we peered out from between two boulders, while I told Ro everything I'd learned.

The compound was a two-story, U-shaped building, painted a dull gray. A small militia guarded the place, their weapons magic, not guns. Some were patrolling the roof with clear sightlines. Others manned the gates in the front and back of the fencing, as well as the three doors we could see from our vantage point.

We'd caught a lucky break and hadn't been seen when we'd showed up.

Rohan adjusted the binoculars. "I recognize some of those men. I've fought with them."

"You think they're always standing guard or is this something new?" I said.

"Because they're expecting an attack?" Ro peered through the binoculars.

"Possibly. Ours or Sienna's?"

He passed them over to me to have a look. "No clue."

The more we watched the men, the more we got the

sense that while they were there to guard the compound, it was more of a routine thing. There was no urgency in the way they strolled the flat roof and the grounds.

Until one of them checked his phone, pulled out a walkie talkie, and spoke into it. All the Rasha ran to containers that had been placed around the property, donning protective helmets and gloves before taking up specific posts. Most manned the fence, while a few remained on the roof.

"No way." I stuffed the binoculars into Ro's hands. "Three o'clock."

An unlikely pack of mountain lions, rangy coyotes, and sleek bobcats prowled their way toward the fences.

"There's more." Rohan lowered the glasses and pointed at the flock of raptors careening out of the sky.

It was an awesome and terrifying sight. Dozens of falcons, vultures, eagles, and owls swooped down at breakneck speeds.

The animal attacks hit more or less simultaneously. The compound may have been warded up against demons, but there was no way to ward it against wildlife.

"Sienna's training them," Rohan said.

"She's compelling them," I corrected.

"Not the animals," he said. "The Rasha. They were expecting it. She's conditioned them so that they expect attacks at certain times and relax at others." He whistled. "Gotta hand it to her, it's pretty brilliant. Fucked up, but brilliant."

Between the large cats attempting to shred the chain link fence with their teeth and claws despite the voltage pouring through their bodies, and the raptors divebombing the men, the hunters had their hands full.

At some invisible signal, any remaining animals still alive trotted or flew back to their desert homes.

Taking the binoculars, Rohan paced the length of the ridge we were on, careful to stay out of view as much as possible.

"Well?"

He dropped down beside me, brushing dust off his pants. "If we turn off the main road a couple of miles back, we can approach this ridge without being seen. Especially if we come under cover of night. It's the last hundred feet that expose us."

"Unless we time it with one of Sienna's attacks. She's not powerful enough to take on all the Rasha and whatever's inside on her own. She needs us."

"It's got to be demons in there," Ro said. "We know Mandelbaum was experimenting on them. But we still don't know Sienna's endgame. Does she want to kill the demons or turn them on us when we're conveniently in one place for her attack?"

I stood up, stretching out my cramped knees and held out a hand. "We'll have to be prepared for every eventuality."

Back at the bungalow, sunglasses firmly in place, I sought out Baruch. "How come you're not at the rabbis' meeting?"

"There's no Executive to force out, and until we've gotten inside that compound and gotten proof against Mandelbaum, I'm holding off speaking to the other rabbis."

"Speaking of the compound." I slapped the coordinates into his hand. "Ro and I scoped it out."

He put two fingers in his mouth and let out an ear-shattering whistle.

There must have been three dozen men crammed into the bungalow. All chatter and activity stopped. Either they'd been briefed about who I was or I'd been gossiped about. Either way, I was glad to be spared a bunch of questions right now.

Ari frowned and tapped his finger next to his eyes, cueing me to take off my sunglasses.

I didn't.

"Listen up," Baruch said. "We have the last piece of our plan. The location of the compound."

Excited murmurs broke out.

"Nava, what can we expect to find there?" he said.

As one, the men turned to me expectantly. Sienna had been wrong. Witches and Rasha could work together. We didn't need to make them obsolete, and there were those who would work with us without relegating us to nursemaid.

I rubbed my breastbone. Lilith's incessant banging around my body was really tenderizing my organs, and she didn't let up her insidious whispering.

I'm looking forward to our reunion. Lilith's power flared up inside me and I absorbed it like the most refreshing water.

I also clasped my hands behind my back because my fingertips had turned black.

You think you're so clever with your plans, Lilith whispered. *You have no idea what's in store for you.*

Shut up, I silently told her. *This is how we save us all. Together.* Lilith seriously needed to watch some *Sesame Street.*

I cleared my throat and began my presentation. I'd only gotten as far as what Rohan and I suspected was inside the compound before Kane raised his hand. "Yes?" Okay, that was teachery and weird.

"Let me bring up a visual." He rose from the laptop and flicked on a projector. One of the aerial view photos of the compound flickered onto one white wall. "Where exactly was everyone stationed?"

I spoke for the next twenty minutes without pause, including Sienna's possible agendas in regards to the Brotherhood.

"Why did she let you live?" one of the hunters asked.

Ro shot me a worried glance but I shook my head. It was truth time. If I meant what I'd said to Sienna about Rasha and witches working together, then it had to start with me.

I fingered the arms of my glasses, took a deep breath, and whipped them off, bracing myself for a mass exodus at the sight of the black-eyed female with the insane power. "I'm a witch."

At the sight of my eyes, pandemonium broke out. There was a lot of furious debate, some curious looks, though some indifference, too. Cisco slapped a ten into Bastijn's hand.

"If we have Rasha, what do we need witches for?" The black Rasha didn't sound antagonistic, merely curious.

"The Brotherhood has been around for centuries," I said, "and there are certain demons that get away time and time again. Why? Because Rasha aren't strong enough to kill them. Witches have that power."

"I've seen it firsthand," Ari said.

"The world needs both Rasha and witches in this fight," I said. "Just like in any war, we need all kinds of abilities, all kinds of brainpower to defeat the greater threat. We need balance, peace, and co-operation between Rasha and witches, or humanity is doomed."

"Witches should have shown up before now." This Rasha had Mediterranean coloring and a Spanish accent. "Not left us to be the only ones fighting. They have an obligation to use their magic as well."

"Get on that and mansplain it to them, Xavier," Cisco said. "I dare you."

"Just because you don't know what witches have been up to," I said, "doesn't mean they haven't been part of the fight all along. We have, and believe me, it's our power that is going to tip the scales."

I had more to say but was drowned out by the Rasha arguing amongst themselves.

"Hey!" Everyone ignored me, busy discussing this turn of event. "Yo! Shut it or I'll turn you all into frogs."

You could have heard a pin drop.

I grinned at them. "Look. A female Rasha is one of those things..." I snapped my fingers a couple of times. "Like jumbo shrimp."

"All you can eat?" a blond Rasha called out.

"It's not an oxymoron," Ari said over the laughter, "it's just incorrect. A woman with magic is a witch. It's reductionist to call her Rasha."

"You are such a nerd," Kane said. He looked away before Ari could see his smile.

"It makes sense," Bastijn said. "Witches are the original hunters and the magic is passed down genetically, so why would any woman with powers merely be Rasha?"

"Hey," Danilo said. "We're not 'merely' anything."

I patted his shoulder, relieved to note that my fingertips were no longer so much evil magic tainted as looking like I'd smudged ink on them. "I know, it's hard being the most badass person around, but I've handled it well."

He tipped his chair back with a cocky grin. "My manhood is feeling threatened."

"Both inches?" Rohan said.

The men hooted.

"Stay with me, people," I said.

They didn't listen to me, so Baruch whistled once more, shutting them up.

"Right now, I have this window where I have mad

power," I said. "Let me use it for good. Let me be the weapon to turn this fight to our advantage. I can take out Mandelbaum's men without any loss of life and I can stop Sienna. I want to stand beside you all and make this a better world. Are you willing to stand with me and my kind as well?"

Rohan and Ari were the first to stand, followed quickly by Baruch and Kane and the Los Angeles crew. The rest of them varied in how fast they got up, but in the end they were all standing.

I flailed my hands in front of my face. "Well, shit, boys."

I handed the floor back to Baruch and returned to my seat by Ari.

He stared at my eyes, his mouth in a grim line, then he tugged his ear lobe. "Your mascara is smudged."

I wiped a finger under my eyes. "Shut up."

We discussed strategy for the next two hours.

Baruch broke down what needed to be destroyed and what needed to be saved as proof to force Mandelbaum out once and for all. He assigned one of the Rasha to videotape every inch of the compound, a couple of others to find any sensitive documents, and the rest to find the demons or destroy dangerous equipment.

Finally, Cisco begged for mercy. And beer.

Rohan stood up. "After you drunks finish happy hour, my parents are putting on a spread for us at the main house. Meet there at six."

Baruch checked his phone. "Discussion with the rabbis broke up an hour ago and Mandelbaum left the premises, saying he couldn't meet tomorrow," Baruch said, "Assume he's headed for the compound. We hit it up tonight."

"It's a three-and-a-half-hour drive," Kane said.

"Meet at the trucks at twenty-one hundred hours." Baruch paused. "Take care of any unfinished business."

"Kiss your loved ones goodbye," Ari murmured as the meeting broke up.

"I can't call Mom and Dad," I said.

"Write them a letter. That's what I'm going to do."

"I'm not writing you one, okay?" I crossed my arms. "Because, no."

"We don't need letters. Whatever happens tonight, we're gonna be fine. We all have each other's backs."

Yeah, but I also had Lilith and if the power of her whisperings was relative to her growing strength, I didn't have much longer before she was free.

"I love you."

"Love you more," he said.

"Impossible and ridiculous," I replied, repeating the phrase our grandmother had always used when we said we loved her more.

He chuckled. "You have to survive because you still owe me a waffle breakfast."

I punched him in the arm. "I paid up months ago."

"Did not."

"Did so."

He shot me a smug glance. "Then you'll just have to stick around and argue with me."

"Guess I will." I cut a glance at Kane. "Are you going to write anyone else?"

"No."

"You're hopeless."

I went back to the bungalow I shared with Rohan. I must have started the letter to my parents a million times but in the end, all I was able to write was "I love you both and I'm proud that I was your daughter."

Leo's letter was a bit longer because I rambled on telling her that if I was dead she should drown her sorrows in orgasms with Drio so I had some pervy thrills in the afterlife.

Rohan entered and glanced at the envelope to my parents. "Ah. Yeah. Billie has mine." He massaged my shoulders. "I checked the dark web and spoke to Leo. Hybris is public enemy number one. The demon realm has been closed to her. If the spawn don't get her by the time we've dealt with the compound, we'll marshal the troops and find her."

I licked Leo's envelope closed and stacked it on top of the one to my parents. "If she's stuck here on earth, I could do a location spell. We have the note she wrote. That should work."

"You want to do that now?"

I placed my hands over his and shook my head. "No. She'll still be around tomorrow. I want to spend this evening with you."

We had an hour before Maya and Dev expected us all for dinner. Lilith was quiet–hopefully all her threat uttering had tuckered the witch out–but she was still weak enough that I was able to put up a mental shield around the box for privacy, just in case.

Ro led me into the bedroom which was bathed in pools of late afternoon sun through the filtered curtains. Our lovemaking was slow and dreamy, both of us relishing each languid touch, each murmured endearment.

We spun out our desire until we lay limp in each other's arms.

Rohan nuzzled my neck, and when I wrote "Nava plus Rohan" with my finger on his chest, the smile he bestowed on me was happy and lazy, while his eyes reflected an appreciation and wonder that filled me to bursting.

It was the perfect opportunity to tell him I loved him.

Except once again there was a knock on the bungalow's

front door. I tensed, bracing for another demon-related disaster, but it was just his dad asking Rohan to come help him find a particular hat of his he was sure Ro had borrowed.

More knocking.

"Rohan?" Dev rattled the doorknob.

"Seriously? Dad, wait. I'm coming." Ro stole one last kiss and left me in the bed, grabbing his jeans on the way out of the room.

It was three little words. Why was the universe conspiring against me?

Dinner was a surprisingly festive affair. While the booze didn't flow, since we were all too professional to get drunk before this mission, the conversation and laughter did.

Rohan rolled his eyes when my reunion with Mahmud turned into a super over-the-top, playful flirtation, then dragged me away to introduce me to the newcomers. I heard an absolutely hilarious story from Bao and An, the Vietnamese brothers, about a naga demon and a stolen boat, discovered a shared love of the old kids' cartoon *The Fairly Oddparents* with Wangombe from Kenya, and tried some delicious Israeli chocolate courtesy of Zvi.

"Who's the Hell's Angel escapee?" I tilted my head at the lone Rasha I had yet to meet. His wild ginger hair was only slightly less bushy than his beard. Tattooed knuckles peeked out of the sleeves of his Harley Davidson shirt.

Ro shot me an odd look. "Go introduce yourself."

The Rasha watched me approach through narrowed eyes. "Fait pas ta neuve, and say hello already," he grunted.

Only one hunter would tell me to stop being a princess in heavy Québécois.

"Pierre!" I squealed and hugged him. "Look at you, Biker Boy. Figured you'd be more the cardigan-wearing type."

"Decriss!" he swore, swatting me away. "Like I'd wear that garbage." He patted the seat next to him. "Sit down, hotshot."

"'Otshot." I snickered.

We got a lot of strange looks in the next ten minutes, nattering away at each other in French, one or the other of us guffawing at the insults flying fast and furious. Pierre also demanded an update on Hybris. He warned me to be careful bringing her in, though he agreed that spreading rumors so other demons would hunt her down for me had been pretty inspired.

I glowed under his praise.

He already knew Ro and Kane, and Baruch obviously since they were stationed in Jerusalem together, so I waved Ari over to introduce him. The two fell into an enthusiastic conversation about hockey–again in French, since I hadn't been the only Katz twin educated in the French Immersion system.

I couldn't get away from the sports talk fast enough. My stomach rumbled and, thrilled I wasn't queasy, I obeyed, beelining for the buffet.

Between Maya's Jewish and Indian sides, she'd provided enough food for a small army–or our bunch. If I wanted Indian, I could help myself to pakoras, samosas, tamarind chutneys, butter chicken, saag paneer, and fluffy Jasmine rice. I could go Cali local with fish tacos, an assortment of salads, farm fresh roasted potatoes or grilled vegetables with balsamic reduction, or satisfy my inner carnivore and load up on steak and sausages, with a side of pesto pasta.

If this was my last supper, I intended to eat all the things. I'd already piled my plate high with yumminess when one of the servers brought out a humongous platter.

I poked Rohan. "Is that fried chicken and waffles from Roscoe's?"

He looked pretty smug. "It is. I had Mom get some to prove to you how good it is."

Ro had waxed poetic about the stuff. I was amazed he hadn't composed a song to the damn chicken. Unless "Rhapsody of You" was about those plump juicy thighs.

I snagged a drumstick. There was no way it could live up to the hype.

One bite and oh, how wrong I was. My breathing quickened.

Ro smirked. "Admit it. I was right."

"I admit nothing," I said through a mouthful of the crispiest, lightest, most mouthwatering fried chicken I'd ever tasted. I got a second plate and helped myself to two more pieces and two fluffy waffles, dousing all of it in maple syrup before sitting down on the nearest couch with my food arrayed in front of me.

While Ari and Kane both seemed to be mingling, it was always somehow with the same group at the same time. Oh, how I wanted to see that finally reach its inevitable conclusion.

And say "I told you so."

Raquel texted me to say she'd found the Tomb of Endless Night and I wriggled my hips joyfully. I was going to stop Sienna. And if that seemingly impossible event could come to pass, then maybe I'd even bully her into giving me a long life.

"Who's that?" Ro asked.

I glanced up over him to answer, struck dumb for a moment that I might really get to be with this amazing man long-term. I ducked my head to hide my moony-eyed look and texted Raquel the coordinates and the approximate time we'd be at the compound. "Raquel. She's got the Tomb."

He rubbed my back. "We're in business."

Maya and Dev were circulating. They seemed to know a few of the Rasha quite well, like the L.A. contingent and Baruch. But eventually they narrowed in on us.

Rohan moved over so his parents could sit down with us. I loved that he didn't stop touching me just because they were there.

I wiped off my mouth and hands, dropping my napkin onto my empty plate. "Thank you so much for dinner. I'm sorry I haven't really seen much of you, just imposed on your hospitality."

Dev patted my knee. The linen fedora he was wearing was pretty cool and I could totally see Ro stealing it. "That's okay. We know this was a working visit. Next time you'll come to hang out. Maybe in a couple months when it's not so hot."

Ro's hand stilled for a fraction of a second, and I knew he was thinking of Lilith.

I leaned against my boyfriend. "Sounds perfect."

"Next time bring your tap shoes," Maya said.

"She better," Ro said. "Now that she has that new floor of hers to christen."

My breath caught. I could picture it so easily. Dancing for Ro at his place, him accompanying me on his guitar as it turned into a dance of another type.

No one, not Lilith, not Sienna, and definitely not Mandelbutt was going to rob me of that future. "Have shoes, will tap."

"I'd like to see you dance in person," Maya said. "The videos never do a performance justice."

"You've seen videos?"

"Ro-Ro found them online and showed us. You're very talented."

I blushed, more from the idea that Rohan had cared

enough to share that with his parents than her compliment. "Thank you. It was my life."

"We're sorry you lost that," Dev said, "but we're glad that path led you to our family."

What would have happened if I'd still been on track with my tap dream when I'd gotten my powers at Ari's induction ceremony? Would I have come to resent my magic? My dancing? If I'd been at the top of my game instead of at my lowest, who would I be now? Because I really liked this woman, one with a deep purpose and a renewed, far more mature sense of self.

A part of me would always grieve the future that could have been, but sitting here with Dev and Maya and the love of my life, I couldn't have stopped the grin that broke free if there had been a gun pressed to my head.

"Me too," I said. "I can't wait to spend more time with you both."

"Good." Maya smiled. "That's settled. Excuse us. We should check on our guests."

Dev stood up and offered her his arm. She gave him a saucy curtsy before letting him escort her across the room.

It was the most adorable sight ever.

Plus, they liked me. They really liked me.

"You have good parents, Mitra."

"Yeah, they produced a top-quality kid." He grinned at me and my heart did a little flip.

We were surrounded by a few dozen people. There was no privacy, no romance, and it didn't matter. I didn't need a perfect moment to say this to him. I just needed him.

"Rohan."

He blinked his golden eyes at me. "What?"

"I want to tell you something. I–"

"No."

I froze at the insistence in his voice. Tried again. "You don't understand. I want–"

"I know what you want to tell me and I'm not letting you."

I crossed my arms, magic sparking off my skin. All right, he didn't love me, but was it so awful to even hear that *I* loved *him*? Did he feel guilty about his lack of reciprocal feelings?

"You're not the boss of me. I can say what I want."

Great start, idiot.

"I can't hear it if you're saying it like some kind of preemptive goodbye." He pulled me flush against him, burying his face in the crook of my neck. "Say it tomorrow."

I'd shut down my magic before he could be injured. "Hmph. I might not want to say it tomorrow, you imperious bastard."

Ro flashed me his rock fuck grin, softening it into something so much more tender. "Say it tomorrow," he implored me softly. "When it's not goodbye. When it's a promise for the rest of our lives."

He didn't know that Lilith was growing stronger with each passing second, her siren croonings that my time of reckoning was coming, growing harder to ignore. My time was slipping away like grains in an hourglass.

I mentally knocked that stupid hourglass onto its side. "Tomorrow," I vowed.

29

Three and a half hours was a long time to be crammed into a jeep with four men when everything on the radio was shit and there was zip to see out the window other than highway, desert, and night sky. None of it stopped my brain from churning at top speed about everything that could go wrong.

Between Ari and I, we could have transported everyone there, but Baruch refused to let us expend our magic on that when we could suck it up and drive. Plus, we needed the armored truck in our convoy.

The first hour wasn't so bad. I sat up front with Baruch who drove, leaving Rohan, Kane, and Ari to squish into the back. I had full rein of the music, my edginess translating to me lasting about a minute on any given song, until Rohan started kicking the back of my chair, griping about the musical torture.

We switched it up in hour two. I was now sandwiched between my brother and Kane, who did the grown-up version of "he's looking out my window," sniping, until Baruch threatened to punch both their lights out.

Then there was hour three. Baruch was bear snoring in

the passenger seat while Kane drove. Ari, still in the back with me and Rohan, stared stonily at the back of Kane's head. Ro had fallen asleep as well and was making these adorable snuffling noises. Less adorable was his dead weight squashing me into the door and smushing my cheek against the window. My left side had gone numb but no matter how I tried to shove him, he didn't budge.

Sienna expected an answer from me. Not any answer either. An answer that involved proving my undying loyalty to all witch-kind by taking her side against the Rasha. And if my undying loyalty involved my actual dying, she wouldn't shed any tears.

I called Raquel on my burner phone to make sure she was on track to meet us, but it went to voicemail. I hung up and immediately received a text.

Rohan startled awake with a snort, jostling my arm. "What?"

I bent over to snag my cell from the floor. "That's what woke you, dude who I've been shoving for an hour? You kids. So tied to your phones. Pathetic."

The text was from Rivka. "The funeral is on Thursday," I said.

"Text back that we'll be there," Ari said.

My fingers hovered over the keys. I had yet to speak to her about Esther.

Another text came in. *She left you something. You don't come. You don't get it.*

I called Rivka. "You sound like your sister."

"I was the original," she said. "I'll give you your inheritance when you come."

"I don't want anything."

"I know. You're still getting it. She was very clear."

"Clear when?" I snapped. "She wasn't an oracle. She didn't know she was going to die."

"Terminal cancer," Rivka said gently. "She knew."

"But she'd done chemo. She looked better."

"She had months at best, so stop beating yourself up about this. She genuinely cared about you. Said you reminded her of her younger self."

"Don't ruin all my fond memories of her."

Rivka barked a laugh and my heart clutched. She really sounded exactly like Esther.

"Thursday. Eleven o'clock at the Jewish cemetery in New Westminster. I'm hanging up before I get maudlin," she said and did just that.

I cuddled into Rohan. "Thursday at 11. You'll come with?"

"Of course," he said.

"Esther said I reminded her of her younger self."

Ari snorted. I reached over Rohan and punched my brother's thigh.

"Not surprising," Kane said. "Dr. Gelman was a total shit disturber when she was young."

"How would you know?" Rohan said.

"I hacked into Brotherhood documents after her death. They had a huge file on her. There was this fifteen-year period they suspected her of killing all these big-time demons before the Rasha could. We're talking dozens and dozens. She was legendary."

"And instead of lauding her for it, she got a file," Ari said. "Nice."

"Exactly," Kane said. "Rasha are a bunch of glory hogs. Present company all included. Tell me you can't all score your kills."

Ari and Rohan muttered their assent.

"Hang on." I leaned forward to see them all. "You guys keep track of how many demons you've taken out? My God, why am I asking this question? Of course you do. Do you circle jerk the numbers or just whip them out one-on-one to compare?"

"Both," Ari and Rohan said at the same time.

The first jeep in our caravan turned off the main road. Kane followed, raising his voice over the whine of the motor as we bumped our way through the desert. "Ready to be legendary, babyslay?"

"We're all gonna be legendary," I said. "Tonight we bring down the old regime and forge a brave new world where witches and Rasha work together. Now someone wake the bear up."

As expected from our earlier reconnaissance, the jeeps reached the ridge undetected. The clock on our dashboard glowed 12:35AM in big blue digits.

Ari immediately left, shadow jumping to the top of the ridge with a pair of high-powered binoculars.

The rest of us stood silently waiting for his return. Well, most of us did. Kane looked decidedly fidgety.

The wind whooshed over the desert as loud as a rushing river, while the sky above was so stuffed full with stars that I swore I could reach up on tiptoe and grab one. It was cold at night, but we had lightweight warm gear that wouldn't restrict our movements.

Ari returned and gathered us into a circle. "Six guards on the roof. No one on the ground. I checked around the compound. Nothing hiding out in the desert."

"You good with that?" Baruch asked me.

I cracked my knuckles. "Child's play. The plan is on track. I'll take them out in waves. First the Rasha outside, then the ones inside. Make sure when you follow me in to secure the men, that you keep barriers between myself and all of you at each stage until I give the all-clear. Don't want you hit with my magic. Once the Rasha are dealt with, I'll track Sienna."

"Is the Tomb here?" Baruch said.

"It will be." I had faith in Raquel.

"The terrain is rocky," Ari said, "but the trucks should make it to the compound no problem."

Baruch turned to Mahmud, Wangombe, Pierre, and Bastijn. "You have the C-4?"

"Ready when you are," Mahmud said.

"Remember your assignments," Baruch said. "Hard proof against Mandelbaum and his men to present to the Brotherhood gets loaded in the jeeps. Demon and blood samples in the lock-up in the armored truck, otherwise, everything gets destroyed. Be thorough." He canted his head up to the moonlight. "Five minutes. That patch of clouds will provide some cover. Nava, get ready on my signal."

"Will do." I pulled Rohan aside for some privacy. "Technically, it's tomorrow."

Ro scowled at me. "Don't you dare."

"Rohan Liam Mitra, you listen up."

This might not be a gazebo or the tap floor at his place, and it might not be as cozy as the two of us waking up together in bed to a rainy morning. Before, I'd hated that I could never find the perfect moment to say it. Now I'd run out of moments. I had to make this perfect by itself, even if the air was thick with tension about our mission and I'd found new places to sweat.

I kissed his knuckles, pressing his hand to my heart. "Being a twin, Ari's always been my other half. But you make me the most myself I've ever been. The most complete as a person in my own right. You found me in the darkness and didn't let me stay there. You pushed me to remake myself into someone better, someone who I am really proud of being. Being with you... it's like living a tap dance all the time. I'm more awake and more alive and at my happiest. I know this seems like the worst moment to say it, but I never want you to wonder or doubt it. I love you, Rohan." I spread my arms helplessly. "I'm yours."

"Nava..." His Adam's apple bobbed up and down.

Oh. I guess all that stuff about saying it like it was a promise had just been an excuse. Well, I was not going to cry. Yeah, I'd hoped he'd still say it back. Yeah, it was stupid. But I was doing this on my terms, and I wasn't about to put up with getting chastised for telling him the truth, for making sure he knew.

I held up a hand and cut him off. "I broke our agreement. Too bad. I said it. Deal with it."

Rohan laughed, his eyes shining, and if somehow that laugh had gotten caught on his album, you'd replay that track over and over just to hear that sound of pure joy. "I love you, too."

He actually blushed when he said it. His eyes flickered to the ground, then once more back to mine, a shy, besotted smile flitting free.

There was no breath left in my body.

"I've never met anyone so full of life and passion as you," he said.

I kind of squirmed in sheer delight. "Yeah? Go on."

"I love your jokes at the most inappropriate moments. I love how you've never met a boundary you didn't take as a personal challenge. And I love how every time something stupid and inconsequential happens, my first thought is to find you and tell you because you're the one person who'll always get it. Because you *always* get me, even when you're giving me shit."

"Especially then," I agreed.

He laughed. "That. Right there." He clasped my head in his hands, his fingers threading through my hair. "Nava Katz, you are complicated and infuriating and extraordinary, and everything I want. How could I not? You're the spark that brought me back to life."

"Damn you." I sniffed, wiping my finger under my damp lashes. "I can't charge in all badass if I'm weepy."

He wrapped me in his arms, and I melted into him, luxuriating in this moment: the chirping crickets far away, the breeze ruffling his hair against my cheek, and best of all the feeling of being cherished by someone so special.

I stepped back, still holding his hands. "We're only getting started, you and I. You and the universe should know that. This love story doesn't end here, got it?"

"Got it." He tugged me to him and kissed me. "I love you so much."

"Back at you, Snowflake. Always and forever."

Baruch cleared his throat. "Can we secure this compound or are you busy?"

"Let's burn this fucker down," I said.

Ro smiled. "That's my girl."

We could have waited for whenever Sienna's next attack happened, but why do things on her schedule when we could do it on ours?

"Get inside the armored trucks and wait for my signal," I said. "I'm going in."

I portalled onto the roof into the shadows and looked down. The guards were barely paying attention. An animal attack must not have been imminent.

I cast out my awareness. There were now eight Rasha outside, their locations pinpointed over the compound grounds by their pale orange life force lights.

Showtime. I reached into Lilith's magic box, scooped up a generous amount and, binding her magic to mine to amp up my attack, flicked my fingers. Eight balls of lightening shot out, each one wrapping itself around a Rasha's head. I didn't even need to be physically near them, which was a hella cool new trick.

The electricity crackled and danced around their brains, the entire thing playing out in my mind's eye like a magic HUD.

Eight men dropped to the ground, unconscious. Their life forces dimmed but weren't extinguished.

Thank you for your contribution to the cause, I thought at Lilith.

I activated the tiny mic pinned to my shirt. "I'm going for the ones inside. Wait for my next signal."

They'd hear me through the ear pieces we all wore.

I checked the Rasha closest to me to make sure he was still breathing, admiring the lightning bolt-shaped burn marks called Lichtenberg Figures that bloomed like vines across his skin.

As I portalled inside, I felt the oddest sensation, like when I'd been in rehab for my Achilles and the physiotherapist had been working on the knots up the side of my leg. He'd press down on a tight spot until I'd feel it kind of melt and give way. That's what happened now for the briefest second, but across my entire chest.

From one blink to another, the sensation changed. I was gut punched from inside my body with the wind knocked out of me. I stumbled my landing inside the building and, doubled over, crashed my shoulder against a wall. Clutching my rib cage, I checked the box.

Lilith still wasn't free, but one of the sides bore an imprint of a fist, like it had been Hulk-smashed from the inside. It had twisted the entire box.

Even worse?

The box itself had lost its matte black solidity. It was paper thin and translucent.

Lilith's cackles filled my brain. *Told you you'd let me out.*

Accessing her magic had eroded the walls of her prison. One more use would blow it away all together.

Fuck! I tried to divest myself of her magic, but we were firmly bound together, a glowing silver spiderweb.

She didn't like that anymore than I did, upping her threats on all the ways she was going to rip me free and destroy me.

"Freeze!" A couple of Mandelbaum's Rasha stormed out of a doorway.

Could I use even the barest level of magic without releasing her?

Try it and find out.

I couldn't risk it, nor could I even use my own magic because there no longer *was* my own magic.

I rushed the men in a flurry of punches, catching them off-guard. Well, that plus the detonation from my team blowing up the fences that rocked us all off our feet. Taking advantage of their distraction, I sprinted past them into the stairwell.

"Ran out of time on my magic," I said into the mic. "Send in a team."

I hit the second floor in a sprint, my progress lit by bursts of light from dozens of different magic outside.

I ran to a window and peered out.

The earth rumbled. Shadows slithered. Even Cisco managed to coax enough life from the cracked desert floor for his vines to trap our enemies who'd run outside at the explosion.

Tree Trunk alone was methodically pummelling any Rasha stupid enough to get on the wrong side of his fists.

Three of our team rounded up the men I'd taken out, imprisoning them in the armored truck that was parked diagonally near the front door.

My earpiece crackled to life. "Team Beta in the east wing on neutralization," Rohan said. "Nava, you okay?"

"Yeah. Sorry. Change in plans," I said. "Keep your men safe."

He had Ari, Kane, Cisco, Danilo, and a dozen others with him.

"Watch your back," Ro said.

I left the fighting to the rest of my team, bent on finding Sienna, though I found the lab before I found her. Thanks to our aerial photos and the expertise of a couple of our Rasha, we'd been able to pinpoint the most likely spots for it. The lab was cordoned off from the rest of the building by two giant sheets of thick, translucent plastic.

I brushed them aside and ducked through. The air temperature dropped to just above freezing and even with my high-tech clothing, I shivered.

The lights were dim, gloomy pools of shadow ringing the corridor that stretched out impossibly long. Every footfall seemed to chime louder than a church bell, but no one came to investigate.

I reached the thick wooden door at the end of the corridor marked "Authorized personnel only." Turning the knob slowly and silently, I slipped inside, sucked in a breath, and wished I hadn't as a slaughterhouse worth of rotted meat gagged me.

Iron cages big enough to comfortably hold a Labrador Retriever rose from the floor to the top of the fifteen-foot ceiling, stretched out in two long lines on either side of me. Every single one was stuffed with demons. Not just one or two, multiples of them crammed in there, dazed and listless.

Mutated, burned, scarred, they stared at me with glazed eyes. Scales, feathers, fur, no matter what they were covered in, they bore the telltale red streaks of iron poisoning.

The hot, swampy stench had so many notes to it from rotting flesh to fungus to excrement, urine to sulfur, that if demons bottled it and sent it into our nightmares, humans would be helpless in its wake.

I kept my sleeve over my mouth as I crept along the narrow pathway, my shoulder blades prickling from the weight of all these demon eyes tracking my progress. At least the noise covered my approach. Raspy caws, feeble growls, claws scraping bars, individually their cries of distress were barely above a whisper but hundreds of them together made the most unholy lullaby I'd ever had the misfortune to hear.

Lilith perked up, a silent fury rolling out of the box. *Destroy these abominations.*

With you on that. Except I couldn't. Not unless I wanted to free her.

It got worse from there, because when I turned the corner, I found the active part of the lab. I ducked behind a metal shelving unit crammed with boxes of gauze and surgical supplies.

One wall held giant glass fridges of vacuum-sealed packs of liquids in various colors. Demon blood? The blood needed to bind demons on a large scale? The "blood to rule the might?"

Scientists in splattered surgical garb cut demons open with whining, spinning saw blades, plucked out eyeballs with dull hooks, and in one case, cranked the voltage to eleven, charring the bucking reptilian body on the metal gurney.

Its one fish eye blinked blearily at me, wordlessly begging me for mercy.

The most benign part were the two scientists discussing X-rays on one of those lit up viewers. I couldn't begin to identify what physiology had made some of the shapes captured on film.

I bolted out of there, racing past the caged demons for the exit, and crashed into Pierre who'd burst through the door with his team. He stumbled sideways to avoid knocking into me, saw the cages, and launched into the worst flurry of swearing I'd ever heard from him.

"Mad scientists." I pointed in the direction I'd come from. "Most are wearing gloves but the couple that weren't didn't have rings. Possibly not Rasha."

I couldn't use my magic, but I still had fists and legs and a battery of fighting techniques.

We spilled into the room, Pierre booming at the scientists to put their instruments down.

Most of the men tried to flee, but some kept at their horrific experimentation. I'd been right and they weren't Rasha, so it was easy enough to round them up.

"The outside has been neutralized," Baruch said over the mic. "Report."

All the team leaders reported in. All had been successful. We'd secured the compound, but there was no sign of either Mandelbaum or Sienna.

I accompanied a couple of Pierre's men to help transport the scientists down to the armored truck. Pierre and the rest of his squad stayed behind to document the demons and blood on camera, keeping a couple as proof then killing the rest before scouring the lab with fire.

The mood outside was festive as our team reunited now that Mandelbaum's men were imprisoned. Yes, we still needed the rabbi, but we'd foiled his plans and had the proof to enact change.

Most importantly, we'd kept humanity safe from the rabbi's nefarious agenda.

And even though, yeah, I still needed to stop Sienna, I

was living in a world in which I had Rohan's love and he had mine. No barriers. No bullshit. Sienna was going to help me keep living that reality.

Pierre and his remaining men came out with a few demons they'd contained that bore the worst marks of experimentation and a couple armfuls of equipment. Their hair was plastered with sweat and soot, but they flashed triumphant thumbs-ups.

We all cheered.

Rohan pulled me inside the foyer, into the darkness of the half-ajar front doors. "How about a celebratory kiss, love of my life?"

I wound my arms around his neck. "Say that again. And again and again."

And as my lips brushed his, a voice boomed out over a bullhorn. "Put your hands up!"

30

Outside, every Rasha on my team simultaneously activated their magic.

"Give yourselves up," the woman on the bullhorn commanded.

No one did, tension rolling over the courtyard like a blanket.

I peeked out through the half-ajar door in time to see the air around the compound's property line ripple.

A dozen women ranging from their twenties to their fifties stood there, expressions alert and bodies coiled to spring. They wore identical black uniforms that seemed to suck all light into them.

Rohan was at my back, the heat of his body pressed against mine, whispering into his mic, asking if anyone was still inside.

"Give yourselves up or we will take action!" Standing slightly in front of everyone and holding the bullhorn, was a tall, broad-shouldered woman who could have taken Tree Trunk in a wrestling match.

I couldn't see who she was consulting with, until she stepped aside.

Sienna.

She took the bullhorn from the other witch.

Fuck. She'd brought the Malfoy wannabes.

"Hello, Rasha," she purred. "We have your rabbis. Don't worry, they're not harmed."

So much for her inability to handle the compound by herself. I'd bet good money that Sienna had known exactly which Rasha I was working with. She'd arranged things so we were all in one place to be dealt with and the rabbis were left exposed.

My old frail Rabbi Abrams being taken like some kind of common criminal caused magic to crackle off my skin.

End them, Lilith crooned.

I grit my teeth and held my fire. I was not throwing away my shot.

"Thank you for your assistance in destroying the demons," Sienna continued. "Now it's time for you to come along quietly. The gig's up. For all of you."

"And if we refuse?" Kane, who'd been standing off to one side, strutted toward her. He struck a pose like a diva supermodel, hand cocked on his hip. "We going to have a good old-fashioned magic showdown like civilized people?"

"Oh, sweetheart, you boys might be the top Rasha, but your magic days are over. These fine women are here to make sure of it." Sienna waved a hand at her allies.

The women began chanting, a low unfamiliar refrain.

The ground boomed and cracked. Brambles sprung up, their twisted branches studded with cacti-needles and tipped with wicked-looking thorns. The Rasha tried to avoid them, tried to cut them down or blast them away, to no avail. The brambles sought them out, forcing them into a stumbled huddle, the ground undulating under the hunters' feet.

I grabbed onto the front door frame, knocked off-balance even inside the building.

The chanting grew louder, the witches now stomping their left feet in a percussive rhythm.

The brambles grew wilder, higher, herding the Rasha closer together, until they were so tightly packed there was no room between their bodies, the branches almost shoulder-height.

The chanting and stomping abruptly stopped, leaving an eerie silence.

"Fuuuuck," Rohan whispered.

Instead of a brambly semi-circle enclosure, Kane had his own special contingent of steely-eyed witches keeping him apart from the others.

"Overkill much?" he said.

"We've learned to be cautious. Especially around men whose leader was planning to unleash demons out of some kind of misguided power play." Sienna wagged a finger at Kane. "Not cool."

Kane was not to be deterred. "Agreed. Which puts you and me on the same side."

"When have your people ever reached out to mine?" Sienna's lip curled. "When we were in trouble, when our magic was dwindling, when did a Rasha come to us and say we were on the same side?"

"Times change." He prowled toward her, ignoring his guard.

The air snapped like an electric wire.

The witch closest to him, rocking an impressively spiked mohawk, made a fist, then blew on it, releasing a stream of icy vapor into the air.

It swirled around Kane, gathering weight and shape until a jagged icicle formed and sliced through his calf, pinning him in place, all in the blink of an eye.

She raised an eyebrow as if daring him to make another move.

He paled. Death was before him, but he didn't cry out. His face was a mask of bravado, as it had always been, except for one moment where he glanced at my brother and pure sorrow broke through his features before it was replaced by gritty determination.

He cracked his knuckles, yanked the icicle from his bleeding leg, and took another few steps toward the witches.

Two massive icicles, about half of Kane's height, coalesced out of thin air and slashed down at him.

Ari burst out of the shadows, grabbed Kane, and whisked him away.

The icicles shuddered into the ground with the force of Excalibur embedding in rock.

I screamed and Rohan grabbed me about the waist, keeping us hidden, his hand clamped over my mouth.

Everything outside the doors had literally frozen: the Rasha and witches powered up for a fight; the bright bursts of magic, showers of earth, weaving vegetation, all was motionless.

All, that is, except Sienna. She stepped forward, surveying the scene with a shake of her head, then flicked her fingers.

Everyone's magic winked out.

Her eyes darted over the courtyard, then, finding whatever she was looking for, she made a "bring it" motion with one hand. "Someone has magic they shouldn't."

Ari and Kane reappeared outside the still half-open front doors, blinking dazedly like she'd plucked them from the shadows.

I frantically scanned them, but they were unharmed. I'd have sagged to my knees if Ro hadn't been still holding me.

"Take two," Sienna said.

The world swung back into motion, all the players looking around, disoriented.

"Magic remains on lockdown. This is not turning into a bloodbath." Her voice was the crack of a whip. "Which Rasha will speak with me?"

The hunters as one turned to Baruch, who stepped forward.

Kane took advantage of Sienna's pre-occupation with Tree Trunk to swat the top of Ari's head. "Idiot. You could have been killed."

"No," Ari fired back. "That's you. Making it your life's work to piss everyone off and damn the consequences."

"Whatever. I made it out okay." Kane waved it off. "You're the most annoying boyfriend ever."

Ari snorted. "*I* got you out–Wait. What?"

Kane's cheeks pinked. "Shut up."

Ari smiled, shy and sweet. "Make me."

Kane clasped the back of Ari's head and kissed him, hard.

I fist pumped, wanting to yell out "I told you so," but Rohan shoved his phone under my nose.

He tapped the text that Drio had sent. *Chapters stormed. Rasha captured. Meet up.*

Gawd. A girl couldn't even get a moment to gloat about two of her favorite people finally getting their shit together.

"We have to get out of here," Rohan whispered. "Find who's still free and regroup."

"First we need to get out back." That's where I'd told Raquel to bring the Tomb. "Baruch won't let them be taken," I assured myself, craning onto tiptoe to see what was happening with the parlay.

Sienna said something that made Baruch clench his

fists. Then he very deliberately stepped back, resignation in every inch of his frame.

Sienna nodded and the witches swarmed my team.

Baruch let himself be captured, though three of the most formidable-looking witches stayed on him, and even they looked nervous.

Tree Trunk's counterpart kept repeating Sienna's directive that no one was to be harmed.

My brother and Kane were prodded into joining the tight circle of Rasha. Kane leaned against my brother's shoulder like he was never losing contact again.

But I was. The last time Ari was captured, he'd come back tortured. And sure, the demon who'd done that to him was dead, but as long as I lived I'd never forget the drop of my stomach on seeing him after Asmodeus had worked him over, seeing my twin transformed into someone I almost couldn't recognize and knowing it had, in some way, been my fault.

I'd sworn I'd never let that happen again, yet here he was being herded away with the other Rasha and I was doing nothing.

"I can't leave him."

"You can't help him from whatever hellhole they're planning to toss them into," Ro said.

"Nava," Sienna called out. "Come out, come out, wherever you are."

Fat chance.

Trusting that Ari would get himself free as soon as the opportunity presented itself, I touched Rohan's shoulder and we raced through the compound to the Tomb, where Sienna and I would have our final showdown. Between Lilith's magic and the Tomb, I was the only one who could wrench control away from her. I'd take away her magic until Sienna agreed to move forward my way, working with Rasha and agreeing to get Lilith out of me.

Raquel could help bind her to her word.

A tiny part of me had hoped that it wouldn't come to this. I wanted to respect Esther's memory as much as Sienna did, and under different circumstances, Sienna and I could have been friends.

I knew better now.

When we burst out the back doors and saw the sarcophagus on the far side of the yard, I stumbled in relief.

The Tomb of Endless Night was made of iron and covered in symbols like the pendant that had held the Bullseye. It looked like something out of a museum. Or a Scooby Doo episode. The heavy door was wide open.

Slap!

I rubbed my stinging cheek, blinking stupidly at Rabbi Mandelbaum.

"You useless girl!" he screeched, spittle flying. "Look what you've done!"

He was apoplectic, his skin splotchy with rage.

"Shut the fuck up, you megalomaniac," I said. "*You* did this and you've cost us everything."

The rabbi rushed me again, but I got him in a headlock with his arms wrenched up behind his back.

His pained wince was so satisfying, I wrenched his arm up higher, savoring his torment.

"Where's Raquel?" She wouldn't have left the Tomb unguarded.

"Raquel?" His confusion wasn't faked.

Icy fear prickled my neck.

"You going to kill me now, witch?"

My hands went sweaty with dread. Mandelbaum slithered free as I cursed myself. "You knew?"

"Not at first. I wanted to know why you were investigating Ferdinand." His smile chilled me. "Given the right incentive, Tessa was very forthcoming about there being no such thing as a female Rasha."

Rohan caught me before I could choke the rabbi out. He faced the rabbi, his blades snicking out.

"Rohan. Enough." Mandelbaum sounded impatient. "You're Rasha. Nava is nothing. A good time, easily forgott–" He screeched as Rohan broke his wrist.

"Say another word about her. Go on."

"Why did you let me live?" I said. What was his endgame with me?

"Rather arrogant of you to assume you were such a scary antagonist that your death was the only solution. So many other uses for you." Hybris stepped out from behind the Tomb. She didn't look much better than those demons in the cage. Obsidian black reptilian skin peeked through the holes in her human glamor: a splash across her collarbone, a curved strip up one cheek, on her left webbed hand and part of her forearm. Her once-lustrous long hair was patchy and scraggly and her red eyes were wild.

Mandelbaum had produced a gun which he dug into the side of my head, his broken wrist cradled against his chest. "I promised Tia first shot at you, but she's assured me there'll be plenty left over for me." He motioned Ro away from me with a jerk of his head. "Give me a reason to shoot Nava. Please."

Fury rolled off Rohan, but at my head shake he kept himself in check. Barely.

My scalp was sweating. I could have disarmed the rabbi, but Hybris complicated things and I needed to save all magic use to stick Sienna in the Tomb. Then Ro and I could take out Mandelbaum and this spawn.

"Left over for what?" I said. Let the windbag talk and buy me time for Sienna to arrive.

"I was going to kill you," Mandelbaum said, "but it seemed more prudent to keep you alive. Watch you to see what the witches with the real power were up to."

Unbelievable. He was still dissing me. I couldn't wait to make him lose that stupid smirk for good.

"But you have more value than I realized," he said.

"I'm not helping you capture Sienna," I said. I mean, *I* was going to capture her, but no way was he getting his hands on her.

Hybris patted the side of the Tomb. "Fun as this is, I'd like my payment. I got you the Tomb. Now, give me the Ring of Solomon."

A ring? And what the hell? *Hybris* had brought the Tomb for Mandelbaum? This wasn't a fortunate last-minute interception of the Tomb. The demon and Mandelbaum had planned this. I shoved my worry for Raquel down tight.

"Of course." The rabbi flicked his wrist.

Hybris gasped softly. A pale silver dart embedded in her cheek glowed in the moonlight. She stood there, twitching.

"That's the poison coursing through you," the rabbi said. "This demon venom really burns."

Baruch's Stinger.

"More of a tiny prick. Like you." Hybris yanked the dart from her cheek. "Not so effective on us ancient ones." She ran directly for Mandelbaum.

Rohan, blades still extended, sprinted to intercept her.

They collided, grappling with each other. A blur of glinting blades, kicks, and punches. For every step the demon drove Rohan forward in her snarled attempt to get to the rabbi, he knocked her back two.

She body-checked Ro, sending him staggering but he quickly regrouped, head down, and charged her.

Mandelbaum's gun fired.

Rohan jerked sideways, blood blossoming on his gut. He crumpled to the ground.

I screamed and ran over to Ro, pressing my hands against his wound and reaching for my healing magic.

"Save your magic for Sienna." His face was twisted in pain.

"Dummy." My voice cracked. I dug deep, but all I got was the tiniest spark. It was like I was walled off from all my power.

My hands were slippery with Rohan's blood, but no matter how much I attempted to send my Lilith-boosted healing power into him, pop the bullet out, and stitch his internal injuries together, my magic was barely a flicker. Nothing happened.

Nothing except Rohan leaching of all color, his skin growing cold and his body spasming as blood pooled beneath him.

I'd used Lilith's magic once too often and now she'd gotten strong enough to cut me off.

Help me, I begged Lilith. *Give me the magic. You'll be free.*

Payback is a bitch, she whispered in my head. She was willing to stay imprisoned just so I could lose him?

I was the spark that brought him back to life. I couldn't leave him alone in the dark. I swore I'd always be with him. I pressed harder on the wound, tears streaming down my face.

"Get help!" I screamed at Mandelbaum, who stood there frozen, the gun in his trembling hands.

"I–I thought I'd hit Hybris."

"You idiot!" I yelled through my sobs. "She's a demon, you know a gun won't stop her. Now run, you asshole! Get a doctor!" One of those scientists had to be able to help.

He jerked into action, but hadn't gotten more than a few feet before Hybris grabbed him.

"I don't appreciate double-crosses," Hybris said.

The rabbi sailed over my head, hitting a concrete wall with a meaty thwack. He bounced on to the dirt, and lay still, moaning.

The demon swaggered over to us. "I told you my face would be the last thing you saw."

"I don't think so," Sienna said.

Hybris spun to face the new arrival, but Sienna waved a hand and the demon crumpled into a ball in short jerky movements.

Rohan gave a choked sob. "I have to kill her. Can't let Asha down again."

His words weren't even a whisper. More an exhale, his breath raspy, punctuated with gurgling noises.

With a roar, Hybris cast off Sienna's magic. "Not today, hunter," she said to Rohan and was gone.

Ro scrabbled weakly at me, his fingers barely moving. "Go. Her."

I turned pleading eyes on Sienna. "Help him."

"You'll turn yourself over to me? No tricks?"

I nodded. I couldn't get her in the Tomb even if I gave a damn.

Sienna crouched down beside Rohan, brushing me aside to take over.

I held my breath, squeezing his hand and praying that between her dark magic and her nurse training that she could save him. Finally, the bleeding stopped and his color improved. A bloodied bullet lay on the ground beside him.

Sienna wiped her brow. "His natural healing should take over now. Say goodbye. You're coming with me."

The gun fired again.

Rabbi Mandelbaum lowered the barrel from where he'd shot into the night sky to train it on Sienna and me. "I'm taking Lilith."

That's why I had more value now. Hybris must have told him and now he had the witch that could bind demons and salvage his plans. That's why he'd arranged to get the Tomb.

"Want to bet on that?" There was death in Sienna's eyes.

I stepped in front of the rabbi.

"Move, Nava," she said. "If you want me to help you live."

Rohan sat up with a wince, swaying slightly. "Nava, step away. We'll solve this."

He must have been broken inside over Hybris getting away, but all I saw was the depth of his feeling for me, shining pure and strong. This man with his passion and his noble impulses and his arrogant certainties that everything would work out.

Except it wouldn't. Not if either Lilith or Sienna emerged victorious or Mandelbaum got hold of either of them. I had to take all three out to save the world.

I wouldn't survive.

I'd loved and been loved for less than half a day and even though I was about to die, my only regret was the time I'd wasted hiding the truth of my heart. The time I'd wasted letting my pride and my fears keep me from being hurt, when I'd failed to understand that opening myself up to love wasn't a vulnerability.

Love was strength.

It was truly go-big-or-go-home time.

"Hey, Rohan?"

He mustered up a strained smile for me. "Yeah?"

"I love you. And I love your nicknames for me. Okay, maybe not Lolita, but Sparky was pretty inspired."

With that I cast my final spark into Lilith's box. It was so thin that the box burned away in a wisp of smoke.

Her magic danced through my body and I lit up the

night like a beacon with pure, unadulterated power. My blood was stardust, dancing with a nebula in a far-off galaxy.

I was the cosmos. I could fly. Hands outstretched, I reached for my foes. I only needed a couple of seconds and it would be done.

But like Sienna had said, the human body wasn't designed to take that much power that fast.

Or ever. Even two seconds was time I didn't have.

Before I could turn the magic on Mandelbaum, Sienna, and Lilith and neutralize them, that beauty dissipated into a million dark magic maggots that consumed me, threatening to flay the skin from my bones.

Lilith's cruel laughter shivered through my veins.

My heart sped up, skipped once, twice, then fell into chaotic convulsions.

I clutched at my chest, falling to my knees, my body bowed backward.

Witches swarmed us from one side, Mandelbaum's men from the other.

Rohan fought anyone who got between them and me.

Sienna was screaming at people to stand down and freezing anyone using magic as fast as she could, but the chaos was too much for her to fully contain. She'd stop six people and two would unfreeze and jump back into the fray.

I had my hands full battling Lilith for possession of my body. She was disoriented, attempting to gather her magic up and disengage from me, but when she couldn't get herself out of me, she forced *me* out of myself.

Although being trapped in that magic prison had fucked with her abilities, I was still outmatched.

My spirit left my body with a whoosh, but the connection between my spirit and my physical self hadn't been severed.

I dive-bombed back into my body, hitting an invisible blockade preventing me from getting in. Again and again, I attempted to regain possession.

And seconds later, there was no point.

You'd think that my death might have registered like some kind of fireworks moment: YOU. ARE. DEAD. But there was just a gentle sag-and-release feeling. An untethering.

Then a lot of shock and me staring down at my motionless form.

Rohan single-handedly carved a path to me and gave me mouth-to-mouth with a ferocity that was terrifying. Nice idea, but pointless.

Lilith flickered out of me, still incorporeal. For a woman who'd been unconscious for a month, she looked pretty good.

And pretty angry.

With a flick of her fingers, she killed a few of Mandelbaum's men.

The witches looked around in shock.

"Get her!" one woman cried. She fell dead, as well.

Sienna sent a rush of magic toward Lilith but the stream broke into prisms that fell harmlessly to the ground like water droplets before they could find their mark. Sienna tried a second time.

"No," Lilith said, her arm carelessly outstretched in Sienna's direction.

Sienna shot backward.

The other witches went ballistic on Lilith, but she was still transparent, and their magic passed harmlessly through her, blowing up a nearby generator.

The lights in half of the compound died.

"I'll deal with you later," Lilith said to Sienna.

Had I been able to laugh at Sienna's look of surprise, I totally would have, but the world was growing hazy and cold. Everything was gray except for a single pale silver thread connecting me and Lilith.

Lilith made a slashing motion through the thread and I shivered, like a saw was buzzing through it, but the thread didn't break. She glared at me like that was my fault.

All around us, the rest of the rabbi's faithful and the witches fell into chaos. No one could get to Lilith, so everyone became a threat.

Four Rasha grabbed Rohan and started beating the shit out of him. His wound opened up, but Rohan was in berserker mode, fighting to get back to my body.

I tried to stop them, but I floated right through the chaos.

Like all cockroaches, Mandelbaum had managed to keep himself alive and untaken. He scuttled out to grab my dead body.

"Oh no, you don't," Sienna said.

Everything crawled into slow motion: the black light erupting from her hands, hissing and snapping toward me, Rohan's distorted and drawn out "No!" as he flung himself sideways and knocked me loose from Mandelbaum, the dark magic that enveloped Rohan instead of its intended target.

From my fading consciousness's vantage point, hovering over the compound, I watched the world snap back into real time.

Lilith stood stock-still with an expression of intense concentration, her ghostly image slowly growing more solid.

Sienna glanced over her shoulder at Lilith, then

scooped me up and stuffed my dead body into the Tomb of Endless Night.

A broken scream tore from Rohan's throat, his body on fire with black magic that danced over his skin. His gold eyes slithered with dark serpents.

Mohawk Witch gasped. "Sienna. What have you done?"

Sienna didn't answer, staring at Rohan with horror stamped over her features.

Go big or go home had reached its tragic consequences. We were all going down.

Even lifeless and outside my own body, I swear I felt tears running down my cheeks.

The Tomb slammed shut, nulling Lilith's magic.

Her translucent form disappeared from the courtyard. She was the architect and she'd designed a very fine product that stood the test of time and the most powerful magic a human had ever possessed.

Hers.

Her time was up, but so was mine.

I winked out of existence.

There was no white light. No fiery pits either.

Just nothing.

Until I came to with a gasp, my nose pressed against the inside of the Tomb door. Somehow it had gotten open again, just a hair, just enough to let me see outside. I couldn't move my hands or my body. Lilith must have kick-started my heart and brought me back to life, but gasping and shaking was all I had energy for.

I couldn't even budge this damn door on my own.

If you're alive, I stay alive, Lilith whispered sadly in the back of my head. It wasn't just our magic that had bonded. Our consciousness or essence had bonded as well. Her barely-there life force mingled with mine.

Was I even still me?

I tried to yell, but my throat was dry and raspy.

If Sienna heard me, she did nothing. Men and women fell to the ground in cascades of magic outside, the action happening faster than my rebooting brain could process.

There was, however, one thing I could see perfectly, even though it haunted me: Rohan, still engulfed in Sienna's twisted black flames, crying out like a man in Hell. Like he was being taken apart, consumed from the inside.

I struggled, thrashed, yelled, but I was too weak and it was useless.

Finally, a shadow blocked my view. Thank God. Help was here. I was nearly crying with relief.

Rabbi Mandelbaum leaned down to meet my eyes, head bruised and wrist still bent unnaturally, and hissed, "You're mine now."

The sliver of light vanished as the door clicked closed and my world went dark.

THANK you for reading THE UNLIKEABLE DEMON HUNTER: FALL!

Start reading THE UNLIKEABLE DEMON HUNTER: BURN.

It's the End of the World as We Know It ...

Nava has come a long way from being a hot mess flying solo. She's now one of the major players on the chessboard, leading the charge against a witch with dark magic, a power-mad rabbi, and the impending apocalypse.

Friends will die and secrets will be exposed. Add imprisonment, torture, and the biggest, baddest demon of them all who has plans for her, and it's a lot for a girl to take in.

Time to rally the troops and make her last stand,

because she's damned if she'll let the end of the world get in the way of her romantic, sexytimes galore, happily-ever-after.

It's trial by fire.

Burn, baby, burn.

Get it now.

Every time a reader leaves a review, an author gets ... a glass of wine. (You thought I was going to say "wings," didn't you? We're authors, not angels, but *you'll* get heavenly karma for your good deed.) Please leave yours on your favorite book site. It makes a huge difference in discoverability to rate and review, especially the first book in a series.

Turn the page for an excerpt from *The Unlikeable Demon Hunter: Burn* ...

EXCERPT FROM THE UNLIKEABLE DEMON HUNTER: BURN

"Come on, Avon. You can't be late for your own performance." Cole pushed his glasses up his nose with a little face scrunch, unwilling to cross the threshold into the Zone of Chaos, a.k.a. my bedroom.

I dug through the pile of workout clothes on the closet floor and tossed a couple Ziplock bags over my shoulder. The one containing hair spray, gel, elastics, and bobby pins hit my fluffy area rug with a quiet thunk, while my jumble of makeup, false eyelashes, and glue sailed onto my mattress.

"One second."

"Let's go already. Parking is a bitch at the—" Cole's irritation cut off with a yelp as a tangle of duct tape and extra shoelaces flew through the air to wing him in the shoulder.

I sat back on my calves. "I can't find the shoes you—"

"I what?"

I shook my head to clear it. "My custom leather taps. I need them for this performance."

"Dropping pricy hints for your next birthday? Noted. Meantime." He nudged my dance bag across the floor. "Your shoes are in here. You put them in last night."

I pulled them out. Black worn taps. Not purple and red saddle shoes with a red heart.

"These aren't them. They don't fit anymore." My voice caught on a half-sob.

Cole crouched down next to me and slid one onto my left foot. "They fit fine."

I ripped it off. "They don't."

Yeah, I was being sulky and kind of childish, but I was a performer. Performers needed the right tools to put on a good show and the shoes I was looking for and annoyingly not finding were it for me. The old shoes would be okay, but I intended to set the world on fire.

"You want to try dancing your heart out in front of a crowd wearing shoes you don't feel absolutely confident in, be my guest," I said.

Cole put the shoe away, then grabbed my hair and makeup accoutrements, and snagged my costume bag from a chair. "Take a moment and breathe. You've got this. I'll meet you at the car."

I dropped my face into my hands. This wasn't my pre-show jitters that I fed off to give my tapping an exhilarating edge. This was a full-blown nightmare of being backstage with the lights dimming and the audience shushing, the first notes about to play, while I stood there in the wings, all my moves forgotten.

Get it together, Katz. People were counting on me to nail this performance. I jogged down to the car, trying to weave my nerves into something more productive.

My phone beeped with a flurry of texts from Leo and my family, even my mom, telling me to break a leg. Nothing from Ari, though. I'd give him shit later when he got home from... I frowned. Where was he?

When I slid into the passenger seat of his hand-me-down clunker, Cole made a big production of ceding control of the radio dial. "M'lady."

"M'thank you."

"Dork." He pulled away from the curb.

I fiddled with the cracked plastic knob, but every radio station was static. I was about to shut it off when I caught the faintest strain of a melody that filled me with hope, light, and deep anxiety. I gripped the dashboard.

"Let's slay all our demons
I'll lay down my knives
For you, I'll lay down my knives."

Cole groaned and snapped off the dial. "This emo crap can't be helping your state of mind, babe."

I scrambled to twist the knob back on, but the song had vanished. Just more static. I spun through radio stations and got nothing.

"Comebackcomebackcomeback!"

Deep in my core, a spark caught with an agonizing electric snap. Current snaked over my body and a scream tore from my throat.

"I know I'm good," said a Southern Californian drawl that was dry with amusement, "but I didn't even touch you."

I clutched his biceps. My body relaxed and my heart slowed its galloping.

Rohan.

I opened my eyes and wriggled closer to him, my cheek finding his solid pecs the perfect pillow. A dusting of dark hair tickled my nose. "If you can't tell the difference between an orgasm and a nightmare, you might need to rethink your technique."

He rolled me over and pinned me against the cool sheets, edging one knee between my legs. "Yeah? You think I need practice?"

I ran my hands down his bare skin to his hipbone. "I mean, it does make perfect. And you are kind of anal about your technique."

"You're getting kind of anal, too," he snickered.

I brushed my fingers over his erection and he hissed. "That's right, buddy. You can crack jokes or go for door number two."

Rohan waggled his eyebrows.

Groaning loudly, I flopped onto my back.

Ro stretched out against me, his lips brushing mine.

If I lived until ninety, I would never tire of feeling him fitted against me. How the ridge of his hip pressed into my soft curves. He was like my own personal docking station. He recharged me, but he always left me better than I was: singing a little louder, shining a little brighter.

"You loooove me," he said.

"Weellllll." Now it was my turn to hiss as he slid a finger inside me. My nipples tightened, and a drugged lust snaked through my veins.

"You are positively dripping with love for me."

"You're hopeless," I laughed, squirming against him as he stroked Cuntessa. I brushed my breasts against his chest, loving the fierce rumble he made.

"Say it," he growled, though he was grinning.

His love shone in the twinkle of his eyes and in the way that he stoked the fire in my body with awed adoration. We were going to grow into that old couple who always held hands and giggled at some inside joke as they tottered along at a snail's pace.

I threaded my fingers into his hair, pulling his face close to reassure myself he was here. For as long as possible, I wanted us to stay like this, where he was my entire world. "I love you so much, Rohan. And I need you inside me."

"Patience, sweetheart."

"Please. Now." My ribcage constricted and I held his forearms tighter so he couldn't fade away.

Rohan wrapped his hand around mine, pressing it to his heart as he knelt on the bed and pushed inside me. But he didn't move, just demolished me with a single volcanic gaze, his eyes amber rum and cinnamon.

I bucked my hips and he cocked an eyebrow at me.

"Oh good," I said. "You remember you're here. Inside me."

"I could never forget that." He fucked me in a lazy tempo. Something in my chest eased as Rohan leaned down to whisper in my ear and I laughed as his stubble tickled my neck. This was it, this was perfect.

"You're my heart, my home. I love you, Lilith."

I gasped, my lungs seizing.

BECOME A WILDE ONE

If you enjoyed this book and want to be first in the know about bonus content, reveals, and exclusive giveaways, become a Wilde One by joining my newsletter: http://www.deborahwilde.com/subscribe

You'll immediately receive short stories set in my various worlds and available only to my newsletter subscribers. There are mild spoilers so they're best enjoyed in the recommended reading order.

If you just want to know about my new releases, please follow me on BookBub: https://www.bookbub.com/authors/deborah-wilde

ACKNOWLEDGMENTS

Huge thanks to all my friends who always answer my many questions, be it about language, local attractions or the latest in douchey clothing brands. You amazing people go above and beyond for me and I love you for it.

A special thanks to Adele for finding me the most appropriate Hebrew swear words and letting me pester her about Hebrew names when I needed to procrastinate with a series I have yet to write. And also to Nisha Shankar for Corn Man. This book and my L.A. trip would have been so much less without that.

I'm always a bit sad when I'm writing my thanks here to my editor Alex Yuschik because it means that it's going to be a while before I have another draft to work on together. This collaboration brings me incredible joy and makes my books infinitely better.

To my snarky, brilliant, wonderful readers, can I just say how much I adore you? Especially my Wilde Ones. Not only do you all make me laugh, pimp me new reads, and virtually hang out with me on a regular basis, you give me the best gift of all. Of the gazillions of books out there, you choose to spend your time and money on mine. Thank you from the bottom of my heart. 🩶

ABOUT THE AUTHOR

A global wanderer, former screenwriter, and total cynic with a broken edit button, Deborah (pronounced deb-O-rah) writes funny urban fantasy and paranormal women's fiction.

Her stories feature sassy women who kick butt, strong female friendships, and swoony, sexy romance. She's all about the happily ever after, with a huge dose of hilarity along the way.

Deborah lives in Vancouver with her husband, daughter, and asshole cat, Abra.

"Magic, sparks, and snark! Go Wilde."

www.deborahwilde.com

facebook.com/DeborahWildeAuthor
instagram.com/wildeauthor

Made in the USA
Coppell, TX
09 March 2024

29927529R00236